Read me an

Behind the Mask
is
Nothing

Behind the Mask

is
Nothing

by

Judy Birkbeck

www.hhousebooks.com

Paperback ISBN: 978-1-910688-27-4
Kindle: 978-1-910688-28-1

Cover design & typeset by B. Julia Lloyd
Printed and bound in Great Britain by
TJ International Ltd. Padstow

Published in the USA and UK

Holland House Books
Holland House
47 Greenham Road
Newbury, Berkshire RG14 7HY
United Kingdom

www.hhousebooks.com

For Tom and Eileen

Often when I think of you
your allness permeates, unfolds.
Like gleaming deer you wander through
and I am forest, I am dark.

The Book of Hours, Rilke

He was a brute, the clumsy juggler. We sat seven-deep in a circle, children and adults laughing at the giant with Atlantean shoulders and bull-chest bulging out of a string vest. He strode over to one guffawing man.

'You think it's funny?' he said in a high-pitched, whiny voice, then brought down a huge hard plastic hammer with a mighty thwack.

The victim flinched and the onlookers shrieked with mirth. Mark and I shrieked too. The juggler bounded over and clouted another man with the hammer. The crowd roared. He marched across to another gleeful man and slammed the top of his head. The laughter exploded. Gulls swooped low, screeching like forced laughter, like the laughter of the crowd, like Mark's and my laughter: it wasn't funny any more, yet we laughed. Everywhere the faces were creased with pain or merriment.

The juggler went back to his skittles till the next drop, and the uproar subsided. Mark and I exchanged looks.

'How do we get out of here?' I mouthed the words behind the juggler's back. Not that I had wanted to rush home after dropping Emma off at the airport. Mark did, but now we were in the middle row on Minehead beach, like fishing boats stuck in the mud. Above the harbour North Hill towered like Leviathan risen from the sea, and beyond the wall shone Butlin's dome; the dodgems bell jingled and the Chair-O-Plane passengers screamed. Mark shrugged and squeezed my hand. His temples were white where he normally brushed the hair forwards over his receding hairline.

'Right,' I said, 'let's go.'

A man in the fourth row half-rose to sidle off with his family. The giant was there in seconds. Spectators parted to let him through. The would-be escapee sat down, and the juggler once more strode round the circle and swooped at random. The audience howled. I couldn't understand why we stayed, why we laughed. Did we need someone else's exodus to give us permission? He wasn't even a good juggler.

Mark's mobile beeped and he glanced at it, then thumbed. I reached across to snatch it, but he had already deleted the message. I sulked. He had received several anonymous sexts, presumably from his besotted thirteen-year-old students; he denied encouraging them.

'How come you never let me see?'

He blushed. 'They're not nice.'

'Manners!' bellowed the juggler. 'This is for your benefit. For your children.' He glared and the audience tittered as though they were mock-glares. 'Show some appreciation.'

He stretched his arms sideways, palms up, and gestured. A slow hand-clap began. He juggled balls, passed them under a leg, caught them between his teeth. Mark and I pulled faces behind his back. How could we leave? It would spoil the atmosphere. Others were enjoying it. It would be un-British. It was all a joke, free entertainment. The juggler's violence escalated but it would soon be over, so we stayed. We stayed to the end.

'I can't believe we put up with that,' Mark said once we were in the car.

'Nor can I.'

'I can't believe we laughed at it. I can't believe anyone laughed at it.'

'We knew it wasn't funny, so why did we put up with it?'

Mark's brow furrowed like waves in a child's drawing. 'Inertia. Inertia kept us seated.' He fondled my thigh and grinned. 'I'll make it up to you, soon as we get home.'

Lovely work I scribbled and stamped it with a red smiley. I grabbed another book from the stacked-up boxes, rushing things because Mark had finished mowing and was festering in a deckchair, waiting for me. The heat clenched my throat like a tight fist. Gulls wheeled over the lowland between the Quantocks and the sea.

'Finally,' he grunted when I appeared after two boxfuls. 'I thought we'd get some us-time now Emma's gone.'

I kissed him and flung myself in the other deckchair.

One moment the bees sang in worship of the sun and black-and-gold dragonflies chased and whirred, while on the hill opposite magpies hopped from sheep to sheep, pecking for ticks and mites. The sunflowers faced the sun, and it seemed that all was right with the world.

Next moment, so it seemed, a sea-mist rolled in. There was no sound of bees or buzzards or dragonflies, only a muffled hiss, as if God had thrown a cold cloth over Somerset. The sunflowers and Mark stared bemused at where the sun had been.

'Right,' I said, hauling myself to my feet. 'No point basking in this.'

We fumbled our way through the cloud to the house smelling of yesterday's potato curry and I checked my emails on the laptop in Mark's study. *Mark*, said the top subject line. I frowned and clicked. The attached jpeg burst into the room: Mark in a green-and-yellow football shirt was devouring a woman with long dark hair and turquoise T-shirt, one adoring splayed hand on her cheek, his scalloped lips enveloping hers. Through the window the gulls screamed like a Greek chorus.

He came up behind me, smelling of cut grass, his fingers sliding over my shoulders, thumbs sandpapering my neck.

'Don't touch me.'

The laptop fan whirred as loud as a wind generator and the woman swelled, filling the room with her flowing hair, his long fingers spread on her peachy face. My fingers wanted to mash the keys, to mash her, scribble all over her in this poxy, sterile boxroom, Mark's room.

'It's photoshopped, Stef. Kids these days can do anything with a computer. Look how blurred it is. Look at the hand.'

'I'm looking at it.'

The silent phone calls made sense now, and the sexts. He just did his bulldog impression, snaggle-teeth overlapping his top lip, wrinkled nose, and the girls giggled and flocked round. And the one time I came home early on a non-football day, he stayed late. So he said. No matter his protests, the image of him locking lips with her in the turquoise T-shirt was indelible.

'Fine.'

He snatched his glasses and stomped off. Was he right? Even my ten- and eleven-year-olds could enhance and manipulate digital images. I fled upstairs to my study, my haven with rows of jars and boxes containing rocks, gems, found objects, cottons, felts, pasta, shells and more, everything comfortingly in its place, all neatly labelled and colour-coded. I opened a jar of sea shells and sniffed. If only I were a fish I could bury myself in the sea, rest in it, be surrounded by the dark, womby waters.

A pigeon on the roof outside my window crooned:
He's *chea*-ting on you,
He's *chea*-ting on you,
He's *chea*-ting on you,
He's *chea*-ting on you.

Outside, the mist rolled away, revealing the hill covered in bright yellow gorse, and sheep munching on as if the sky had always been blue. A pair of ravens swept down the combe.

That night we lay in bed separated by a question mark. A bluebottle tangled in a cobweb kicked and buzzed, broke free and hurled itself from wall to wall in a frantic ballet.

'I wouldn't—'

'I don't want to hear it,' I screeched.

His stance in the photo was that of kissing passionately, so to create the image they must have obtained a photo of him kissing me with that stance and airbrushed me out. No such photo existed.

*

Gran sat like a tree, tall and beaming, hair pinned in a neat bun, elegant but for the floury mauve pinafore.

'It was all right till the new head with her vermilion red power suit came and decreed every child must learn the recorder,' I burst out. 'Imagine twenty-seven squeaking beginners in one room! Can you imagine it, Gran?'

'But I thought you were the music coordinator?' She poured tea from the teapot with the red and purple-chequered knitted tea cosy and offered Thumbelina-sized cinnamon cakes.

'I am, but she ignores me. If Hatchet Man says jump, she jumps.'

'Who's Hatchet Man?'

'Her old deputy head. The one she brought with her as if we were a failing school. Hatchett by name and Hatchet by nature. There's no time for Stomp-style music-making now. And she makes us log every single piece of work by every single child in every single lesson. Mark moans at the work I do, but he hasn't got Evelyn for a head. He dashes off his marking before leaving school and breezes through lessons.'

It was good to offload about school, but Gran had heard it

all before, many times since last September, and what I really wanted to talk about was the photo. Only I couldn't. We sat in the green dralon wingback chairs facing the cast-iron fireplace at which we used to toast teacakes on a toasting fork, and she listened to worries about school and Emma, now off canoeing down the Zambezi. Hippos kill more people than any other animal in the world, I told her. Gran's house was all musty books and moths, my sister Lisa said now, but to me it was cosy, unhurried, the place of childhood holidays. The acquisitiveness and style obsession of the eighties, nineties and noughties had passed it by. A fading, shiny print of Degas' desolate absinthe drinker hung on the chimney breast.

In the dining room, calmer now, I sat in front of Gran's computer and increased the font size in her memoir. She couldn't centre, tabulate or paginate either. I wanted to type out the memoir for her as well as do everything for my class and school choir, but it wasn't humanly possible, not even Stefly possible, and Gran said no, I had enough to do and must get back to that lovely husband of mine after shopping or she wouldn't forgive herself. Lovely?

I stiffened at the name Hitler on the screen: '...in love with Hitler.'

'When I'm gone you can read it,' she said hastily. 'Close it down now. It's time for Diabelli.'

Saturday was shopping and Diabelli day. We played duets on the old Bechstein grand and giggled and cackled over mistakes. As toddlers, Lisa and I would sit underneath and watch Gran's feet go up and down on the pedals like cartoon cats watching a mouse on a trampoline.

Afterwards we crawled along The Avenue brimming with lurid purple and magenta petunias and pink stone buildings glowing in the sun, to the other side of Minehead. A car behind hooted and I accelerated.

'Don't speed up.' She grinned, tannin-stained teeth pointing all ways like battered wicket stumps. 'When I was driving, if anyone tooted I always *made sure* they were held up.'

With a chuckle I dabbed the brake.

Back in Gran's street after shopping, another car behind hooted. My foot patted the brake and we exchanged sly smiles. I slowed down more and we burst out laughing.

On the doorstep before leaving, my hands clutched a box of raspberries and home-made cherry cake for Mark and the grandfather clock in the hall sounded the quarters, gathered up its strength with a hum like the quivering of orchestral strings before the battle charge of Egmont and struck four booming bass notes. I took a deep breath.

'Do you think Mark would cheat on me, Gran?'

'Stef! Not in a million years. Why...?'

Her hand gripped the doorpost. She had angina and I regretted asking. At my explanation she shook her head.

'Darling, that boy is a treasure. These thoughts will steal your happiness if you entertain them. If Mark said it was photoshopped, then you must believe him.'

I kissed her cheek, carefully because the skin was thin, soft as a rose petal, might break.

2

Hilda strolled among the raspberry canes and the warm fruits in her mouth collapsed and drizzled down her throat; but sweet berries and sunshine could not mask the sourness. A marriage could pall so easily, love disappear like the sea-mists, and this was Stef's second one. But it wasn't just Stef's fears: the fire hydrant cover in the car park had upset her. For years she never saw the swastika patterns in the ridges, but now her eyes sought them out every time. If only Fred were here. He was calmer and more sensible about such things—that was part of why she married him—but he left Germany in 1934, three years before Hilda. He didn't know the half of it. She went indoors to type her memoir, which she was too ashamed to let anyone see before she died:

I don't know why I followed the dancing bear. We were all mesmerised by this huge brown creature staggering like a drunk over the cobbles with front paws dangling. The gypsy banged his drum with every other step and it lumbered forwards. We children marched in time with the drum and never took our eyes off the hapless bear. Maybe we liked the danger, though it was muzzled and Herta said they took out the claws and teeth, and it could only go whichever way it was pulled by the lead attached to the pin through its nose.

'Do you know how bears kill you?' Hanno said with his cheeky grin. He pushed past to get nearer, but I grabbed him by his sailor-suit collar. I had strict instructions to look after him. 'They hug you to death,' he said and shoved me so hard I put out my hands to stop myself falling and touched its back. It dropped on all fours, but got up again with a wincing grunt because the gypsy walked on. The gypsy stopped and turned.

'Who touched him?' He stepped sideways to see who was behind the bear and glared at me from beneath bushy black eyebrows and a wide-brimmed hat. He had a large hole in his trouser leg and a moustache that hid whether he was smiling. But he wasn't smiling. 'It was you, wasn't it?'

The people behind bunched round in a semicircle, looking at me. I shrank. Herta, hair tied with a giant emerald bow, looked accusing. She held Hanno by the shoulders for me with both hands. Sharp-nosed Elisabeth, who was jealous of me because our teacher had singled me out for good work, smirked. The bear swayed from side to side.

'No,' I said.

'Keep away if you don't want to get mauled,' the man growled and walked on. He pulled the rope tight, and it reared up and bellowed.

I could have left then. I knew it was cruel, but we all marvelled and laughed to see the bear stand like a human being, back straight, head high. I didn't want to be left out.

I laughed too.

We headed for the square. I prayed that Papa wouldn't be there. After losing his job as an actor when the theatre closed, he had taken to doing acrobatics on the street with Herr Stresemann the theatre director on the barrel organ. We stopped under a giant advertisement for Lux soap flakes. There he was on the next corner, in his cable-knit sleeveless pullover, doing contortions. When he put his legs behind his ears you could see the holes in his soles. Elisabeth pointed them out. Herr Stresemann, in his black, red and yellow knitted tie, spotted me, so I hid behind a woman who had stopped to watch the bear while a yellow tram ringing its loud bell rattled past.

Every so often the gypsy did a fast drumming routine and the bear jumped up and down on its hind legs, which looked comical. Everyone laughed. Even toffee-nosed Elisabeth cackled. The gypsy never smiled. The crowd trebled in size, but no one was watching Papa and Herr Stresemann. Hanno copied the bear and all we children followed suit. Its mouth hung open all the time. Then Hanno slapped his knees in the air, because its front paws touched the knees of its back legs, and we were all doing it and laughing ourselves silly. Later, I learnt that often part of the bear's nose is torn out. Bear dancing was banned in 1933. Then we followed other processions instead.

3

The acrid smell of lilies and incense pricked the atmosphere. Grinning grotesques looked down on the choir from stone pillars eroded by centuries of passing hands and the walls were covered in stone plaques in memory of rich people in search of immortality. As the cathedral filled up to the sweet, stinging high tones of the organ, the murmuring grew louder. Lisa and four-year-old Jack sat in the second row of the nave next to Mark and my parents. I waved and Jack's face broke into a big smile. Rachel envied me my family.

'Mark's only here out of loyalty and my father's just a snob. It's the shiny shoes, tails and white cummerbunds and bow ties he loves.'

Women with long dark hair swarmed throughout the cathedral like a nest of winged ants about to take flight. A turquoise jumper caught my eye. But if Mark were cheating, I reasoned, he could have skipped the concert. Wailing bints, he called us, and he hated the smell of incense.

'Here they come.' Rachel secreted chewing gum into her big rush bag and waved. 'At last I've persuaded them.'

A dozen people trooped in and sat erect as hyenas' ears in a side aisle while the audience chatted and fidgeted.

Conductor and soloists walked on to applause and a cough-fest started, rasping and hacking enough to last to the first pause in the music. The conductor smiled, or grimaced; it ended with a final sputter, the audience bristled with impatience and he raised his baton to warn, no more coughing. *Elijah* began

'Help, Lord!'

and the evening sun gleamed amber over the heads like the fiery sun over drought-ridden Israel. I caught Mark's eye and launched into an orgy of emotion: the wooing of sweet-voiced angels hovering over the earth, plaintive moaning in a parched land, and angry hammer blows blaming other people's gods.

After the interval the second half zipped along till the earth shook and the fire from heaven reached fever pitch, and in the embers was the still small voice at the centre. Even Mark sat up straight. Ecstasy or peace, which was better? Before we could answer, the string players bent their heads, bows sawed as one, and the choir broke forth like a fire, our words were like burning torches and a whirlwind swept us up to heaven in a fiery chariot with fiery horses. We finished in a blaze that lit up the nave.

Amen.

Flying high, up there among the rafters and the grotesques. Before the music ended in our heads, while it still throbbed in the lofty spaces, the audience clapped, intruding. On and on they clapped. Was it appreciation, or did no one want to be the first to stop clapping?

The choir floated out, intoxicated, and Rachel and I headed for the nave. My family crowded round with congratulations. Even Mark gave a thumbs-up.

'Well done, Stef,' said Lisa, and I prickled at the suspected put-down.

'Wonderful,' said Mum and Dad with one voice.

'I loved the angels,' said Hilda, beaming.

Rachel's friends, a motley crew, stood in a triangle like snooker balls set up for a new game. At the head was a young version of Captain Mainwaring with round wire glasses and a ponytail. This must be Oliver, the counsellor Rachel had eulogised. The idea of spilling my heart out to him did not appeal.

'Well done, Rachel,' he said.

Well done Well done Well done echoed through the triangle. On Captain Mainwaring's right stood a frosty-looking woman with a moon-white face, wearing a boxy-shouldered jacket and leopard-spot dress. On his left a man with bushy eyebrows stepped forwards and held out a hand.

'I'm Simon,' he said in the warm, relaxed cadences of a Somerset accent. 'Wonderful concert. You must be proper proud.'

Rachel glowed. 'These are my friends from where I live.'

'It's lovely to see you all here,' I said.

They stood stiff and fish-faced and strangely earthbound. My stubborn euphoria seemed out of place: they were as unmoved as Odysseus' crew after plugging their ears with beeswax to escape enchantment by the Sirens. Poor Rachel. Her friends came to her concert for the first time ever, then sat like stones.

They left and I picked up my nephew Jack. He gave me a slobbery kiss and I hugged him tight. I loved the bold innocence, the way he trod carelessly through uncharted waters, his blond curls dancing and shouting, waving not drowning.

'Do you know why you have a crease there?' Dad placed his finger in the dimple above Jack's upper lip. 'It's because,' he continued as Jack shook his head, 'every baby in his mummy's tummy knows everything there is to know, but the moment he's born an angel puts a finger over his lip and says, 'Sh, don't tell.''

Jack gazed open-mouthed as though Dad were that angel. Lisa laughed because Dad had spun us the same yarn.

Sitting in the back of the car with Gran, I was still soaring among the rafters.

'Rachel's friends were a funny lot,' said Mark. 'Like zombies. So was the guy at the front with glasses this marvellous counsellor? Didn't look like someone I'd want to share with.'

'No, Rachel said he wasn't there.'

Gran frowned. 'Hasn't Rachel got any family?'

'No. Well, she has, but they don't communicate.'

'Shame.' She squeezed my hand.

We drove through the wooded Exe valley in darkness. The towering trees on the off side leant over the road, like a great cloak completing the canopy. They looked as if they might fall off the steep slopes – and sometimes did so in strong winds. On the near side was a precipice down to the Exe and misty meadowland beyond. The road snaked its way round the side of the hill.

'Look out,' I screamed and clutched the grab handle.

The car screeched and juddered to a halt on a bend. A herd of red deer with young sauntered across. Two of them stopped and stared, long necks craning round, ears proud, dog noses pointing at us. One by one they bounded up the slope on the other side and their pale underparts gleamed in the dark.

4

Hilda turned a loaf onto a rack, warm and yeasty-smelling with a bulbous shape and glossy ginger crust. The music had been glorious, but all through the concert her eyes were drawn to one window. The way the light fell, the lead cames at the top formed a pair of sig runes, the SS insignia. She had tried to focus on the choir, but her eyes kept drifting up to see the symbols. The concert was ruined. And then there was the email photo. She should have given Stef more attention when she minded her and Lisa after school. Lisa was such an easy, placid child, but Stef... Stef was demanding, never satisfied. Lisa could be fobbed off with reasons not to hear her read, not to teach her to do up her laces, not to play duets with her, not right now, dear. Go and read to yourself, dear, go and play a solo piece, dear. But Stef always strove after the unattainable. Hilda should have done more. 'Don't beat yourself up, Mum,' her daughter always said.

She sat at the piano and Chopin's nocturnes lulled her into a dream of playing in the Tiergarten when Hanno pushed her in the pond, or jumping up to bite sausages hanging from a clothes line strung between trees, or hunting for the Easter eggs Papa had hidden in the woods. Rose-tinted spectacles; lying spectacles. Her parents eyed her from the photo beside the piano: Papa leant his elbow on the field gate on which Mama sat. They looked very much in love. Mellow sounds filled the room and all thought of then or now faded, her eyelids drooped and her fingers stole like a spider over the keys. Here in the piano was rest. She no longer knew where she ended and the piano began. The honey-sweet lotus fruit of Chopin's music carried her away to a quiet place, calm and serene, where there was no thought, no worry, no regrets, nothing.

The grandfather clock in the hallway chimed the hour. In the dining room, the bold blue flowers on the wallpaper blurred and the heaviness in her chest spread to her left arm. She popped a tiny pill under her tongue.

Oma (Papa's mother) lived in the same block as us in Berlin-Wilmersdorf, and kept us supplied with fruit and vegetables which she magicked from bare soil in her wonderful allotment garden and brought home on a handcart. Every Sunday the whole family went there with a picnic to weed and harvest. After Opa died, Papa did the digging, and then he would give us an acrobatic performance and sing the Internationale. For us children it was a labyrinth of secret hollows and tunnels through bushes, and trees to climb. My parents and Oma sat on deckchairs outside the shed with a table and Primus stove and the silver samovar Papa had brought back from Turkey, while Hanno and I feasted on gooseberries, raspberries, whitecurrants, redcurrants, blackberries and apples until we got collywobbles. Like the pigeons, we didn't wait for fruit to ripen.

One day we sat among the raspberries and scoffed the lot while the adults chatted. Oma, who had cataracts, later bent over the canes to inspect and mistook the stripped plugs for a failed crop. 'They must be past their best,' she said and got Papa to dig them out and plant new canes. We never confessed.

The neighbour on one side was friendly, and Papa and Mama often talked to him over the brambles. We spied on him from the space behind the currant bushes and pulled faces. The scarecrow we made was a replica of him, the body bulging above and below the waist-string, and teeth bared like a radiator grille, stitched in black in an oblong mouth.

After Opa's death Oma took in lodgers, a couple with a fourteen-year-old son. He was a sly, unpleasant boy who dropped things on the floor so he could look up my skirt. They took over, shifted Oma's silver-framed photo of her and Opa off the mantelpiece and into a niche to make room for a photo of Hitler. 'Just put it back and tell them,' Papa said, but she was afraid. She spent more and more time in the allotment garden, and often I accompanied her. She kept a stock of my favourite cinnamon biscuits, for which I still have the recipe. Not that bribery was necessary. I loved Oma. She always smelt of lily of the valley, as did her bedroom which Opa had wallpapered with 1000-mark banknotes in the hyperinflation of 1923.

One day when I was eleven we went with the empty handcart after school to pick runner beans and tomatoes. She was wearing her old navy dress with the Paisley labyrinths that I loved to run my finger round, and on the way we sang An Die Freude and laughed as each outvied the other in lustiness. When we reached the wrought-iron entrance gate, the key didn't work. Someone had changed the lock. She peered over the bushes and there, sitting at her picnic table with the tablecloth embroidered by her mother and the samovar, smoking and drinking from her cup, sat the friendly neighbour, smirking. He had replaced Papa's flag with the three silver arrows by a swastika banner on the shed roof. Without a word she fled, still pulling the cart. When we reached the street door to our flats, she broke down and told me to go home. Mama and later Papa went and spoke to her, but she never returned to the allotment garden. Papa said she was a spirited lady in her youth and once used a hatpin to stab the groping hand of a man on the tram. But this broke her spirit.

Some weeks later Onkel Eduard and Tante Luise came.

Oma wasn't there. 'She had it coming,' they said. 'She's not a good German.' Papa defended her, but after that my visits to Oma were less and less frequent, and when she came down for tea, there was darkness in my heart.

5

From now on there was no respite until break-up. For the beginning of Healthy Schools Week I went into auto-smile. The stick insects escaped during *Goodnight, Mr Tom* and they were all in the curtains, Lauren got caught in a hollow bramble thicket and the school choir learned the Volga boat song so that Natalya, who arrived three weeks ago with no English, could sing it in Russian, while Ellis and Kevin took the opportunity to make up silly words. At the staff meeting Evelyn chided Wendy and me: 'In future please do not exchange looks on contentious issues.' A typical day, but every moment the photo invaded.

'Right,' I tried on the Tuesday. Kevin was entertaining his companions by squashing up alternate nostrils, and Ross was probably on his X-box in his head. 'Can you take out – pencils and rubbers,' I sang to the tune of O When The Saints.

'We can take out – pencils and rubbers,' came the gleeful response on the same notes.

The girls put on a pageant of glittery pink pencils taken from glittery pink pencil-cases. One of them could have sent the email, the girls swooned over Mark when he came to my school fête. Nothing was private or secure these days. The malice of ten and eleven-year-olds equalled that of adults, but the sophistication, the ability to get at anyone – that was scary.

Evelyn brought in a maths specialist, a tall, lynx-eyed man who sat at the back of the class with stiff politeness.

'Twice I noticed,' he said in the staffroom, 'when a pupil asked you to explain, you said the same thing again, just louder.'

The heat rose to my face. Evelyn watched like a sparrowhawk biding its time in a tree.

'And you should be able to solve the percentage problem.'

Later, I overheard Hatchet Man telling Evelyn a duck could do it with its eyes shut.

*

In a quiet Taunton backstreet stood a row of dingy tenements of decayed grandeur. We stopped at one and looked around. A bottle and crisp packet were wedged in the hedge. Like debutantes descending ballroom stairs in reverse, we mounted the steps and pressed the bell marked D, which didn't work.

As we waited, unsure what to do, a man came past us up the steps, unlocked the front door and held it open; inside, the dust lay thick. We climbed the windowless stairs. On the first floor the light went out, and we fumbled in vain for a switch before trudging up two flights in darkness. At the top a door opened and a man in his mid- to late forties stood in the doorway silhouetted by the light. He was tall and wiry with a face like an Aztec eagle, piercing blue eyes and feral auburn hair which the sun lit up a dark orange marmalade, and a dazzling shirt of Smarties on a black background.

'Oliver Diamond.'

He offered a firm hand first to Mark and then to me. He smelled of Floris Santal aftershave, my favourite.

In the main room we left our shoes by the door. Oliver's own feet were bare. Through a small, dirty window the sun made a triangle of light across the floor and up the wall and over the Smarties shirt. The room was empty but for two red and purple beanbags at one end, and a larger one opposite. We sat side by side on the smaller beanbags like naughty children while he limped from wall to wall as he talked, dragging the right leg and stopping at intervals to view us from beneath his eyebrows like a charging bull.

'Right,' said Oliver, and I recognised a superior rightness. When I said 'Right', it was probably because I wasn't sure I was right, but this Oliver oozed rightness, the way he said right and straightway glided across the floor, telling us he'd been in the business for two decades, led personal development workshops in countries as far flung as New Zealand and Canada and helped some five hundred people.

'Of course the pragmatic approach might be to observe the phenomena of inner processes and then deduce the deep-seated personality problems of concern. So of course it could be said that the received wisdom is that...' he said. Our eyelids drooped. The wall-to-wall figure dance stopped. The jute floor covering with large square mesh must have hurt his bare feet. 'Where were we?'

We stared blankly.

'Shall we talk about why you're here?'

It exploded out, the maths specialist and the new head who made us log every piece of work by every child in every lesson, everything I did was wrong, and we had a fantastic music scene before Evelyn but what Evelyn said was gospel.

'Everything I do is wrong,' I repeated.

Oliver jumped up and paced. 'Something is rotten in the state of Denmark. I was a teacher myself, so I do understand the stresses of the job. In fact I ran my own vocal school for many a year and helped countless youngsters to get gigs that were of untold benefit to them in their personal lives.' He talked at length about his school, striding back and forth, finally perching on his beanbag. 'Where were we?'

We stared. The beanbag granules rolled about and we sank to the floor.

'Ah yes. Hard-pressed teachers.'

'Mark said I should get another job.'

'Hmm.' Oliver moved off again. 'When I was in the West

End I had directors telling me how to sing, do it this way, do it that way, when I knew better.' He rambled on about the illustrious career cut short. 'In the end I did the only thing possible: I set up my own school.'

The jute dug into my soles. 'But I love my job and it was fine before Evelyn.'

'Don't blame Evelyn,' said Mark. 'You've always done more work than me.'

'It's a gender thing. His head and parents drool over him because he's male.'

'She's such a perfectionist. She's got rows and rows of jars and boxes, six shelves each with forty-four 100-gramme Co-op Fairtrade coffee jars on one wall, four shelves each with thirty-eight 200-gramme Co-op Fairtrade coffee jars on another, and four shelves each with six two-litre Co-op ice-cream boxes on another, all labelled. I know because I counted them, and d'you know what? They're all the same. I bought Sainsbury's coffee once and she threw out the jar. They must all be Co-op Fairtrade.'

'So you like order, Stef?' said Oliver, the toes of his bare feet twitching.

Life was in bits. You couldn't do one thing, all day and all week one thing. No, you had to think about different things, or there were no proper endings, and just when one was finished, like waving Emma off to Africa, you found it was still in your head, pecking away. Then you started a new thought, Mark or marking or email photos, and your head was full of thoughts you couldn't file in coffee jars or boxes. They weighed you down, fragments of this, fragments of that. It would be wonderful not to think, just exist like a leaf on a pond.

'Yes, I like order.' Wasn't all of life an attempt to create order and meaning out of chaos? 'I worry over my daughter

Emma who's left—'

Oliver leapt up and paced. 'Ah. Empty-nest syndrome, that's hard.' He stopped at the other wall. 'What do you think, Mark?'

Mark glanced at me. 'I think you're jealous. *You* went canoeing on the Limpopo.'

'That was different.'

'It's not.'

'So how do you think the rot started, Mark?'

Mark hesitated. 'I feel neglected when Stef spends so much time on work.'

The wall-to-wall figure dance resumed. 'Well, the question is, do you feel neglected as an outcome, or do you just feel neglected? I mean, it might be said that the very essence of the universe is dynamic, that the structure of...'

Maybe too many late nights made it seem soporific, something about formative years and repression and infantile wishes.

'Perhaps you'd like to say more about those feelings of neglect.'

Mark's brow furrowed. 'I just feel ignored.'

A police siren droned in a distant street.

'Stef, how about you? Or shall I call you Stefanie?'

'Stef. Stef with an eff,' I added.

'Okay, Stef with an eff. How do you feel about it?'

Mark's face was expressionless. 'The teaching is very demanding,' I said, thinking I should be talking about the email image.

'Okay.' He sat down. 'I do understand, of course. I kept up the school for years before I had to acknowledge I'd had enough of pushy parents. A small percentage took up a disproportionate amount of my time. I loved the job, loved working with the kids, but...' He gazed at each of us in turn.

'Why don't you tell me a bit about your background. Mark first, tell me about your childhood. Then Stef.'

Mark grew up in Norfolk, his father died when he was thirteen and his mother became clingy. Mark escaped, but his sister remained as an unappreciated slave. 'But I'm the golden boy.'

'Gran raised me and Lisa while our parents went to work,' I said. 'She taught me to sing and play the piano. In fact, she taught me everything.'

Oliver sat up and the Smarties on his shirt gleamed in the sun. 'It's a little odd that you talk about your grandmother first, rather than your parents.'

'Oh, I'm on the best of terms with my parents. It's the new head teacher that's the problem.'

'I see. Big changes. The thing is, it could be said that the aim is to understand the relations of consciousness and nature. By nature I mean a plurality of events that are external to each other and yet connected by relations of causality. And perhaps...'

And so on and so forth for fifty minutes while we stared, uncomprehending.

'Sorry we're out of time.' The legs made a scissor shadow in the shaft of light and the Smarties shimmered. 'We'll save the rest for next week, though there'll be no primrose path. I need commitment.'

But we hadn't talked about the photo. We paid ninety pounds and left. For two teachers accustomed to talking all day, we had said remarkably little. And we couldn't remember a word he said, apart from 'commitment'.

'That man could talk a glass eye to sleep,' said Mark.

*

Another email came: '*Mark seen with other woman last Sat*

a.m.' No picture, no proof. My scalp tightened and at the sound of Mark's footsteps I pressed Delete and pocketed the phone. The Russian Giant sunflowers outside the French windows made eerie figures in the dark with their fluttering heart-shaped leaves.

Above the piano the Laughing Cavalier twisted his lips into a smile beneath handlebar moustaches. Schumann floated into the room and calmed me with his dreaminess, the mellow bass notes, the warm timbre like a hand stroking my face, soothing away the photo, the simple melody always coming home. Home, where the heart is. Except that this home was tainted by vicious emails that might or might not be true. The feathery sounds filled the room and the familiarity of the tune drew me in, but the worries swelled like dough.

Mark scoffed when I confronted him, told me not to listen to them and thought it okay not to listen to me either.

Gran was my refuge. Gran always listened and the smell of warm cinnamon greeted me at the door.

'He admitted he was in town last Saturday morning, Gran,' I said over tea and cakes, sitting facing the cast-iron fireplace, 'but he denied he'd been with anyone. He told me each shop he went in. But why would someone make that up? Why would they, Gran?'

'Sometimes people say things to spite someone.' She gazed at the empty fireplace with lacklustre eyes.

The grandfather clock struck the quarter-hour. We dissected the email, then Evelyn and the maths specialist.

'The emails are the worst. Mark dismisses them. I got more comfort from the counsellor.' Actually, I couldn't remember what he said, apart from the stresses of teaching. We were getting somewhere, there would be no primrose path but, with commitment on our part, Oliver could help. 'I feel I've come home, Gran. I feel he understands me.'

'Darling, you mustn't worry, do you hear me? Give Mark the benefit of the doubt.'

Like a drowning spider that clings to the finger it rejected on dry land I clung to her words and let Diabelli duets wash everything away, thumping out the bass chords, the grand finales. Melodies were easy, it was the bass that complemented them, like a conversation but more beautiful. Gran played the melody, like a stream flowing on and on until in the end it trickled away and we sat in contemplation. Or we teased each other, wove in and out and collapsed in laughter over wrong notes in a fast dance, or stomped and swaggered over the piano and dissolved into giggles. The familiar tunes were like warm cakes.

Hilda patted the piano and said, grinning, 'Ein gutes Tier ist das Klavier, still, friedlich und bescheiden, und muß dabei doch vielerlei erdulden und erleiden.'[1]

Back home, empties were stacking up and Mark and his friends were playing Grand Theft Auto.

'Thanks for doing the hedge, Mark.'

'You could put a spirit level on that hedge,' said a friend.

'That's how the boss likes it,' said Mark.

'Who won the match?' I said.

'Spain, of course,' said another friend. 'They controlled the play.'

'Bit like marriage,' said Mark, laughing like a chimpanzee, eyes on the screen. 'I should have let Adam keep her.'

'Thanks a bunch,' I said.

---

1 'The piano is a good animal, quiet, peaceful and modest, and yet must endure and suffer much.'

6

Germany's forests were full of sick spruce trees, Hilda read with dismay. And now here in England sudden oak death was spreading through the West Country. She loved the forest, magical and dark, a place to wander and get lost, where witches and wolves ate little children. It echoed her own darkness, or perhaps replaced it. She pulled a large leather suitcase thick with dust out from under the high wrought-iron bed. Stef and Lisa used to hide among the boxes and cases under the bed while she counted to fifty. She took out a letter dated 1.8.1919 she had found after her mother's death, on thin and frail yellowed paper. Inside was a pressed gentian, still faintly blue.

She read:

My darling Ilse, I wander through the Tiergarten and think of our walks in the Thuringian Forest, the leaves rustling and birds singing for us, and I yearn for your gentle touch. Every moment I think of your beauty and my heart longs for the day we will be together forever. Your Stefan.

She typed:

Every summer we stayed with Mama's mother in the Thuringian Forest, the green heart of Germany. Thüringen-Oma was the salt of the earth, like a little Wichtelmännchen who comes out at night and does the housework and baking the humans are too tired to do. With her hair tied up in a bun with hundreds of pins, and wearing one apron on top of the other to save her best apron, she was permanently bent over the range stirring a pot of potato dumplings in gravy. She put all her heart into feeding us. Mama's sister Tante Elsbeth and Onkel Karl lived in the same village. There was a brother too, but he died in the First World War. He was only eighteen. Thüringen-Opa died of consumption three years after the war.

Back home, Hanno and I often walked to the Grunewald forest, but it was two hours away, so to have the forest on the doorstep was wonderful. You could breathe among the spruces. It was so quiet you could hear things growing, and after rain the droplets clinging to the needles glistened and the fragrance was heady. We and the three cousins were allowed to go off and play all day, as long as we looked after Otto. Otto was older than me, but had learning difficulties. We teased him that there was a wolf behind him or took toys off him, but he was a sweet boy who wouldn't harm a fly. He held us back and sometimes we wished he wouldn't come along. He was a cry-baby and never wanted to be the bear when we played Bear Driver. Once we put a dead black-and-yellow fire salamander in his bed, and another time we hid inside the old German oak with knobby eyes and gaping mouth-hole. He dawdled home, crying all the way, and although we kept him within sight, I am ashamed. We went to bed with no supper.

One year we travelled with Berlin-Oma by third-class rail to Thüringen-Oma's for Christmas. Our carriage had hard wooden seats and we scraped the frost off the windows with our fingernails. We arrived to find a thick blanket of snow. I wore two pairs of knickers, thick woollen ones on top, and we went tobogganing. Bedtime was early, with warnings about the night raven that devoured children still up after the last sound of the church bell.

On Christmas Eve Papa brought in the tree and we

decorated it with baubles, candles and lametta, then crunched through the snow to church, me in my new blue washable velvet dress with frills and flounces round the neck and cuffs, Thüringen-Oma in her smelly fur coat, and Tante Elsbeth and Onkel Karl and our cousins too, then back to Oma's with lighted candles to light the candles on the tree. Bits of spruce decorated every clock and picture. We children each sang a song – Otto sang O Tannenbaum very loudly – before opening the presents under the tree. I had a musical box which played the tune of Daisy Bell and a mouth organ and a jointed teddy bear stuffed with wood wool. Onkel Karl worked in a teddy bear factory. After the gifts we had a Yule boar dinner, then Papa sang the first verse of In Dulci Jubilo solo, and we all sang carols with Mama on the piano and the two grandmothers sitting on the settee.

On Christmas Day Onkel Ernst and Tante Grete arrived. They came in their bright red Steyr car, bringing biscuits shaped like sig runes which Tante Grete insisted on hanging on the tree, and pralines, nougat and truffles from the factory which Onkel Ernst had bought together with the car and house with antique furniture from a Jewish man desperate to leave Germany. Papa said angrily he hardly paid any money for it. Their daughters Waltraud and Sofie were fifteen and fourteen and had cascading curly locks like Dürer. Their parents called them the blonde one and the dark one instead of names. We had roast goose with potato dumplings and red cabbage for dinner, and Otto said it was the best dinner ever, and best of all were the marzipan sweets.

'You made them?' he said to Mama and me. 'That's wonderful,' and we laughed at his simple delight.

We didn't like the girls. While we moaned at Otto

and teased him, they beat him with a stick for disobeying their commands to dance in Bear Driver. While we threw snowballs, at which he laughed more than anyone, Waltraud and Sofie made him stand still and encased him head to foot in snow. Liesl and I objected, but Waltraud dug the end of her stick in Liesl's neck and threatened to have us thrown out of Jungmädel if we told. Tante Grete was a regional leader.

Otto was shivering and ill afterwards. We never told the adults and nor did he. After they left, Thüringen-Oma took the rune biscuits off the tree and binned them without a word. We had Oma's Stollen and Pfefferkuchen instead. I loved the presents and Oma's baking and singing carols round the piano, but Mama and Papa said Christmas was spoilt by Onkel Ernst and Tante Grete.

'Never again,' said Papa.

7

'Come in. Sit down. I'll be with you in a minute.'

Evelyn's head was bent over what she was writing. She was wearing her red suit. The new maple furniture made the room less forbidding, she said, but I would rather have kept Stella and Jane and the old furniture and forgone the six-foot-high philodendron and the rare orchid and the Axminster carpet. A mizzly rain started, but Mark and his football boys would still carry on playing.

'Stef.' Evelyn laid down her pen, looked up and folded her arms on the desk. 'I feel things are getting on top of you and I've been considering ways to lighten your load. That's difficult, because I could have, *should* have asked you to run the after-school club since you have no children at home. I had to think of other options.' She smiled. 'I'm transferring you from Year 6 to Year 3. It'll give you more time, less pressure.'

Outside, the voices of the last few children dwindled to a murmur. Beads of sweat amassed between my shoulder blades and trickled down. Evelyn's smiling face looked like some hideous, mocking gargoyle.

'But I'd have to swot up a whole new curriculum.'

'And eight-year-olds are more manageable.'

'But I manage the eleven-year-olds perfectly well.'

'We have one particularly unbiddable boy, Thomas Rankine, moving up to Year 6, as you know, and John is good with him.'

Thomas had done an amazing picture of his teacher holding the globe on strings, with a speech balloon that said, 'Now I have you all in my power.' Every teacher loves a challenge.

'You'll find the new Year 3s very willing and endearing. You already know five of them from the choir. But you mustn't feel obliged to keep doing the choir. Sally will happily do it in your place.'

'But—'

'I don't want you to have any unnecessary stress, Stef. I know you'll make a good job of Year 3.'

'But I'm not stressed, I love doing Year 6, you know I do. No one else thinks I can't handle it. Ask the parents. Ask the children.'

'I think you'll find Year 3 easier. My mind is made up.'

My brain felt like a shrivelled walnut. 'That's it?'

The gargoyle smiled again. 'That is it, Stef. The job is less demanding. You'll have more opportunity for creative pursuits. Of course, if you're unhappy about it, I'd let you go at the end of this term instead of serving three months' notice, but I'd much rather keep you. I'm doing this to make things easier for you, not harder, you know.'

The children's voices outside had stopped. A marble bounced at first slowly, then faster and faster over the corrugated tin roof outside.

'Sleep on it and let me know in the morning. You'll think differently about Year 3 by then.'

I staggered to my feet, walked to the door and turned, one hand on the door handle. 'I don't need to think about it. This school's gone down the pan since you came. It's like an avalanche. I'll leave at the end of this term.' I lurched out into the brilliant fluorescent light of the corridor.

On my classroom walls were the children's artwork and photos. Jonathan, the tallest boy, stood under a sunflower that measured three metres and fifty-five centimetres to the underside of the flower. Now everything must be moved out. Evelyn had done it on purpose to make more work, push me out. All the good staff wanted to leave. Try as I might, I couldn't concentrate. Evelyn had put the after-school club in the hall next to my classroom and the shrieking and yelling were intolerable. And Lauren had spelt 'there' and 'their' persistently wrong today. In the cupboard were rows of identical box files and ice-cream tubs, colour-coded, indexed and cross-referenced. Pink paper? Stef will have some. Spare scissors? Go to Stef. The boxed reams of government diktats covered every subject imaginable. Six thousand pages last year alone, more than twice the complete works of Shakespeare. The crunch of the guillotine blade slicing through stacks of paper was some kind of music. 'Support for school from the National Institute for Clinical Excellence', covering alcohol, obesity, social and emotional wellbeing, atopic eczema: damn Evelyn with her faux niceness, crunch, the silky words, crunch, smiling mouth, crunch, the skin creasing round dagger eyes, crunch. I did have a good reputation, and if people like Kevin Connor's father hollered, Evelyn should take no notice. I brushed aside the shredded paper and seized another stack. 'Workforce race advisory group workplan executive summary': things getting on top of me, crunch, lighten my load, crunch. If Evelyn wanted me to run the after-school club, why not ask, crunch? 'Guidance on the inclusion of Gypsy, Roma and Traveller pupils': think you'll find Year 3 easier, lying toad, crunch. She'd done it on purpose, crunch, driving me out, crunch. 'Let's fight it together – cyberbullying resource pack': you mustn't feel obliged to keep doing the choir, crunch, smarmy woman, crunch, I built that choir up from nothing, crunch. Kevin had changed from urchin to angel. Seeing Kevin, mouth wide, not poking the others, made everything worthwhile. 'Equality and sexual orientation': on and on I shredded and brushed the strips onto the floor.

The mountain was as high as the table when I spotted a solitary figure in the playground, in the rain: Kevin with no jacket, trying to look nonchalant, darting glances towards the gate. His spiked hair with the forked-lightning bald patch dripped. Never mind the terrible din when Kevin and friends fixed drawing pins along the undersides of their desk lids, then simultaneously slammed. Never mind his bullying of sweet, gentle Amy. I opened the window and told him to come and wait in the classroom. His father was supposed to collect him, but his mobile had no credit. No one replied on mine, so after clearing the shredded paper I dropped him off.

'You're home early,' said Mark, arriving later, soaked and muddy.

'Evelyn is transferring me to Year 3 and she gave me the option of leaving now instead of at Christmas so I'm leaving in two weeks,' I said and burst apart like the innards of a pen springing out when unscrewed.

*

The jute carpet cut into my stockinged feet and in one breath out tumbled the maths specialist again and the choir and oily Evelyn with her fancy Axminster carpet, grotesquely smiling and speaking in the voice of someone giving a child their favourite ice-cream.

'I'm sure she thinks I'm too old. The other Year 6 teacher is twenty-eight and the kids all love a younger teacher.'

'Stef, this is awful. This person should be sacked. Your choir sounds wonderful, and I'm sure your maths is fine. As for your age, I know plenty of teachers older than you.'

The mirror eyes of the embroidered elephants on his maroon and black waistcoat gleamed.

'You could get Evelyn for constructive dismissal,' said Mark.

'Whoa,' said Oliver. 'You don't want to jeopardise chances of a decent reference. Teachers can always find jobs. If you have no success, I know a couple of head teachers. So how do you feel now about the lack of time you spend together?'

'If she doesn't get a job,' said Mark, 'she'll have all the time in the world but not for me.'

'I've got a whole classroom to clear out in four weeks. That's my summer holidays gone.'

'Good job we're off to Norfolk for five days, then. We were supposed to book a proper holiday on lastminute.com.'

'We can't afford that now.' Five days of cycling with only each other for company sounded like a penance—not to mention staying at his mother's on the first and last nights, with her sly little asides skirted over before they could be answered: 'Doesn't she make you spotted dick and custard?' and 'You don't know how to remove a bloodstain?'

'When I said get another job, I meant before quitting this one. You could go to Evelyn cap in hand.'

So as not to cramp his freedom to meet *her*? 'No way.'

And so on—all the old chestnuts: it wasn't just Mark who suffered from my obsessive schoolwork, Sadie and Emma did too; perhaps it was a good thing I had no job; I had torn him away from his mother and sister; his mother liked him to herself...

Oliver glanced at the clock. 'Sorry, have to stop you there.' He smiled. 'And the bad news is that I'm giving up this room. The landlord and I have never seen eye to eye. But the good news is that you can still see me. At the Academy. A better option is to come to a residential workshop. There's one in eight days' time. Come and strut and fret your hour upon my stage, Mark. Ask for Amelia.' He scribbled a number on a piece of paper. 'And any teacher who can play the piano can get a job,' he added. His eyes lit up. 'What do you get if you drop a piano down a mine shaft?'

We stared.

'A flat minor.'

The more I thought about it, the more I laughed. His eyes sparkled and his lips sucked like an amoeba engulfing a piece of food as he spoke. With his piercing blue eyes and woody smell of Floris Santal, Oliver was irresistibly sexy.

On a soap-bubble of hope I floated out, having quite forgotten the photo.

*

'What do you get if you drop a piano down a mine shaft?'

'Go on, tell me,' said Gran.

'A flat minor.'

We shrieked with laughter. Jack and I were building a railway track on the patio after going to Lynmouth on the open-topped double-decker. All the way there and all the way back, on and on he had pestered, 'Why didn't Mark come?'

'He's out canoeing for the day,' I replied, but seeing the charcoaled, contorted gorse skeletons from last winter's swaling on Porlock Hill, doubt muscled in. He could have come.

'Outrageous,' said Gran when I told her about Evelyn. 'But you'll easily get another job, as soon as anyone sees that you're a *good* teacher.'

'I've had another email. It said, 'We're glad you've gone.''

'It sounds like children.'

'If the photo is real, their age doesn't matter.'

We played The Arrival of the Queen of Sheba, but all Handel's joyful noise could not shake off the sense of doom.

Jack said, 'I'm glad you haven't gone, Auntie Stef.'

8

It hurt more than if Hilda had received the hate mail herself. She took an unfinished Schubert sonata from the stack. A barren landscape. In her youth she liked muscular playing, but now she preferred mellow, to escape old marching rhythms that forever impinged on her consciousness. Remorse and regret seeped into the room and no music could cure that. There was space in her head only for creeping away with mouse-like steps so delicate she barely touched the keys. It ended with a dark going-down.

Afterwards she typed:

When I was ten, on Monday evenings I joined the youth club run by the Lutheran church. My parents were not churchgoers, but they didn't mind. We played games and sang songs and listened to Bible stories, or went on swimming trips on the Wannsee on the outskirts of Berlin.

One Sunday we lined up after church, about forty of us, and marched, giggling and chatting, along the Charlottenburger Chaussee. In the Großer Stern we stopped and waited. After ten minutes a Hitler Youth march came from the same direction with a band, and girls at the back. The procession stopped and the two leaders faced each other, gave the German greeting, shook hands and spoke a few words. They gave the German greeting again and the Hitler Youth marched off. As the end of the column went by, our leader shouted for us to march behind that column, left, right, left, right. They were singing the Horst Wessel song, which meant nothing to us, but they had bugles and fifes and drums which was exciting. No longer the chattering, higgledy-piggledy line of boys and girls, we became neat and serious, and when we fell out of step we quickly rectified it. Marching in time was thrilling. We wished we knew the words. We soon would. We marched to the Hitler Youth headquarters where they divided us into under and over fourteen years old, boys and girls, and assigned us to our new squads, told us where next to meet and dismissed us. Eva and I giggled as we walked home. We had become Jungmädel.

My parents said, 'Do you want to be in the Hitler Youth?'

I said, 'All my friends are there.'

They said, 'If you leave you can still see your friends.'

But I neither could nor wanted to. We had more fun with our new leader Gisela, who was not much older than us, sailing on the Wannsee, puppet shows, recorder trios, putting on plays in the forest, roasting sausages on a camp-fire, and singing and dancing. We clapped hands and linked arms in all the wrong places and ended up laughing so much we couldn't do the dance. We had day trips to the country and summer camps lasting four whole weeks. Most girls had never left Berlin. Life was no longer just schoolwork and family outings. On sports afternoons at Jungmädel Gisela would say, 'Line up – head count,' and we lined up in order of height on three sides of a square in black shorts and white tops, heads facing right, then the first girl said 'One' and faced left, the second said 'Two' and faced left, and so on. They made us feel grown-up and important. We loved the uniform – the brown velours climbing jacket with extra pockets that we called a monkey skin, and the skirt that buttoned onto the shirt with mother-of-pearl buttons. And the marching. As we marched we sang Alle Menschen Werden Brüder, All Men Become Brothers. I was hooked.

Everything we did knitted us together: singing, games,

stitching our own pennant which we placed in the middle of the circle while Gisela gave her sometimes boring lectures. We were a community, and the whole nation was a people's community. We were comrades of the people. Those who were not with us were against us.

'A people helps itself,' was the slogan, and the second Sunday of every month from October to March was Eintopfsonntag, one-pot Sunday. Dinner was stew, and the money saved was donated to the winter relief fund. One Sunday in front of the Kaiser-Wilhelm-Gedächtnis-Kirche I saw a banner: 'Berlin is eating its one-pot stew today.' Opposite were a portable canteen and tents and a brass band wearing pillbox hats with peaks and jackboots, and people in fox stoles and heavy square-shouldered coats queuing.

Sometimes I collected door to door for the winter relief. I had to report where I was sent away empty-handed and where no one was in. I didn't appreciate the mockery in Mama's answers to my question, 'What's for dinner today?' 'Today is one-pot Friday' or 'Today is one-pot Monday.' She said the winter relief fund was a swindle, and she preferred to give money directly to people who'd lost their jobs because of the regime.

9

The car groaned uphill. At each summit another summit appeared; there were endless swathes of brown, dead-looking heather and tawny grass, with a few trees stunted by harsh winds. We stopped and got out. The ling was turning mauve. I stepped over a bog-pool on to turf, but my shoe sank in inky black water. Mark stared into the distance.

'I have a good feeling about this weekend,' he said. 'This could be the saving of us.'

Tiny yellow tormentil flowers were still out here. Back home they were long since finished; back home Mark and I were half-finished. Lost my job, losing my husband. Here was hope. After the hullabaloo of the classroom, here was peace in spite of the twittering of invisible birds.

We got back in the car and drove and drove, tired of the never-ending moor now. Sitting in the car was like seeing a silent film without the outpouring of the lark or the tickle of the wind, without the smell of fresh air. Mark drove faster, braking on every bend, while I clutched the grab handle and depressed an imaginary foot brake.

'I'm sure we passed that rowan before,' I said, not sure at all. The orange berries were bright, conspicuous as a piece of plastic on the beach.

'You've got the map. I can't drive *and* read the map.'

'I don't know where we are. Somewhere round here.' My hand circled over a large area.

'That's no use to me.'

'I'm not God.'

He stopped the car. 'Sometimes you behave like it. I can't think why I agreed to come. I've always thought people who live in communes are odd.'

'Rachel's not odd.'

'Rachel's great. Here, give me the map. '

I spread it between us and he drove on. The sun was sinking. On a bend two Exmoor ponies with mealy muzzles as if they had stuck them in a bag of flour and a foal with wonky legs stood in the road and nibbled at the grass edges. I screamed and he braked.

'I wish we hadn't stopped earlier,' I said.

'I wish you'd directed us better.'

'Oh, for God's sake, stop it. We should have started earlier. You know I hate being late.'

Yet here the horizons kept coming and time no longer seemed precious. The ticking clocks of the towns could tick themselves to death and the moor would still be the moor. The school maelstrom and the pressure to get a job in five weeks had faded.

The ponies ambled off and we sped up and down. We stopped to study the map again. A kestrel with chestnut plumage hovered with outspread wings and fanned tail, unbuffeted by the wind, eyes trained down over a combe, its position unchanged.

On we went, slowly because sheep were on or near the road, and I flustered and tried to phone, but there was no signal. No signal, no instant communication, no instant gratification of every wish.

By chance we spotted the sign: The Diamond Academy for Spiritual Development. A flock of rooks cawed over nearby woodland and a long, winding drive lined with beeches like a guard of honour led to an old manor house, a red sandstone building with battlemented tower and Georgian windows. We need not have hurried, because we were greeted only by a voluptuous rosy sky and bats popping one after the other out of a hole in the wall. A bird flew out of the sausage-trunked ivy next to the door.

'Fancy making a nest near the door.'

'Probably a female making the decisions,' said Mark, which earnt him a look.

A Border collie came round the corner, wagging its tail as it shepherded us to the door. In the lobby with its palatial black-veined marble floor and broad sweeping staircase was a stag's head with lips drawn back, and a huge gilt-framed photo of Oliver. The ice-blue eyes watched us whether we stood to right or left. Beneath it was the legend 'Work is an end, not a means.'

A pompon chrysanthemum-headed woman with shifting lemur eyes appeared, her T-shirt emblazoned with Oliver's face. I struggled to concentrate on the talking face.

'I'm Claire.' She grinned and proffered a dish marked Visitors. 'Can you hand over your mobiles, please.'

Mark took out his mobile. 'There's no signal anyway.' He put it back in his pocket.

'I'm sorry, it's what we've all agreed.'

'But there's no signal.'

The woman with the leopard-spot dress who had stood beside Captain Mainwaring at *Elijah* appeared, and her heels clicked across the marble floor. 'I'm Amelia,' she said in a crisp voice like a ballet teacher's. She smelt of sun cream. 'We don't have mobiles here. Just ask in the office if you need it.' She smiled.

Mark smiled back as we put our mobiles in the dish.

She strutted off and called, 'Take them straight in, Claire.'

Claire popped the dish behind a door. 'You'll love it here. Everyone does.'

She led us down a corridor into a vast room with a lofty scrolled ceiling. Men and women with eager faces greeted us like children at a circus; they were mostly in their thirties and forties, some in their fifties and sixties. We sat on a sheepskin rug on the flagstones between Rachel, who wore a hand-made multi-coloured patchwork skirt, black tights and red cloth shoes and hugged the huge woven-rush shoulder bag she always carried, and Simon with the tufty eyebrows.

'We've been looking forward to your coming,' said Simon in his warm Somerset accent with the rhotic r's. 'Where've you been to? Did you get lost?' He told us he grew up on a farm on Exmoor, but went to London for the bright lights and joined Oliver's Alexander technique class. When the manor house and farm came up for sale after the foot-and-mouth epidemic, Oliver said it was meant to be.

'Is Stef your wife?' said Amelia, joining us, bringing with her the sickly sun cream smell.

'Nah,' said Mark, 'I hired her for the weekend,' and we all laughed. His eyes fixed on Amelia. 'Why are married women heavier than single women?'

'I don't know.'

'Single women come home, see what's in the fridge and go to bed. Married women come home, see what's in bed and go to the fridge.'

Amelia let out a peal of giggles. 'You are funny, Mark.'

'At last,' said Mark. 'Someone who appreciates my jokes.'

I groaned.

Another door opened and the buzz stopped. Oliver stood in the doorway, wearing a bright red satin waistcoat with gold dragons which gleamed in the light from the chandeliers. His head with feral chestnut hair was cocked, and on his lips was a faint Mona Lisa smile. The ice-blue eyes took in the gathering in one sweep. The air bristled like the moment before a concert begins, and fourteen pairs of eyes converged on Oliver. The room held its breath.

His face broke into a big smile which spread like a bush

fire, the room let out its breath, the statues relaxed. Still he waited.

'Thank you all for coming,' he said quietly at last, stepping across the threshold. 'It's good to see new faces. This community will die if it doesn't get new blood.' The penetrating eyes lingered on each person in turn. The faces were rapt, like a class of six-year-olds at storytelling time. 'I feel a prodigious energy in this room. We've come a long way from our beginnings eight years ago. We were nothing then, just people disillusioned with our lives, trying to make them better.' He trembled and his voice rose in a crescendo, reverberating round the walls. The eyes reached me. 'We're like springs that well up to the surface and end up as mighty rivers. We were forced out, but look how strong we are now. We're not quitters. So screw your courage to the sticking place and we'll not fail.'

The applause was loud and immediate. Mark and I joined in the clapping without cheering. Rachel and others gave a standing ovation.

'Do we feel positive about this weekend?'

Mutters of 'yes' went round the room like a never-ending echo.

'Are we all ready to work?'

'Yes,' they chorused.

'Right.'

He strode to the door, leg dragging, and everyone funnelled through behind him, hugging as they went. Mark was at the front. Rachel hugged me by the waist as we climbed the stone stairs, and admired my hair which Mark hadn't noticed was loose instead of tied in a ponytail.

The walls of the workroom were half-clad in oak panelling, above which hung Persian carpets in brilliant carmines and ultramarines and viridians with tulips and sickle leaves and

Herati patterns. A huge bay window reaching down to the floor overlooked the brooding moor: all trace of pink was gone from the sky. In a corner was a scuffed baseball bat. We heaped up our shoes by the door and sat in a circle on cushions on the thick cherry-red carpet, Mark and I between Rachel and Simon. Oliver sat on a larger, plumper cushion in the bay, with a respectful gap either side. We waited. Oliver grabbed his cushion and limped across to a position between Mark and Simon, who fanned out to make way, and the movement went round the circle in both directions like a wave.

'We'll start with a round-up,' said Oliver. 'Mark, tell us why you're here.'

Mark hesitated.

'Take your time, Mark, we're all with you.'

'Relationship problems.'

Oliver's face softened. 'Could you say a little more for the group?'

'We're both teachers and we never spend enough time together. We feel we're drifting apart.'

'Stef?'

'It's only in term-time. I've lost my job now anyway.' For the moment Mark's insistence that the image was photoshopped outweighed the doubts.

'My feeling is that Stef is a conscientious teacher. I feel she will get another job soon. A better job. And we will be rooting for Mark and Stef as a couple.'

He smiled and I reddened.

'Right,' said Oliver at the end of the round-up. 'Swimming pool sculpt.'

He indicated an imaginary pool and directed us to position ourselves according to comfort level. Oliver sat at the poolside on the only chair in the room, bare feet resting on a bar, arms resting on splayed thighs. I dangled my legs in the water at the opposite edge, while Simon was about to dive into the deep end. The rest were in the middle, everyone facing Oliver. Mark stood beside Amelia, with a foolish grin.

Each of us described how we felt.

'I'm looking forward to the workshop,' I lied.

Mark said 'Very comfortable', which annoyed me because these people all knew each other well and hugged freely, while Mark and I knew no one. The least Mark could have done was stay with me at the far edge instead of standing next to Amelia like a bee headfirst in a flower.

'Right,' said Oliver.

In groups of three we discussed our given names. Amelia commandeered Mark. I joined Rachel and a sad-looking, sallow-cheeked woman in her sixties with dyed black hair and shiny black leggings. She was named Donna after a dog that died. She didn't mind. They buried it under a lawn which Donna the dog had decorated with yellow circles. The lawn was weak and yellow while the dog was alive, but grew green and strong after its death. So the name was a compliment, she said. Her husband used to tease her about it. They were in a cult together, and the leader drove a wedge between them. The leader called her Donna the dog, and then her husband did too.

'I don't mind,' she said again, curling her bare toes.

Rachel hugged her. 'Bastards. Thank God she found us.'

Bear hugs were the thing. The other two in Mark's threesome were hugging as well. Mark and I looked on nonplussed—as teachers, we had learnt to be non-tactile. Yet it moved me. These people were hungry for contact. Imagine that scene in the staff-room every morning. Imagine hugging Evelyn or Hatchet Man. Wendy and Bill were good friends, but daily hugs would be unthinkable. But these people loved each other and I envied them.

Rachel had changed her name because her parents kept calling her by her older sister's name.

'My mum calls me Lisa all the time,' I said dismissively. 'I do it too, to Sadie and Emma. Everyone does it, don't they?' Though Gran didn't. Rachel looked stung.

I was named after great-grandfather Stefan. 'He was German, and he was imprisoned by the Nazis,' I hastened to add in case they thought he was a Nazi. 'My dumb parents didn't think to spell my name with a 'ph', so I spent the best part of forty-two years telling people it was Stef with an eff. I was nicknamed Eff at school.'

'Okay, Eff,' Rachel and Donna chorused. Donna's face creased into a smile.

'You've made quite an impression, Eff,' said Oliver afterwards. He touched my arm and I blushed. 'You have the makings of a diamond.' Everyone laughed.

At the end we joined hands in a circle and sang Amazing Grace, moving in with raised hands and out again, in and out, in and out. Mark cringed and mimed. Someone started on another note, then someone else on another, and the harmonies stirred me to such a pitch of feeling that the past was forgotten.

We said goodnight, hugging people whose names we didn't know or remember, and Captain Mainwaring with the ponytail took us to the shippon. He wore black, red and turquoise trainers and looked less fearsome when he smiled. His name was Joe, but he was nicknamed Joe the Toe because of an extra toe; fellow medics had got hold of his mobile and changed his ID to Toe.

A black shape loomed out of the shadows, a Tyrannosaurus rex-shaped shrub.

'Simon's idea of a joke,' said Toe.

The moon grimaced over the dark outline of the moor and the wooded slopes of the combe. We walked for fifteen minutes.

'Sorry you're a long way from the house, but the shippon is more comfortable. We hope you're enjoying it so far. Oliver's very caring.'

On the rough-plastered, whitewashed wall was a poem:

The fly's eye
The eye
or should we say eyes
they see
this one sees the way ahead
this one sees the trees to left
this one sees the hungry bird to right
this one sees the way just travelled
fifty eyes with fifty messages
I am the real eye
they all proclaim.

Oliver Diamond

'Sounds nuts,' said Mark.

We lay facing each other under a feather-light quilt with the smell of fresh air on crisp cotton linen. A fly buzzed, wings snagged on a cobweb, while the spider watched from the edge of the web, sallying forth and retreating at intervals.

'I didn't know you were named after your great-grandfather. Your gran never talks about Germany. In fact you'd never know she was German.'

'She's been here since she was fourteen.'

'So what happened to her father?'

'Don't know. She never talks about him. My mother said

the war took him, and she made it sound like a trip on a magic carpet to a fairy-tale land.'

We lay contemplating, nuzzling, with the hard muscle of his upper arm under my neck.

'I was wrong about these people,' said Mark. 'They're very friendly. But why didn't you say about Evelyn?'

I shrugged. The way he said it, our differences were all down to Evelyn. No mention of the photo, the sexts, the silent calls. 'It felt like you were attacking me.'

'I don't think I said anything against you.'

'Maybe not. It was okay afterwards.'

His scalloped lips plucked at the end of my nose like a sea anemone over a poking finger and he kneaded out a frown on my brow.

'Oliver's very sexy,' I said. 'He has an amazing touch. In a healing kind of way.'

'Yes, Stef.'

'Oh, come on, Mark. You know you're the only one.'

The photo of the woman in the turquoise top danced before my eyes.

10

Simon wanted to skip assembly to show us his beloved Red Rubies but Oliver said no, so he pointed out the cattle through the window. They were the same auburn colour as Oliver's hair.

Assembly was for everyone, including some who didn't live in the manor house because they had children. Oliver had bought a house for them in the nearest village. The children were not allowed in the workroom. Three of them kicked the skirting board in the corridor. At assembly the adults aired grievances. Discussing grievances outside was frowned upon because it divided them into subgroups. We sat in a circle, waiting. At length Oliver entered and limped across to the bay.

A woman with a sky-blue bandanna tied at the back and a copper ankh on a leather cord round her neck raised a hand. A tongue-stud glimmered as she spoke. 'Rachel kept me awake with her snoring.'

Snores disturbed others too, but Claire, who was in the same room as Rachel, had heard nothing.

'It's not my fault.' Rachel finger-twisted her hair.

'It's no one else's,' said Amelia.

More voices swelled the chorus.

'Hold on a minute.' Oliver raised a palm. 'Rachel has sought Toe's advice since time immemorial. I won't have anyone blaming Rachel.'

No one spoke.

'Toe, what do you think?' said Oliver at last.

Toe wanted to put himself and Simon in the quiet east wing with Oliver because he had a stressful job as a general practitioner and contributed more financially, with Claire and Rachel in the shippon. Claire and Rachel sulked, and others also craved being near Oliver. So that wasn't fair.

They could squeeze more beds into other rooms, leaving Rachel and Claire alone in a large room. But Amelia detected snores across the corridor, and why should those two get a whole room to themselves? So that wasn't fair.

They tried Simon, Toe and Oliver in the shippon. But where would visitors go? And they needed more workshop participants. Besides, Oliver *belonged* in the main house. So that wasn't fair.

They bickered, they bitched, they scrambled, and bare feet thumped the carpeted floor. In the corridor the children punched and kicked each other and the youngest bawled, so their parents were excused. Mark and I stood by the door hopefully.

'We're very unwelcoming,' said Simon, 'putting our visitors in the shippon or the lodge.'

Then someone had the solution: put Rachel in the tower. Amelia went up with a tape measure and returned triumphant. Claire volunteered to join Rachel in the tower. 'How come Donna gets to keep her own room?' said the bandanna woman who had started it all.

Oliver, who had kept silent throughout, resting his chin on a cupped hand, said, 'Children, children. Enough. What will Eff and Mark think? And you know why Donna has her own room.'

'I know why, but I don't think it's fair,' muttered the bandanna woman.

Not fair, not fair. Like the school playground. Like my constant retort to Sadie and Emma, life isn't fair, so get over it.

'Right,' said Oliver, 'everyone to the pond site. Nothing like a good bout of physical activity to get rid of grumbles.'

We joined hands and walked round singing Kumbayah, and the murmured voices filled the room like snow falling. No one wanted to break the spell after four verses. We stood, still with hands joined, deeply moved, before dispersing.

Oliver limped over to Mark and me. 'I am so sorry. I wouldn't want you to think we behave like this normally.'

Outside Mark said, 'What a carry-on. Rachel would be better off sleeping with the dogs.'

Grey smudges hid the sun and the swallows flew low. We borrowed wellies and traipsed with the others through the grounds with spades and forks and wheelbarrows to dig a pond. As we dug, Rachel told us seven people from Oliver's extramural singing classes had formed a close-knit group and followed him here eight years ago. Oliver had put her in charge of boarding kennels and liked to boast they were run by an ex-guide dog trainer. They managed the farming organically and sold the surplus, and got grants for sustainability, which was Simon's idea. Oliver had helped Donna through a mucky divorce, so she gave her half of the proceeds from the sale of a six-bedroomed house in Epsom.

Rachel rammed her spade in the ground and stretched both arms up to lowering clouds, her face upturned. 'Come, gentle rain, come fall on me. This pond, this is about promoting wildlife.'

'Feels to me like it's about cheap labour,' muttered Mark. 'We paid a lot of money to come and dig someone else's pond.'

'Think positive, Mark, it's more fun doing it together. Can't you feel the energy? It's this place.'

The moment Oliver had crunched over the gravel before the house, he said a wave swept through him, a flood of something indefinable. 'This is it,' he'd said to the seven who came for the viewing, and they were silent for several minutes till he spoke again: 'There's a river of energy.' From then on he had carried them all along with his river.

The red-brown topsoil heaped up beside the hole and we forked the sticky pink subsoil into spadeable lumps and carted it off in barrows. A spadeful of subsoil flew past Toe's ear, and he spat out a piece.

'For God's sake, Claire.'

'It wasn't me.'

A shower started as the elephant bell rang for lunch. In the dining room Oliver offered quiche Lorraine.

'I was lying in bed last night thinking how to help you,' he told me and Mark.

'I'm a vegetarian,' said Mark.

'And you want to become a carnivore?' Bystanders tittered. 'Sorry, Mark, couldn't resist that. You don't look like one. You look too athletic for a vegetarian. Did you know that vegetarians don't live longer?'

We stared.

'It just seems longer.'

He guffawed and the company sniggered.

Back at the pond Simon sang Frère Jacques, thrusting and chucking in time. Others joined in with gusto, thrusting and chucking on the same beat. Someone started singing a bar behind, then someone else, and the round went on and on, the weirdest, most comical thing, like some jolly musical, only this was real camaraderie, they would not wave each other off on Sunday afternoon. The fight over the rooms was all in good fellowship. I thrust and chucked and sang along, but after a while feigned exhaustion so Mark wasn't the odd one out, though I could have dug six ponds single-handed. And it wasn't the hard labour getting to Mark. He had more muscle than anyone here. The hole deepened.

Bits of blue sky appeared and the clouds with their fat

grey cheeks slid off. On impulse I tapped my spade against a barrow on the third and fourth beats of every bar. Simon stopped singing and tapped his spade against his neighbour's on the first and second beats. Others laughed. Soon everyone was banging and clanging and clinking and jingling in time to the unsung tune, skipping and leaping. It was like school music lessons before Evelyn.

Oliver appeared with a spade. 'You seem to be having a good time without me.' His lips pouted like a child on a school outing when the van runs out of chocolate ice-cream.

'Eff's the champion,' they told him.

He left, and soon we lined the hole and paid out the hose, and a cheer went up at the first spurt. We moved off to dig up potatoes.

'What? Now we have to dig up our own dinner?' Mark grumbled, but Rachel and Amelia chuckled and frogmarched him to the kitchen garden.

The sun came out. Under a damselfly-blue sky we dug potatoes. It was like finding buried treasure, rooting with bare hands through the soft, crumbly soil to find every last little knob, holding each one to my nose to drink in the earthy smell.

'Right,' said Oliver when we reassembled upstairs, and we worked in pairs, smiling, crying, shouting, screaming, laughing. The moor gleamed in the sun.

At the end, while everyone clamoured round the shoe heap, Oliver asked us how we were getting on. We both answered at once.

'Fine,' said Mark.

'I'm enjoying it,' I said, beaming.

'Come and see me if you need anything. Always go straight to the top.' He walked off.

'I thought you were fed up with ponds and potatoes?' I

said.

'I got over it.'

*

How strange to sit opposite a row of Olivers. That massive hair, those piercing eyes, on three T-shirts in a row at the other long refectory table. Triple vision. Oliver was proliferating. But which face to look at – the one on the chest or the one on the head?

In the middle of the top table sat Oliver, flanked by Toe and Amelia and wearing an emerald-green brocade frock-coat with a black velvet stand-up collar and white lace jabot. On the wall above him an oil painting of his head and shoulders with lurid copper hair gleamed brighter than the real figure. I tore my eyes away and looked at the three chest faces. People were cramped, elbows tight, wielding knives and forks at difficult angles.

'Bide still,' came Simon's loud voice from further up the row opposite. 'Everybody, left elbow out, right elbow in,' and they laughed and twisted their upper torsos to sit obliquely.

Oliver gave him a withering look. Claire giggled and mumbled about growing numbers. She liked sharing a room between six, she said.

'Bit of a dampener for sex,' said Mark.

'Doesn't stop people, mmm.' She made little pleasure noises while eating.

My eyes widened.

'Perhaps we should sleep in a dormitory tonight,' said Mark. 'After the football, of course.'

I knuckle-punched him.

'We don't have telly here, mmm.'

I tucked in Claire's peeping name tag. 'Are you related, Claire Diamond?'

'No.'

Mark looked at the top table. 'So what does Amelia do?'
'She does the admin, mmm.'

On cue Amelia, wearing an elegant black dress with a gold-embroidered sash, stood up and tapped a glass. Silence fell. 'This morning the Diamond Academy received planning permission to convert the big barn in the lower field for residential use,' she said in clipped tones. 'Our dreams of a growing community are coming true. And we'll have plenty of spare rooms for snorers.' Everyone laughed, Rachel the loudest. Amelia raised her glass. 'A massive thank-you to Oliver for making it all possible.'

Cheers and glasses went up, with cries of 'Speech!' Oliver leant back with an artful smile, his auburn Afro lit up by the sun, and a slow hand-clap started. He rose and a frisson went round the room. Through the open windows came the burr-burr of a raven. His eyes panned up and down as he waited for absolute stillness, and the smile skulked round the corners of his mouth. We picked it up like a radio signal, amplified it but not too much. At last Oliver gave us the full smile, gave us permission to smile properly, and spirits soared like feathers on the breath of Oliver.

'We are such stuff as dreams are made on,' he said quietly. 'My break in the Cantabrian mountains has renewed my strength. Sometimes I forget how exhausting this work is. But for me the act of listening to you, loving you, is instinctive. It heartens me to see the changes in you.' He paused and cocked his head first one way, then the other. 'Donna has made great strides in personal relationships. You've laboured at examining yourselves to discover the jewels in your hearts and no one can steal those jewels.' He trembled, fulgent in the glow of the setting sun. 'They thought they could stop us, but we're just beginning.' His voice rose. 'We won't be camels, we'll stand and be counted. The dragon says, 'Thou shalt,' but the lion says, 'I will.'" On the last two words his voice boomed and echoed round the walls.

A cheer went up and cries of 'Bravo', and Mark and I clapped with the rest. Oliver stood with chest heaving, one hand clasping the other wrist, head high and shoulders thrown back like a lion rampant. The roar ebbed and flowed, reverberated between stone floor and ceiling, and the chandeliers tinkled. When it died down, he sang The Ash Grove in a beautiful lyrical tenor voice, pitch-perfect, that brought tears to my eyes.

*

The moon was paralysed on one side of its face. On a hilltop near Titchworthy Barrows we stood round the woodpile, more of us now with five children, two asleep in back-carriers, and the rooks cawed over Beechcleave Wood.

Oliver began 'John Brown's body lies a-mouldering in the grave' and we joined in. Five women with burning wax torches stepped forwards and danced inside the circle, arms snaking, while the torches drew circles and figures of eight in the dark then were thrust into the woodpile, which crackled and spat and heaved. The singing stopped, yellow tongues licked the air, a cry went up and so did the fire.

'Campfire's burning,' Oliver's voice rang out above the roar. More sang 'campfire's burning, draw nearer,' then more 'draw nearer,' and finally everyone sang 'in the gloaming, in the gloaming,' but softly while the fire roared. A man on the far side started 'Campfire's burning' while the rest sang 'draw nearer,' others followed, the fire settled into a steady melody and the harmonies of the round hovered over the moor. The air was hissy and prickly with the heat. The people in the combe must have thought it was one of those fiery dragons seen flying and lighting on the barrows. After all, what sort of people spend hours on a hilltop, singing round a bonfire long after the rooks have finished their noise?

'We are one family,' Oliver declared, Amelia by his side. 'There are no classes among us, no cliques, no rich and poor here. We live in harmony and I'm proud of you all. You've worked hard for our goals, steeled yourselves against hardship. This community was born out of nothing. Today we reached a milestone, and each and every one of you is lifted up on the wings of your generosity. This is a magic moment for me, to be surrounded and loved by such willing, giving, loving people.'

While the moon made its slow climb, we sang songs until the fire was nothing but embers, then joined hands in one big circle and sang Amazing Grace, moving in with raised hands and out again, in and out, in and out. We hugged each other goodnight, exhausted but happy.

*

'That was very moving,' said Mark.

We lay side by side in the shippon and drank in the smell of wood smoke in our hair and on our skin.

'Oliver's quite something, isn't he?' I said.

'That Amelia is something else. I've never seen anyone like her.'

'I noticed you kept staring at her.'

'It's the white skin. She's very striking. She could probably make me lick her soles.'

I was silent.

'Sorry, I forgot.' He kissed the end of my nose. Outside, some creature of the night stepped over the gravel.

'Simon's funny. He reminds me of Hatchet Man to look at, without the nastiness. It was probably Hatchet Man's idea to move me to Year 3, the bastard.'

'No shop talk.'

'Sorry. I was forgetting why we came.'

'No worries.' Mark grinned. 'I wasn't. Come here.'

'I will,' I boomed and we collapsed in a tangle of laughter and kisses, and soon we were sailing high on the sweet sound of Amazing Grace and Mark's face was a phantasmagoria of shock and strain and bliss and I sighed louder than the wind howling up the combe at home, and the moon smiled its lopsided smile.

*

I sat up with a start. The dream carried on in my head, a swimming pool full of angry, open-mouthed hippos. I got up and stood at the window, thinking of Emma. A bat swooped past. The moon scowled. Maybe the strange cry of a fox had entered my sleep and turned into the hippos. I had heard it earlier, from the hilltop, and later, the shrill kew-wick of a female tawny owl right outside the shippon.

'Once more unto the breach, dear friends, once more,' said Oliver to the ring of red-eyed faces at assembly.

'Claire has something to tell you.' The bandanna woman again. The tongue-stud quivered in the cavernous mouth.

Claire sat with bent shoulders and neck forwards like a ripe barley stem so that Oliver's face on her chest was crumpled. She was one of those people who looked guilty as soon as she thought someone suspected her, or might do so, with shifting, bulging, watery, blame-me eyes. 'I got a letter.'

'Sit up, Claire,' said Oliver.

Claire sat up. 'From an old friend in an acting cooperative. They've invited me to audition.' Her eyes flitted round the room. 'I was only thinking about it.'

She stared at her purple toenails.

Silence. Then, 'Nothing would make me sadder than to see you go, Claire,' said Oliver. 'You're a hard-working, team-spirited member of this community. We'd miss you terribly. My heart aches to hear you, after all we've done for you. But I would rather you be your true self than feel obliged to do the work.'

No one spoke.

At last Toe said, 'It takes courage to do what we're doing here.'

'Now, now, Toe, we must become who we are. If Claire doesn't feel the energy here, she must seek it elsewhere.'

Claire wilted. The air was close and clouds hunkered down over the moor.

After assembly those not doing the workshop filed out. Oliver asked Donna to lead while he attended to some business. I wished she hadn't said her husband called her

Donna the dog. With her dyed-black hair, bent back and weary step she reminded me of the black greyhound my mother rescued from the roadside. But she came alive now, told us to lie in a circle, each with our head on the belly of the next person. Someone tittered. The titter went round the circle. My head wobbled up and down, a comical sensation that made me giggle more. Someone sniggered on the other side. Round and round the circle went the snigger with a rotating groundswell of bobbing heads, chortles and chuckles grew louder, ripples turned to waves, a cackle broke out, then lots of cackles, heads tossed and rolled, gales of laughter sounded. Simon's guffaws were the loudest. Every time the laughter faded, Simon guffawed anew, and the guffaw went round. The room was awash with merriment when Oliver returned. We stopped and sat up like string puppets hoisted aloft.

'Just having a bit of fun,' said Donna, grinning.

Oliver sat on the chair after lunch with the statutory respectful gap either side. We waited.

'Claire.'

Claire beamed. 'I'm writing to thank them and say no.'

'You would have found it difficult.'

There were mutterings of assent. The round-up became a blur of voices outside my bubble till Oliver uttered my name. I mentioned sleeping badly and the dream, and he asked me to relay it. His face softened.

'My daughter's canoeing down the Zambezi now, but in the dream she was back home. Water kept welling up at the corner of her windowsill and all I could find to mop it up was two pairs of knickers.' There were sniggers. 'Then I discovered Emma was dropping her grey socks along the road. I picked them up and put them in her cupboard, but she did it again, and again. Then water spurted out and her bedroom turned into a swimming pool full of hippos and I couldn't get Emma out.' I was shaking. 'They warned us parents about the dangers at a meeting. I googled it and read that hippos kill more people than any other animal in the world.'

Oliver's scrutiny pinned me to the floor. At last he spoke: 'All those socks and not enough time.' Laughter rippled through the group, but he whipped round. 'It's no laughing matter.' He turned back to me. 'It's about time management and prioritisation, Eff, and relinquishing control. Let go of Emma and all your problems. Let go of your hippos.'

The pale blue eyes sparkled like a stardust marble, a kaleidoscope of mica flakes endlessly reflected, depths you could fall into and never come out of again. Oliver had pinpointed my troubles exactly. I must dismiss fears about Mark and accept his explanation. The smiles in the room lifted me. There was hope. Like a buzzard riding a thermal I spread my wings and soared, breathless.

'Thank you.'

We covered one long wall with paper and painted flames, a heart with an arrow, moon and stars. I painted a buzzard with spread wings at the top. Toe painted a pentagon house with a single square window, and water spouting. Amelia giggled and painted knickers with pink polka dots above the water. The bandanna woman and Rachel strewed grey socks along the bottom and someone put a giant pool round the whole lot, with waves of blue. Seven people rushed to fill the pool with hippos. Toe made a hippo with jaws wide. Mark did a bikinied swimmer over the jaws, with a speech balloon that said 'Eek'. Tears flowed, faces gaped, cackles filled the room with a forestful of Rabelaisian kookaburras, and bodies rolled round the floor in uproar.

At the end we joined hands and sang Amazing Grace,

moving in with raised hands and out again, in and out, in and out. The warmth of the group and the Persian carpets on the walls cocooned us, like Gran's knitted patchwork tea cosy. The sound floated over us all, greater than the sum of its parts.

'Working with you is absolutely delectable,' Oliver said to me and Mark, 'Something to leaven the lump. The work is like a window at night: sometimes you see yourself reflected, sometimes you see through it. In three weeks I'm running an Open-Up workshop which you'd find useful, transformative even. It will soothe the savage breast, Eff.'

We all hugged. We had shared our souls, given away a bit of ourselves and gained bits of others, gained more than we had lost.

'I heard the two of you were out walking at the crack of dawn,' said Oliver. 'Where did you go?'

'To the moor.'

'Ah, the moor. Take care. The bogs are treacherous, especially at night. Only fools, drunkards and demons go to the bogs at night.'

12

It was raining on Wales, but the sun shone on Minehead. The beach glared back and gull shadows swam over the sand. Eight three- and four-year olds in pink and turquoise sunsuits, caps with neck shields and jelly shoes clamoured for wheelbarrow races, then shovelled sand on a supine Mark, aided by Sadie.

'Auntie Stef,' Jack called across to the little gathering where Gran and Lisa were knitting, 'come and help us.'

Mark's protests were drowned out by squeals of delight. The mound grew high over hips and legs and we joined hands and walked round, chanting 'Ring a ring o' roses.' As we sang 'one, two, three,' we leapt up and so did Mark with a roar; he proceeded to chase the screaming children. Sadie and Emma hadn't had as much fun when they were small. Adam wasn't such a good dad and schoolwork was demanding. The best gift to any child was time and I had not given as the apple tree gave its apples, but grudgingly. Now here was Sadie, warm and lovely, giving back what I never gave.

Angry clouds loitered, outnumbered by rays of sunshine, and the adults huddled together. A cheer went up at the arrival of my parents with the dog. Dad snorted in and out to waggle a bindweed flower on his nose, to hoots of laughter. I laughed too at the ridiculous nose covering.

'You're not allowed dogs on the beach, Dad,' I said.

'Pfff. Sally won't do anything.'

He patted the hangdog-faced greyhound.

'You can't just flout the law.'

'I'll put her in the car in the shade, Dan,' said Mum.

'You'll do no such thing, Margaret. I'll be responsible for what the dog does. Any luck with jobs, Stefanie?'

'Not yet.'

Gran, sitting on a beach chair without the support tights which normally covered the Stiltonian veins on her legs, said, 'You look happier anyway.'

'I've been away from that awful woman and her Hatchet Man for nineteen days.' School was as far away as the distant sea, but even as I spoke, Evelyn stood before me, chastising in her snidey way that sounded like a compliment.

Out came the party food and the birthday cake and they sang 'Happy birthday.' Jack tried to blow out the candles from a distance.

'He singed off his eyelashes last time,' said Lisa.

A small turquoise boy politely thanked Lisa, another began singing 'Please and thank you' to the tune of Frère Jacques and the others joined in:

'Please and thank you, please and thank you,
we should say, we should say,
when we ask for something, when we ask for something,
every day, every day.'

The grown-ups cheered and clapped, so they did it again.

'How lovely.' Gran grinned. 'So confident.'

Arms waved, heads jigged, feet itched in the pink and turquoise uniforms. One marched and swung his arms, then they all strutted in a circle, arms swinging and singing, 'Please and thank you, please and thank you,' over and over and over again, no longer driven by the chortling audience, but caught up by the familiar words and tune. Louder and louder they sang, swung their arms higher and stomped their feet.

Gran asked about the workshop, and Mark grumbled about handing over mobiles like schoolchildren and digging a pond.

'We played lots of games,' I said. 'I was thinking about

great-grandfather Stefan.'

The chatting and the click of knitting needles stopped. The Chair-O-Plane passengers at Butlin's screamed.

'What on earth made you think of that?' Gran said at last.

'At the workshop we told why our first names were chosen.'

A look of anguish crossed my gran's face. She stared out to sea. 'It was a long time ago.'

After an awkward silence, Lisa said, 'This doesn't sound like your cup of tea, Mark, organised games. And you paid money and they got you to dig a pond?'

'True, I'm not into that sort of thing, never liked the Cubs.'

'It was weird the way they all hugged each other at first, but we got a taste for it in the end, didn't we, Mark? They had something special going. Even Mark was moved by the singing.'

Mark nodded.

'I'll have you singing yet,' I said, and the pair of us rolled about, laughing, while the others looked on nonplussed.

'Sounds freakish if you ask me,' said Dad.

'Please and thank you,' sang the pink and turquoise children again. They marched in a circle, stomped their feet and swung their arms to shoulder height. 'Please and thank you, please and thank you,' over and over and over again.

There was just time to finish off the sandcastle before the advancing rain-clouds evicted the sun and the beach-party.

Back home in the warmth of the Moroccan red walls with the smell of yesterday's curry, Mark slid an arm under my long hair, his nose nuzzled mine and our mouths swam together. Sex was a distant memory, and spoilt by teenage girls flashing bits at him on his mobile, by suspicions about his lack of reaction, by the sixteen-ton weight of joblessness and worry about Emma hanging over my head, like the magpies pecking at the sheep's backs.

In the bedroom I closed my eyes and began an ascent to a place where I wavered, incredulous, on a solitary note. We vibrated in sympathy. The waves came and came. A spark inside me ignited, the full orchestra coming in after a single thread of violin, hot and heady, the kundalini snake quick-uncoiling, shooting up to the brain, dissolving every cell. I sighed and opened my eyes. His lean arms shuddered and his mouth was set in a knot of concentration. Then back to the violin, streaming away into the ether, and more violins shimmering on the high notes, excruciating, as if we were lying in a meadow on a summer's day. Whether to laugh or cry?

Rudely the air was split by a blast from the bedside phone.

'Don't answer that,' said Mark in mid-stroke.

He carried on, but my attention was elsewhere. I half-twisted towards the phone. 'It might be an emergency.'

'Leave it,' he snarled; then, more gently, 'It won't be.' He was shrinking.

With a heave I grabbed the handset. He sighed, withdrew and flopped on his back. I listened with screwed-up face and held my breath. I fancied I heard breathing. I replaced the handset.

'Sorry. The ringing got on my nerves.'

I slid an arm across his chest and fondled a shoulder.

'Don't bother.'

He pushed the arm off. He had shrunk to a chafer grub.

'Sorry. I thought it might be Emma with a problem.'

He said nothing.

'Or one of your infatuated pupils. It might put them off if I answered.'

'Or we could not answer at all. We could have sex on a Sunday afternoon, why not?'

He flipped his head away and his chest rose and fell like bellows. The hairs on his arm fluttered in the blast from his nostrils. I kept silent. Three sorries would be annoying. He flung the quilt aside and got dressed, his back turned.

'I'm off out.'

With my desire to know everything, control everything, I had ruined the long-awaited union, the quicksilver finale. From the sheep shed came a bleating. A bluebottle lay on its back on the windowsill, spinning in a wild break-dance.

13

Hilda went down the steps into the scullery with rows of Kilner jars, jams, the mammoth copper pan for jam-making, heavy aluminium saucepans with deep indentations, and the big black encrusted omelette pan which was never washed, only wiped clean with newspaper. She stirred sultanas, sunflower seeds and chopped apple into melted suet, then poured the mix into large yoghourt pots to set for her beloved birds. The contents of the other pan – fifty grammes of minced meat laced with half a bottle of Tabasco – she spooned into a plastic tray which she carried outside and placed on the path. That black-and-white killer would learn a lesson he would not forget. Fred would say she put all her anger into the cats instead of the real target.

Back inside she put on a CD. Margaret had given her two, bless her, but the other one Hilda hid: Schumann's *Kinderszenen*, including *Träumerei*. Mama wouldn't let her play it until her hands could stretch to an octave, but later into this one piece she put all her feeling. In the nebulous, lingering notes of *Träumerei* she would seek refuge from torments of memory. So tranquil, so peaceful. Until, at the age of thirty-six, she found out it was Mengele's favourite. He made them play it, a few metres from the gas chambers. After that she couldn't listen.

By the window she watched for the cat to come for his bounty and listened to Richard Tauber passionately singing *Dein ist mein ganzes Herz*. Papa often sang it to her or told her the story of Rapunzel or the runaway pancake that ran kantapper, kantapper into the wood. Birds danced round the feeders like autumn leaves in the slipstream of a car. The goldfinches in their red and yellow livery stayed and stuffed, but the rest perched nearby and checked for cats before a quick sally to the feeder and back. She tolerated the sparrowhawk or a gleaming blue magpie poking under the eaves to get at sparrow eggs and chicks – they had to eat – but cats... There were so many: the tabby, the ginger, the white Persian, the all-black, and most murderous of all the black-and-white. As much as Hilda fed the birds to offset loss of habitat and chemical garnish, the garden was populated with killers, torturers.

Feline eugenics. 'It's what cats do, Mum,' Margaret said and shrugged, but Hilda hated the waste. For twenty minutes the day before she had watched, horrified, unable to tear herself away and too late to help, as the white Persian sat with pseudo-benevolent mien and waited for the mutilated wren to flutter again, and again, and again. Hate... why did she gloat over the prospect of some cat leaping with the Tabasco aftershock? She was as bad as the cats, like a bad apple rosy on the outside, maggoty and brown and foul inside. She was eaten up by hatred. And guilt, that parasite for which there was no remedy. Blaming cats was more palatable. She could live with them more easily than with herself.

There he was now, the black-and-white, sniffing his way to his mince treat. He sauntered up the path, hesitated, stepped gingerly round the tray, lowered his head and jerked back. Hilda leant forwards, agog. He nibbled. Suddenly he leapt into the air and sprinted kantapper, kantapper up the garden. Something akin to joy flooded every cell in Hilda's body.

The cat's cruelty—or was it her own?—reminded her of the summer camp on the Baltic coast when she had found the amber. She fetched the biscuit tin full of buttons, picked out the black velvet bag with drawstring and took out the large golden fossil inside which was a tiny fly with sprawling legs. Papa had it polished. They all found pieces, but Hilda's was the only one with a trapped insect. She held it high and it glowed an orangey red. Every joint, every hair of the creature was visible. When she left Germany she had treasured its warmth to the touch, its fiery glow. Now, the amber held all of her past up to the light. She replaced it, then went to the computer.

I never had so much fun in my life as at summer camp. I had never seen the sea! We travelled by train to the Baltic Sea, where there were almost no tides. The fine white sand trickled through the fingers and the waves sounded as though they were giggling and whispering. We changed into our costumes, and Inge and I ran hand in hand and embraced the cold. Everyone screamed except Gisela, our leader, who laughed. Gisela was only a couple of years older than most of us and could walk the length of the meeting hall and back on her hands.

Christa stayed in the shallows because she couldn't swim. She was new at Jungmädel. At first I befriended her because I had fallen out with Inge. She looked strange, with green eyes, a chin that melted into her neck, bushy eyebrows and fuzzy hair that stuck out in a wedge. She was sweet-natured and always willing to help. But shortly before camp I made it up with Inge and dropped Christa like a brick.

Christa walked in up to her ankles that first day at camp, wearing a hand-knitted woollen costume with green and white stripes. Someone pushed her over, and when she emerged the legs had stretched down to her knees and the neckline had sagged below her nipples with the weight of the water. It shrank back up as it dried. She crept off when we did handstands and cartwheels and crabs. She could barely do a head-over-heels and was afraid to leap into a makeshift cradle of arms. We were exhorted to be swift as a greyhound, tough as leather, hard as Krupp's steel. Christa was none of these.

Back at the camp Gisela assigned us to chores, putting Christa in the kitchen. Everyone protested, but Gisela overruled the objections. Elisabeth said Christa would be the worst person to cook. And so she was. The meat and vegetable stew with a uniform colour and texture tasted disgusting. I emptied my plate into the slop bin and others followed suit, including Gisela, who then allowed us extra bread.

But dinner was forgotten in the excitement of a game of rounders, followed by gathering sticks and lighting the bonfire. Sitting cross-legged in the clearing in the forest, we were all mesmerised by the flames. We sang folk songs like The Lorelei and the national anthem and danced round the fire holding hands. I cannot describe our happiness. From Elisabeth with her rich parents to Christa whose mother was poor since her father died, all our differences dissolved.

We carried on singing softly, tucked up in our blankets on prickly straw with our feet towards the pole in the middle of the tent like the spokes of a wheel. Inge and I lay side by side. One by one the voices stopped as girls fell asleep.

Inge grumbled next morning that Christa's snoring had woken her in the night. She was not alone. We hatched schemes to stop it. Those who had lost sleep revived that afternoon with the swim and the walk over the dunes and through ancient woodland with beech and pine trees straining to reach the light. The sun shone and the sea glittered. We came to a meadow full of flowers and warm feelings flooded us. Inge said we were privileged to live in such a beautiful country. We sang as we went, swinging arms, feet sinking in the sand. We picnicked on a different beach, where we found the amber pieces.

In the night I woke up. Christa was snoring again. The girls either side poked her in vain. Gisela ordered her to sleep outside the tent, some distance away. In the morning we had to wake her up to tidy her things for inspection. She was sullen but never said much anyway, and nobody spoke to her except when necessary. She held us back on walks with her flat feet and complained of septic mosquito bites, and her singing voice was raucous like a market trader's. When Gisela insisted she swim, she came up spluttering and gasping and we had to help her out.

Christa's mother couldn't afford the proper uniform with the shirt buttoned into the skirt, so she wore an ordinary shirt which flapped loose when she bent over, and a skirt a paler shade of navy blue. To trick her into bending over we threw the ball short during games or dropped a piece of paper instead of handing it to her, to see the shirt come untucked, which annoyed her. One day Anna, marching behind her at the back of the column in the forest, cut off a lock of fuzzy hair without Christa noticing. Anna paraded the trophy round the camp later and we all laughed. Christa must have hated us, yet she clung to us.

One day she got out of the walk because of blisters. Her shoes pinched, she said. Gisela allowed it. But next morning Inge's pocket-knife had disappeared from the bottom of her kitbag. Others emptied out their bags: money and a torch powered by pumping a handle were missing. Two girls pounced on Christa's kitbag, but didn't find the stolen items. Anna accused her of hiding them, and Inge suggested we follow her everywhere, even to the latrine pit. But it didn't spoil the campfire singing. We were eleven years old, the future belonged to us, we would not vanish from the earth, choked by weeds, we were healthy budding saplings ready to straddle new spaces and flourish. Old-fashioned things were dead, we sang. The glorious sound carried on in the dark between the trees and ended with the Deutschlandlied. Christa kept her harsh voice low and I felt sorry for her. It wasn't her fault she snored. I hugged her. But in the end I was no better than anyone else.

One night I was woken by a kerfuffle. Everyone was awake. Christa had sneaked back in out of the rain and was snoring again. Several girls pounced. Four grabbed an arm or a leg, and three more followed us out.

Our nightshirts were soaked by the downpour. We ducked Christa in a puddle and she screamed. Anna said that was for thieving. She didn't protest her innocence. We dragged her off, kicking and screaming.

I could blame Gisela for staying inside, but that would be facile. We just kept going. No one needed to speak, we were so mad at being drenched. We passed the blackberry bushes we had stripped that afternoon, cursing the arching branches which caught on our loose clothing and tore at our skin. The path grew narrow and we half-trailed her along the ground with one at each end, taking turns. She struggled, which maddened us all the more. The rain lessened, but not our anger. There was only one way to go now.

When we reached the beach, it was empty and still but for the trickle of the waves. The rain had stopped and the moon was visible again. We dumped her near the water's edge and stood round in a semicircle, smug and shivering. We looked at each other. Christa sat up with fear in her eyes. We didn't know what to do. Someone must do something. I clapped and the others joined in. I'm ashamed to admit I enjoyed the terror on her face – her punishment for our lost sleep. The clapping grew loud and rhythmic. Inge laughed and soon we were all laughing and stepping in time with the clapping, one step forwards, one step back. Christa crawled into the water on hands and knees. Her head turned back and the moon lit up the green eyes. I will never forget that look.

We bounded back up the path, joking and chattering, but guilt nagged at me. As I turned round, a cloud passed in front of the moon. I screwed up my eyes, but the beach was in darkness, and all I could hear was the waves whispering and giggling. I stood waiting for the cloud to pass, but Inge grabbed my arm.

Her body was washed up further along the coast next morning. We were sent home after talking to the police. They called it suicide. Now, I cannot go to the beach without thinking of Christa. Yet part of me looks back on those days with nostalgia for the camaraderie, everyone working together and helping each other, so much laughing and singing. How can I marry those fond memories with my shame?

14

The car bounced along the edge of the moor. On our right, cotton-wool clouds hung over Wales like the front row at a concert – we were going via Porlock Hill – but on our left the sky was forget-me-not blue. The heather was more mauve now, dotted with blobs of yellow gorse. Leaving behind the audience, we turned inland and the car raced downhill and up again, as though eager to get there. Oliver awaited its return. Oliver with his piercing eyes awaited us for the Open-Up workshop. He had said so and Mark had relented.

The car cut across the moor and over green fields, and slowed to a halt for cattle crossing. 'Red Rubies,' we both cried at once and laughed. After them came the moor again, the air heady with the scent of heather and the rowan berries a brighter orange. We stopped to admire the view. For ten years this numinous place had been on our doorstep unnoticed. On top of a barrow we stood while big black St Mark's flies sailed through the air with legs dangling like paragliders. Mark and I were sailing, our hearts were sailing through the air to a place of hope.

'Do we know where we're going this time?' I said.
'We do.'

No we didn't. We drove through the same village with the thatched cottages through which we had passed twenty minutes earlier.

'I remember those hay bales. Let's go the other way.'

'I'm saying nothing,' Mark said and drove my way.

We climbed, ears popping and engine fluttering. Go left, go right, this way, that way, every which way, I said. Chubby sheep wandered over the moor and on sinuous roads. The mauve was dimming and the bracken was turning brown.

'You're deliberately keeping quiet so as to blame me,' I said as we passed once more through the village with the velvet-roofed cottages. 'I'm not saying another word. You choose.'

So he chose a different way while I sat gloating. But fretful thoughts intruded. Oliver said people who were late didn't want to be there. It was Mark's fault. I would have left an hour earlier and holed up nearby if we arrived too early. I did want to be there, but not with Mark, the doubting Thomas who closed himself off from new things. Or maybe I subconsciously caused our late start because of Mark, and all because I was going with Mark. He drove half a mile down a track, then reversed at speed between a ditch and a stone-faced earth bank.

'Gently!' I snapped.

The moor just went on and on, darkening purple and brown, invaded by squares of lurid green farmland that seemed out of place amongst the rawness. In the west the sun sank.

When we arrived, the sky was speckled with rooks croaking over their roost, fluttering heavenwards like flakes from a bonfire, and the big house frowned in the dusk. Oliver stood in the doorway of the unlit lobby, a silhouette in the dim light, hands in pockets. I almost levitated with relief at our unforgivable lateness being forgiven: Oliver was smilier than a yellow smiley. Rachel appeared.

'Take their mobiles, Rachel, I'll be in in a minute.'

He disappeared and after warm hugs I ceded my mobile – 'I left mine at home,' Mark said – and we followed Rachel down the corridor. Huggers mobbed us while new faces looked on, confounded. A church-like hush fell and all eyes were on the doorway in which Oliver had appeared like a magician waiting in the wings. Mark and I half-smiled. This routine was familiar. He wore a smart shirt with white pinstripes on pale blue – 'his Park Authority shirt,' Rachel whispered. When the silence was complete and only the chirping of crickets was audible through the open window, he stepped forwards into the light of the chandelier and stood like an oak with outstretched arms and wild red hair.

'Good to see you all here, both diamonds and new faces.' He spoke softly. Everyone was riveted, all eyes fixed on him, like traffic heading towards a capital city from all directions. 'I've had a sublime, restful five days in the Massif Central, and now I revel in the prospect of work. As you know, in the middle of Exmoor is the desolate bogland called the Chains, of which Mr Fenwick Bisset, MP for West Somerset in the nineteenth century, said, 'I would far sooner be anywhere on Exmoor (except on the Chains) in the thickest fog, than in the House of Commons.' There rise the springs that are the beginnings of the rivers Exe, Barle and West Lyn, tiny trickles in a blanket bog, yet look how they flow and grow. North and south to the sea they run: slow and gentle to the south, ending in the great sprawling mouth of the Exe. But in the north they crash down a thousand feet over a short distance.' He scanned the company. 'We are those mighty rivers. This weekend, you've come here as mice, but you'll go away as lions.' He waited while people opened their mouths and roared their approval. 'To kick off I'll read out a little poem I wrote.' He cleared his throat and stretched tall.

'The Horticultural Show
Behold the onion
beautiful and brown as autumn bracken
firm, unyielding
proud on its plate
it bears a sign: First Prize.
Under its skin a layer

of creamy flesh
and then another layer
and then another
layer upon layer
upon layer
and in the middle
nothing.'

A slow hand-clap began. He beamed.

'Right.'

We crowded round the bottom of the stairs behind him and spilt out into the upper room, discarding shoes by the door. Sitting on cushions on the cherry-red carpet with the Persian carpets on the walls and the familiar faces, with Oliver on a chair in the bay, was cosy. After the round-up each one said their name with an epithet having the same initial.

'I'll start. Outraged Oliver.' He paused to look at the dismayed faces. 'And why am I outraged? I'm outraged because today, no sooner had I got back from my much-needed rest, than I saw a man from the Park Authority who thought he knew better than me, whose sole objective was to obstruct me. I know more about sustainability than his whole team put together, but that arrogant, conceited, overbearing, flap-mouthed, beslubbering, bald-headed clod...'

His fists clenched and the eyes flashed. His audience radiated rage too, ready to rise up and lynch the man from the Authority. Simon's eyebrows knitted into one continuous bushy strip and the anger in the room on Oliver's behalf leapt out and touched me like tongues of fire. I too fumed at the thought of some petty bureaucrat thwarting Oliver.

Efficient Eff was my choice because of my immaculate filing system. Evelyn called it obsessive-compulsive disorder. Mark chose Master Mark because he was a teacher.

'Not very character-related,' said Oliver. 'Got any better ideas, Eff?'

'Mocking Mark? It's an in-joke,' I added as Oliver raised an eyebrow. 'I have these rows of identical coffee jars and Mark changed one to a different type to see if I'd notice. I kept quiet about it.'

Mark smirked.

'He has quite a sense of humour, does Mark. Right. We'll do the symphony of emotions.'

We stood in three rows while he assigned the whole gamut of feelings, with passion for Mark and grief for me. Then he conducted, weaving us in and out, groans and roars and shrieks and wails and boos, Donna's nasal monotone 'Woe is me', Simon's guffaws, Rachel's high-pitched sung hallelujahs, Amelia's growly 'dis-gust-ing'; a kaleidoscope of the heart in one body of sound. Above it all Mark uttered orgasmic sighs, unlike my orgasmic sighs, and I thought of the woman in the turquoise top. My grief was an act, not supposed to be real grief. But then something stirred inside me, choking me, and I howled like a dog, as if a lifetime's sorrow had risen to the surface and exploded in these few moments. I wanted them all to hug me there and then. Still in our three rows when the symphony finished, we spoke in hushed tones. Even cool Amelia was thrown out of kilter. Like the boatmen lured to their deaths by the Lorelei sitting and combing her golden hair on a rock in the middle of the Rhine, our hearts dissolved, our minds were numb, our fingers hung limp.

'*That* was something else,' said Mark as we lay side by side in the shippon that night.

'Yes,' I said, still silently howling.

*

'Right. A little trust exercise. In this one we fall back into the arms of someone behind us.'

Ah, the joy of surrender, the total release when you know you will be saved; all cares belong to the past or the future. I remembered this game from teacher training. We sauntered round the room, crisscrossing, and I grinned to myself. Let go of your hippos, Oliver said. Relaxed in the knowledge that someone, or several, would rush to my aid, I fell back through the air with the grace of a buzzard riding the thermals, thinking how good it was to be there, then not thinking of anything, drifting in blissful nothingness, gliding in a dream on a summer's day.

I hit the floor. I lay there, shocked. Faces appeared: Mark and others looking concerned, while Oliver thrust forwards and stared open-mouthed.

'Are you all right, Eff?' he said at last, peering down.

'I thought someone would catch me.'

Mark pushed through and held me by the shoulders. Too late now, Mark. 'You didn't hurt your head? Or your back?'

'No.'

'You were supposed to wait for someone to touch you from behind.'

Silence followed, but for the patter of rain on glass.

Oliver wiped his forehead. 'I've never known a person so trusting.' He threw his arms wide in a gesture of helplessness.

Simon guffawed. 'You made the Thin Controller speechless.'

The room echoed with laughter.

'Right. Everyone sit down.' Oliver was white-faced. He undid the neck of his shirt and took deep breaths. On recovering, he rolled a ball of string across the circle while hanging on to the end. 'Melanie.' The woman with the blue bandanna and ankh picked up the ball. 'I like your honesty, your willingness to disclose whatever comes up.'

Melanie flushed and beamed. Holding the string, she rolled the ball to Simon. 'Simon. I love your laugh.'

Hither and thither went the ball of string, at times kinking its way to the wrong person. The new people were last. At the end the circle held a spider's web of string. At Oliver's instruction we rose and carried it gingerly to the bay where we laid it on the floor. Oliver sat on his cushion in the middle of it.

'Right.'

We lay on our backs with knees raised and sighed loudly. I stifled a giggle. If Simon sighed any louder, I would burst into hysterics. He bellowed like a cow robbed of her calf. I sneaked a look. Oliver's long legs stepped over bodies like a string puppet's, the right leg trailing.

'Let it all out.'

He demonstrated a descending scale of an octave, which spurred Simon to sigh even louder. We all sighed louder, the whole octave starting on the same note as Oliver, in unison, but some rebel started on a higher note and went out of sync, then others copied, cascades of moaning, with Simon the loudest and longest, so I took a gulp, knitted my brow and sighed my best.

'Magnificent,' said Oliver, which brought forth a resounding sigh from Simon. 'Let all your sorrows out.'

Oliver's stentorian sighs, over and over, set the room once more in unison, another orgasmic chorus. He stood and stretched both arms out sideways, priestly palms raised, and sighed with renewed vigour, eyes heavenwards, shoulders rising and falling with every chanted moan. The room sounded like a ward with seventeen women in labour.

'Eyes shut.'

I closed my eyes, but felt the piercing gaze still on me. My eyelids flickered, my sighs shrank inside me.

Then a woman howled in earnest. The room fell quiet but for the wailing woman. I peeped and everyone was sitting up watching a woman in her seventies named Angela. Oliver stood over her like a hunter with his dead prey. At a click of his fingers six people gathered round and stroked her hair and the howls subsided into sobs. Then at a scoop of the hand from Oliver they formed two rows, one either side, slid their arms under the supine woman, joined hands, then lifted and rocked her to and fro, babbling a lullaby, la-la-la, then two sang la-la-la on a higher note, then two sang it still higher. Her face changed from agony to bliss at the trickling voices.

'Right. Stiffen the sinews, summon up the blood.'

They laid her down and she stood up, smiling.

So much emotion all in one room. Open up? I would rather close down. Mark pulled faces at me. We sat in a circle, clapping rhythmically, fortissimo. I wanted to block my ears. Louder and louder we clapped, thunderclapped, and rain beat on the window and I don't know why I was blubbering, I couldn't stop, the convulsions kept coming. No one said anything: we just carried on in perfect unison, exuberant and forceful, one body clapping on and on for ten minutes.

'What happened?' Mark said when we finished, but I shrugged. It was the noise, the rhythm, the force of it.

'Come and see me in my office after lunch, Eff,' Oliver muttered in passing. 'Claire will show you where it is.'

*

'Wait here.'

Claire slipped through an inner doorway, beaming as if she'd won the lottery, and re-emerged soon after. The waiting room was bare but for a chair and a carved oak bookcase with books on hang-gliding, rock-climbing, sky-diving and sailing.

On the walls were photos of Oliver soaring, floating or spread-eagled on rock, and one standing on a lawn, grinning and wearing a ship's captain's cap and a sweatshirt with the logo The Thin Controller. Another showed Oliver planting a tree with a group of Africans. After twenty minutes he appeared.

'Sorry, I have a headache. Bear with me.'

In the consulting room above a corned-beef marble fireplace were more photos of Oliver hang-gliding, sky-diving and mountaineering, and one of Oliver with pouting chest, dwarfing the snow-capped mountain behind. Two walls had bookshelves from floor to ceiling with names like Heidegger, Shakespeare and Meister Eckhart. A white volume stood out, with the title 'Life Is Real Only Then, When I Am'. On the floor was a Persian carpet with orange hexagons and pineapples. Oliver wallowed in a sumptuous leather chair behind a vast oak desk with green inlay covered in messy papers which I itched to tidy, and a lamp with a globe shade of marbled opaline and an alighting bronze eagle on its base.

'So, Eff, what's it all about?'

I shrugged.

'Tell me about your old head.'

I shifted. 'She changed everything, completely undermined me... I love teaching, but Evelyn spoilt it and all my job applications are unsuccessful.'

'Don't you worry. Teachers who play the piano easily find jobs, and someone as conscientious as you will always succeed.'

'But I'm sure Evelyn's giving me bad references. My maths wasn't good enough and she said I was stressed out.' I pressed a fist against my mouth. 'I don't know what's happening any more.'

Oliver sat up. 'Of course you were stressed out. By her.

Get a better reference from your old head.'

'I've got one, a good one, and from the old deputy head, but they still say they'll ring Evelyn.'

'A bad reference from a new head and two glowing ones from people who worked with you for years – I know which I'd believe. And remember, I can get you a job any time.' He gazed with unswerving focus like a kestrel. 'Tell me a bit more about your marriage. You have a daughter.'

Two jade sphinxes on bookends on the mantelpiece half-smiled.

'I've got two but they're not Mark's. I didn't want any more.' I paused. 'Now I regret not giving him a choice.' We had always discussed everything, but on this one issue I had stonewalled him.

'So what's the story this morning?'

A tremor began in my legs and lips and spread through the whole body like the uncontrollable shuddering of a child who has played too long in the snow.

'The phone rang while we were having sex.' My voice came in bursts, involuntarily shouting the word sex. 'I picked it up. Mark was completely frustrated and humiliated. I feel so ashamed.'

He stroked and fondled an imaginary beard. 'Well, I suppose the question is, was he frustrated and humiliated as an outcome, or was he just frustrated and humiliated?'

'Yes. I don't know. Yes. He was just frustrated and humiliated.'

'I understand. I have myself experienced extreme humiliation.' His upper body shuddered as if to throw off the memory like a dog shaking off water. He gazed at me, caressing his chin. A swallow swooped past the window. 'There's more, isn't there?' He came round the desk, squatted, took my hands in his and looked into my eyes. 'What is it,

Eff? Tell me what it is. Tell me what it was in the whirligig of time that brought you to see me.'

A pumice-grey cloud eclipsed the sun, but the rays escaped all round and lit up the sky a brilliant silver. The shivering began again, a violent shaking, my whole body convulsing. Oliver grasped my shoulders and hugged me wordlessly. I erupted.

'Someone sent me a picture of Mark kissing another woman,' I gasped. 'He says it's doctored. He says it's kids.'

Oliver rubbed up and down my back. 'That must have been terrible.'

'And silent phone calls. And sexts to Mark.'

'Dreadful for you. Appalling.' His hand stroked my hair over and over and the shaking subsided.

'Do you think he's lying?'

'Mark, lying?' For once Oliver faltered.

'Mark can't see why I'm upset and it makes me suspicious. I don't know what to do.'

He stood up, perched on the edge of the desk and stroked his chin with finger and thumb in a circular motion.

'Have you had an HIV test?'

I stared in horror.

'Eff, you've taken a huge first step, sharing this with me. You're a strong person, you are. You like to help others, but now you need help.' He nodded. 'You must ring me any time you feel the need, Eff.' He hugged me again, rubbing his hand up and down my spine. 'Everyone here will support you. I suggest you do go for a test. Are you finding the workshop helpful?'

I heaved a sigh of relief. 'Yes.'

'Of course these things take time. Come and see me on your own. I charge sixty pounds an hour for singles, but this session is free because it's an emergency.'

'That's very kind, but I'm broke. We have got savings for a trip to Australia next year, but I've got no job.'

'The question is, Eff, what is more important: working on yourself or luxury holidays?' He perched on the edge of the desk. 'You know, Eff, you can do things without Mark. You need to nurture yourself after all that's happened. Give yourself space for healing. It will benefit your relationship with Mark in the long run. We can't connect with one another when we're worn down inside. And you don't deserve to be mocked.'

'You mean the coffee jar? That was just a joke. He thought I wouldn't notice he'd swapped a straight jar for a *woman*-shaped jar.'

'A *woman*-shaped jar?' He straightened up, limped back to his chair, then studied me. 'A woman-shaped jar. You know it's perfectly sensible to be systematic, Eff. People who have a system get things done. I suspect you are one of those people, and you do nothing at all unless you can do it properly.' He raised an eyebrow and I nodded. 'Every joke has a giant grain of truth in it. I want to help you, Eff. Unfortunately I'm away for a month on Wednesday, to Australia. Hang-gliding. Riding the Morning Glory.'

I stared.

'The Morning Glory is a spectacular wall of cloud that rolls in off the sea at dawn at sixty kilometres an hour.'

'Isn't it dangerous?'

He chuckled. 'Only if you land in a swamp full of saltwater crocodiles.'

He waxed lyrical about occluded fronts and the Coriolis effect and katabatic airflow.

I listened, struggling to follow.

'Here, we watch the buzzards to see where the thermals are, and they watch us for the same reason.'

I said nothing.

'Cheer up. Here's a new joke. Man to woman: Why don't you tell me when you have an orgasm? Woman: I would but you're never there.'

I roared and blushed.

'Let me hug you before you go. Your hair looks nice loose, by the way. Talk to Rachel while I'm away.'

The sun-cloud had dispersed. I left flying ahead of the Morning Glory, immune to crocodiles.

'What did he say?' said Mark downstairs.

'Oh, all sorts.' I beamed. 'I feel quite hopeful now. See, the sun's come out again.'

'I like your hair loose rather than in a ponytail,' he said.

'I've worn it loose for over a month now.'

'Have you?' His eyes widened. 'So what was it all about, in the clapping?'

But he learnt nothing, nor could he squash my spirit. I was like a blown feather till I remembered Oliver's headache. I had forgotten it, being so selfishly wrapped up in myself.

*

At dinner the Oliver-faced T-shirts were out in force – there were five at the refectory table opposite. Those eagle eyes, times five. Oliver himself wore a sapphire-blue poet's shirt with baggy sleeves and cross-laced neck, and Amelia beside him wore a Japanese black satin dress with pink flowers. Out of uniform Toe sat in animated conversation with Meredith, a weekend visitor with long dark curls. She sucked up tubes of spaghetti, spattering orange globules of Bolognese sauce in a wide radius. The merriment spread further than the globules, but subsided at Oliver's stare. When he looked away, Toe licked his lips in a circle and Meredith copied.

With the last dessert spoon laid to rest, Toe stood and

banged a spoon on a glass. 'Meredith wants to read a poem she's written.' He smiled at her and she smiled back. 'It's a very spiritual poem.'

She stood up and from her cleavage took and unfolded a piece of paper. Without looking round, she waited for the fidgeting to stop.

'I can't imagine what this will be like,' Oliver murmured to Amelia, resting his chin on his hands.

A shifting went down the rows, and once more Meredith waited for stillness.

'This isn't my best effort. It's work in progress. It's based on a friend.' She stretched tall and read:

'The earth is still.
Birds have gone to roost,
even the blackbird has finished
its last chuck-chuck.
The dandelions have closed,
the bees retreated to their hives.
The light is dying...'

'I knew there'd be death in it somewhere,' Oliver murmured, and Amelia tittered.

Toe glared.

'Sorry.' Oliver clamped his lips and made a show of concentrating on Meredith.

'The light is dying and they sleep,
their souls have merged,
melded with the earth as one.
One soul, one sleeping soul.
Or is it the sleep of death
that takes their life away,

the death towards which all creatures strive?
In death we shrivel,
shrink into the earth.
Only a whisper of ourselves
lingers, follows the living
in their lives, pursues them,
fills their every waking moment
'til they beg for mercy,
beg for the peace of their own death.
The dead devour the living.
Greedy death.
His breath, like a volcano's fumes
enveloping us all.'

She folded the paper and looked round.

'That was very poignant,' said Toe to murmurs of agreement.

She sat down, blushing and glancing at Oliver. There was an uneasy silence until Oliver thanked the cooks and the chatter resumed.

All sign of rain had receded. After dinner, taking a walk before the bonfire, we found Meredith sitting on a staddle-stone.

Mark said, 'I liked your poem. It was heartfelt, passionate. You had something important to say. Always write about what matters to you. It shows in the writing.'

'You must carry on,' I said. 'You've got talent.'

'Carry on...?' She swallowed. 'Have you seen Toe?'

'He was back at the house,' said Mark. Best not mention we last saw Toe chortling at one of Oliver's jokes.

Claire came bounding along the path, beaming, her chrysanthemum mop-top bouncing.

'There you are, Meredith. Oliver wants you.'

'I'm going for a walk.' She stepped off the staddle-stone and headed for the woods.

'But what will I tell Oliver?'

'Young love,' said Mark as we walked on.

Had Mark wanted a child of his own? The woman in the photo was much younger than him. We had stopped talking about poison emails now. We used to share everything, talk about things over and over, but a shadow had fallen across us.

*

We stood round the woodpile on the hilltop while snaking bodies with burning torches made curlicues and figures of eight in the moonlight; then we thrust the torches into the pile. Flames lit up the ring of faces and roared.

'Next time I'm in London to give a talk at a champagne dinner, you shall come too.' Oliver's hand squeezed Meredith's shoulder. The hand strayed across the top of her back under the jungle of curls and she leant her head on his shoulder. 'I'll introduce you to some theatre friends from when I was in the West End. They'll get you all the parts you want.'

Toe was not there. The wood smoke and sweet sounds of Kumbayah wafted across the hills, and the pink cloud-slivers over the horizon turned slate. 'Someone's laughing, Someone's crying,' we sang—appropriately, because they laughed and cried a lot, these people. Mark and I had stepped out of our shadow-world and into this new one in which individuals merged into a single body, yet we were each more alive. The melodious singing, the heat on our faces against the cool night air, the laughter of flames crackling and curling, the smell of smoke, all filled our senses and nothing else mattered. Here we could forget ourselves, not be ourselves anymore.

*

'So what did Oliver say to you?' said Mark in the shippon. 'Did you talk about me?'

From outside came the short, shrill yap of a female tawny owl and the male's long quavering hoot.

'I told him about the emails, yes.'

'And that you believe them?'

'No.'

Mark snorted. 'I don't know. You come to an Open-Up workshop and close down.'

I scowled. In my head Oliver's voice was saying, 'Come on your own.' It was unrelaxing with Mark making negative comments. His laughter at the orderliness of my coffee jars contained more than a grain of contempt and now he was critical of the workshop.

15

The sky went from white mackerel to grey and white mackerel. Mackerel sky, mackerel sky, never long wet, never long dry. The clouds were still, but the leaves of the solitary ash tree in the field fluttered. Mark came in from an early walk while I was brushing my hair.

'Guess what I've seen inside one of those big barns down the track with two huge security lights and an alarm. Two luxury off-roaders, a three-litre BMW, a Merc and a Maserati. No rich and poor here?'

The brush stopped mid-stroke. 'Could be for everyone's use. They'd need four-wheel drives.'

A tickling drizzle started as we reached the house. After assembly we bombarded a partner with compliments, and I paired with Melanie, the bandanna woman whom I hardly knew and hardly liked. I stared at the glistening tongue-stud and tried 'You've got wonderful energy' and 'You're fun to be with', but the lies fell flat. Melanie said, 'You're really trusting' and 'You're very open.' It was just as bad with Craig, a gangling young man with hunched shoulders, hands in the pockets of his rustling combat trousers. Craig and I stood in the middle to demonstrate.

'Come on, Craig,' said Oliver. 'You may be the youngest, but make it sound like you mean it.' He shoved him aside. 'You're fantastic, Eff, marvellous, so trusting, your class must be sorry you've gone. We all love you to bits. I'd love you to be part of this community. You're a great teacher, they all know that from the pond-digging.'

Oliver breathed fire and gold till I glowed from head to toe. But the next pair were feeble. Jogging round the room ten times, star jumps, sit-ups – all failed to revive the flagging participants.

'Right.' Oliver ran his fingers through his hair like a comb. 'A short sharp walk should galvanise you all.'

He started towards the door and several groaned.

'We can't go, Olly,' said Amelia. 'It's raining.'

'A bit of rain never hurt anybody. In fact, those most willing to embrace challenges, be they rain, be they emotional obstacles, are the ones taking this seriously. And they are the ones I will treat seriously. I hope that will be all of you.'

Once more he headed for the door and we shuffled after him.

The mossy dry-stone walls were like rows of grinning green teeth. None of the people were grinning. Oliver strode ahead in spite of his limp, with Claire and Amelia close behind, unsquashable, while the rest straggled out, wet and miserable. Mark especially was not grinning. He sidled along at the rear with two newcomers. Simon turned a black beetle onto its back to reveal an iridescent turquoise belly, to my delight. The path went down into a deep valley, then ran parallel to the river. The rain pelted on our black cagoules with the Diamond logo, and after an hour we entered a dry conifer wood where we sat on fir-tree stumps and peered out at fields lashed by rain.

'We're felling these conifers in the goyle and replacing them with deciduous trees,' said Simon. 'It would be great if you and Mark came when we replant. An environmental expert will be speechifying and the media are coming too. Back along in the fifties they wanted to cover swathes of Exmoor in conifers and it was only a few people craiking that stopped it. We're proudly following in their footsteps.'

Melanie said, 'If Oliver keeps doing walks in the rain it might be better to leave the fir trees standing.'

'But you can't hear a single bird. These firs support only

sixteen insect species. They're nearly as bad as sycamores which support only fifteen species, whereas an oak supports two hundred and eighty-four.'

'You're so right on, Simon.'

'My viola's made of sycamore,' I said.

'You play the viola? You should bring it with you.'

'I haven't played for years.'

The firs were dark and eerily silent, giants fighting over the stingy light of an overcast sky. The needles were soft underfoot and dry as dust and the resin smell was comforting.

'Right, everybody turn back,' said Oliver. His hair had turned into a mass of squiggles.

We trudged back up. Mark and the two newcomers fell to the rear again. At the top the bedraggled column dribbled across the open fields; in the driving rain the moor was a blur. The few trees were all crown and no trunk and there was no sign of life, not even a slug. The wind buffeted my face, washing me raw. Conversation tailed off and we slogged on in single file with ballooning cagoules.

Then above the dirge of the rain came the tinkling melody of the overture to William Tell: Mark's ringtone. Oliver stopped and turned, as did those behind him. Mark ignored the glares, turned it off in his pocket, and when they caught up with the next person, Oliver carried on. We walked back in silence.

'Expecting a call, were you?' Oliver said when we reached the shippon.

'Not at all,' Mark replied and went in.

'Fifteen minutes to change into dry clothes and we'll start again.'

They plodded on to the house.

'This is too much,' said Mark. 'You go back up if you want. I'm not. If he wants an apology he'll be unlucky.' He towelled himself dry.

'He can't predict the weather.'

'Come on, Stef. Exmoor's one of the wettest places in Britain. He knows.'

Drips fell from my hair to the floor. 'I found it bracing.'

'Bracing? I do sports every day. I didn't come here for bracing.'

'You're being negative, Mark. This place is beautiful in any weather. I saw this amazing black beetle with a brilliant turquoise underside you'd never guess was there. This place is magic.'

'I haven't paid all that money to look at beetles. Twenty years' experience of helping people with relationships, he said. Utter wank-speak. And so have you paid a lot and you haven't even got a job.'

'Thanks for that. Oliver was so encouraging, assuring me I'd get a job, which is more than you've done. And he had a headache, which he apologised for. How can you criticise when he's helped so many people? Give it a chance, Mark. You may as well get your money's worth.'

'Right now I'm staying here. I'll join you after lunch if I feel like it, so unless you're happy to go home now, go on up to the house and I'll wait.'

He didn't want to come, and now he regretted coming. He'd rather be with his younger woman. I should not have persuaded him. I wanted him to come of his own volition. I had issues of control-freakery, my desire for order, everything in its place and as I chose. But I couldn't make Mark want it too.

*

'Mark's wet through and he's had enough.'

Oliver gazed at me from the web of string. Everyone stared. The faces said, I knew it, you poor thing.

'Perhaps Mark wanted time on his own,' said Melanie. 'Perhaps he wanted to return a call.'

'I don't like the way you said that,' said Rachel. 'If you're suggesting Mark has a secret lover, I don't believe it. Mark's a lovely person, and I know him better than you.'

'I'm not suggesting anything.'

'It's a bit odd, though,' said Amelia. 'A bit off. Leaving Eff all on her own.'

'She's got us.'

A ring of smiles surrounded me. Oliver was solemn-faced. Gradually the smiles faded, all shiftings and murmurings ceased, the rain subsided and became a faint patter on the window.

Into the silence walked Mark. He crossed the room, kissed me and murmured, 'Sorry, love,' then sat beside me.

The kiss was like a warm bath. I took his hand and leant over for a proper kiss.

'Good to see you back, Mark,' said Oliver.

We played guessing the name of a famous person on a label pinned to our backs by asking yes or no questions. At the end I alone hadn't guessed and we each said how we felt. There was a lot of saying how we felt in this place.

'I wonder why you failed to guess, Eff,' said Oliver, watching quick-eyed from his web.

'I think Eff is distracted,' said Toe.

'Confused, more like,' said Melanie.

'Why does it matter to guess right?' I said. 'It's only a game.'

'It's not whether you got it right,' said Toe. 'It's what you learn about yourself from it.'

I prickled. 'I didn't think it mattered.'

'Obviously it does matter, because look at you. You're very affected by it.'

'I'm affected by the fact that you think it matters. You're making me feel stupid.'

'That says more about you than it does about us.'

Crisp-voiced Amelia said, 'If you don't want it to matter, then don't let it. It's you that's making an issue of it.'

'But I'm not making an issue of it. I don't care. What's the problem?'

'You're the one with the problem.'

'If there's no problem, can I ask why are you speaking about it, then?' This came from Donna, who usually said little.

'Because she was asked,' Mark shouted.

'Yes, because I was asked.'

'Perhaps you like the attention,' said Melanie.

'But I didn't ask for attention. I'm just defending myself.'

'Look at you,' said Toe. 'You say you don't want the attention, but you've got the whole group focusing on you.'

'Attention-seeking,' said Melanie.

The tulips and sickle leaves and Herati patterns on the Persian carpets curled and swirled.

'Children, children,' said Oliver. He crossed the room and grasped my shoulder. 'I know you want to help Eff, but this is no way to treat a guest. We'll do some nice trust exercises. Eff's good at those.'

We played leading the blind by hooked little fingers only. We held hands in a circle and individuals fell inwards or outwards, almost to the floor, without crumpling at the knees. We took a running jump the length of the room and launched ourselves into a cradle of arms.

'Right,' said Oliver. 'The sinking ship.' Everyone rushed into the middle. 'Vote one person overboard at a time. Remember this is work. You must be your true selves to benefit, so no passive-aggressive behaviour, please.'

There was no passive-aggressive behaviour, just aggressive behaviour. First they threw out the two newcomers for contributing least. Only Mark and I objected. Next they threw out Mark for the same reason. Only I voted in his favour. No one defended Angela who had howled in the sighing exercise, unfairly disposed of for being the oldest. The concept of comparing people's worth was anathema to me, but my view was dismissed. They threw me overboard for being stupid.

'Stupid how?' said Mark.

'You're drowned, Mark,' said Oliver. 'You have no vote and no voice.'

Simon and Amelia, the last two, wrestled round the floor.

'Just because you grew up on the land doesn't make you indispensable,' said Amelia. 'This place would fall apart without me.'

'Let's see if it falls apart then.' He pushed her off the mat by brute force, ignoring the pain of a pulled earlobe with nails digging in. The onlookers screeched and shouted.

Oliver grinned. 'They're not quitters.'

Finally we held hands and sang Amazing Grace, moving in and out, in and out. In the bay the web of string was a tangled mess. Then hugs all round. Mark asked Oliver about Meredith.

'She's gone back to London. Don't worry about Meredith, she's a drama queen, tough as old boots. Lovers and madmen have such seething brains.' He squeezed my hand. 'There's another workshop in three weeks' time. Unlike Evelyn, we will always welcome you.'

The sun came out. Driving over the rolling country with the rosebay willow herb by the roadside more fluff than flower, inside the car it was as silent as a world without birds, silent as the moor with its raven-black bogs.

Mark opened his mobile statement, folded it and turned away. The back of his T-shirt hugged his shoulder blades and hung loose at the waist.

There were three more hate mails. 'Were glad uv left.' 'Ur a lousy teachr, a lousy lovr, u cant even keep ur man.' 'Ur a rubbish teachr, evryı h8s u.'

'Come on,' said Mark after dinner. 'Let's go to bed. Hard words can't harm you.'

He pulled me towards his side of the bed. His lips slunk over my cheekbones, plucked at the nose, and he slid a leg over my hip. Happiness flooded in and our movements merged as if there had always been one beat only, one primordial rhythm, till a woman with long dark hair intruded and I went flat. He slumped and shrank. I spat him out.

He rolled off. 'Why do I bother?'

That night I tiptoed downstairs, the sound of my breathing magnified like an astronaut's, and looked through the letter rack three times. The statement was not there, but on the table lay his phone. Blood pounding in my head, I unlocked it and fumbled through the menus. The inbox had been wiped.

Next morning bright sunshine streamed in and beside me was an empty space. A pigeon crooned from the roof:
Your *life* is rub-bish,
Your *life* is rub-bish,
Your *life* is rub-bish,
Your *life* is rub-bish.

Minehead Station buzzed with activity: people scrubbing and polishing locomotives on the siding, oiling the works, watering the hanging baskets.

A few weeks earlier, I had been busy with the endless stream of lesson preparation, marking, choir, reports, precision-mounting artwork and so on. A few weeks earlier, I had smiled as brightly as the African marigolds and black-eyed Susans tumbling out of the tubs on the platform. I had revelled in the jollity and camaraderie of school, the forest of hands when I asked a question, the fine detail in which they drew the owl after I pointed out the complex marbling and streaking of the plumage, the feeling that I was making a difference, I was important and respected. Now I had hours to give away, but filled them with nothings.

For her eighty-eighth birthday Hilda had chosen a trip on the steam train with the family. My parents were down from the Midlands, staying with Lisa, and it was a double celebration because Emma was back, full of sunshine and self-confidence and ready to leave for university in a month's time.

'There's no need to inspect my bedroom every day any more, Mum' and 'If I want an apple I'll take one, okay?' she said firmly.

Books of old railway photos showed people with long coats and battered leather suitcases, and big enamel-plate advertisements boasted: Wills's Gold Flake, The World's most famous cigarette; Read The News of the World, Best Sunday Paper; Nestlé's Milk, The Richest in Cream.

'Stef, the Best Music Teacher in West Somerset,' said Gran with a grin.

'But still jobless two weeks before start of term.'

Mark and I took Jack along the platform to put ten pence in the slot for the Princess Victoria model train in its glass case. It didn't move. Some wheels turned, that was all, and Jack's face fell.

'Never mind, Jack,' said Mark. 'The big train will move.'

The tannoy announced the imminent departure to Bishops Lydeard and an engine on the siding whistled and shuffled off, then reversed, with hisses and puffs, on to the brown and cream train on the platform. The excitement rose, but with no class to direct or choir to conduct I was flat, bereft. The plans to perform Joseph with three other schools next July and the planned repeat visit to the care home at Christmas were all for nothing. The coming year was a black hole.

The family crammed into two compartments and ordered teas and sandwiches.

'How many teaspoonfuls of sugar is it now, Stefanie?' said Dad, and they teased me for cutting down from two to nought by reducing half a teaspoonful every six months. 'Can I not tempt you to skip a few months and go on to the next reduction?'

I laughed. On the first of February I would go from half a teaspoonful to none. I didn't know where or how or, horrors, if I would be working, but I knew I would have no sugar in my tea.

The train chugged along, children waved from station platforms, fanatics with tripods stood by the road bridge. Gran asked about the workshop.

I sighed. 'It was all rather emotional, Gran.'

'Oh. Is that a good thing? What do you think, Mark?'

'Frankly, I think Oliver's a little Hitler.'

Gran raised her eyebrows like railway signals.

'Rubbish. Oliver is the kindest, most caring, most selfless

person I know. He's like you, Gran, he gives his time to everybody.'

Mark sneered. 'What's kind and caring about making us do a five-mile walk in belting rain?'

'Well, now I don't know whether to be flattered or displeased, being compared to Oliver.'

'Be flattered, Gran, ignore Mark.'

'Yes, ignore me, Stef does it all the time. Sorry, Gran,' he added, reddening. 'Not the time or place.'

The train chuntered on and the family looked out of the windows.

'Auntie Stef, what's a little Hitler?' Jack's high-pitched voice broke the silence.

'Be quiet, Jack,' said Lisa. 'Auntie Stef doesn't want to hear your nonsense. This is Great-Grandma's birthday.'

The chatter resumed and the gentle contours of the Quantocks sloped by. The guard entered in triumph, bearing a birthday cake topped by a solitary candle, and the happy gathering sang Happy Birthday.

The small brown leather suitcase was wedged between boxes and grey with dust. Hilda pulled it out from under her high metal-framed bed. Seeing those photos of people with old suitcases at the station had reminded her. She wiped the dust with a yellow duster which she then shook out of the window; she opened the case, its hinges squeaking with rust.

In the conservatory she settled in the upholstered cane chair, took out the contents of the envelope, and unwrapped the tissue paper: a fragment of silver birch bark, almost flat, broken in three, and bearing a collage of a landscape composed of bits of plant matter. There were fields of different hues of tow colour made of grass seeds and pieces of stems, faded forests made of scraps of fir, clouds made of pressed seed pods and down feathers and dandelion seeds, and in the foreground two leafless trees made of minute twigs. The hermit had fixed each particle with tree rosin and they still held after all these years. She didn't even know his name.

She went into the dining room and typed:

Nobody said not to go near the man in Grunewald forest, but that was probably because nobody knew he was there. Eva and I found him one day when we were wandering among the birches and pines, looking for an oak or beech to climb, looking for adventure; what we found was a log cabin in the clearing. Although it wasn't made of gingerbread, we knew we should walk away. But curiosity rooted us to the forest floor. He came to the door and still we didn't run, because he looked sad, with big blue eyes and a cross round his neck which tightened over his Adam's apple and stuck out when he swallowed. 'Maybe he's a saint,' Eva whispered. 'Hallo,' I said, embarrassed by her whispering. He smiled and mumbled hallo, then turned to a rack made of twigs on which different leaves and catkins and bits of bark were laid to dry. 'What are those for?' Eva said, so he showed us his pictures propped up on shelves and hanging on walls: beautiful landscapes of seeds and twigs and bits of plants and feathers stuck to dried birch bark. We were speechless. The rough hair and beard, the holes in his trousers, the frayed hems, horse-flies which he kept swatting with an old newspaper, the bare floor made of tree trunks sawn lengthways—it was all so grim and sparse, yet the pictures were... immaculate. He gave us each a plant picture, small enough to hide under our blouses.

After that we visited frequently. We stole food from our larders for him. He wept the first time we presented him with a quarter of a loaf of rye bread and butter wrapped in greaseproof paper and two slices of Black Forest ham and blood sausage. 'You shouldn't do that,' he said, but we explained we were allowed to take a picnic lunch. Then he cooked us chanterelles, which smelt like apricots and tasted peppery. We had never eaten them before. He took us foraging for chanterelles and ceps with their soft, sticky, leathery caps and showed us what to look for, but in the same breath made us promise never to pick mushrooms on our own.

One day my parents took me and Hanno for a day in the woods, picking ceps and blackberries. They made us promise never to pick mushrooms on our own. It was strange, hearing those same words. I couldn't stop thinking about the hermit all day. I wanted to tell them, but Eva and I had cut our fingers and mingled our blood and sworn secrecy. I wanted to say the mushrooms taste better after three days of heavy rain in a full moon, and they should handle and cook them lightly to allow them to talk, but they would have asked questions.

It was one of those sultry August days, a year later, that Eva called round and we went out because Papa was giving German lessons to some Chinese students at home. Oma upstairs wasn't in, so we went to the park and played on the swings and seesaw. That was the park where Papa had carved our initials in a linden tree, SK + HK, and a heart with an arrow. Eva and I sang Der Lindenbaum as we swung. But it was boring, so we made our way to Oma's allotment garden to see if she was there. This was before it was taken over. We were in luck: she gave us homemade lemonade and cinnamon cakes and we sat among the blackcurrant and whitecurrant bushes to scoff. Eva said, 'Let's go and see the hermit.' We took blackcurrants and plums and maize cobs – we used to eat them raw. Oma put them in a bag when we told her we were off for a picnic.

He was gone. His artwork was all over the floor, broken. His mattress was sliced open and the straw scattered. Two plates and a cup were smashed. Next to the tripod structure he'd built outside for cooking was a frying pan, overturned. Beside it in the dirt lay a bream with gaping mouth and stary eye. For a long time we couldn't speak. We walked home in silence. 'Oma said to give these to you,' I said to Mama, handing her the bag, because we hadn't had any appetite. She looked at me strangely. I went to my room and took out the delicate picture. I have never eaten ceps or chanterelles since.

Eva told her parents and was forbidden to play with me. Inge said that was Eva's loss. Six months later, Eva and her family moved away. I was aggrieved that she didn't say goodbye. I never asked where she had gone, or why, nor did I ask where the hermit had gone. People didn't ask, and I didn't ask. Now I am asking myself all the time why not.

Gran was holding a picture on her lap in the conservatory when, clutching a potted orchid, I entered.

'Did you make that, Gran? It's beautiful.'

'No. Someone I knew in my childhood.' She took out a handkerchief and blew her nose. 'I want you to have it.'

I put an arm round her shoulders. 'Why, thank you.'

She wrapped it in its tissue paper and put it back in its envelope placing it on the coffee table, which was inlaid with a beach scene in miniature mosaic tiles, and smoothed down her T-shirt. 'Sit down and tell me about your weekend. I'm concerned because it was supposed to unite you and Mark, not divide you.'

'Just because he got a bit wet,' I sneered. 'Everyone else enjoyed themselves, Gran.' I stood the orchid on the table, straightened the table, and sat down. 'For you.'

'Thank you. What a lovely thought, and what a beautiful plant.' She sat up. 'What's wrong?'

I told her about the messages and Mark's mobile and the statement. 'I shouldn't have done it, but I keep thinking of that photo, Gran.'

'Have you asked him? It's not right to spy on each other. There'll be some explanation. Mark is a good man.'

A dragonfly headed for the pond. Devil's darning needles, Simon called them. Oliver and the group were an icon dimly lit by a candle. I wanted to kiss it back to life, or maybe kiss the memory of me and Mark in our early days.

Things were stuck like the Princess Victoria model at Minehead station. The wheels turned but I was going nowhere. No matter how much Mark told me he would never be unfaithful and the picture was a fake, I doubted.

'Why stay with me if you think me capable of that? It's insulting.'

'I still love you,' I replied.

'I want to shake you. What is it you love? A partner who you think cheats on you?'

I didn't protest. All day I moved things between jars and boxes with a liturgical sameness and hummed Amazing Grace. The marshmallow tones of the piano seemed flat. I read *A Truthful Existence*. The James Grieve apples ripened and the night-mists started. I was as dull as a much-travelled coin.

At the first choir rehearsal of the term, Rachel and I hugged like long-lost friends, rocking from foot to foot in tandem, and people stared, unaccustomed to such emotion. In Taunton streets they passed me without recognition and no one socialised afterwards. Choir members were people who sang together every Tuesday; the voices blended but the souls were apart. We ran high on adrenaline and endorphins in the concerts, buoyed up by the music and audience appreciation, then went home on individual clouds. Oliver's group was not like that.

'Mark wants me to do a poetry teaching workshop with him. But I want to do Oliver's workshop.'

Rachel squeezed my hand. 'Didn't you do poetry teaching in college?'

I had, and my poetry teaching was fine, I thought. 'Mark

called you a pack of dogs.'

She flinched. 'We criticise to help you. It was con*struc*tive criticism. Were you upset?'

'No, no, it's just Mark.'

The hall resounded with full-bodied voices singing warm-up scales. Spirits were high as we launched into Haydn's *The Seasons* and all thought of Mark and that photo faded. Haydn's joy at spring warmth carried us along, like the group singing and dancing round the bonfire on the moor, creating an ordered world of simple melodies where your thinking was done for you: where you slept, what you ate, what work you did. I liked to hold the reins, but Evelyn and the bureaucracy had killed the pleasure, and now home was tainted by a woman in a turquoise T-shirt. Out of that chaos I had stepped into a world of uplifting music where everyone smiled and brightened the sound. We finished with the rollicking *Ewiger, mächtiger, gnädiger Gott*, Everlasting, mighty, bounteous God, which made me wish I believed in an Almighty, one who could give me a job and stop emails and make Mark faithful, one who would make everything right. Rachel and I exchanged knowing smiles.

While I waited to give a lift to Janet, a soprano who wore the same unwashed crimplene dress and dirt-speckled glasses every week, Rachel grumbled about the sister she stayed with on choir nights when the lanes were icy. Her sister sneered at the farm on Exmoor. 'You never do what you want,' she said. 'You just want me to do what you want,' Rachel retorted.

'You could stay with us.'

'Thank you. I've stopped speaking to her now.'

I raised an eyebrow.

Rachel finger-twisted her long half-kempt hair till the fingertip turned white and stared at the scuffed parquet floor. 'Working with Oliver is transformative. I was a resister, a hardened resister. My sister thinks our father's the sweetest thing since sliced bread. He sexually abused me.'

The following week, after Sadie and Emma left, Rachel and I burst into song with *Ewiger, mächtiger, gnädiger Gott* to the accompaniment of the CD, and our voices wove in and out in the semi-fugue. We grasped hands and spun round and praised an almighty and bounteous God, becoming more and more animated. Finally we sank laughing and sighing into the easy chairs.

'I miss Oliver,' I said.

'We all miss him. We feel as though we've lost a tooth.'

I went into the downstairs study to check email and stopped dead. Mark's mobile was on the desk. I gazed at it, every muscle tense, my arm drawn to it like a dog pulling on the lead. I dabbed it and its luminous turquoise symbols and my eyes gleamed at my touch. Then I snatched it up and thumbed through. *The odds are good, but the goods are odd*, I read with horror from Ed, whoever he was. In the sent messages was one to Ed: *Go for it*.

I put the mobile back and checked my emails: six from six different addresses. *I saw them*, said the first one. I pressed Delete six times before seeing any more, but then read them in the trash. Rachel walked in and I crumbled and told her the whole saga.

'I don't normally look at his mobile.'

She was silent for a long time. 'Surely not Mark?'

'I don't know, Rachel. I just don't know.'

Neglected old friends were out or at work. The swallows had gone and the blackberries were too small and seedy to pick after the dry summer. Three days' supply teaching boosted me with the success of singing the register till I found out they'd cheated. Behind my back they were laughing me to scorn. Only the sea comforted with its constancy, its rhythm, its muscular lashing at the wall, lashing at me. Aeroplane blips made their way across the sky like tadpoles of light in the sun's gleaming goodbye.

Mark drove Emma to university with a hamper of home-made fruitcake, jams and cheeses. Blu-tack dotted the walls of her room and clothes covered the floor, and on the windowsill was a jar used as an ashtray – she'd slipped that one past her mother. I pored over old school reports never before read properly.

In the supermarket an eight-year-old voice called Mum and I turned round.

Just when the days seemed most pointless, Oliver phoned and kindly offered me four hours' work on Wednesday in return for an hour's one-to-one session. Perfect: Mark did football club after school on Wednesdays. The house was filled with the sound of Amazing Grace. Worries about losing supply teaching proved needless. The autumn term was moving on without me. Dragonflies were mating, the female clinging to the male and dipping her rear end into mud or water. The eggs lay in the mud, then hatched into nymphs which stayed underwater for years before emerging as adults. Stuck in the mud like me.

At choir we sang The Hunting Chorus. Back home Rachel and I practised with the CD, exulting over the exhausted stag while braying horns, baying trombones and the galloping rhythm all hastened towards the final triumphant mort.

Mark pulled faces in the background.

'Never mind, Mark,' said Sadie. 'They're happy.'

Happy indeed. The music jerked our heartstrings into quivers of ecstasy over the hapless creature. 'Halali,' we sang, 'halali,' and one final, prolonged 'halaaaali'.

23

The cast sheep was helpless with legs in the air, eyes half-closed, lower lip hanging sidewards, teeth peeping out.

'Now, heave.'

Simon and I hauled her onto her feet, and he straddled her and clutched her neck and belly. Protruding veins like Celtic knots sprawled up his arms. The weight of the fleece combined with pregnancy made the sheep unstable, he explained, and the poor beasts could die in half an hour without help. Gases built up in the rumen and compressed the lungs and they suffocated. On his forehead were worry lines like the waves representing the sea in children's drawings.

'I did wonder whether it wasn't too late or no. But she's fine.'

He let go and she tottered off over the reddish-brown heather. A cloud-shadow stretched its fingers across the moor like an advancing amoeba.

'I'm really glad you're here. We all are.'

'I feel alive today,' I confided, and he squeezed my waist.

With the dog we trod between clumps of heather towards the quad bike. Heather gave way to tussocks of rushes and faded purple moor-grass and my gumboots sank in thick black mire. He pulled me out like a stubborn cork, and the bog protested with loud sucking noises.

The engine blasts of the bike shattered the peace. I clasped his waist and sat with zigzag legs while the wind rasped my face. The moor was stark and dark, one hill flowing into the next, with lozenge-shaped pastures cutting into it. As we passed a herd of Red Rubies he slowed down and shouted, 'Hallo, my lovelies,' and they looked up. At last the bike plunged down a combe with wooded lower slopes and stopped by a row of eight monumental compost structures. Amelia and Toe threw down pitchforks and rushed over to hug me.

Simon said, 'Eff's coming on her own for the weekend.' He put an arm round my shoulders. 'I'll take you at dusk to hear the nightjars in Beechcleave Wood if they're still here. Oliver will approve.' He chuckled. 'We've been declared nationally important for our nightjar population.'

'Oliver never misses a chance for a moment of fame,' said Toe and they laughed.

I set to like a bird uniting with its shadow when it lands. The compost was a bracken and wool mixture, bagged and sold under the Diamond name. Simon had gained extra Brownie points for that idea. A wet stripe appeared in the middle of his back and veins protruded over the clenched biceps. The work had a structure, a rhythm, and I slowed down to half their speed to keep time, but Oliver had kindly let me work, so I thrust the fork in faster to catch up. Our bodies flowed from swan-neck to arabesque, forks lifted to the clouds.

After lunch I worked at the kennels.

'Brilliant,' said Rachel. 'Craig's glad you're here too. He's escaped mucking out the dogs.'

We drove two miles down the beech-lined drive, along the road and up a dirt track headed by a sign: Diamond Kennels. Past cornfields, sheep fields and rough pasture. If the wind was right, you could hear the barking from indoors, but close up the racket was deafening. Rachel hated keeping them on leads; a dog should run free. Still, each cage had a pen six metres long. A Jack Russell wore a red hunting jacket with brass buttons down the back. A Border Terrier, Pip, which came three months ago and was never collected was trusted off the lead and romped while sad faces watched. Oliver, who avoided the place because he loathed dogs, didn't know about Pip. Rachel dreaded betrayal. For their first visit clients came to the house where they admired the lavish marble and furnishings, then someone took them to the kennels. She hid Pip in the back room where she kept records. She didn't trust anyone with her secret.

I picked him up and cuddled him, and he relaxed and closed his eyes, opening them for the occasional lick. 'But you trust me?'

'You're different.'

Craig drove me back to the manor house. Oliver led me into his consulting room, then left the room. The papers on the desk formed a shambolic heap. On the wall hung a new picture of a hang-glider in front of a long bank of cloud, the Morning Glory. The figure was too small to make out, but I pictured him soaring with the kite, arms outstretched, baggy red T-shirt ballooning.

An agonising ten minutes later he reappeared and lounged, with his elbows on the arms of the slouchy executive chair, forefingers pressed together and pointing at me, and stared. After being desperate for his help, I had nothing to say. The clouds emptied themselves over the dark land. He broke the silence.

'I have a soft spot for you. It's a peat bog on the moor.'

I giggled.

'I wanted to be a singer. I was in the West End, you know. I could have got gigs all over the world, but it didn't happen, for reasons best known to their precious selves.' He gritted his teeth. 'But the work I do here is infinitely more important.'

We fell silent again and I stared at the floor.

'I'm reading an unputdownable book about a woman,' he said, studying my face. 'As she is. Unputdownable.'

I laughed.

'Here's a good joke. Three women shortlisted for a job at MI5 are waiting in the corridor. The interviewer hands the first woman a gun and says, 'Go into that room where you'll find your husband sitting on a chair and kill him.' She goes in. No sound. After five minutes she staggers out, slumps on a chair and mops her brow. 'I couldn't bring myself to do it,' she says. The second woman takes the gun and goes into the room. Again there's silence. After five minutes she crawls out, sweat pouring off her brow, tears flowing, and collapses onto a chair. 'It's no good,' she says, 'I just can't do it.' The third woman goes in. A terrible noise follows, crashing and shouting and screaming and banging, that goes on for ages. Finally after twenty minutes she emerges, scratched and bruised, clothes in tatters. 'You could have told me the gun wasn't loaded,' she says. 'I had to kill him with the chair.'"

I roared and he grinned and nodded.

'I hear Mark thinks we're a pack of dogs.' He raised an eyebrow.

'Well, *I* don't think that. It was con*struc*tive criticism. Mark doesn't want to see you again. He didn't like the long walk in the rain.'

'Or perhaps Mark has something to hide.'

Blushing, I told him about reading Mark's mobile. 'I feel ashamed.'

'Ashamed? No wonder you're so fucked up. It sounds like two blokes comparing potential conquests.'

'I keep sneaking downstairs in the night to look at his phone. I don't know what to do.'

He stroked his chin, nodding; the ice-blue eyes gazed at me and the jade sphinxes on the mantelpiece smiled their inscrutable smiles. 'Have you had an HIV test yet?'

'No.' While Oliver soared ahead of the Morning Glory, I had plummeted at home, jobless, betrayed, benighted. 'I was hoping you could mend our marriage.'

Oliver squeezed his lips between thumb and forefinger, never taking his eyes off me. 'I climb mountains, I don't move them.'

24

The stone-floored lounge buzzed, like the audience chatter before a concert. Claire's mother, who had driven all the way from Hastings, had Claire's thin-lipped smile that didn't know whether to spread or shrink. Two other visitors and twelve familiar faces made me a veteran now. Several wore scarves and gloves.

A door opened. Oliver's eyes swept across the gathering. The noise ceased but for the muted hiss of held breaths. He smiled and thanked us for coming, and Claire's mother beamed as if he had thanked her personally. Simon winked at me and I winked back. Oliver was telling the MI5 job joke. I listened intently and roared with the others at the punch-line, then joined the bottleneck at the foot of the stairs.

'Right. You must all be nice to Eff this weekend,' Oliver announced from his chair. 'She deserves to be looked after.' My cheeks burned. 'Mark isn't coming back. He doesn't like us,' he added in a whining, high-pitched voice.

Cries of outrage filled the room.

'He went to some poetry teaching workshop,' I said. 'He wanted me to go, but I wanted to come here.'

Silence.

'Perhaps you'd like to tell the group about the email you received?'

My heart thumped.

'It was a photo of Mark kissing another woman.' I pursed my lips. 'Mark said it was photoshopped.'

Here it was, back again in full Technicolor, the woman's figure-hugging turquoise T-shirt, and Mark.

'So you think he's meeting another woman there?' said Amelia.

'Don't be a noggerhead,' said Simon. 'He wouldn't want Eff with him if he was.'

'Could be a cover, knowing Eff would rather be with us. He could have bought two tickets and then...'

Oliver watched with arms folded. 'Now, now, children. Enough.'

We finished late. My bed was in a dormitory with five other women, between Melanie's and the window. Melanie, who wore her ankh in bed, said Oliver got his limp from a mountaineering accident. For a long time I lay awake, thinking of the pack of dogs remark and Oliver's accident and what Mark was doing, till the strangeness of the surroundings evaporated and my mind spilt out into sleep.

*

'Speak up, Claire,' said Oliver. 'Claire is an only child,' he explained to the group, 'she's used to getting attention, so she's never needed to talk loudly. And can you not slouch when we're working? Otherwise your mother will think I'm no good for you.'

Claire sat up. Her mother and the other visitors were having a lie-in in the shippon.

'Yes, Claire?'

'I just wanted to say Rachel's snoring isn't that bad, and could you reinstate her in a bedroom?'

A gush of vitriol came from Amelia and Melanie, who said they heard the bear-like roars from the corridor below. Brickbats flew back and forth till Oliver ordered us to work. We sang Kumbayah, and when it ended we stood suspended by the magical sound that still hung in the air.

We built oat sheaves into stooks. Simon said the oat had a good ear on it. The clouds looked like giant heaps of ice-cream sitting on top of invisible cones. Rachel and I sang

The Hunting Chorus, and in my head was the hullabaloo of the horns, the galloping hooves of the lower strings and the followers' cries. Over and over we sang it and the merry throng joined in with the triumphant Halali, halali, and again halaaaali. Hurrah, the stag is dead. By the time we returned indoors, it was the theme tune for the weekend: Halali, halali, halaaaali.

At lunchtime Rachel approached me privately. 'I shouldn't tell you this because you're supposed to concentrate on the work, but there's a text for you.' She squeezed my arm.

In the office she handed me the phone.

'It's from Mark.' I read: *Found out something about Oliver. Be very careful. Love M.* I deleted it. 'He's just sending his love,' I said without missing a beat. I doubted it was serious. Mark was determined to swipe at Oliver.

*

'Give a man a mask and he'll show you the truth. Who said that?'

'You did,' said Simon, and the group tittered.

Oliver ignored him. 'Oscar Wilde.'

He handed out full-face white masks with holes for eyes and nostrils, as expressionless as the hazy moor beyond the window. 'Le Coq said there are three masks: the one we think we are, the one we really are, and the one we have in common. The neutral mask allows you to take off all the other masks. You'll discover a state of pure presence, no past, no future, just the present. Be calm and open to whatever comes your way. A blank page. It will put you in touch with your core being, your true self. It'll empower you. So find a space, lie down and put it on.' He waited. 'Right. Now you are six years old. You wake up in the school playground. No speaking, no sounds. Off you go.'

I sat up and shrank like a touched slug. Not a blank page, but a whirl of photoshopped images and job worries and missing the teaching and thinking be careful and wanting to be part of this group. Rachel and Simon approached me, but it was not-Rachel and not-Simon. The smiling eyes and mouths were gone. They terrified me, my head was like a poked ants' nest, and Mark was in another place with other people, maybe with one other. I shrugged Gargantuan shoulders. They held out their arms and I copied, but my own felt like extending robot arms. I had a vacuum in my skull and colossal gestures. They looked about to throttle me, but instead they took my magnified hands and the three of us held hands in a circle and danced round. I let them guide me, all body and no mind, forgetting why I was there or who I was. If this was my true self, it was loathsome.

'I felt disturbed,' I said in the round-up afterwards. 'Out of control.'

'Good,' said Oliver.

Beyond the wildness of the room lay the moor with shimmering horizon.

In the next exercise I was still spinning, till Oliver's hand clasped my shoulder and the whirling in my mind settled.

'Remember, Eff, there's no primrose path, but I know you're not a quitter.'

*

The gorse bushes shot out prickly arms across the path; the cobweb of cloud turned from gold to pewter and the rooks croaked over Beechcleave Wood.

'Come on, it's getting dimpsy. You're lucky the nightjars are still here. They should be gone. That would've been hard cheddar.'

We quickened our pace. The lower trunks of the beeches on top of the stone-faced earth banks were laid and wrapped round each other like tongues. All these enclosures on the former Royal Forest of Exmoor, Simon explained, were made by John Knight and his son, who bought it from the Crown in the nineteenth century and drained and dug up the land for farming.

The wood was dark and quiet but for gentle rustling. It was a mixture of oak, beech and birch, Simon said. Conifers were all right for nightjars for five years, but then, without clearings...

He looked at me quizzically. 'Sorry, I'm speechifying. Was it the mask exercise?'

'I was a bit put out.'

'Oliver's good at getting to the heart of things.'

He raised a forefinger and cocked his head. A churring filled the night air. We stood spellbound, smiling at each other, and tiptoed towards the sound. He waved a tissue because a white handkerchief was supposed to attract nightjars – not that he'd ever succeeded. The strange low trilling went on and on, changing pitch at intervals. We lay down side by side in a grassy clearing on the solid earth and the afternoon's turmoil waned. I could have lain there forever.

'What went wrong in the mask exercise?'

'I don't know. I felt weird. Scared. Didn't you?'

'No, I felt peaceful, as though the emotional floodgates had opened and everybody was my friend. Which they are, of course. Were you upset because of the photo?'

'Yes.'

The churring subsided into a throb, then stopped. The birch trunks gleamed in the dark and the earth smelt damp with dew.

Simon squeezed my hand. 'Don't say naught you don't want. Let's join the others. They'll be flippin' moaning about waiting.'

The moor was black with only a sliver of moon, but the bodies round the bonfire radiated light, flames licked at the darkness and the air smelt of burning fir resin. The faces shone and the singing drifted over the hills till only embers remained.

I slept fitfully. Sharing a room with five others was strange, and I kept thinking of Mark at his workshop. A house cricket chirped outside, its tempo hardly dropping with the cool of the night. One time a whirring woke me. A bat swooped a hand's width away from my face at speed, swished round and round before thudding into a wall and hanging there, then took off again. Bats are not supposed to bump into things, but again and again it hit the wall and stuck there, throbbing. At last I got up and opened the sash, but it clung to the wall with wings folded over the pulsing body. Using a glass and card, I trapped it. The tiny thing was too spent to struggle. I released it through the open window, exhausted myself, and fell into a deep sleep which was unbroken till the elephant bell rang.

*

'Exmoor has the highest cliffs in England and a plateau of unglaciated upland approximately two hundred million years old,' Amelia announced. Oliver had asked her to lead a short walk. 'The moor is covered in blanket bog due to an iron pan just below the surface and an annual rainfall of up to two thousand millimetres.'

We bunched behind her in the lobby.

'Amelia likes to show off to new people,' Rachel said to me at the back.

'Only because the Thin Controller told her to,' said Simon.

Amelia glared across and marched out.

The walk was long and I was tired. Suddenly Amelia

stopped and raised a hand, and a hush travelled down the column. On the hillside before us were red deer, one stag and seven hinds, thick necks craning round, noses pointing at the walkers, and those at the back tiptoed forwards. Amelia still held her hand in mid-air. The deer stared, the people stared. None moved. For an age we stood, the deer on the hill, the people below, and every cell in my body buzzed, till at last one deer lowered its head and carried on grazing and the rest copied. The voices resumed in a murmur and we let out our breaths and trudged on.

The red sandstone walls of the house glowed pink in the sun. Oliver was waiting upstairs, his tall figure silhouetted against the moor and his hair like the bracken gleaming orange. Melanie had a headache. Oliver directed three people to cluster round, touching her shoulders, hands and ankles. He squatted in front of her, took off her ankh and bandanna, stroked out the long, silky hair and looked deep into her eyes. Her cheeks quivered, her mouth fell open. He laid hands on her temples and she groaned, then howled at the ceiling, and the tongue-stud gleamed under a coat of saliva. She screwed up her face, eyes closed, shaking. Finally she gulped air and calmed down. The headache was gone.

Amelia cackled. 'You had an orgasm.'

Melanie blushed. Oliver stood up and shuffled off.

'Melanie's secret is out,' he said.

After the goodbye hugs Oliver said, 'Come and see me any time. Tell Mark we're sorry he didn't come. I should have rung and persuaded him. Mea culpa.'

*

Driving back over the moor with the hills greyed out by rain, I listened to the new CD and Oliver's sexy, assured voice eased itself into my consciousness like a warm, smooth Jack Daniels.

Maybe that was why I lost my way. The CD finished before anywhere looked familiar, but no matter. I replayed it and kept on through the rain which dropped on the windscreen like a waterfall and blotted out the roadside beeches turning orangey red, the ponies' coats dark with wet. I suspected Mark's great discovery was nothing of the kind. He despised Oliver and would say anything to demonise him. Halali, I sang, halali, halaaaali.

25

Authorities investigate African ecological charity

Life's Rich Tapestry, *Oliver Diamond's story of how he came to dedicate his life to promoting the environment in Tanzania, recounts the accident in which he fell 200 feet down Mount Kilimanjaro and suffered multiple fractures of leg, pelvis and arm. After 6 months in hospital and a year being cared for by a family in Moshi, he set off, only to be robbed, beaten and left for dead on the road. The people who took him in helped him get funds from England, which they then stole. Hitchhiking his way out, he was kidnapped by terrorists. A run of bad luck.*

But according to a website created by journalist Alan Crathorne, none of that happened. Crathorne was so moved by Life's Rich Tapestry that he donated £5,000 to the Tanzanian tree planting charity founded by Diamond. Film stars and politicians equally moved by the book also donated large sums. Why Crathorne changed his mind is unclear, but he went to great lengths to find witnesses, a difficult task because Diamond was not forthcoming with names. The kidnapper turned out to be a man who gave him food and shelter for three weeks. Martin Ng'hoboko said his reputation is ruined. His hospitality was repaid with slander. Friends who climbed with Diamond said there was no serious accident. His account of living among the people by the Kikafu River describes them as khat-chewing thieves and liars. But khat is unknown in the district, and honesty is a prime principle. Diamond claims literary licence and condensation of the facts. He said if he included everything he did from 1990 to 1997, it would take six mammoth tomes.

Now the police and HMRC are looking into allegations of tax fraud and extortion.

Suddenly Mark had taken away all the sweetness of Oliver. The ice-blue eyes stared out from the printout. He looked shrunken, sorry for himself, while the real Oliver was bold and caring. The hair was less marmalade and more dead bracken.

'It was 1998.' My voice was flat and lifeless. 'Not relevant.'

'The leopard never changes its spots.'

'The paper might have published errata and hidden them in a corner.'

'I would find them, Stef. I looked hard. Here are two more articles from the same period, all reputable sources.' He watched my face as I read. 'I wish you'd come to the poetry teaching with me.'

I wished so too. Even the robin sounded wistful.

Next day, browsing for Oliver Diamond yielded more results. Only a few were scraped. What a fool, placing so much hope in Oliver. A leap of faith. A mistake. Like a vine twining itself through the air in search of something to which it could cling.

On Tuesday the midday sun strove to get above the rooftops or trees. Sadie was plugged in to music all of the two hundred miles to university, then a quick hug and she was gone. Back home the fridge shuddered to a halt and a deadly silence reigned.

After choir I told Rachel about the articles. She twirled a lock of hair. 'It must be lies. I would have known.'

We sat glum-faced while waiting twenty minutes for Janet.

'I don't know why you still give her a lift,' said Rachel. 'It's out of your way now.'

'I don't mind.' I couldn't bring myself to stop the lifts, though the smell in the car was unbearable.

I didn't expect to see Oliver again. But on Monday he rang and told me not to believe everything in black and white, even in the quality press.

'I'd hate to lose you because of a pack of lies.' His voice was anguished.

'It wasn't just one article. Mark showed me several and I googled it too.'

'I have to wonder why Mark has taken against me so, when all I've ever done is try to help. Sometimes people are disappointed because I can't help, and they blame me. But you, Eff... I can help you. That I do know.'

'How can you help me without helping Mark? And what about the articles?'

'I'm not prepared to argue over the phone,' he said. 'If you want my help, I'll see you in return for four hours' work on Wednesday.'

I bit my lip. 'Tuesday.'

'I feel hurt that you believe these fabrications so readily, but out of the goodness of my heart I will fit you in tomorrow.'

*

One moment the bracken glowed in the sun, the next the valleys were hidden in mist. A crow sat at the top of a solitary Scots pine. On a verge with parked vehicles, people with binoculars watched a stag leap up the wooded slope and crash through the hazels, followed by a cavalcade of lusting dogs and riders.

'Beautiful,' said one. 'Look at the strength of those haunches.'

'Beautiful. All his rights and three atop.'

They argued about the number of antler points. Only those long enough to hang a crop on were counted. I drove off at speed, disgusted.

Claire was waiting in the doorway with dyed-black pompon-chrysanthemum hair and black fingernails. I was to help in the bottling shed. She showed me where the spring bubbled out at the surface on the moor. It probably came from Wales under the Bristol Channel. They sold seven hundred litres a week and were allowed to take unlimited water. At first they'd argued all that waste plastic was environmentally unfriendly, and, as it was a democratic community, everything was debated and put to the vote, but Oliver said they needed the money. Silence reigned in the shed but for the plink of bottles till the elephant bell rang.

Lunchtime was frosty; I felt cold stares on my back. Only Simon, who came in from tree-felling wearing ballistic dungarees and steel toecaps, hugged me. Oliver was not there.

Afterwards I helped Rachel muck out and walk the dogs. The fog clung to skin, hair and clothes and muffled voices. She strode ahead as if her three were pulling her forwards, and the dogs on their long leads were greyed out. We wandered over bleaching grass and heather, the black ground beneath, then towelled the small dogs dry and searched for ticks. We were walking back in silence when Claire came running along the path like a dog with a ball.

'Oliver will see you now.'

He barked when I knocked. He stood with one elbow on the mantelpiece like a male model. With wounded face he read out an article, then dropped his trousers to reveal a scar the length of his thigh.

'Clearly the accident did happen.' His eyes impaled me

and I blushed. He pulled the trousers back up and sat behind the desk. 'This Alan Crathorne... Sometimes people blame their failures on a scapegoat. He was an ardent advocate of my work till he fell in with a certain woman. Alan was ruled by the women in his life. As for Martin Gobbledegook saying he wasn't a kidnapper. Well, he would say that, wouldn't he? Gave him food and shelter for three weeks... Of course he gave me food and shelter. If you want a ransom, you keep your victim alive. I never heard such stupidity.' He broke out laughing. 'Di-da-di-da-di-da... The accident we've dealt with. Khat unknown... Honesty a prime principle... Again, they're bound to say that. Shows what liars they are. As for tax fraud and extortion, the allegations were dropped for lack of evidence. Years ago. I never heard any more. So there you are. That's why I discourage people from using the internet.'

I gaped, ashamed that Mark had persuaded me, and apologised profusely. Shame gave way to outrage at Mark's exultation and my own naïve belief in this fabrication. Mark was like this Alan Crathorne, attacking just because it didn't work for him.

'I forgive you,' he said, still looking wounded. 'Don't listen to others. Listen to your heart. We'd all be sorry to lose you.' Following my gaze he added, 'I'll take you up in a two-seater one day.'

He gave me a hug like the amniotic fog outside, clinging and glistening and cosseting and perfect.

*

'I've been to the Academy and it's not what you think,' I told Mark after choir. 'It was all fabrication.' Though a corner of my mind still questioned this.

Rachel chewed gum and studied the floor.

'I'd like a private word with Stef, please.'

'No. Rachel should hear this. Otherwise we'd be talking behind her back.'

'Right, if that's the way you want it.'

And so it was. Rachel pouted and joined in with 'Oliver doesn't operate like that' and 'He has the scars to prove it.'

'It feels like a cult,' Mark shouted at last.

'There's no restriction of food, sleep or contact with family and friends,' said Rachel without hesitation.

Every day the pigeons courted in the trees with noisy wing-beats, while Mark and I had abstained for ages. In bed he pulled me close and his hand groped like a pair of pliers looking for purchase on a deformed screw head. Thankfully he came quickly. He shrank and withdrew, grumpy. I turned my back.

26

Football was rained off and Mark called on Hilda. He wanted her to persuade Stef that this man Oliver was running a cult. They talked over tea and cinnamon cakes in the conservatory, enveloped by triffids.

'Can't you persuade her, Gran? She listens to you.'

'*You* have to speak to her, Mark.'

'I can't get through to her. It's like wading through deep snow. I've even studied her Facebook page for clues and given her articles denigrating this Oliver, but he persuades her it's all lies.'

Hilda raised her eyebrows. 'But Rachel seemed such a lovely young woman.'

'She is. They're all great individually. They're friendly, they're fun. But together... They stand united, they become a single person, they're all moonstruck or they're all jubilant or they're all sad. They bicker over who should sleep where, but they're like one body. Oliver clicks a finger and they come running. Right from the off we were steamrollered into handing over our mobiles in the lobby like schoolchildren. The second time I kept mine, and I almost got the death penalty when it went off. And in the name game they were a pack of dogs. Oliver just sat back and smirked. He doesn't do anything, all he has to do is appear and open his mouth. Whatever he says is gospel. Those people are like a pearl forming round a piece of grit, the way they cluster round him.'

Hilda sipped her tea. The grandfather clock in the hall struck a quarter to and the rain pattered on.

'If I were you, Mark, I would speak to him, express your concerns.'

'What? Tell him I think he's a fraud?'

'Tell him you're worried that Stef thinks this computer image is real. She respects what he thinks. I remember you did too at first.'

'I was touched, it's true. I envied them the tight-knit community, the great community spirit. It made a refreshing change from people talking on mobiles and ignoring the person next to them. Maybe you're right. I *will* go and talk to Oliver.'

'So what's he like?'

'He's as slimy as the underside of a sink plug,' said Mark.

*

After Mark left Hilda sat for a long time, shocked. Like the sparrowhawk, you never saw it coming. If Mark was right she could not prevent it. Suddenly she leant forwards. Every morning she had looked out past the rubber doormat outside the patio doors. But now she saw that the geometrical Greek key pattern of its border was full of swastikas. All day whenever she passed, the hated symbols leapt at her. Before the day was out she could stand it no more. She dragged the offending object across the back and into the six-inch gap between garage and wall.

If only she could help. They also serve who only stand and wait, she told herself. But she doubted it. She thought of the last time she'd had dinner at Stef and Mark's, that awkward, telling moment when Stef asked Mark to take the bowls out and he snatched them up and muttered, 'Sometimes I think she thinks I'm the butler.' At the piano Hilda sang *Dein Ist Mein Ganzes Herz* and her voice quavered on the long notes. Fred always said she should forgive herself, but she didn't know how. The grandfather clock chimed nine. She closed the piano, lit the candle inside the clock to keep it warm and went into the dining room to type:

Papa used to sing me *Dein Ist Mein Ganzes Herz* on bended knee and hold up one of my plaits as I sat by the tiled stove with feet tucked under between coal bucket and kindling box. 'Leave the girl alone, Stefan,' Mama would say, but I could listen all day. He sang every evening in a restaurant in Berlin-Mitte. 'Not a real job,' Onkel Wilhelm said, twirling the ends of his handlebar moustache with spit on his fingers. Not like himself, a real warrior with his Iron Cross for South-West Africa. 'He's jealous,' Papa would lean over and whisper. If my uncle wore his Iron Cross to make his brother look bad, he failed. My hackles rose in defence of my hero. Papa also had a war medal and he could sing to me forever.

But later I changed. We didn't hold with the old ways. We were true Germans who defeated the Romans at the Battle of the Teutoburg Forest, and my father's generation were degenerate like the Romans. I forgot the war medals.

I was jubilant at being selected to go to the Nuremberg rally. My parents said they couldn't afford it, although it was subsidised. They were lying. I asked Tante Luise and Onkel Eduard for the money. Papa was furious.

We went by special train, to camp for seven days. The town was a sea of red flags, pavements seethed with people as we tramped through, and the air sizzled with excitement. We felt grand. Each girl had the location and number of her position in the tent city. On the fourth day, Youth Day, we got up early and marched to the stadium. The drum rolls and trumpet fanfares tightened every nerve. Eighty thousand of us lined up. When Hitler came on, we were told to greet him with the triple Sieg Heil, but we just carried on repeating it, shouting for joy. I can hear those endless shouts of Heil now. We fought back tears when he spoke, telling us to be peaceful and obedient and courageous. 'You are flesh of our flesh, blood of our blood,' he said, and his words lifted us sky-high. We were together, joined in spirit, we had new values, refined in the fire. Only later did I find out all our noise was made to drown out our cries and the cries of those we trod on in the scramble for self-esteem.

At Nuremberg I became friends with Veronika who was in my class at school. I slept next to her in the tent and I was green with envy because Hitler gazed at her. After that we both vowed to devote our lives to the Führer, and we each wrote him a letter and received a reply. He didn't write it himself, but he did sign it. We used to take out our letters and kiss the signatures. Her mother liked me because I played snakes and ladders with Veronika's little brother and fetched potatoes from the cellar or bread from the baker's, and she fed me cake and liquorice sweets and fresh lemon squash. Every Sunday Veronika and I went to the cinema. We were thick as thieves. Not only was she good at sports and clever, but she was Nordic-looking like me. After Nuremberg we walked to school together.

One day, the day after the Graf Zeppelin flew close by, a removal van was outside her flat and the men were carrying out all their furniture. I never saw her again. I was hurt that she left without saying goodbye.

27

People had stopped mentioning jobs on Facebook, but there were emails.

Hi Eff,
I hear from Rachel you still have doubts – I thought I explained the articles. Come and see me if you need clarification. I know others here miss you and would be most upset if they thought you weren't coming again. You can work for four hours in exchange for an hour of my time as usual.
Yours affectionately,
Oliver Diamond

I read it again twice. Yours affectionately. I smiled.

Hi Eff,
I'd be most upset if I didn't see you again. Think of the laughs we've had. ;) Look forward to seeing you again soon.
x Simon

'Bless,' I said out loud.

Dear Eff, You have great potential and I for one would be extremely sorry if you did not come back. This place could use your talents.
Regds,
Amelia

See you Tuesday. ☺ Talk to you then.
x Rachel

Hi Eff,
Please come back. It was really nice talking to you.
x Claire

cant get a job cuz ur a lousy tchr ur a lousy lover saw
mark with her agn.

Attached was a photo of a couple hand in hand from behind: the long dark hair and turquoise T-shirt again, and what looked like Mark, with a metal-strap watch and charcoal-grey jumper like his. Their heads were turned towards each other. I put the phone back in my pocket, but every last pixel was carved in my memory, the hang of his jumper from the shoulder blades, the woman's snub nose, the ease of their togetherness, the way his lower lip hung down. Above all, the love and tenderness on his face.

I hunkered over the piano, hammered the keys and let Beethoven's Tempest Sonata sweep through me in a torrent of emotions, taking me now this way, now that. The piece was fiendishly difficult, but then, I was fiendishly angry. My fingers were unstoppable with the buzzing inner voices and rumbling bass tremolandi. It grew darker and darker, livid, and the light gleamed for a brief moment before it was smothered. Like an Aeolian harp I perched at the centre of the storm and let my heartstrings be pulled, let the florid, raging tunes flow from my fingers, and the brief rests were enough to go on.

Later, waiting for the Minehead bus from Taunton and humming Kumbayah, the distant sky filled with a nebulous black mass moving in waves, dividing and merging and changing shape, one moment an ink blot, the next a tornado. At last I realised they were starlings, thousands of them reeling, swirling, soaring, diving, in perfect coordination. If one turned, all turned, yet they never collided. After half an hour of turning, in one final, massive swoop they were gone to the Levels.

That evening, during a singing lesson, my right hand drummed fast like a galloping horse, while Mark tramped from room to room and clattered dishes.

'Your voice has a wonderful timbre, Aaron.' His cheeks flushed as red as the walls. 'But take your space. This is *your* song, *your* gift to the listener.'

Aaron sang lustily. Louder, my God, to thee. I hated imperfection in myself and others. At my instruction he went through and paraphrased Goethe's poem.

'The father's riding fast at night, clutching his son,' said Aaron. 'But the boy's afraid because he can see the Erl-King. His father says it's nothing, just the mist. But the boy hears the Erl-King ask him to come away with him. His father says it's nothing, just the leaves rustling. But the boy hears the Erl-King promise that his daughters will sing and dance with him, and sees the daughters. His father says it's nothing, just the old grey willows. The Erl-King tells the boy he loves him, he's beautiful, and if he won't come willingly he'll use force. The boy cries out that the Erl-King is touching him and hurting him. The father rides faster, but arrives home to find the boy is dead.'

He didn't say it was nothing then. I asked Aaron to sing it again with more dynamic and emotional variation, the boy both afraid and enchanted, and the Erl-King wheedling, saying anything to get his own way. The fast-paced ostinato imitating the galloping horse, with the father clutching the boy and hanging on to the reins, tree trunks gleaming in the moonlight, and the child's terror, made me tense.

We started again and the Erl-King's hissing promises, the

boy's fear, the father's blind assurance were more heartfelt. Over and over he sang, and the grausets with its guttural g and rolled r and the ow like a cat spoiling for a fight was chilling. Maybe, I suggested, the father is afraid and putting on a brave face. Maybe the boy wants to go with the Erl-King, maybe he likes someone telling him he's beautiful, offering attention and affection.

'Children will do anything for a bit of love.'

*

Knurre, schnurre, knurre,
schnurre, Rädchen, schnurre.

On and on went the Spinning Song, the same phrase again and again like the three Fates spinning the thread of life, like weird, conjoined sisters. The choir suppressed the impulse to join in with legs and arms, but Rachel and I swayed and our heads parted and came together in perpetual motion. *Knurre, schnurre, knurre,* the wheel whirred, round and round, wore down the sharpness of the day, the poison of the photos. It lured with its constancy, and that was comforting, knowing the simple tune with just six notes. But it was strange being in the choir, social yet solitary, like sheep all in one corner of the field, each munching on its own personal grazing area, ignoring the rest. Not quite ignoring. We listened and blended and rolled our r's. *Knurrrre, schnurrrre, knurrrre.* Long after Janet was delivered home, the melody carried on in our heads.

28

We woke up with the wheel still turning, and drove over the moor. The sodden bracken was the colour of Red Rubies and the grass shimmered like silk in the wind.

Oliver stood in the doorway, hands in pockets, wearing a red satin waistcoat covered in gold dragons with curly arrow-headed tails. He led me to the consulting room where screwed-up balls of paper engulfed the wastepaper basket, and the eyes of the alighting eagle on the lamp base narrowed. He slumped in the voluptuous chair behind the desk. A sphinx-like smile lurked around his lips.

'Mark came to see me. He asked me not to tell you, but of course my duty is to you. He thinks you're menopausal.'

'What?' My jaws clenched and fingers curled like the dragons' outstretched claws.

Suddenly the room seemed airless. I told him about the new photo, quivering.

He spread his arms with palms upturned. 'That explains everything. And the three days in Venice from Boxing Day for the two of you. But don't mention it,' he added, seeing my face, 'it's a surprise, but he just wants to buy you off, have his cake and eat it.'

I fumed. Venice? Worse, my parents were coming to stay for a whole week, for the concert. They had always, *always* stayed with Lisa before.

Oliver settled into his chair.

'Perhaps Mark is behind it. What are they like?'

Like chalk and cheese. They hardly talked to each other, except in the garden where prize-winning roses vented their perfume and shouted their colour, static and beautiful, expressing what the humans could not. Their carers glided among them, admiring, sniffing, squashing bugs, spraying, snipping with secateurs. They grunted at each other all through my childhood, and boredom seeped like an insecticidal spray into every pore. Then came light in the form of Gran and the piano when Mum returned to work. 'They mean well. They come to all my concerts. Loyalty.'

'Or guilt.'

I looked at him quizzically.

'For farming you out.'

'But I loved being with Gran.'

He asked what my mother was like.

'Sort of sweet. A bit dreamy, a bit churchy.' I pondered. 'Once, on holiday, she took me and Lisa out to this grass-topped rock in the sea where people picnic on top and explore rock pools. We were about seven and eight. On the way out everyone else was going back to the shore. When we were on top she twigged the sea was coming in and surrounding the rock. Instead of waiting for the tide to go in and back out, she grabbed us and dragged us through the water, clutching buckets and spades in our spare hands. People on the beach stood and stared as the water rushed round into the empty space in front of us. It was up to our armpits. But we made it. She'd checked the tides before leaving, but misread the height of low water as the time.' I rocked with laughter. 'Mum got it wrong again.'

Oliver puffed out his cheeks. 'I'm not surprised you're fucked up.'

*

Like a city-dweller in a city I disappeared into the sea. I didn't want to go home after the Academy. The seaweedy smell beckoned and the sea took me in its wide arms and whispered sweet nothings in my ears. In the sea-womb was no time. The

October air was cold but the warm water licked my skin as I floated, long hair fanned out, like a boat in the harbour, cosseted by dabbing waves. Each wave was a member of the group reaching out to touch me, sluggish waves, and I sighed at their touch. The rhythm was soothing: *Knurre, schnurre, knurre.* Somewhere I ended and the sea began, but it no longer mattered. Here somewhere was self and there somewhere was sea. The sea moulded itself round me or I moulded myself to the sea. I conformed to my surroundings and the sea was a willing surrounder and a calmer of rampant thoughts.

In Gran's garden, where the meadow had been cut for the winter, a great green bush-cricket chirped like a squeaky saw. Gran and I marvelled at how long it sang, on and on for three minutes, a brief pause, then another three minutes, over and over.

'Dad used to show me how different crickets and grasshoppers make their sounds by scraping leg on wing, or wing on wing, when we came here on holiday,' I said. 'He took me to this field which was like this amazing symphony. And once we walked through wet grass, and with every footstep fifty tiny grasshopper nymphs bounced in all directions like a box of fireworks.'

'You and he made a football rattler out of cardboard, to imitate one.'

'The common green grasshopper.'

'And maracas made out of a purple plastic eggshell and mustard seeds.'

'That was the great green bush-cricket. And for the short-winged cone-head, curl your tongue behind your front teeth and suck, and purr like a drum brush. There's a great green bush-cricket now.'

I didn't want to go home.

'Can I take you shopping today, Gran, because Mark's

visiting his sick mother at the weekend and I'm busy.'

She looked at me suspiciously. 'Today will be lovely. I'm looking forward to the concert. Will Rachel be there?'

'Of course. And her friends from the Academy,' I added with more enthusiasm than I had meant to betray.

'I don't remember seeing the friends before the *Elijah* concert.'

'There'll be some reason,' I snapped.

While she changed I sat in the lounge where a bowl of potpourri of dried baby rosebuds and tiny pine cones sat next to the television. I took out my MP3 player, closed my eyes and breathed deep.

'Picture a warm, safe, comforting fire,' said the warm and comforting voice. 'A purifying fire. You relax in the warmth of this safe, comforting, crackling, purifying fire. Now picture all the negative people, negative emotions nesting in your mind, those intruders. Write each one on an imaginary piece of paper.' I wrote Mark and Evelyn, people who reject job applications, senders of poison emails. My pen hovered and then wrote Dad, Mum, Lisa, and should I add Gran? Yes, I'd felt negativity just now. 'Take a broom and sweep them into a heap, take a dustpan and brush and gather them up and throw them on the purifying fire. Watch the paper singe, blacken and ignite. See all those intruders swallowed by flames.'

'Ready, dear,' said Gran.

'The snake which cannot cast its skin has to die,' said the lilting voice, and the warm memory of hilltop flames melted me.

Gran asked, 'Are Rachel's friends supportive of you too?'

But I fended off her questions. I sensed a prying mind clawing its way into mine, like the badger I once saw through the patio doors at night, pincering

a squealing, rolled-up hedgehog in its sides till it
unfurled.

29

The leaping flames of the fire laid by Stef comforted Hilda, but a sudden dread filled her as she pictured the zombies, as Mark had called them, standing in formation after the concert, with Stef among them. Such things could overwhelm a person unwittingly, like your own shadow creeping up from behind in a lamplit street. She herself had been in a cult of the most dangerous kind and never knew it until a year after leaving. How could they be wrong when everybody was doing it, Berni, her secret boyfriend before her mother snatched her away, and Inge and all her friends? Don't beat yourself up, Fred had said, but Hilda ached.

Berni was Inge's older brother, tall, blond, blue-eyed and fit. I untied my plaits, and Berni put a blue columbine in my hair. When my father found out about our trysts after the Wednesday afternoon meetings, he went mad and forbade us to meet. I was too young, he said. We ignored the ban.

One winter's day we headed out to the River Havel, me, Hanno, Inge, Berni, and my three cousins from Thuringia. We could roam where we wanted as long as we looked after Otto. At sixteen he had a mental age of eight. We bought cheap liquorice from a shop we knew. It was a poor area, and the grocer saved on lighting and heating and wore fingerless gloves instead. His fingers were red-raw. A man in a dark coat and black Homburg was questioning him for giving a tab to a Jew. The grocer said, 'How can I tell if they're Jews?' They went quiet when we came in, and we thought no more about it. But later the man in the dark coat followed and stopped us. He wanted our addresses and our ages, and wrote them in a notebook. We forgot about it as we walked along, and sat on the beach by the river to eat our picnic of cold pork chops and rolls and lemonade, near the spot where Herta's father drowned himself.

On the way home a gypsy woman with thick black wavy hair pinned back with hair grips came up. She wore a brightly coloured ankle-length skirt and a cameo brooch with a bear at her neck. She pressed a sprig of heather against my collarbone and said, 'Buy some heather for good luck?' I said no, but Berni, in a good mood, said, 'Only if you read her palm.' So we gave her two Reichsmarks and I held out my hand.

'Lucky devil,' she said. 'You'll always land on your feet.'

Without being asked, she took Berni's hand and held it palm up alongside. 'That's a couple like Max and Klärchen,' she said, which meant we were ideally suited.

The others clamoured, 'Read mine, read mine.'

Hanno would be a man of courage. Inge would rise to great heights. Liesl would have a wonderful husband and children. Walter would lead an honourable life. She refused to read Otto's. I was outraged on his behalf.

I told Mama about the gypsy, without mentioning Berni.

'Take no notice,' she said.

Three weeks later when our cousins were back home, Otto was taken away by the Gestapo. Tante Elsbeth was beside herself. A month after, she received a letter saying that he had died of bronchial pneumonia after an operation. In my school maths book at the time was a question: The construction of a lunatic asylum costs 6 million Reichsmarks. How many houses at 15,000 Reichsmarks each could be built for that amount?

30

On a dark night I left the house in stillness. The smell of gunpowder hung in the air and a flame inside me guided me to a greater flame. No one saw me go. The bright headlights lit up the woods of the Exe valley like a cavern, and the thrill of going for the weekend without Mark knowing fanned my flame. Gusting winds buffeted the car on the top, but it kept on, a dot of light gliding over the moor on a moonless night. They wouldn't start without me, and no wind would stop them on the fifth of November.

A mile away I stopped on a hill and wound down the window. The sound of Kumbayah drifted across on the wind. It ebbed and flowed, and when it flowed, my flame whooshed like a hot-air balloon, taking my breath away, and I sighed at the flood of pleasure.

Simon was waiting at the manor house. He hugged me long and hard and I drank in the warm, earthy smell.

'Come on, let's go out over. Bring the viola.'

On top of the pile of fir branches was a guy with wrists, ankles and waist tied with string, with a lurid red lipstick mouth exaggerated like a clown's.

'That's Graham.' Rachel giggled. 'Oliver's idea.'

'Was Graham a quitter?'

'He was asked to quit. He was difficult. Those were Graham's clothes he never collected.'

Oliver started 'John Brown's body lies a-mouldering in the grave' and everyone joined in, then Melanie and three others with torches stepped forwards and danced inside the circle. Their arms snaked and zigzagged and looped, then thrust the torches into the woodpile, which crackled and spat in the gusting wind. The fire erupted and the guy's rug-wool hair sizzled and melted. People jumped back as the sooty flames lashed out like lizards' tongues. Oliver, wearing a metallic silver puffer jacket which gleamed in the firelight, spoke, but the roar of the fire and the wind drowned him out. He beamed across at me.

We shared out sparklers and the night was full of whizzing circles and figures of eight, to the children's delight. I wrote Purify in the air. Our cheeks were rosy as we feasted on potatoes and marshmallows baked in foil round a bed of embers. Oliver gestured drawing a bow across a stringed instrument and I held the viola aloft.

I played What Shall We Do With The Drunken Sailor? Angela, who had howled in the sighing exercise, cried 'Wahey,' linked arms with Craig and they lifted their knees high and slapped their thighs. Everyone copied them except Oliver. The firelight flickered on the thick varnish of the instrument and the sea shanties continued till Oliver gestured with both hands, palms down. I launched into a brief intermezzo followed by Amazing Grace. My claw-like left hand fluttered.

'If the Devil sleeping on Tarr Steps had heard that, he'd leap up and skip over the stones in delight,' said Simon as we strolled back. 'Your sycamore viola.'

We smiled at each other. Oliver walked ahead and his path seemed to shine with the silver colour of his puffer jacket, like a sparkler leaving trails of light.

I could have fallen straight into bed, but no, we went up to the workroom. Claire, only the bottom half of her hair black now, and Stick, a new woman with smoker's yellowed fingertips and a multi-coloured hand-knitted jumper like Oliver's, had bumped into Graham in town. He'd set up his own business forest gardening and said leaving was the best thing that ever happened to him.

'That young cockerel wouldn't have had a clue without me,' said Oliver.

'With his partner,' added Claire.

'Partner?' said Amelia. 'Who would go with that fucking creep?'

'She seemed nice. And he did too.'

'I think you had a soft spot for him, Claire.'

'Weak spot, more like,' said Toe. 'Graham never completely deumbilicated.'

I yawned. The argument washed over me. Just when I thought they were all grahamed out, Melanie complained that Donna was in the British Red Cross shop on her own. Donna said no one would go with her. Oliver said she should have come to see him. They ranted on and on. People rested chins on knees or slumped like the guy on the bonfire, or slept.

'You stay up very late talking about things,' I said to Donna as we went up to bed.

Donna had been working on the cider press and smelt of apples. I envied her having her own room. The dormitory smelt of stale body odour with the window shut. No sooner were my eyes closed than the sound of heaving bodies and lips on flesh made them spring open. Between my legs was a wetness that had long been unfamiliar.

*

Melanie woke me. My neck was stiff and my fingers sore from the viola.

Assembly was soporific. Stick was knitting a red-and-black striped jumper.

Suddenly Rachel's voice sounded: 'Eff asked why my friends weren't at the concert before?'

I jerked awake. The faces stared and the logs in the wood-burner glowed. Rachel twiddled her hair.

'I didn't expect Rachel to repeat it.'

'Keeping secrets is not my modus operandi,' said Oliver. 'Any complaints should be brought to the group.' He paused. 'Well, I think you should all go and support Rachel at the next concert. And Eff. I might even come myself.'

Rachel beamed, while I shrank in shame. I hadn't meant it as a complaint. Had I?

As if to defuse my embarrassment, Oliver said, 'Why is a viola like premature ejaculation?' Nobody knew. 'Because you know it's coming, but you can't do a thing about it.'

The room rocked with laughter and my face burned.

All day we stacked logs on a trailer, and were glad when it ended. The beech trees blazed orange everywhere and the bracken gleamed chestnut in the dying sun. At dinner Oliver chided Claire for clacking her teeth on the spoon.

'My kids used to do that,' said Donna. 'It annoyed their father no end.'

'You have kids?'

'Yes. But I haven't heard from them for twelve years. They could be in Australia for all I know.'

My spoon stopped in mid-air. 'You poor thing. I'd be gutted.'

'I'm fine with it. All my family are here.'

I stared at Donna's sunken profile, which sat oddly with the lacy top and short skirt.

After dinner Oliver squatted like a toad in the bay. 'I hear Mark called us a cult.'

An angry response followed: there was no deprivation of food, sleep or contact with family and friends. And only stupid people joined cults. I gasped on learning they were all graduates, even postgraduates. Simon had a degree in agriculture, Toe was a doctor of medicine, Amelia had a master's in business administration, Melanie did clinical psychology, Claire was a history teacher, Rachel had studied English. The only one without a degree was Oliver. Rachel was a stockbroker till she got sick of the City, the dark satanic tills, and took up guide-dog training.

On Sunday morning Oliver excused me from woodland clearing. 'Simon will take you to Watersmeet. Think of the springs bubbling out of the ground on the high moor when you see the water rushing downhill, joining with other streams, carving a channel deeper and deeper, swelling into a mighty river.' His blue eyes looked deep into mine. 'We are that river.'

An hour later we stood on the wooden footbridge and stared at the rivers fighting to get down the steep rock face, spitting pieces of water the colour of beef jelly. Clouds of vapour drifted up and the rushing was tremendous. The birds had to shout. All around, water tumbled down the slopes and the oaks dripped. The spume seemed to rush towards me as if I were hypnotising it. I breathed in the energy.

'We'll come back in spring when the Devil gets in the rivers. The bluebells will be out too.'

Back at the Academy we assembled upstairs.

'I can't come next Wednesday because of my parents,' I moaned. 'They insisted on staying with me. They never stay with me, always with my sister. They like her better.'

'Tell them you're giving lessons.'

'I can't lie.'

Oliver grinned. 'Then you'll have to give somebody a lesson. Any volunteers?'

A forest of hands shot up.

Back home the soothing voice said, 'Picture a warm, safe, comforting fire,' and a smile hovered round my lips.

31

They came with a bootful of home-made compost. They came with a rose called Deep Secret which he planted straightaway. They came with Sally the sad-faced black greyhound who reminded me of Donna. My father was too jolly, like some clown who hates children at a children's party.

'Rich velvety red, smells wonderful.' He bent over and inhaled so that the petals clung round his nose; then he stroked it. 'Like a baby's skin.'

My mother had the wheelbarrow out and was spreading two sacks of compost over the vegetable patch and round the new rose. They hadn't even had a cup of tea. The dog stood mournfully by. I retreated into the kitchen to prepare a traditional roast dinner, to avoid comments like 'mixed-up food' and 'where's the meat?'

After dinner I left them with Mark and fiddled about upstairs with jars and boxes or sipped a bottle of Diamond cider to the sound of Oliver's voice. But instead of being soothed, I ached for the warm, safe, comforting fire, the purifying fire.

I was bored. The company was uninvited and unwelcome. Yet another job had come and gone without me. Private lessons needed preparing but I couldn't be bothered. My existence was as skeletal as the rowans on the high moor. Teaching was losing its appeal. I preferred red soil sticking to my hands and digging – you stuck your fork in and came up with roots and tubers plain and simple, whereas teaching came with reams of paperwork and stroppy heads and parents. Oliver wandered through my mind all day. Was blind, but now I see, I sang unceasingly.

At choir we ran through *The Seasons* and ended with the

hearty final chorus. Amen. Amen. Back home with Rachel I told my parents I had singing lessons all day on Wednesday.

'Can't you cancel? We've come specially to see you.'

'They're trying to lay a guilt trip on me,' I said to Oliver next day after giving a jokey singing lesson to a group of eight.

Oliver loosened a black tie with luminous gold roses which clashed with the pearl-studded black velvet waistcoat embroidered with curlicues of silver thread. He rested his elbows on the arms of the executive chair, hands clasped. I was discovering my true feelings, he said, but when he probed more deeply I shrugged, could think of nothing to say. As for Mark, I wasn't sure I loved him any more. It had been lust at first sight, a magnet. That was gone.

'I thought you could fix our marriage.'

The sun flashed through the window and the clouds twirled in patterns, a giant thumbprint in the sky.

'Some things can't be fixed,' he said solemnly. 'The best anyone can offer is to make separation less painful.'

The word separation struck like an axe.

*

'Oliver's not there.' Rachel waved at her friends sitting in the cathedral dimness.

I waved too, from the choir benches in the glare of spotlights hung on the pillars below the grotesques. In the second row of the nave sat my family. Mark slouched and wrinkled his nose, perhaps at the whiff of incense (which he hated), while Dad sat upright, eyes wide.

The oboe sang out an A, which prompted a burst of musical phrases scattering in all directions. The audience stopped chattering, shifted and coughed instead. The leader came on, the soloists and conductor came on, and the conductor frowned at Janet who had warbled a top D in a poignant silence in the afternoon rehearsal. Then he bowed his head while the fidgetings and coughings grew louder and louder till finally they fused into one squirming, spluttering mass and subsided. The Seasons began.

The sound of one hundred and twenty voices and orchestra filled our bodies with light which we radiated out into the dark beyond the orchestra, and out into the night. We blasted the Song of Joy to an everlasting, mighty, bounteous God in the direction of the group, and they echoed back our smiles. We raged in the storm, and with the evening bell we sang softly in harmony like whispering waves, fused into one.

In the interval the choir filed out into a back room.

Rachel's eyes were watery. 'He promised he'd come,' she said bitterly.

The bubble of joy created by the bouncy, melodious music was punctured. We hugged long and hard.

Later in The Hunting Chorus the group bobbed up and down in the pews and mouthed Halali. Rachel and I grinned as we sang the final Halaaali. The magical encounter with the deer on the hill was forgotten in the excitement at the kill, the braying horns and baying trombones. We shouldn't enjoy singing these words but we did. Music could make you say anything.

In the drinking song we bubbled over and the bodies of the string players swayed, while the audience were polite and impassive. I pictured them all getting up and linking arms. My own feet itched to move, which was strange because I never got drunk, and hated losing control.

Rachel nudged me at the beginning of The Spinning Song. *Knurre, schnurre, knurre,* the choir sang repeatedly, and the group grinned and swayed from the aisle. A pity Oliver had not come. After the fog and anguish of winter came the last chorus: the gates of heaven open, the holy mountain appears, a new dawn is breaking. Sam waved his arms around on the podium like a swan flapping its wings before take-off, a warm yellow light bathed the nave and boundless happiness streamed through my body, like crowd-surfing. Trumpets and timpani sounded, and we sang two triumphant amens to the vaulted roof. The music was this magic thing that hung in the air and cast its spell over everyone. With the final note Sam kept his arms held high, prolonging the moment, then let them fall to uproarious applause.

We wafted out. In the hall at the back Rachel and I clasped each other tight, rocked from side to side and rubbed cheeks, tears flowing, then made our way to the nave. Behind a pillar the group waited in a knot.

'Halali,' Simon sang while the rest grinned sheepishly.

Amelia stepped forwards. 'Oliver's sorry, he was tired.'

Mark gazed at her and the group drifted off after a final hug between Rachel and me. My family stood by the pulpit and Jack ran a finger round the scrolls of the wrought ironwork.

'We thought you'd come through to see us in the interval,' said Dad.

'Never mind that,' said Mum. 'That was lovely, dear, and the flowers are lovely too.' She pointed to an array of purple alliums, blue delphiniums and white roses on a pedestal.

Mark and Lisa smiled.

'Haydn is so optimistic,' said Gran. 'That wonderful amen. I think it's still there among the rafters.'

'Are those the people who... live on Exmoor?' Dad reddened. The trippy herringbone pattern of his jacket rippled under the spotlight.

'I suppose Mark told you it's a cult. Well, it's not. Mark just doesn't like the man who runs it.'

'Now,' said Mum, 'let's not spoil a lovely evening.'

But it was already spoilt. The yellow light which had bathed everything was gone.

'They're very touchy-feely,' Dad persisted.

'That's nice,' said Mum. 'Young people like to hug a lot.'

'They're not young people, Mum. Some of them are older than me. Some of them are older than you. Angela's seventy-six.'

'Let's go home.' Lisa started towards the door.

The darkness of the car park masked my frosty goodbye to Mum and Dad, who would spend Sunday with Lisa.

Back home I feigned exhaustion and went to bed, but exhilaration from the singing and fury at Dad and Mark, or all of them, kept sleep at bay. In my head the gates of heaven opened, the holy mountain appeared, a new dawn was breaking.

When I woke up, Mark had gone cycling, leaving a note. A pigeon on the roof crooned:

Hur-*rah*, ha-lali,
Hur-*rah*, ha-lali,
Hur-*rah*, ha-lali,
Hur-*rah*, ha-lali.

*

We sat on the cane chairs among festoons of triffids. The garden feeders overflowed with woodland birds returning for winter and a great tit sang, 'Teacher, teacher' like a squeaky saw.

'I love the hair,' said Gran. It was cut short and dyed dark copper. 'Any joy with jobs?'

'Maybe.' I plucked at a jumper thread. 'Someone I know is asking on my behalf. He sounded hopeful.'

'Who's that?'

'No one you know.'

'That's very kind.' She thanked me for the wonderful concert. 'I'd never heard it before. It made me think of a Brueghel painting of merrymaking peasants.'

I left after a short time. On the doorstep I kissed her goodbye.

She hung on. 'Whatever happens,' she said, 'as long as I live I'll be here for you.'

32

Hilda sucked a jelly baby and drew a damp cloth over the leaves of the Swiss cheese plant, a present from Stef seven years ago which now reached the ceiling in the conservatory jungle. A Red Admiral hit the glass, fluttered off and lurched again towards the light. She took the folded paper from the coffee table, guided the hapless creature to the open casement and shook it into freedom.

She hummed The Hunting Chorus. The joyful music with galloping horses and barking dogs both attracted and repelled her. She distrusted joyful music: she was being tricked into joy. It swept her along, made her bloom more brightly than the peace-lily flower at her shoulder, the creamy-white cup with curled lips and thrusting yellow tongue. She thought of the Handel aria, The Trumpet's Loud Clangour Excites Us To Arms. No it doesn't, she always wanted to shout back.

The soprano sunrise with low strings slithering up and up, violins adding layer upon layer of brightening sky, the inevitability of ending in dazzling brass and the full choir hailing the sun – the beautiful sounds had swept her up into the lofty spaces of the cathedral, unbearably, spine tingling, head aching and shouting no, yes, no, yes, every cell in her body blazing with the trumpets, howling with the choir at the rafters.

As she wiped round the holes in a leaf, from a corner of one eye she saw that the black squares in the half-finished crossword formed a swastika. She stiffened, tearing a leaf, and the cloth fell in the bucket. She picked up the paper at arm's length, averting her eyes, carried it to the recycling box, then fetched a pill, put it under her tongue and clutched the door, panting.

She sat at the piano and began Schumann's Des Abends, a gentle picture of dusk. Let Schumann trick her any day. She stepped lightly, moving in and out of keys in the striving after the light, as she strove to reach Stef. Higher and higher she reached like a buzzard to grasp at the light, but eventually it must all come tumbling down. When darkness came it could only be accepted, like her sadness that Fred had died before grandchildren were born. She sighed herself away like Alice's gnat, a lingering decline, a calm disappearing.

I had been close to my father. The shame I felt at our poverty in his years of unemployment turned to pride in his new dark trenchcoat and fedora, and in his singing. He sang all over the flat, and would grasp both my hands, swing me round and sing. I sang with him, and he loved me to sing The Lorelei to his accompaniment, because Papa played the piano too, though not as well as Mama. 'You're my Lorelei, Hildchen,' he said and quoted Heine: 'Where words leave off, music begins.' In the early evenings I hung round the restaurant and watched him sing. People put down their knives and forks to listen. Later, ten horses couldn't have dragged me there.

I became friendly with Sabine when we staged The Brave Little Tailor at Jungmädel. She was the tailor and I was the giant, being tall. Because Sabine was poor, I was allowed to bring her home for lunch. Mama made soup from a Knorr soup sausage, then we played Zehnerball on the windowless wall of the block. The day after Herr Schmidt the biology teacher left we had pea soup, but it was raining, so we pushed back the furniture in the sitting room, tucked our skirts into our knickers and did handstands. We needed to strengthen our arms because it was hard keeping your arm outstretched through three verses of the Deutschlandlied.

Then we did headstands on the armchairs with the tassels and I moved the doll with the purple silk and lace dress to the other side of the settee, to avoid kicking it. The scar on my head from a tussle between Hanno and me over the carpet beater still hurt. My parents were in the kitchen, which smelt of boiled handkerchiefs, and Sabine and I had stood on our heads for three and a half minutes according to the brass carriage clock on the mantelpiece, which we counted upside down, when Papa's voice came through:

'I'm afraid, Ilse. He comes to the restaurant frequently. He and his two officer friends sit at the corner table, smoking and playing skat. He mentioned a job for me with some important people. I tried singing badly...'

'Stefan,' hissed my mother, and they fell to whispering.

The blood rushed to my head, whether from headstands or shame, I don't know.

I asked Hanno if Papa was one of those unreliable elements. Papa's friends never came any more. One day Mama and Papa were talking about Anton, but they went silent when I appeared. Later, in England, Mama told me he was arrested for being Jewish and sent to Sachsenhausen.

I saw more of Sabine. Sometimes she was absent because she helped in the allotment garden or with little brothers and sisters. But when she was at school she often came to my flat for lunch. We used to pass the home of a woman with learning difficulties and shout insults. We thought we were superior, and I felt superior to Sabine because we were better off.

'She can't help it if her cuffs are frayed,' I said to Mama one day. Mama had lifted off the top of the tiled stove in the kitchen by its three cast iron rings, and picked up a piece of coal from the coal bin. The tongs stopped in mid-air. 'Don't ever think you are better because you have neat edges,' she said. It was one of the few times I saw her angry.

A fortnight later Sabine was caught having stolen three Reichsmarks and two Reichspfennigs from Marianne Hoffmann's coat pocket at Jungmädel. We lined up on three sides of a square with Sabine in the middle and sang O Deutschland, hoch in Ehre.

Gisela made a speech about honour and loyalty to each other, to our country and to our Führer. 'When a member forgets the soil from which she rose, the blood that flows through her veins,' she said, 'then she is no longer worthy to be a member.'

She stepped forwards and removed Sabine's leather woggle and black kerchief. Sabine kept her head bowed. She stood in the middle, crying, while we sang the Deutschlandlied and the Horst Wessel song. The meeting hall rang with the sound of our voices. I still know all the words of these songs. They come to me unbidden, against my wishes. They are in my blood.

33

'Were they good singing lessons on Wednesday?' Mark's eyes were as stary as a yellow-ringed blackbird's eye. I fiddled with the keys in my pocket. 'Your parents told me.'

'I knew you'd be critical. And them.'

'What do you want to go there for, anyway?'

'I like going there. What difference is it to you?'

'You go regularly? What on earth do you do there?'

'I work.'

'For free?'

'Why are you so negative?'

'You're being used.'

'I am not being used. If you had been more supportive after I lost my job... Oliver is more caring than you.'

'He wasn't caring in the name game.'

'Oh, that old chestnut. I told you, they were being helpful, pointing out the truth.'

'Look, I've had a rotten day with two disruptive boys. Remember why we went to see Oliver? He was supposed to help fix our marriage.'

On the Moroccan red wall, above the piano the Laughing Cavalier's ruby cheeks and lips glowed and the red and gold arrows, flaming cornucopiae and lovers' knots twinkled in the glossy black cloth of his garment. The lips hid beneath the moustache, the eyes sparkled but with what? Not with laughter.

'Some things can't be fixed,' I said.

*

Unknown to Mark, who had taken the car to visit his mother for the weekend, Rachel picked me up. Cloud-shadows turned the moor from chestnut to burnt umber and deep cleeves looked spooky in the failing light. Ivy clawed at the windows of the manor house and the leafless ash swayed in the field. Oliver had transferred Rachel from the kennels to mailshotting. Pip got sick and was put down, she said.

All day Saturday she was gloomy. She twirled her hair and complained she was just a dog-minder and not even that now – forty-two years of underachieving. Oliver objected to the inclusion of the last eight years in that bracket, but she remained sullen.

That evening after the bonfire Claire stood with bent shoulders and glazed eyes in the middle of the workroom while they bombarded her with accusations. Oliver sat on his chair with the mandatory respectful distance on either side. The room was charged, dark pulses aimed at the centre.

'You think you're better than the rest of us.'

'You thought of deserting us.'

'You're difficult to work with.'

Claire pursed her lips and tears rolled down. Oliver was silent.

'You look a tart with scarlet fingernails,' said Pete, who reminded me of a dog watching for its owner to come out of a shop. He looked venomous as he spoke, then reverted to little dog lost.

'You look a tart with half a head of black hair,' said Neil, a blond, ruddy-cheeked man who always sat beside Pete. They repeated each other like Tweedledum and Tweedledee, and each had a forelock which moved in time with the music when he danced.

Claire flinched and turned to me. The shifting eyes pleaded.

'You're not easy to work with,' I said meanly, but it was true.

Claire winced. Oliver, the last in the round-up, sat like a mountain.

'Since everyone says you're difficult to work with, you should take note. My criticism is, you never do what *you* want. You're a wimp, a milquetoast.' Claire crumpled. 'All right, Claire. Your turn to respond. Speak up.'

She took a deep breath and faced Amelia. 'You're the one who thinks you're fucking better than us with your posh accent. You think you're closest to Oliver and that makes you superior.'

To most she said it wasn't her fault she couldn't multitask.

To Pete she said, 'You look ugly anyway. You should try painting your own nails,' at which the room shook with laughter.

Finally she turned to Oliver. 'I can't win with you. If I do what you say, I'm a wimp, and if I don't, you say I never listen.'

Oliver wore his Mona Lisa smile.

Amelia leapt up. 'The trouble with you, Claire, is you don't listen. Ever. You don't see how much Oliver does for you.'

Claire protested, but Oliver interrupted.

'Don't get your panties in a twist, Claire. Accept the feedback.'

He ordered a round-up with each person saying one good thing about her. Most chose her willingness. Oliver said, 'Nice bum.'

'Oliver likes to challenge our nice safe perceptions,' Rachel said when I privately questioned his remark afterwards.

On Sunday morning he leant back in the copious leather chair in his consulting room and stroked his chin. 'I guess the hair is symbolic. Time for cutting.' Bits of cloud trailed across the sky. 'Love the hair, by the way.'

Which was more than Mark had said. Oliver talked at length in trumpet tones.

'The work,' he said with a thrust of his lips. Throughout his long diatribe I kept hearing the words 'the work' and 'now.' Now was what mattered, and observing oneself. 'You will go far, Eff.'

The weekend had passed in a flurry of cleaning and digging up Jerusalem artichokes.

'I wish I lived here,' I told Rachel, laughing.

Her fork stood still. She looked solemn. 'If you find a pearl, you should give up everything to get the pearl.'

*

Late afternoon, and the sheep in the shed were bleating for their supper. Pheasants roosted in the leafless trees and blackbirds squawked. The frost had stayed all day, coating the garden like whitewash. The bell rang and I opened the door. The Maréchal Niel rose which Dad had planted years ago clambered round the porch, still covered in lemon-yellow flowers in December, and breathed its essence over Mum and Dad.

'Come and say hallo to Grandad,' said Dad in a dinner jacket and bow tie, the lit-up eyes fastening on Jack, arms outstretched, and 'Hallo' came the bold reply as Jack moved forwards and up into his arms.

'Hallo, hallo,' Mum clucked, looking taller in long black velvet skirt and floral blouse under her overcoat, flushed and all smiles.

In the kitchen Lisa whipped egg whites into meringue, Gran clanked saucepan lids, Emma talked wildebeests. Verbal fog. The smell of meat fat filled my nostrils. Mum bent over the tray, silver Celtic-cross earrings and silver crucifix dangling, and bayoneted the hunk of flesh with a fork. Blood bubbled over the potatoes turning ginger and scrunchy and the fat bubbles sang a hallelujah chorus.

Dad disappeared with Mark into the garden, followed by Lisa.

'Your hair looks lovely, Stefanie,' said Mum. 'I don't know what it is between you and Mark, but tonight everything will be perfect. Mark got the best lamb and your sister's making your favourite—Baked Alaska. Your father's excited. You could join him in the garden.'

Mum was tiddly. She was not averse to a drop of Dubonnet. Beyond the patio where Sadie and Emma sat talking and smoking, Dad was boring Mark with his rose talk, making him smell the new rose. Once I had shared his pride and stood by while he stooped and scrutinised and clipped, and he handed me the dead heads to soak in water to make perfume. Now I disliked the prickly things.

Outside, I ignored the little coterie and crunched over the frost past the fuchsia Mum grew from a cutting, the magenta rhododendron and red-hot pokers still in bloom. Once, as Mum bent over red-hot poker stalks, I'd silently urged Lisa to push the voluminous rear. Mum cried all night with a pierced cornea and I told Dad Lisa did it. Then Lisa cried all day. Beyond the apple trees were the raspberry canes Dad planted. The bottom of the garden was shady, lush with Mum's hostas and Solomon's seal. Everything in this garden bore my parents' fingerprints.

'Stef. What's up?'

I spun round to see Lisa advancing. 'Nothing.'

'This is supposed to be our birthday dinner. You're not going to spoil it, are you? Mark and I have put ourselves out for this evening. And Jack begged me to let him come.'

'I thought you brought him because Tony was working.'

'I could have got a babysitter.'

I started back through the frosty autumn leaf carpet.

'Just don't spoil things for Mum and Dad,' she said.

*

Home. It suffocated with its smells of cooking, caked mud in the back porch, tired red walls, the dusty rug from the edges of which spiders sallied forth over the maple floor, the old mahogany piano. The table was laid, the candles flickered. Dad folded his paper serviette into a mouse, grinning at Sadie and Emma, as if he still needed to amuse the children. Melon was served.

'Shall we say grace? Lord,' he continued without waiting for an answer, 'we thank you that we have food enough on our plates and remember that many are not so fortunate. Amen.'

'Amen,' I murmured with the company and pressed my elbows into my sides, because elbows were an undesirable part of the body at table.

'Well, this is a wonderful occasion.' Dad beamed and raised his glass. 'Let's hope there'll be another like this one.'

'We do it every year, Dad,' said Lisa.

'Tuck in, everybody.' Dad thrust his spoon into the melon.

'It's good of you girls to come all this way for the weekend,' said Lisa.

'Just try and keep us away,' said Sadie.

'Only place we could get a decent meal,' said Emma.

I curled my lip over the spoon like a camel and nibbled off tiny pieces.

Dad sat opposite me, towering and rooted as an ash tree. 'You're not leaving all that melon, are you, Sadie? You've left half of it on the skin.'

I laughed. 'You know your grandad can't abide waste.'

She gave him the bowl and he scooped the melon into his mouth. His cheeks rose and swelled like nectarines. He handed the bowl with limp skin to Mum, who hovered behind him, and she scuttled off, busy-happy.

'You're looking well, Stefanie,' said Dad. 'But why did you cut your beautiful long hair?'

The air was thick with unspoken intensities. Mark sat immovable and stolid like a garden gnome. He had said he liked it at the time, but grudgingly. He said nothing now.

'*I* think it looks lovely,' said Gran, but the words fell on stony ground.

'You had such gorgeous flowing hair,' said Dad.

'Take no notice, Mum,' said Emma, 'it's cool. Shabby chic's all the rage, Grandad. Great-Gran's more up to date than you are. Love the colour, Mum.'

Lisa placed a steaming dish in front of Dad. He plunged the big fork in and picked up the carving knife. It cut into the surface, slithered through the yielding, bleeding flesh and squeaked across the porcelain. Like a boil he tended it, carefully to inflict the minimum of pain, drew the knife to and fro with head bent, and the steam spread misty amoeba-fingers over his glasses. Slices of pink lamb lay limp on the platter. He passed round the plates.

'You haven't given Mark any meat, Dan.'

'He doesn't eat meat, Mum. You should know by now.'

Mum looked at Mark open-mouthed as if this was the first time she'd heard it. 'You'll waste away, Mark.'

'Here's to the future.' Dad raised his glass of apple juice after the food was served and wine poured and Mum had plied Mark with extra of everything 'so you don't waste away.'

'The future,' we echoed.

'Tuck in,' said Mum as if she and Dad were the hosts.

Her cheeks were ruddy with a tracery of tiny blood vessels. The cutlery clattered. Eat up, don't talk, no elbows on the table, elbows in, don't slurp, don't blow your nose at the table, don't reach across, don't talk with your mouth full. And if you're small, don't talk at all. Thankfully no peas to balance on top of the fork's humpback rather than scooping them up in its hollow. Sadie and Emma escaped all that.

'Any luck with jobs yet, Stefanie?'

My mouth was full. Hastily I swallowed the lot. 'Not yet.'

'I suppose beggars can't be choosers.' Dad lifted his serviette to his mouth to dab at a spot of gravy.

I picked at a roast potato. My stomach clenched like a rolled-up hedgehog.

'So what should Stefanie do, Mark? Retrain?'

Dad had a knack for making people believe he liked them by asking their opinion.

Mark hesitated. 'I think Stef will do what she wants.'

I cut off a sliver of lamb and chewed. Dad stared at me, his pupils sucked me in like black holes and I guessed Mark had told them of my deception about lessons on Wednesdays. I was like a sheep before its shearers.

'Eat up, Stefanie.' Dad's lips pursed and plumped with each chewing.

The swollen traitor lodged in my mouth. I placed knife and fork side by side on the plate.

'You can't leave all that good food. Here, give it to me.' He reached across and grabbed the plate. 'You're not still going to this place on Exmoor, are you?'

The candles flickered. Not an eyelid flickered. I glared at Mark.

'Why do you want to go mixing with people with problems?'

'They're not people with problems. Who told you that? They've chosen that way of life.' No one spoke, so I added, 'They're sincere people. They lead a truthful existence. Oliver is a man of principle.'

'He must be rather special,' said Gran.

'You'd like him, Gran. He wanted to be a singer too.' I stood up. 'I'll go and check on Jack.'

Light from a lamppost fell on Jack's face and a tawny owl hooted from the woods. The tight blond curls lay in all directions, his lips were parted and his arms were flung out in surrender. I love you, said the arms. I love you all. No boundaries, sit on anyone's knee, hug them, kiss them. I climbed in and snuggled close. He stirred, turned and clasped my neck and the clutching fingertips tickled. One of his ringlets fluttered in the airstream from my nostrils like the gentle rise and fall of trailing wing-flaps.

In the kitchen Lisa was spooning meringue over raspberry ripple ice cream on a sponge base with pears. Fierce heat swept out as she opened the oven door.

'What's wrong with you, Stef? I've made a huge effort over this dinner. *Huge*. You could show some appreciation.'

Four minutes later, Lisa carried Baked Alaska topped with brown peaks of meringue into the lounge.

'Let your father serve,' said Mum.

He handed me a bowl of Baked Alaska and a smile seeped across his face like the already-melting ice cream creeping towards the rim. 'You won't carry on going to this place, will you? We're all concerned for you.'

'You know nothing about it.'

'I know enough to know there's something funny about it.'

'Judge not.'

The group shifted. There was a welling-up, like an

underground spring that has roamed the darkness through the ages in search of a weak point to burst forth. And springs that have travelled the bowels for so long might become too great, might flood, might erupt and not stop, and the vessel that contained them might sink below its own contents. So un-British. Must stiffen that upper lip, keep the springs down. But the ground is never quite firm and my ground was near breaking-point.

Mark said, 'Are these your pears, Gran?'

'Yes.' She grinned. 'I remember the year I tied brown paper bags over the pears to keep the wasps off, and when I untied them I found Stef and Lisa had eaten them. Left the cores on the tree and tied the bags over them. Little minxes.'

Everyone laughed.

Mum said, 'Guess what I found behind the bookshelf the other day, Stefanie.' She fondled the cross round her neck. 'An old Sunday School prize of yours. *The Little Donkey.* You could recite the names of all the books in the Bible in the right order by the time you were eight. Would you like it back?' She gazed at me. 'Don't you go to church any more?'

'No.' No, had enough of all that God and sin stuff. Let my mother pray for me every day, as she undoubtedly already did. She had wanted her daughters to replicate her own zeal and for a while I obliged. Stef the chameleon, be whatever you want. Mum looked on with delight, noticed how I cared for the less fortunate and involved myself in the church. Well, Lisa could make up for me now. Mum knew perfectly well I no longer went to church.

'Lost interest, have you?' Mum's eyes sparkled. 'God hasn't lost interest in you. You used to be such a good little churchgoer. I remember when you were six Uncle John sat you on his knee – he was a hardened atheist if ever there was one – and you looked into his face and said, 'Uncle John, is

Jesus the King of your heart?' He nearly died.'

We all laughed. Mark smiled at me and I smiled back, but his smile felt treacherous. In my bowl was a picked-over mess of meringue and ice cream and pears and sponge cake.

'Mark, I'm sure you can finish this Baked Alaska. It won't keep. Besides, you haven't had any meat.' Before he could answer she took his bowl and filled it.

The table was cleared and coffee drunk. Sadie and Emma sneaked off for a smoke.

'Let's have a sing-song round the piano,' said Mum.

The dinner in my stomach tumbled and glooped like mixer cement. 'I'm too full,' I said, but 'Come on,' Dad said, and I rose obediently. The Laughing Cavalier's moustaches smirked at the little gathering as Gran played and we sang Guide Me, O Thou Great Jehovah. I sang: 'Feed me till I want no more, Feed me till I want no more,' and I wanted no more, no more of any of them. Mark was squirming.

It was over. We sat on comfortable chairs and sofa round the coffee table with stacked Times Educational Supplements underneath.

'I didn't know you could sing,' Dad said to me.

'No,' said Mum.

I frowned. My childhood was one long song and they had not noticed.

'Stef has always had a lovely voice,' said Gran.

Emma showed her photos of Africa. Dad took an album off the shelf and opened it to a photo of me aged eight, massive smile, wearing a Titian-red dress with broderie-anglaise hem and yoke and holding up a coin.

'You were a happy child, Stefanie. Always smiling. Wasn't she, Margaret?'

'Ye-e-es,' came a voice from the sheep shed.

At last they stood up to leave. Lisa went upstairs and

carried down the sleeping Jack.

'See you at Christmas, darling,' Mum said.

Dad gave me a bear hug. 'Take care.'

In the kitchen something in my handbag shone: Mum's crucifix which gleamed like a silver dagger, engraved with tiny scrolls and swirls, spirals radiating out or drawing me into its centre, and at the top in feathered script the monogram INRI. Angrily I tossed it in the bin.

*

'Teaching, singing, haikus, gardening, tidying up, directing the school choir, cycling, canoeing, watching Mark have sex with another woman,' read my interests on Facebook. My photos were now all of Mark kissing, Mark hugging, Mark caressing the other woman. Fifteen of them. Then followed eight hundred fake comments: love the new page Stef lol; always knew you had it in you; wow what a goer; what a teacher; and vile remarks on the size of my vagina, its shape, its rotting-cabbage smell, what might be inserted in it, with more f words and c words than anyone could imagine. Reading it was like stepping over a cliff believing I could fly, and plummeting. I rang Oliver, hardly able to speak, then ran the mile and a half to Gran's.

The ground had been frosted all day. Her coat hung loose as she topped up the bird feeders. Her grin faded and the hand holding the jug of seed stopped in mid-air.

'You're leaving us.' She shuddered. 'Let's go in. It's chilly out here.'

Over a cup of tea I told my worst nightmare, my fears and suspicions. To stay was unthinkable.

'But darling, it's not like you to do things on impulse. Is this what you want?'

'I don't know, Gran. I think so.'

She urged me to go to the police again, confront Mark, wait till after Christmas, after Sadie and Emma went back, but my mind was made up.

'The police can't or won't help and I'm done with confronting Mark. I just want to disappear, forget it all.' I talked about the Academy, about the herd of deer and how the two groups, people and deer, had simply stood and stared at each other for fifteen minutes. 'I felt honoured to be there, Gran.'

I picked up the knitting-needle holder I had made as a child from a cardboard tube covered in black velvet, complete with pink bow and whiskered face, touched that Gran had kept it.

'Come and see me sometimes,' Gran begged on the doorstep and we hugged tight.

Back home the phone rang.

'How could you do this to Gran?' Lisa shrieked. 'And just before Christmas. You do realise this could finish her off, don't you? And I've ordered a huge turkey. And what about Mark? How did he put up with you all these years? You may be my sister, but anyone who lives with you needs the patience of a saint. And what will I tell Jack? You'll break his heart.'

She hung up. The lambs in the shed bleated. Little machine guns, not yet silenced.

34

Hilda sat down with a leaden heart. What made people believe things? The heart has its reasons which are unknown to the head. There was something terrifyingly attractive about the certainty of belief, especially shared belief. Margaret and Dan and Lisa had their faith and it buoyed them up like corks on an ocean. She herself had embraced an ideology with her whole being; Mephistopheles had whispered in her ear and she had said yes, three times yes. Energy, beauty, strength. It felt good, it felt wonderful, until she found out it wasn't. Not wonderful at all. But who was this memoir for? Margaret was taken up with devotions and flower arranging and the parish needy, Lisa wouldn't understand, and Stef would think she wanted to manipulate her.

What will Mark do, what about Sadie and Emma, what about Christmas, what about me? All things she'd wanted to say, but couldn't. She had to bite her lip. She couldn't cry. Like the crickets Stef used to keep in shoeboxes with holes punched in the lids. They never sang. How could they sing? She sat at the piano and played Liszt's *Sunt Lacrimae Rerum*, her head drooped at the low churning and from her fingertips anger struck like forked lightning. The bass notes growled in the depths. She hammered out her despair, the dying of the light. Her mother stared cat-lipped from the photo on the wall, a smile that would later conceal black thoughts, while her father beamed. The piano wept. And if the piece ended on a high note, it was only because hope like the phoenix always rises.

She typed:

Mama and Papa must have rummaged in my room and

seen my diary with the columbine pressed between the pages. I came home one day to find Papa sitting on the black and gold-striped settee with the continuous wooden rim round the arms and back, shirt sleeves rolled up, wearing the red braces with the black-and-white guitars. Sit down, he said. He stared with a wounded expression at the wall where The Absinthe Drinker had been. Mama sat beside him and pretended to be engrossed in her embroidery. I sat on the leather chair which made a rude noise, but I didn't laugh. I was breaking his and Mama's hearts by my deceit, seeing Berni behind their backs. Then he droned on about how else I had changed lately. I glared. 'Hard as nails,' he called me. He had fought a war to give my generation a better life, and the young these days had no idea what they had suffered. After all they had done for me, this was how I repaid them.

'I'm your father,' he said. 'You're my flesh and blood. You of all people should understand that.'

His cheeks were as scarlet as his braces. I fumbled with a handkerchief in a pocket and counted the flowers in the carpet. I hid the diary and carried on seeing Berni. We resolved to run away if we had to.

I criticised Papa for everything, even smoking. He rarely smoked after he got the singing job, but still had the occasional cigarette. He was poisoning his body with tobacco, I said. I chided Mama too after I got ticked off at Jungmädel for a dirty blouse. She complained about washing an extra four shirts a week between me and Hanno. To me this was blasphemy, but it was rare for Mama to carp. Papa was the one whose disapproval of Jungmädel drove me further and further into it. Had he buttoned his lip, things might have turned out otherwise, but I had the long teeth and claws of a thirteen-year-old. I asked Hanno, 'Do you think Papa and Mama are Sozis?' That's what we called the Socialists. I compared my parents with Berni and Inge's parents who stood to attention when the Führer came on the radio. In school we learnt that Tacitus said the Germans were courageous and virtuous, had fierce blue eyes and large frames and never polluted themselves by marrying foreigners, so their blood was pure.

'Keep your blood pure,' we heard, 'it is not yours alone. It comes from afar and flows far onward.'

I began to see Papa differently: unlike Mama, who was blonde and blue-eyed and tall, in fact taller than him, he was short and slender and dark with brown eyes. At the age of twelve my hair darkened and my nose grew longer. I was scared. I hated Jews as much as any of my classmates, but if he was Jewish, what about me? Hanno and I consulted our textbooks and agreed that maybe Papa was westisch, which is Mediterranean, one of the five racial types of Germans. He had the narrow face and olive skin too.

A classmate asked the new biology teacher which race Hitler belonged to. There were giggles from the back. He replied: 'Herr Hitler is a healthy mixture like most of us. He has the Nordic strength of will, bravery and truthfulness and the Dinaric creativity and love of his country.'

Twice a year, in December and June, Mama held a concert in our flat for her piano pupils, including me and Hanno. The partition between sitting and dining rooms was folded back and parents and pupils sat round on the black and gold-striped settee and rush-seat chairs. Some I knew from school, and I was embarrassed by the plain wallpaper and curtains, not patterned like my friends'. At the end Papa always leapt up to take his turn. I am not sure whether other parents thought him vain, or whether they relished this moment.   After all, he was a professional singer. He stood with his thumbs in his scarlet braces with the black-and-white guitars and sang *Der Lindenbaum* or *Wien, Du Stadt Meiner Träume* or Schubert's Serenade, and always followed with an encore of *Dein Ist Mein Ganzes Herz*, leaning one elbow on the piano and gazing into Mama's eyes. We applauded, myself the most passionately.

But when I turned twelve and thirteen I saw that he was taking the limelight away from children who, though less impressive, outshone him in effort and progress and, unlike him, needed encouragement. He was a café crooner, not a serious singer, he just sang to entertain and I doubted he had any patriotic feeling. His attempts at learning Sütterlin script, which had become standard in schools, were half-hearted, and when he sang heroic songs he smiled as though they were just songs, as though it was a joke. I despised him increasingly. I felt ashamed of him and begged him to buy a flag to hang out of the window on celebration days like everyone else. He pretended the window-box with the geraniums was in the way, but the man upstairs gave him his old flag and insisted on helping him to fix a bracket. I caught Mama and Papa laughing about it afterwards. That was when I discovered I could silence their laughter with a look. I had been a daddy's girl, so his attitude felt like a betrayal of my childhood years. This man I had loved, still loved, had turned into an enemy of the people.

One time Hanno was not at the concert because he'd given up the piano. Papa had begun his encore, elbow on the piano, when a fanfare blared out from Hanno's room. Hanno had sneaked his bugle home from the Jungvolk.

I burst out laughing, at which Mama glared. I can still picture the mortification on Papa's face. It was a turning point. I despised him all the more for his lack of humour. I loved to sit cross-legged on Hanno's floor while he blew his five notes in different orders, ending with The Last Post, after which we both observed a respectful silence. He let me blow it, which brought the blood to my face, a rush to my ears. How I envied him – girls weren't allowed to play the bugle or drum. Kirche, Küche, Kinder (church, kitchen, children) was our destiny. Later, much later, I realised the significance of The Last Post.

At the dinner table that evening I kept my eyes on Hanno, exchanged sly smiles with him throughout.

35

The quad bike stopped in front of a pink rubblestone cottage with tiled roof on the edge of woodland. Thick ivy vines clung to the walls, crossing over and under so they could never detach, never leave. Rachel took one suitcase and the bag of wellies and shoes, while I took the other suitcase and the viola. Inside it was cold and damp. Rachel lit the tiny range with logs from outside and showed me how to use the Tilley lamp.

'People find the work hard the first week,' she said.

'I thought I wouldn't be working during the Intensive.'

'Work on yourself. The real work.'

She held me tight for a full minute, then left.

The cottage had one room with bed, desk and chair, range and sink with cold tap, and a separate toilet. The walls were rough-plastered and whitewashed and on the concrete floor were plushy Persian mats and sheepskin rugs. There were no curtains. On the wall was written in black marker pen: 'Only when you recognise your nothingness will you be open to change.'

The house was miles away. I had expected hugs and cheers, people clamouring round, a big welcoming party, not this. The land in front of the cottage plunged out of sight. Beyond was endless grass and heather moor dotted with gorse bushes in flower and a few sheep. The sky was thick and white. Fourteen harlequin ladybirds clustered in a top corner of the window frame.

The fridge was a cupboard outside, locked against badgers. I took out milk, then boiled a kettle, but there was no sugar. My plan to give up the last half-teaspoonful on the first of February, not for another six weeks, was thwarted. I skipped tea and went out. Down in the damp, earthy-smelling cleeve, velvet moss smothered the trees up to the upper branches, and thick ivy tentacles crisscrossed and knotted their way up to the sky. Birds flitted everywhere.

After eating I boiled water for washing up. No tea. I unpacked, but it was bare without jars and boxes. The candle in the toilet lit up the words on the wall:

The Tittle

Once upon a time there was a little tittle, which is a dot over the i (˙). It thought it was the universe. It thought everything was all about me, me, me. Until one day it spotted the stem of the i nearby. It looked round and saw there were other tittles, other stems and other strange markings. They were not alone. In fact there were dozens of them: letters, words, sentences. One day a breeze came and it noticed that the paper on which it sat was translucent and there were other words visible through the paper: hundreds, thousands. Then one day it looked across the room and saw that the wall was covered in words from floor to ceiling. In fact, words covered all the walls, because this was a library. The little tittle realised how insignificant it was. It was nothing. Nothing in a universe.

Oliver Diamond

How profound, I thought, and re-read it several times, then stoked up the stove and sat at the desk with a questionnaire: sexual orientation, hobbies, ambitions, faults, strengths, greatest secret, why I wanted to live there. After the previous night's argument I would never go back to Mark. I had hugged Sadie and Emma goodbye and left.

Toe and Stick appeared after dark, wearing matching

quilted black jackets with the Diamond logo. She was the nurse in Toe's practice. 'Stick' was short for stick insect.

'That's Oliver for you,' she said with a skeletal grin.

Toe glanced at my HIV certificate, then examined me. He stared at the stretch marks that spread from bust to thighs like silver snail trails.

'Did you really get that from being pregnant?'

I blushed. 'I hate them.'

He scribbled in his notebook.

'I'm sure they were worth it.' Stick smiled at Toe and the backs of his fingers grazed her cheek. She stroked the sheepskin over the back of the chair. 'The Intensive is really tough. We're all rooting for you. Can we help with anything else?'

'There's no sugar.'

'I'll tell Oliver to bring some in the morning,' said Toe.

'We could go and get some. Tea without sugar is horrible if you're used to it sweet.'

'I don't want to sound mean, because Oliver's very caring, but it's important to keep to the plan.'

They left and I put the last two logs in the stove and sat down to write. In bed the soothing voice whispered into my ears; ivy stems squeaked against the window and the leaves fluttered against the night sky.

*

I woke up to a white world. Snow covered more than half the window and the sky was blanked out. Wrapped in the quilt, I climbed on the bed to look out. The sheep were belly-deep, grubby against the background, heads buried or snowy-faced. Trees, fields and moor beyond were all white. One ladybird had defected to the opposite top corner of the window frame.

It was too cold to wash. I threw on a thick jumper and jeans and jacket to fetch logs and milk for tea, which I had now decided to endure. The door didn't open. I kicked hard. Over and over I launched myself at it shoulder first or foot first, bellowing and then weeping with rage, but it was stuck fast. I was trapped, helpless as a baby. I was nothing in a Narnian universe.

The tap yielded no water. Slumping on the bed, I searched the sky through the uncovered part of the window for sun, hope, anything, unable to tell how much time had passed. I shivered under the quilt and my hands and feet were numb. What if no one came? My stomach growled. The ceiling was bare truss and tiles draped with cobwebs, perhaps low enough to be buried. Now and then I stood on the bed again and willed someone to appear. A pheasant with copper plumage hunched against the snow, the sheep huddled, and outside the window was a beech with feathery twigs that curved like the arms of a ballet dancer. Simon said if you say a prayer under a beech it will rise straight to heaven. I could hear his warm voice saying it. I curled up in bed. Hours went by.

At last a tractor engine throbbed. It grew louder, then stopped, voices sounded, and scraping shovels. Simon and Pete, the one who had called Claire a tart, burst in.

'Never known snow this bad,' said Simon. 'You poor thing, your first day.'

They took hay to the sheep and dug out a path to the logs and fridge. They lit the stove and damp wood-smoke filled the room.

'Sorry we can't stay,' said Simon. 'Oliver'll be along this afternoon.' He tried the tap, scooped snow into a pan and set it on the stove. 'Make sure you boil the snow for water first, mind.'

I stood and stared at the door for a long time after they left.

I wondered what Mark was doing. Probably planning Venice with the floozie.

*

Oliver counted out and pocketed the three thousand pounds, then straddled the chair, his arms resting on its sheepskin-covered back. 'We had to dig out the drive first, and the kennels. Can't leave people's precious pooches without food and water. The phone lines are down too. So much for global warming. Amelia closed your Facebook and email. You can use the group hotmail account.'

'Thank you.' Mark would not echo that sentiment when he found the Australia savings gone.

'Right, Eff. Show me your magnum opus.'

He read aloud from the questionnaire, 'Strengths: Affectionate. Hm. I think most people are looking forward to your coming. Like to do things properly. Is that another way of saying others don't?'

'Oh no.'

'The lady doth protest too much, methinks.' A glimmer of a smile crossed his lips. 'For your homework I want examples of things you've done properly and others haven't. Good at teaching, running a choir, running a recorder group. Faults: Adultery.' He looked up. 'Is that it?'

I spread my arms helplessly.

He snorted. 'In twenty-four hours? I suggest you are not someone who likes to take direction, and you'll find it impossible to live here unless you learn. I want a full account of your control freakery by tomorrow.' He tossed the paper onto the desk behind him and handed me the biography. 'Read it out.'

I read:

'I was born in Edgbaston in Birmingham. I have a sister, Lisa, one year younger. My parents are retired. My father was a teacher and my mother worked in an office. After school I did teacher training, specialising in music. My grandmother taught me to play the piano and sing. I have Grade 8 in singing, piano and viola. I got married while I was still at college. I adore teaching. Apart from maternity leave, I have had teaching jobs continuously, till last summer. I have two daughters, Sadie and Emma. I left their father ten years ago for Mark.'

I looked up. 'The rest you know.'

'The rest I know? Eff, this tells me nothing. You don't even say what happened to the first marriage. If you want to fit in here, you need to trust me, let your guard down. Forget the other homework. Incorporate it all into your biography, strengths, faults, the lot. No judgementalism. When you walk in here, you leave your logic at the door. We work in a different reality here.'

With that, he left. No hug. No sugar.

The snow was at the top of my wellies. The wind bit, but not as painfully as Oliver's coldness. The moor lay under a white fleece and the sun gleamed between the horizon and lowering slate clouds. Gorse in flower was covered in a fur of ice crystals longer than a thumbnail. My eyeballs were chilled, cheeks and lips numb. Climbing back up was hard, even with ready-made welly-holes. I fetched in logs and food and collapsed on the silky velvet mat with geometrical shapes blurred into leering faces. My viola lay nearby. Still lying down, I took it out and cuddled it. One edge was chipped where a flatmate had kicked it after I vomited on his heirloom rug. Star-lights came on in a clear sky, a gibbous moon cast a white square on the quilt, and the defecting harlequin was still solitary. I stood and played, at first visceral scourging rhythms, harsh scrapings that scarred the ears, then laments and Bach's Chaconne, flowing like the streams that run over the moor, till the repetition and the stove's warmth left me drained.

*

Oliver glanced through the sheets of homework, then I read out the new biography:

'I was born in Edgbaston in Birmingham. I have a sister, Lisa, a midwife, one year younger, though she behaves as if she was the elder. I don't think I'm a control freak with her – it's the other way round, or maybe it's revenge for all the times I pulled rank when we were children. My parents are retired – he was a teacher and she worked in an office. After school I did teacher training in Reading, specialising in music. My grandmother taught me to play the piano and sing, and I had private lessons in viola. I begged my parents for them because my best friend was learning viola. When we played together, it sounded like a catfight. I got Grade 8 in viola, piano and singing. I nearly went to music college, but I wanted to teach like my grandmother. She gave me so much, and I wanted to give something back. I never knew my grandfather, and we only saw my paternal grandparents once a year because they looked down on my mother. I married Adam while I was still at college. I adore teaching, or I did. Apart from maternity leave, I've had teaching jobs continuously, till last summer. I have two daughters by Adam, Sadie and Emma, aged 20 and 18. I met Mark while the three of us were still all at Reading. He was best man, and we got drunk and had sex a year later. I felt guilty and so did he, so we avoided each other. But when the girls were 3 and 5 years old, we met by chance and started again. Adam never knew at the time. He thinks it started 10 years ago. The girls don't know either.'

Silence. The red, white and gold flowers in the centre mat

squirmed, some round, some elongated, some with perfect edges, some crooked. My hand fumbled with the sheepskin on the bed and searched its rust-red depths beneath the golden sheen.

'And that's good work, is it?'

I stroked the sheepskin, pressing hard as though I was kneading dough. He wanted details of my family, whether my mother was a good mother, what my father was like, my grandmother, my daughters, what they thought, my sex life with my husbands, how things had changed between Mark and me in the past six months.

'I asked about your controlling of others and you give me some spiel about your sister. What about your mother nearly drowning you? And I don't buy this wanting to give something back.'

'Ants and bees do things for others. Bees sacrifice their lives for the colony.'

'You're not an ant or a bee.' He squashed his lower lip with his upper teeth. 'So what did Mark say?'

'That I'm selfish, and if I come here I can forget about him.' And a lot more besides. He wouldn't tell me the other woman's name because there was no other woman; my obsessive tidiness got on his nerves; he'd kept me for six months, for me to go and leave him; I never had any time for him, the hems of the lounge curtains were still held up by pins, and he couldn't imagine what I did with my time, unless I went to the Academy every day. And stuff about mighty rivers speeches, posturing in eighteenth-century garb and a bunch of eager slaves. I left Christmas presents for him, Sadie and Emma on the kitchen table. The others' presents I left with Gran.

'He said he'd been paying to keep you supplied with slave labour.'

'People don't like it when their partner puts their own desires and ambitions first for a change.'

Oliver talked about the lack of self-awareness of most people, about how they reacted blindly to external forces like machines. Blinds lived life on the surface and engaged in rampant consumerism to fill the void in their lives. Diamonds eschewed materialism and learnt to do one thing at a time with their whole attention, as he was giving me his whole attention now because he cared for me. 'You have to lose the density of your conditioned mind structures and become transparent to the light of consciousness. The greater the suffering, the greater the possibility for productive work, provided you work consciously. The energy expended in active inner work is transformed into new energy; that expended in passive work is lost forever.'

His eyes were like large balls of pale blue ice-cream with spidery fingers of caramel sauce spreading out. No comment on me and Mark having sex so soon after I married Adam. No hug. No sugar.

The session had gone badly, but already I was dreaming of the following day, or dreading it. The viola lay untouched.

*

The snow glinted in the sun. An old beech in the combe offered solace, wider than a double bed, its trunk in folds with gaping cracks and lurid green velvet moss, woodlice and tiny white toadstools, and branches reaching almost to the ground.

I steeped myself in the work, but it was never enough. He came at different times, unexpectedly so I had to stay in, sometimes till after dark. It was light by the full moon, but as eerie as all the bass strings of a large orchestra together, and the sky was a graveyard for stars. One day I heard the dogs barking and set out at daybreak along the cleared path towards the main house in a pink and gold sunrise. After two or three miles uphill it stood, broad and welcoming with its snow hat like a Disney house, pink stone gleaming and windows flashing in the sun. The holy city.

He said I was obsessed with my stretch marks because of guilt at denying Mark children. In his experience, 'I don't know' meant 'I don't want to know'. It was the gravitational pull of my conditioning. He was determined to discover what I was hiding; he would crack the tough carapace. I should heed my appearance. Women should look good, not dress in baggy clothes.

'How lonely you must be,' he said one day.

'True.' The solitary harlequin had rejoined the cluster, clambered over the others and made them all shift. Was I lonely? I missed my jars and boxes more than Mark, as if I had defined myself by my possessions. Oliver said no jars or boxes. No books either: too much intellectualisation. Blinds' lives were too frenetic, too divorced from their origins. Diamonds lived close to the earth. Yet he had books.

He was kind to me, he said. I was lazy, would never find my true self, I was a weasel, a subversive, too crazy, fucked up. Every day before he came, I expected the sky to cloud over like a slate behemoth crouching over the horizon. Every day after he left, I wept. Then I walked through my grief over endless moor till I stood under the old beech. I was a speck in the snow. By the end of the week I was absorbed into the landscape, the whiteness, the silence.

On the last day the clouds were a penitent grey. Drained but alert, I read out the final version of my biography. He hugged me and I wanted to capture him like a butterfly and keep him. Afterwards I took up the viola, but the sound that issued was insipid, watery. I trailed over the blurred-out moor.

The following day Rachel collected me in the tractor and we drove in triumph up to the house. Everyone cheered when we entered the workroom.

'Welcome to the family,' said Oliver.

In a grand ceremony he presented me with a pack of labels embroidered with my name, and the whole sky was a song.

*

Melding into the group was bliss – the forgetting of self and its horrors, which sank beneath waves of love and peace. Every afternoon we went tobogganing with sledges or builders' bags stuffed with straw, and shouts and screams echoed across the goyle.

After three days off for Christmas the late sessions were a shock. The workroom was chilly and we wore scarves and gloves. Every night we worked into the early hours, growing and developing, and the following morning the elephant bell burst in. Nevertheless I threw myself into it: lots of trust exercises. Those who faltered joined the losers' group and repeated the exercise while the winners bayed and jeered. Oliver sat aloof in the bay in the Dennis the Menace jumper knitted by Stick. One loser would be left, with a measured attack in which Oliver participated. Mark would have hated these sessions, but then his mind was closed.

During a blind foray the muffled echo of our stockinged feet told me we were in a music room.

'It does have a piano,' Toe said warily in reply to my question, 'but it's not used.'

His voice rang out loud and clear. I dropped to the floor and felt the smoothness of thick varnish unsoiled by the passing of shoes.

'Take me to the piano.'

He waited while I played with eyes still closed. It was painfully flat.

'Come on. We're not supposed to be doing this.'

I stood up and hooked my little finger round his.

Oliver suggested Rachel and I form a choir with me conducting, instead of the choral society.

'The piano's flat.'

He humphed and grumbled. 'Just for you, chick, I'll get it tuned.'

*

I worked at the kennels for a fortnight. Rachel was back in charge. More snow blew across the face of the earth and the dogs grew excited, while Rachel grew sad.

She was always sad at Christmastime because it reminded her of her fucking father. Not that she ever spoke to him, nor her sister any more. She had deumbilicated completely and now cured her sadness through mock fights, two or three against her one, rolling round the floor, scratching, fighting and hurling abuse. Her patchwork skirt was hand-stitched from her mother's favourite blouse and wedding dress, her father's best shirt and a red damask tablecloth.

'Come on, Rachel,' we urged and 'Go for it, Rachel,' while the three family taunted her, 'Lavinia, Lavinia.'

'I'm not Lavinia, you fucking bastards,' she shouted.

Pete slipped his hand up her skirt, at which she sprang at him, hands round his throat. Others pulled her off but then let go, and she kicked him in the balls. While Pete lay gasping, comforted by Stick, Rachel was lifted on a cradle of joined arms. They rocked her and sang a babbling lullaby. Later, Pete and Rachel bear-hugged. I hugged her too. How could someone do that to any child, let alone his own?

One evening Rachel cried how lonely she was.

Oliver raised his eyebrows. 'But you have all of us here.'

'I have all of you and I have none of you.' She finger-combed her hair and her cheeks turned fuchsia. 'Inside, I'm on my own.'

'Could you leave your hair alone?'

He sat her on his knee and stroked her. She howled like a dog.

The snow stayed and the roofs were fringed with icicles as long as arms. A rabbit hopped tentatively across the pure white moor and vanished and I felt myself hopping over the surface, falling down rabbit holes. Every night the group cocooned me.

One day I found out Pip was not put down sick, but because someone reported him to Oliver, who said they couldn't afford freeloaders.

*

'18th December?' I grunted at the letter Claire handed me.

'Amelia said it got buried under a heap of papers.'

My darling Stef,

I hope you have settled in well. I'm afraid Mark is devastated, as am I. He will go to his sister's in Norfolk for Christmas, and I will go to Lisa's as planned, with Sadie and Emma.

I didn't say goodbye properly because your announcement took me by surprise. Now that I've had time to think, I want to wish you well. I'm very sorry you've left, but I hope I shall see you soon for more Diabelli! The thought of it makes me laugh. I've been practising. Practice makes perfect, as my mother used to say.

Sadie and Emma say hi and asked me to tell you your email is not working. Emma says whatever you choose to do, it's cool. The young are so easy-going, aren't they? Mark hopes you will come home.

*Your mother and father think you are making a big
mistake, but I know you have to do what is right for you,
and when you find what you want, then everything will
become clear.*

*Write to me soon, darling, and let me know how you
are getting on.*

Your loving Gran.

I frowned. I had found what I wanted. Gran had dismissed
it out of hand. All day it stayed, the annoyance.

That evening we lay with knees raised and eyes closed,
emptied our minds, felt the breath enter and leave our bodies
while Oliver droned through a guided visualisation.

'Then you think to yourself, when did someone last say, "I
love you".'

Probably when he wanted sex. Mark was like that, said he
liked my hair when he didn't, to get sex. We opened our eyes
and rushed round telling everyone 'I love you', and a hubbub
followed like a high wind, accompanied by the ubiquitous
hugs.

'I've never known so much love and openness as here,' I
said in the round-up. 'Everyone is so accepting, I feel myself
held in a cradle of love.' But the exercise brought back Mark,
who was always in my thoughts but not welcome there.
Annoyingly, it was good things like stuffing snow down each
other's necks, sharing a laugh about some naughty child's
exploits or orgasming together. Then I remembered the train
trip.

'Mark called you a little Hitler.'

A stunned silence followed, but for the hum and crackle of
the wood-burner.

'That's rich when he's cheating on you,' said Amelia.

'He's jealous.' Rachel twirled a wisp of hair that curled over a temple.

'Perhaps *he*'s a little Hitler,' said Melanie.

The air was filled with mutterings.

Toe said, 'If I had to choose between listening to Oliver and listening to Mark, I'd choose Oliver every time. I mean, I thought Mark was an OK guy at first. But Oliver has more wisdom than all of us here put together. He has more compassion than any doctor I've ever known. He'll listen to your troubles for hours on end. He understands, he knows when you're going down the wrong path and he'll tell you straight, you're heading for disaster. He works above and beyond the call of duty. When my wife left me, he took me into his own home for months till I could cope on my own. I'm eternally grateful for everything he's done for me and I know many here will echo that sentiment. So if that's being a little Hitler, give me Hitler any day.'

A chorus of 'Hear, hear' resounded through the room.

Oliver sat tall throughout this paean. 'Hitler was a man who achieved great things,' he said and beamed.

*

Like harlequin ladybirds we clustered together, lost without Oliver who was hang-gliding in the Dolomites, with Amelia as his retriever. More snow fell. From dawn to dusk a thick grey-white mist clung to the moor, pressed us down against the snow and sucked out the energy, leaving cold droplets on the skin. The trees with their ivy leggings were a blur. Sheep knocked Simon over in their desperation to get at a bale of hay he was carrying. In the evenings we sang spirituals and laments and retired early.

*

Toe collected Oliver from the airport, and with him came the music of snow-melt—it melted and froze, melted and froze till the tops of fern and heather poked through—it crashed off the roof and icicles dripped to nothing.

When we moaned at his long walks, he raged.

'Try flying at fifteen hundred metres above sea level with only thin gloves between flesh and aluminium, or running through much deeper snow than this with a seventy-pound hang-glider on your back for take-off. Then you can moan.'

Later he relented.

'What's the difference between a viola and a sarcophagus?' he asked. No one answered. 'The sarcophagus has the dead person on the inside.'

The shrieks and hoots that followed, mine included, would have sent the Devil flying over to the Quantocks, Simon said afterwards.

Melanie was all smiles these days, the ankh and bandanna replaced by a silver chain with pendant O. One morning, wearing jeans and sweater, she was standing on her head with legs in a V when Oliver entered and limped across to the bay.

'Would someone like to say what Melanie was doing just now?'

No one moved.

'Well, Melanie. Tell us what it means.'

The wood-burner crackled.

'Melanie, you have zero emotional intelligence. It means, I want to be fucked. Hands up who thinks Melanie's being a tramp.'

Amelia's hand shot up. Others followed. Some wavered.

Melanie, red-faced, protested it was a question of balance. No one defended her. Amelia was vociferous. I was one of the waverers, but since Oliver pointed out it was tramp-like, I could see what he meant.

'And your sweater is showing half your tits,' said Oliver. 'You can take it off for the rest of the evening so you can see your seductive behaviour for what it is.'

Melanie rubbed her thighs and stared at the red carpet. The room was like musical statues after the music stops. Oliver was purple-faced.

'I'm not giving you an option. Take it off.'

Slowly she removed the sweater and folded her arms over her bra, still wearing scarf and gloves. Everyone sat with lizard-like equanimity. No one looked at her for the rest of the evening, whether to punish her or to save her further embarrassment was unclear. In bed I faced the window, glad not to be in Melanie's position, although twenty years in teaching should have accustomed me to scrutiny. But then, I wasn't a tramp.

*

We must no longer be camels feeding on acorns and grass, burdened with guilt and fear like the blinds.

Oliver wrote and drew in marker pen on an easel, ripped off pages and tossed them aside.

Camels in the wilderness must find their true selves and become lions. The lion wants freedom, wants to be lord in its own desert. When it meets the dragon, scales glittering with the values of a thousand years, sparkling with the words 'Thou shalt', then the lion must roar 'I will' and slay the dragon and become a child and create its own values.

Diamonds must forget old values and see with a child's eye. Diamonds forget the compulsion to dominate and colonise nature, they live in harmony with the earth, in harmony with each other.

Or something like that. The words glided over me like a buzzard, unattainable but magnificent.

Outside, Simon squeezed my arm. 'Don't worry, just work at it. Just carry on being a lion.'

'I will!' The words roared out and I laughed.

My old life receded like the planet below on Google Earth, small and unimportant, and my gratitude was overwhelming.

*

One day Oliver handed me a letter from Dad and invited me to read it aloud.

My dear Stefanie,
I am writing to tell you your mother has been unwell with high blood pressure. We are both very sorry you have left Mark. However, I know a counsellor in your area who is willing to discuss the relationship or any other problems. He's an old friend from years ago and would do this for me as a favour. Please give this your best consideration. I will gladly pay the fees.
Your mother and I are praying for you.
All our love in Christ Jesus,
Dad.

Oliver talked about the subtext, that I had made my mother ill, and their rejection of their own daughter's account, to which they preferred Mark's version. Did they know Mark had his own agenda? They were blind. Of course, I assured Oliver, I wouldn't dream of accepting the offer. Gran was the only one I could talk to about the Academy. She wasn't biased like the others.

'I'd love to meet your gran. Invite her for a weekend. She sounds important to you. Much more than your father.

What's he like?'

'He's... charming, gregarious, always has a story to tell, does lots of good works. Ex-teacher, school governor, hospital volunteer, Samaritan, Rotarian, rosarian and on all the committees – pillar of the community. You name it, he's on it.'

'A busy man with little time for his daughter while she was growing up?'

I pondered. 'He did take me for nature walks. He taught me all I know about crickets and grasshoppers.'

Oliver nodded.

'Now give me the letter.'

He screwed it into a ball, put it in a pewter dish and set fire to it. It rocked as the flames leapt, then shrivelled to a blackened heap. The bronze eagle narrowed its eyes.

*

For centuries, Simon said, Exmoor's bogs were drained. Ploughs smashed through the thin iron pan into the subsoil and the moorland dried out, scarred by a network of ditches. Drier was better for grazing, for access. The peat which had stored water and carbon was cut for fuel, but then there was nothing to hold the lashings of rain, stop it gushing downhill in one go. At Watersmeet two rivers plummet down steep rock faces, disembowelling themselves as they join forces and rush to get to the sea, currents pushing past each other. At Lynmouth they pushed too hard.

Now the ditches are being blocked up to form hummocks and hollows with shallow pools, and bright green sphagnum mosses soak up the heavy rain.

Bloody daft idea, Oliver said, till he heard money was available. He sent Simon on a course. Not for Oliver the specialist contractors. He had twenty-five willing pairs of hands at his disposal. Already some bogs were restored and attracting snipe and dragonflies.

'Aren't they dangerous, the bogs?' I asked.

'No,' said Simon, 'they're not that deep. There was a girl called Mollie Phillips supposed to have drowned seventy years ago on Codsend Moor. The locals were sceptical, mind. I had a herd of cows panic and run into a bog. Proper floundering, we all were, and one beast was up to her chin, but she got out. Normally they avoid the bogs.'

The grass and heather heaved themselves out of the snow, leaving bare patches of land. The mire restoration party consisted of Simon, Donna, Pete and me, wearing the black quilted jackets with the Diamond logo. Titchworthy Moor was wild. Clammy mists stayed for days. A pair of ravens often flew over, scissorhands-wingtips almost touching. A good omen, Simon said and smiled at me. They somersaulted in the wind as if they were playing with it, rolled over and over sideways or corkscrew-dived or hung in mid-air. Then they swept across the moor and disappeared. My feet squelched in the silty black water inside the boots. No matter how carefully I trod, testing the tussocks of sedge and grass to see if they could take the weight, I sank in the greedy slime, while Simon negotiated the mires easily. His upper body swung the scythe, the sinews of his forearms bulged below the cuffs as he pulled the baler cord tight, and his breath steamed in dragon puffs.

One day he stopped the quad bike by a high barrow to show me the view right across the Bristol Channel. The ground was so spongy we bounced over it like Teletubbies. Yellow gorse flowers covered the snowy hillsides. Last summer I had stood on a barrow like this with Mark, full of hope.

'How come the gorse always seems to be in flower? Even with snow.'

'There are two species that cover most of the year between them. We have a saying: When the furze is out of bloom, kissing's out of season.'

We both blushed. He smiled and the smile spread like first light coming over the horizon. Then he leant over and kissed me on the lips as lightly as a thistle seed wafting down on its wispy umbrella. For a moment we gazed at each other, smiling, then I reached up for a long, meandering kiss.

That night he came to me. At first we were anxious, as tentative as the stumblings of a beginner violist, and I kept seeing Mark's scalloped lips. Then confidence grew as we revelled in boggy smells and like the ravens we soared, rolled and tumbled, wild as the moor. In quiet interludes we folded over and over. That cold winter's night was gold with a warm chocolate sonority. Again and again deep called unto deep, we mingled, moaned and grunted, cried each other's names as we were swept up above the heights of the clouds. We came to a quiet close, brooding over the perfect harmony. I opened my eyes and smiled.

36

The rush of melted snow through the drains had long since finished, as had Mark's distress, which shocked Hilda.

'Stef thinks he's got another woman,' she told Lisa over coffee.

'That's men for you. Can't live without a woman.'

'She thought it started long before she left. I don't think it was true.'

'It will be if she doesn't come back.'

Hilda put her head in her hands. She just wanted eternal rest, though the word eternal had sinister resonances. Some things never ended, like the old tins of Libby's milk which showed a white-clad nurse holding a tiny tin of Libby's milk, which showed a tiny nurse holding a minuscule tin of Libby's milk, which showed... Or like guilt.

'Mummy, when will I see Auntie Stef again?' said Jack.

Lisa pulled a face. 'Depends whether she comes back.'

'Why?'

'Because she might not.'

'Why?'

But Lisa was hostile to the why-why-why of four-year-oldness.

On the doorstep Jack shot up both arms like a windmill. Hilda picked him up, hugged and kissed him.

Later, a letter arrived from Stef:

Dear Gran,
I hope you're keeping well. Everything here is fine. I've learnt so much. Recently I've been restoring the bogs with Simon, the friendly one with expressive eyebrows, remember? We need the bogs to store carbon and hold water. Simon showed me

one they did two years ago, it was just grass and now it's full of sphagnum mosses and other plants. Of course I get covered in black mud and it's freezing, but it's salutary here and everyone is lovely and it feels so right, the way we're looking after the land, being thoughtful about caring for the animals and everything. Coming here is the best thing I've done in my life.

Rachel and I have left the choir because we're starting our own choir. There's a proper music room with a piano, although I think it'll all be a cappella because Rachel won't conduct and I'm the only one who can play, apart from Oliver who's too busy.

I am still jobless, but it doesn't matter because my days are very full, and I left the car for Mark to make up for taking our savings. Did he say anything about that? We did argue about the circumstances of my leaving, but I didn't mention the money because I knew he'd blow a fuse. Is he okay?

I hope you're keeping warm, Gran. Have you still got snow? It's only partly melted here. We had nine inches of snow the night after I arrived. Freezing cold!

I'll come and see you with Rachel soon. We'll ring first.

I haven't heard back from Sadie or Emma, so I hope they're okay. Give Jack a big kiss from me.

I'm hoping you'll come and stay for a weekend some time. Oliver is looking forward to meeting you. When you meet him, you'll understand why I've given up everything, Gran. He is a true pearl.

> Love Stef

PS. Looking forward to the Diabelli.
PPS. My new email address is diamondacademy@hotmail. com.

A pearl... that was how Mark described him, though less flatteringly. Selfishly she wanted her granddaughter's venture to fail. If Stef was happy, then so should Hilda be. Mark might be wrong. She slipped an angina pill under her tongue and sat at the piano. Schumann flowed from her fingers as easily as the snow had melted. Streams of gold and saffron energy poured into the room, overlapping and blending, and washed away all past and future, all fragility.

Afterwards she typed:

As a child I was Papa's Hildchen. I ripened like a soft plum in the sun. Then came adolescence and the Third Reich and I found a new sun. Mad wasps flew out of me. To Gisela our squad leader I had described my family as idyllic and myself as virtuous, but at home the tension grew. Papa was a socialist, a Volksschädling, a people's pest. Hanno was my ally.

My parents didn't want to go to the Richtfest, the roof-raising party for Tante Luise and Onkel Eduard's new villa in Tempelhof. 'They're too spießig,' Papa said, which means something like bourgeois, conservative and stuffy. 'It'll be full of people with whom I have nothing in common, all showing off.' Tante Luise was his sister, but she married into money. Mama pushed him into going, to be polite. The neighbours and builders would be invited as well, she said. 'The neighbours will be the same,' said Papa. 'The builders, then,' said Mama. Oma was excused because of leg trouble.

The villa was surrounded by high white brick walls and in the grounds were several large motor cars. We children – me, Hanno and their six – were allowed to sit in a cream-coloured Mercedes with giant headlamps and beige satin furnishings. A photographer with camera and tripod took a photo. He said, 'Watch the black box and a little bird will fly out soon,' then disappeared under a black cloth.

Under the villa was a real air-raid shelter with tunnels and rooms off and an emergency exit into the garden. We had a whale of a time. There were fireworks and a brass band and we fished sausages out of a huge cauldron.

Himmler was there. I didn't much like cousin Ada, a sickly-looking girl who'd recently recovered from diphtheria, but we were united in our worship of Himmler. We loved the Bavarian accent and pudgy cheeks and the way he blinked through his pince-nez. Papa wore his best suit with bow tie and handkerchief peeping out from a breast pocket, and Mama wore a close-fitting polka-dot suit and a brooch with real sapphires, but I was ashamed of them. The overcoats hanging on the hooks all had party badges. Papa and Mama were the only non-party members.

A woman with a pearl necklace said how wonderful it was that there was no more street fighting nor inflation. Another woman said on a country walk she had seen groups of young people holding hands and singing at the tops of their voices. Mama and Papa nodded politely.

A maid with topknot and frilly cap and starched white apron was offering drinks from a silver tray when an SS officer approached Papa and said, 'Don't I know you from somewhere?'

'I don't think so,' said Papa.

'But yes. We spoke in a restaurant. I was admiring your beautiful tenor voice. Unfortunately I was called away out of Berlin for a time. I'm so glad to catch you here. You must come and sing for us sometime.'

'I would be most honoured.'

Papa bowed his head and I felt immensely proud, but

he was tense, uncomfortable.

At that point our cousins came and asked me and Hanno to play hide and seek. Cousin Ada and I were responsible for the younger ones. She boasted what an important person her father was. 'My father's been invited to sing for officers,' I said. I was impressed by her cigarette card collection. She had three whole albums of painters with none missing. I tested her and she knew all the details on the backs of the cards by heart. Mama said later that Onkel Eduard's father had bought a cigarette factory. She also told me Papa's employer would not release him from his job because many important people came to his restaurant to hear him sing. I was disappointed.

37

'Siiiix thirty-thirty-thirty-thirty, siiiix thirty-thirty-thirty-thirty-five, siiiix forty-forty-forty-forty, siiiix forty-forty-forty-forty-five...'

The music of the auctioneer's voice went on and on, the same two notes at the speed of galloping horses, while farmers raised rolled-up programmes. There were over a thousand lots to get through. No sooner was one beast out than the next was in the ring, covered in muck, not like the Red Rubies. Or maybe their bowels had given way to fear. The farmers chattered excitedly, the café buzzed. Simon knew everyone. A neighbour of his father came over.

'Your father's sick, lad,' he said, although Simon was fifty. 'He hasn't got sufficient sproil to get out of his bed some days. Your brother said your father's asking after you, and your mother's begging.'

Simon thanked him and he moved off. It was five or six years since Simon had seen his parents.

'I'm a cow-baby,' he told me. 'He was ill before, but I stayed away. Parcel of old crams about how the farm's gone downhill since I left. Big guilt trip, that's what we all think.'

Next morning he raised it at assembly. Oliver pursed his lips and snapped at Stick to stop clicking her knitting needles.

'Why see them after what they did? After all your hard work on deumbilicating. We're your real family. I feel insulted.'

'What if he dies?'

'What if he does?'

'I'd feel guilty.'

'So it's all about how you feel. Isn't that rather selfish?'

Cries of 'manipulative' and 'controlling' and loud mutterings filled the room, till Oliver said, 'Let's hear what

Eff thinks.'

Still burbling like a chaffinch in spring from the newness of the romance, I said, 'What harm would it do? He might not forgive himself otherwise. Besides, Simon's his own person.'

The hubbub rose again. Oliver put up a hand. 'Go this morning and take Eff with you and that'll be an end to it.'

We crawled along through thick mist. Because of the beech-topped earth banks on either side, five-feet-high piles of snow lined the lanes, leaving only a narrow passage down the middle.

Simon exploded when we drew near. 'They've replaced the sheep with horses. Never mind food security for the nation. Get rid of the livestock and fill the fields with rich people's playthings.' He stopped to take deep breaths. 'Sorry. It makes me proper mad.'

'It's the same round where I lived. The horses are free while the sheep are cooped up.'

The old oak door of the slate-roofed farmhouse had no bell or knocker or letterbox. Simon knocked and a voice called out to come in. We walked past a deer's foot on the wall into the hallway. A woman in a flour-dusted pinafore appeared, gasped and fell about his shoulders. His father lay on the couch in the living room. In a dark corner an old man with hands like root ginger and shoes tied with baler cord said, 'Dang I if it ain't young Simon. You still with those pixie-led people in gurt big old manor house?'

'Yes, gramfer.'

'What you been doing?'

'Blocking up rhynes.'

He shook his head. 'Daft beggar. How will the lambs get out of the bogs?'

Simon's father said, 'They've got new ideas these days, Dad. It stops the floods. Don't listen to your gramfer, Simon, it's good to see you. Are you walking out?'

'Yes, Dad. This is Eff.'

'Mind you don't end up at the bottom of Pinkery Pond, maid,' said Gramfer.

Simon trembled.

'Sit down, sit down,' said his mother.

She plied us with tea and apple cake and they talked for an hour. All was well till his father said the next farm had bovine tuberculosis.

'I told them,' said Gramfer, 'get an apple and put eight paracetamol in it and place it near the entrance of the badger sett.'

'Leave it be, Dad. They don't want to know nothing like that.'

Simon stood up to leave, shaking.

'Afore you go,' his mother said and dashed out, returning with a foil-wrapped fruitcake. 'You'll always be welcome back, Simon,' she added on the doorstep. 'Don't mind your gramfer.'

He stopped the Land Rover half a mile away. The badger culling method had upset him, and the popular rumour that Pinkery Pond contained the body of someone from the Academy upset him more. We crawled back through the mist. By the barrow of our first kiss we got out and did it again while cold clouds swirled past and drips ran down our faces.

Later Oliver pressed me for details of the visit. I hesitated.

'We don't keep secrets here,' he said sternly. 'It's about sharing. You want to help Simon, don't you?'

'They talked about farming.'

'And?'

I took a deep breath and relayed Simon's upset. Oliver hobbled up and down behind the desk, red-faced and shouting. His shirt snagged on a window-catch and he whipped the arm away, tearing the sleeve.

That evening he ordered a batting session because, far from gaining clarity, Simon was now even more fucked up. Simon stood with knitted eyebrows by his cushion in the middle of the room, holding the baseball bat.

'I don't know what to say, mind.'

'My father is a tyrant.'

Simon pushed a hand through his hair. 'A beggaring toad he may be, but he isn't no tyrant.'

Oliver raised an eyebrow.

'You said we don't have to do naught we don't want.'

'You don't.'

Oliver sat with deadpan face on his chair in the bay. The spectators glared. Amelia arched her back like a cat about to pounce.

'My father is a tyrant.' On the last word he whacked the cushion so hard, a cloud of dust rose several feet.

'Louder. My father is a wanker.'

Simon hesitated, then screeched, 'My father is a wanker!'

The whole company flinched as he lashed the cushion with all his strength. Fifty, a hundred times he walloped it like one possessed, face knotted with anger, knuckles white. This was the person who that same morning had chatted amiably with his family? Finally he sat back in the circle.

That night I told Simon my guilt, telling Oliver.

'Don't worry.' He pulled my shoulder towards him and I embraced the waves of doubt and certainty, my fingers whispered into his neck and his rough hand clasped my vulva. We languished and thrilled like a wave-tossed ship, like a flock of gulls going all ways.

The days followed in a blur of bogs, mist and sex. My clothes and skin smelt rich and rotten and gorgeous. Because darkness came early we sloped off and made love, or I sat and read *Life's Rich Tapestry* or *A Truthful Existence*. Do one thing with your whole attention, said Oliver, and I worked hard. The moor still wore its winter coat of dead-looking heather and straggled, bleached grass like old mop-heads, with flecks of snow. The mist smothered sounds and its cold fingers fondled the moor and slithered over its surface and condensed on necks and faces. The ghostly silhouettes gliding about in black jackets, the muffled voices, the air glistening with excitement, with strangeness – it was a world away from my old life, a grey prelude of shifting, ambiguous harmonies that brooded over the land.

*

'Right. Let me bend my eye on this letter.'

Dear Mum and Dad,

Sorry you've been unwell, Mum. Hope you're feeling better now. I expect you're looking forward to the end of this cold weather and being able to get out in the garden. It's a bit cold on the hands, even with good gloves, but I'm loving it here.

Don't worry about Mark. He's a dark horse. As far as your other suggestion is concerned, Dad, there's no need. I am living in a space of joy and gratefulness. I know you won't believe this, but God is in this place. I have never known so much love and openness as I have found here.

Love
Stefanie.

PS. I'm hoping Gran will come for a weekend, and she'll tell you how happy everyone is here.

'What do you think? I put in that bit about God because I'm trying to talk on their level. Or maybe to annoy them. Annoy him.'

Oliver smiled. 'I do think there's a real disconnect between you and your parents. I suspect your father wishes you were still under his thumb.'

'They'll be praying for me.'

'I wonder what the origin of those feelings is. I get a real sense of a child held down by a giant hand.'

His gaze was unswerving and for a moment I couldn't breathe, and the rivers of Watersmeet were rushing towards me, spume filling the room. I was drawing in gulps of air which I couldn't expel, like an asthmatic I kept gulping more, and the air between us was running out and I couldn't speak, there was no air, the air was all his. His voice seemed far away.

'It's all right. Just let it out, let it all out.'

I breathed out and breathed too much back in but he was saying soothing words, a serenade of calming words, slowly does it, a gentle slap of warm waves, rhythmic, washing all my sins away and lifting me skywards. Gradually I breathed in time with the voice.

'Your letter is perfect. Do you want to call yourself Stefanie?'

The setting sun struggled through the mist.

'You're right.'

I crossed it out and put Eff.

*

Oliver started it. News travelled fast: go and look at his suite. There was a mass expedition from the kitchen. Screwed to his door was the blue and yellow Lions badge with two open-mouthed lions in profile, as wide as the door.

'I didn't know you were in the Lions, Olly,' said Amelia.

Oliver sat in the bay like a thin Buddha, resplendent in the jumper in blended autumn colours knitted by Stick. 'I'm not.' He chortled. 'I stole it.'

'Those people have plenty of money,' said Toe.

'They've got a cheek to call themselves lions,' said Melanie.

A discussion followed on the boldness of Oliver's action, ending with his challenge:

'So are we lions or aren't we?'

A few days later a sign appeared on a dormitory: Trespassers will be prosecuted. Pete and Neil glowed with pride. Soon there were more: Private; Slow; and pictures of a camera and a dog with a steaming turd.

So when Rachel turned the Land Rover into a potholed lane, stopped and prised a canary-yellow Danger of Death sign with a picture of forked lightning and a collapsed body off a pole, my heart leapt. With the sign rattling in the boot we drove into Minehead, cock-a-hoop. Rachel wore dark glasses and chewed non-stop round the town, hugging the rush bag. Nothing in the charity shops could match that feeling of power, so we saved our money.

'People don't consume goods,' said Rachel. 'Goods consume people.'

However, I did 'buy something decent to wear' with the money Oliver had given me. He liked his women to wear figure-hugging clothes, not like the cardigan with opal buttons knitted by Gran, which I donated to the charity shop.

There was no sign that snow had ever existed in Minehead, and the cherry tree and periwinkles in Gran's front garden were blossoming. The smell of cinnamon greeted us at the door. Oliver was in New York, so we stayed for lunch, then the three of us went to the supermarket. The shelves stacked high with BOGOF bargains were empty, soulless, while the sign in the boot sparkled. Rachel and I giggled.

Back at Gran's for a cup of tea, she asked whether there was any chance of reconciliation between me and Mark.

'I'm afraid you'll lose Mark.'

'I already have, Gran. I'm more valued at the Academy. I feel like a mermaid who's got her legs. Oliver has changed my life.' Blood rushed to my face. 'And Simon is my partner now. But we don't believe in attachment to people or things, we believe in being open.'

On the doorstep Gran said, 'I have a request, Stef: I want to visit the place in Germany where my father died, and I would very much like you to come with me. I'll pay the fare and accommodation.'

'Germany?' I stared. 'What about your angina?'

'It's stable.'

I hesitated. 'I'll let you know.'

She hugged me. 'I'll tell your parents you came.'

'No need, Gran. I know they'd prefer me in a nice suburban house with a front lawn and church on Sunday and a husband and photos of their brilliant graduate grandchildren on the piano, but I'm happy where I am. We don't hold with rampant consumerism.'

She flinched.

Driving back, I felt pangs of guilt, not at the booty in the boot, but at the hurt on Gran's face. My father had probably pestered her for her alliance. Not till we screwed the sign to the door at the top of the tower and announced it at dinner, did I feel the bond of shared criminality. I was part of this community as surely as the veins in the marble. The sun had struggled to stay up in the sky all day, but I was bursting with energy. The things of this world so highly prized were nothings. The group was everything, an ocean in which I dissolved as we sang The Quartermaster's Store and clapped, an ocean inside and outside me, and the waves all talked to each other, talked to me. We laughed till we cried as we made up rhymes with each other's names – There Was Eff, Eff, Danger of Death. The singing and clapping hung in the air long after.

'There was Melanie, Melanie,' I sang softly from my bed by the window, 'lion enough for felony,' before sleep came.

38

Hilda unpinned her bun. That rebuff was so unlike Stef. And no duets. She was disappointed that Stef didn't immediately say yes to Germany. Germany would be difficult. Some people looked back with nostalgia and brushed off atrocities. She had done so herself. The moments of union and happiness kept returning. But spring was here, the chiffchaff had spoken for the first time this year, the pheasants had changed from same-sex flocks to groups of one male and his harem, and Schumann could always take her to another place. She typed:

We had ideals. We swept away everything degenerate. I wasn't sure what degenerate meant, but my parents must have known, because one day when I was ten I came home to find Mama had lifted off the top of the tiled stove in the kitchen by its three iron rings, and Papa was handing her books which she put in the stove. They were choking in black smoke. The window was open only a crack. Papa fetched The Absinthe Drinker from the sitting room, broke it with his bare hands and handed the pieces to Mama. I wanted to ask why, but their faces told me it was best not to. The models in the painting were friends of Berlin-Opa, who was dead by then. I worried over it for months. Then later I did ask. Mama said, 'They were classed as degenerate. We're forbidden those things now.' Papa sighed and said, 'An elephant never forgets.' The elephant held it in her head for future remembering. She also remembered hearing them whisper about a bonfire in Opernplatz, and going with Hanno to look at the smouldering remains of books and papers. Papa, quoting Heine who wrote it a hundred years earlier, said, 'Where they burn books, they'll end up burning people.' Mama shushed him. I fell out with Renate, Papa's old schoolmate's daughter, over the book-burning. Our fathers were no longer friends at the time. 'Where they burn books, they'll end up burning people,' I told her. She flinched and changed the subject. After that, we never talked about politics. Two years later, I would happily have burnt those same books. I would have pushed my own grandmother in the oven.

Papa's brother was a Jehovah's Witness. Sometimes he came with his violin and played duets with Papa, who had a viola which he rarely played, or trios with Mama on the piano. Mama called him holy behind his back, and we children cringed when he preached at us, which was all the time. He was sent away for saying Grüß Gott instead of Heil Hitler. One day Papa read out his wife's letter to say he had been killed. 'Who will be next?' said Mama.

39

Everywhere was soggy, but spring had come early. Bats popped out of their hole in single file every evening. I stumbled and slopped in the rich-smelling bogs, scooped up handfuls of black slime, held it to my cheeks and let it ooze over chin and neck, biting back the cold. Real earth, ancient, not poisoned by humankind.

Oliver took off his belted camel coat and calf-leather gloves as I entered the consulting room. A large gold ingot sat on his desk. I asked about the piano tuner.

'Hang on, chick, I've only been back two seconds.' He blew out his cheeks. 'Be not afear'd, you shall have your tuner. More importantly, Mark has communicated.'

Mark wanted me back. He claimed to have posted two letters and sent more emails.

'Perhaps the floozie left him,' I said.

'If he wanted you he'd come in person.'

'Could I have my own email address?' Immediately this felt too bold, and ungrateful.

Oliver huffed and puffed. No one else had their own address. He went away for six days and came back to nothing but demands. He was disappointed. I should learn to give up my ego. Of course I was new and it had taken him years to attain selflessness, but he expected better. 'Very disappointed,' he repeated. 'Very.'

Just when I wished I could crawl out unnoticed, Amelia danced in.

'Fantastic news.' Her eyes fixed on Oliver like a hunter's on a prize stag. 'The American Spiritual Enlightenment Society has donated five thousand dollars. On top of your fee.'

Oliver threw up both arms and yelled, 'Yay. A few more

like that and we'll be rich.'

'They're recommending you to associates, Olly. They called you a subtle, redeeming force and a beacon of light in the twenty-first century.' She tittered.

'Excellent. Ask if we can quote them on our website. This is it, Amelia. We're in the wrong country. What d'you think, Eff? Shall we all go to America? Amelia, Eff thinks her emails have been deleted.'

'Not deliberately.'

'Accidentally, of course,' he chuckled.

Amelia stared at me with bloodless white face.

'I told her it happens all the time. They float away in the ether and the postmen can't find us.'

Amelia swivelled on her heels and left.

'You look nice in that, by the way,' said Oliver, nodding towards my new sequin-chested top.

*

The piano was tuned to a round, clean sound and I played in the breaks, Romantic music of yearning and striving after some infinity which transcended the senses. It calmed me. The piano was my still, small voice which silenced all my noise, but Oliver said it was selfish.

'But if I don't practise, I'll lose it.'

'You nincompoop. If you practise in all your spare time, you'll lose the group's support. You'll certainly lose mine.'

I yawned. A bad dream had woken me early, I explained, about a raging flood outside my door, like Cockermouth or Boscastle. He perched on the desk with legs extended and hands gripping the edge and asked about childhood nightmares, and I related one of swimming in a river in the Norfolk Broads, chased by a crocodile. Just when it was about to touch me I woke up, every time. Oliver stared so long, I lowered my eyes to his shiny shoes beside the hexagons and pineapples in the carpet.

'There is a tide in the affairs of men,' he said, 'which, taken at the flood, leads on to fortune; omitted, all the voyage of their life is bound in shallows and in miseries.'

I stared, uncomprehending.

'Who does he represent, the crocodile?'

I wanted to say I didn't know, but Oliver would say that meant I didn't want to know.

'Was there a time in your childhood when a parent was really angry?'

I pondered. 'One time when I was nine my father and his friend both let me look after their raffle tickets at the rose show. The friend's ticket won, so I went up on stage and was asked for my daddy's name. So I told them. Daddy was mad at me for causing embarrassment.'

Oliver leaned forwards, his eyes gleaming and his hands clutching his thighs. 'Did he punish you?'

'I can't remember.'

'Perhaps he punished you in a way you wouldn't want to remember.'

'He used to say the reason we have a crease above the upper lip is that every baby in her mummy's tummy knows everything, but the moment she's born an angel puts a finger over her lip and says, 'Sh, don't tell.''

Oliver snorted. 'Classic. Absolutely classic.' He crouched in front of me and squeezed my arm. 'You're safe here, you know that. Close your eyes.'

His voice nursed me like a mandolin serenade, like mist seeping through my clothes, touching my skin, and I was in the lake, the reedy eight-year-old in the orange costume with the big bow, and the sun was warm on my back as I swam breast-stroke towards an overhanging willow on the bank. Then I saw the crocodile, mouth wide open, jagged teeth, gaining on me, and my thin limbs kicked and fought against the water but the crocodile was closer, I reached the willow branch that dipped in the water and started to climb out but the crocodile was right behind, it was going to touch me.

'He's going to touch you, he's going to touch you,' Oliver urged. 'Who is he?'

'I don't know, I don't know,' I cried, clenching my fists.

'Could your father be your crocodile?'

'I don't know.'

'All right, open your eyes.' He stepped back. 'You've got in touch with something deep inside you. Hold on to it, it's the key to your recovery. Everyone here is rooting for you.'

For a moment the ice-blue eyes looked fiercer than any crocodile. He squeezed my arm.

'Here's one for you. Violist: Doctor, doctor, will I be able to play the viola after my op? Doctor: Yes. Violist: Good, because I never could before.'

I giggled and a smile crossed Oliver's lips.

That night I woke in a sweat, the crocodile swimming after me, the first in a series of nightmares.

40

March, and already the sun was playing spoons with the earth against a Chartres-blue sky, as if it had decided to skip spring and go straight into summer. The red soil waiting for the sun need wait no longer. Ribbons of water hurried with laughing, lilting voices down the slopes. Cattle were shedding their mahogany winter coats and everywhere were new lambs with waggy tails.

Hilda looked towards the moor and breathed in the freshness.

Stef and Rachel led her into a marble-floored vestibule with a stag's head and a massive photo of a man with eagle eyes and a bush of red hair, the same as the one on Stef's T-shirt. As she stared he appeared, limping. He was everywhere.

'I've been so looking forward to meeting you,' he said. He was tall and lean, in his late forties, and reminded her of someone she once saw gobbling a piled-up roast dinner alone in a carvery. 'I've heard so much about you, Gran. Your granddaughter's a real treasure.'

His charm dispatched any misgivings, but as Papa used to say, *Schön ist, was schön tut*, Handsome is as handsome does. She handed Oliver a home-made Dundee cake.

His eyes gleamed. 'That looks delightful. Eff told me you wanted to be a singer, but the war put paid to that. I wanted to be a singer too. I was in the West End, a great success, but then I became a teacher, like you. I wanted to give something back to the community. In fact I had my own vocal school in London. I love the bright lights, but this place is more conducive to spirituality, I find, being closer to the land.'

The land... blood and soil. National Socialism had hijacked her own love of nature, and for years afterwards she smothered it until she met Fred and the spirit of the forest re-emerged.

'I'd like to go for a walk in this beautiful place,' she said.

'I'd never guess you were German.'

Her face burned. Since coming to England at fourteen, she had tried to hide her Germanness. The man with expressive eyebrows walked through.

'Simon, Eff tells me Gran has angina, so I'd be happier if you accompanied them on their walk.'

Everything here was idyllic, the hills with bleached grass and bracken and dots of bright yellow gorse. And the woods – not a forest, but still... The trees were leafless, but the blackthorns were clothed in bridal white and the hazels dripped with catkins and last year's beech mast crunched underfoot.

She loved the way everyone called her Gran. The people seemed to really care for each other. In the warm light and waxy smell of flickering candles, amid the conviviality of chicken and roast potatoes washed down with cider, Oliver, sitting beneath a giant oil painting of himself, announced an impromptu concert.

'I had the piano tuned specially for your coming, Gran. I want to hear this choir.'

The wood-panelled music room rang with the sound of Diabelli duets, the scratch choir of fifteen, the viola. Oliver cut a striking figure in his bottle-green brocade frock-coat with black velvet stand-up collar and white lace jabot. He played virtuoso jazz piano and six blues numbers which he sang with a haunting beauty that made her cry. She thanked him for a wonderful evening, and his eyes twinkled more than the sequins and silver thread on his frock-coat.

'There's more.'

He drove her himself on a quad bike to a hilltop with a woodpile. Heather and grass sprawled across the moor under the full moon. The fire was lit, happy faces glowed and Hilda's cheeks prickled with the heat. The flames settled into a regular dance, the cold night air was filled with the smell of burning resin and the warm timbre of voices singing spirituals, and Hilda was uplifted, transported to another world where only the music mattered, and anything was good if it was done with music.

At the end they all hugged. Hilda was deeply moved. The people were unexpectedly friendly and Stef was happy here, so why was Mark so opposed to Oliver?

*

Oliver insisted that everyone fetch chairs so Hilda was not the odd one out. It was all perfectly civilised and the games were fun, or affecting, especially the symphony of emotions. Guilt, Oliver had said to her with an apologetic smile when allocating emotions, and she had looked up in surprise. They stood in three rows and he conducted a polyphony of grunts and squawks and moans and yelps that ebbed and flowed like the comings and goings of a busy city. Stef whooped for joy, while Hilda beside her groaned and yowled, at first just making the sounds, but then came a flood of genuine sorrow that shocked her, poured out unstoppably, a raging torrent of biblical proportions. The symphony would stay with her long after.

While she packed, Stef asked whether she had enjoyed herself.

'Very much. I feel they killed the fatted calf for me. Oliver seems such a thoughtful person, not overpowering at all. I can't think why Mark called him a little Hitler.'

Stef gathered up the bed linen and said, 'Hitler was a man who achieved great things.'

Hilda clutched the pillow and flopped down, grabbed her

bag, took out an angina pill and put it under her tongue. 'Don't ever say that again, Stef,' she gasped when she had regained her calm. 'Never. Not ever. Hitler was a man who achieved great evil.' Her voice wobbled. 'Great evil,' she repeated. 'And don't ever forget it.'

Stef frowned and bowed her head. 'Sorry, Gran.'

Stef and Rachel took her home. As they went over the cattle grid too fast, the rat-a-tat echoed in her head, and the moor groaned under the dying embers of the sky.

Back home she lit a fire because the flames were comforting. Sparks drifted up the chimney and pockets of moisture sizzled, and bits spat out over the mat. In her head she heard the harmonies on the moor. They held her prisoner. She was shocked by what Stef had said. Her gut feeling was that Mark was right, the commune was like a metropolis, all glossy on the outside, underbelly crawling with misery. But how could what was happening there be wrong, when they looked so happy and the sounds were so beautiful? It must be the music. She was tricked by the music. It reached into her deepest parts and laid claim, forced her to rejoice and ignore suffering. What was it about belief, the way it held you in its grip? She envied Margaret and Dan their faith. Nothing would shake it. They adopted faith because they wanted to, then looked for ways to justify it, and hey presto, it worked. While she, Hilda, was in limbo, longing for the certainty of believing something. Of course, she had once believed in something, truly believed. Fred said they should believe in themselves.

She went to the other room.

At summer solstice, at dusk we marched to the woodpile in a clearing in the oak forest. I had hoped to be selected to collect branches and stay behind afterwards, but I was unlucky. 'Next year,' Gisela said. We formed a ring round the pile, about forty girls linked by outspread arms on shoulders. All was still. Not a leaf rustled. While the twelve best dancers danced inside the circle, we sang and our sounds pierced the night. I loved these old songs like Der Lindenbaum and Das Veilchen that we had sung with Mama at the piano. It felt as if the music would lift us off the ground. The dancers picked up torches made of hessian soaked in wax, lit them from one to the next and flew through the air making fiery patterns. At last someone shouted 'Fire' and they thrust the torches into the woodpile and rejoined the circle. The woodpile flickered and spat, and when the tongues of fire leapt, we held hands and danced round slowly, chanting 'Our sun, our strength, our life, we give you back our life,' louder and louder, and when the fire roared, we sang Flamme empor. When we reached the top E, the flames burst out violently and lit up the faces. We were happy, joined together and singing, we were one. We pledged our loyalty until death and listened to a speech about how we were the future and must steel ourselves against hardships to come. Then we sang and sang of our love for each other and the land that gave us life and the faithfulness of the old German oak. When it was over and the fire had died down, Inge and I held hands and jumped over the embers, laughing, and as we leapt we recited this verse we had written.

41

Blinds live in a kind of waking sleep, said Oliver in his back-to-basics lecture. Like automata. Which makes them open to outside influences and liable to be swept along in wars and other crimes. They must wake up. Diamonds work hard on themselves and each other. To thine own self be true, was the aim. But – and here, using easel and felt-tip pen, he drew a large circle and crosshatched it, like a fly's eye, and in each section he wrote 'I' – we have a plurality of selves, scores of false selves or I's that bully each other and fight for supremacy. Depending on our mood, different I's come to the fore, each pretending to be the true self. All this fighting wastes energy, so we put up barriers and go to sleep. We are blind.

'Understanding is acquired from the totality of information intentionally learnt and from personal experience; whereas knowledge is the automatic remembrance of words in a certain sequence. We suffer from abnormal functioning of the psyche without objectively true information, without the participation either of the abnormally crystallized factors already within, or of the factors which might newly arise from the results of external perceptions obtained from the abnormally established form of ordinary being-existence.'

'I'm confused,' I said at this barrage. 'I must be missing something.'

Oliver stared, silhouetted against the window. 'Ask the others.'

We funnelled down the stairs.

Donna said, 'We have to work it out for ourselves. We're not spoonfed.'

Which was no help at all.

Still, it was the last day of slopping and splashing in the

bogs. Spring had come too early. The sun bewitched us all, drew shoots from the ground and smiles from winter-weary faces. But that day the sky contained endless rain with which it beat the earth.

'We'll finish early,' said Simon. 'You must be scrammed.'

There were just the two of us, so we stopped at a pub, dashing from Land Rover to door. We removed our sodden jackets and I crouched over the log fire while Simon fetched two glasses of scrumpy. The walls were covered in antlers, hooves and a snarling fox's head. Beside me were photos of tight-lipped, flint-eyed masters of the hunt, and a photo with the caption Exercising the Hounds: one man leading the way, flanked by two behind, all on foot, mouths set hard, while the dogs walked thirty wide and five or six deep. The dogs at the front looked eagerly at the leader, tails high. All kept obediently close.

Rain lashed the windows. The scrumpy prickled the inside of my mouth. Simon chatted to the landlord, then joined me. He had opposed Oliver's choice of Exmoor because everyone knew him and disapproved of his change of name by deed poll to Diamond. My eyes widened.

'You changed your surname?'

'Lots of us did. After I deumbilicated, I hated having my father's name. I regret it now, mind. He was only doing his best. Come with me to see them again, Stef. They liked you, I know they did.'

The staccato of rain on the windows grew louder. The fire spat and a burning fragment jumped out onto the tiles.

'But you called him a tyrant and a wanker.'

Simon took a gulp and wiped his upper lip with the back of his hand. 'He's still my father. Imagine if it was your gran you hadn't seen for ten years and she didn't have long to go. I wanted Rachel to come ages ago, but she wouldn't. I think she was projecting her issues with her own parents on to me.'

I raised my eyebrows.

'Rachel and I were an item. After Amelia and Claire. And Donna. Don't look surprised. It's inevitable when you live in close contact.'

That night we lay side by side. I loved his breath warm on my ear, his muscled arm lying hard on my belly, his dick sandwiched between our thighs, but the passion of old times was gone. It was deceitful, visiting his parents again secretly. Secrets were bad. Nightly sex with Simon had palled, but sleeping alone was worse. The night was a giant boa constrictor. 'Don't go,' I said, or, 'I don't want to go,' when we were in his bed. The bats twittering in the roost and the grunts and groans of copulation in the other beds entered my sleeping and waking.

I didn't mean to tell Oliver about Simon. Whether or not to go to Germany with Gran was the issue.

'Maybe your gran wants to get you away from here.'

The bronze eagle and the gold bar gleamed in the sun. Oliver's sweatshirt bore a lighthouse and the words Beacon of Light. He told me not to decide about Germany yet, then probed my relationship with Simon. I stopped short.

'Go on.' He sat up straight. 'You were going to say something.'

'No no, it was nothing.'

His voice was clipped, urgent. 'It wasn't nothing. What did he say?'

'Nothing important.'

'I'll be the judge of that. What did he say?'

I hesitated. A burst of sunlight blinded me.

'I don't like being dangled on a string, Eff.' His face looked like a coming celestial pummelling and the rooks over

Beechcleave Wood uttered cries like a discordant harmonica.

'He said he regrets changing his name.' I pulled my fingers and cracked the joints and gave him a blow-by-blow account of the visit to Simon's parents, the warm atmosphere, how his father had called me a spurrity woman. 'Maybe his father has mellowed with age.'

'Eff?'

'Yes?'

A cloud passed over the sun and he glowered, like a piece of paper lolling on top of a log fire, about to burst into flames.

'Just stick to what you know.'

*

Simon's mouth fastened onto mine and his tongue burrowed. I lay leaden. The second hand of a clock jerked round, like petals pulled off a dandelion: he loves me, he loves me not, he loves me, he loves me not... A rose scent drifted from the flickering candles. The candle-shadows lifted and lowered like bats' wings. The black satin sheet, at first cool against my skin, had warmed up, and now the brandy was warming my insides, spreading me out on the king-size bed, bigger and bigger, filling the room like Alice after drinking the potion, uncontrollable. With jellied hand I held him. It was weird, too weird, the shrinking bed, the shrinking room, and Simon somewhere above me with his rough hand on my breast. The smell of Floris Santal filled my nostrils and the blood thumped in my ears. Simon was fuzzy. The wall light above the bed cast an orange glow on his face, the enormous eyebrows twitched, but the rest was a blur. I was still growing, ballooning – I would fall off the bed if I grew any more.

'Go down,' said a tight voice.

On the bedside table was a stack of books. Beside the bed a black silk dressing gown with gold pheasants hung either side of a bony knee. Long fingers parted me, the proboscis dip-dipping for nectar, thick hair buried between my legs, tickling the thin skin. I let out a moan like the long, meandering lament of an oboe that drowned out the stertorous breathing next to me. The room swam and darkened. My moans grew louder, the other voice grunted, a punched teddy-bear grunt. The slam of a large wave hitting the shore sent me reeling, whinnying, with flashes of brilliant pink light that kept coming like a Roman candle. It was over. My eyes would not open and my limbs were ponderous. I lay naked, interrupted.

I woke up in my own bed, gloss-eyed, shaken by Simon. Lunchtime. What happened?

'You don't remember? The Thin Controller helped you overcome your fears around sex. We had sex in his bed.'

My eyes widened. Memories of satin cold on my back and Simon warm on top trickled through.

'Don't worry. You were fantastic. He was impressed.'

'He was there?'

Simon squeezed the back of my neck. 'It's all right. We all go through it. You did agree to it.'

*

The day passed in a daze. My head was thick. At the sound of the elephant bell the light came crimson over the horizon, clouds slithered across the sky and midges fast-scribbled in the air round my head, like the scribbled mess inside it.

After dinner we waited in the workroom, the door opened and Oliver limped to the bay with the viola and beckoned to me. He hummed a tune for me to accompany him.

'This is Eff's song,' he announced.

He sang tenderly, eyes fixed on mine, and I gazed back and drew velvet notes from the viola. His hair glinted copper in the sun and his voice quivered. My left hand fluttered in an ecstasy of vibration.

'Love is a flood.
Its joyful waters sweep
over my stony ground,
a river full and deep.

'Love is a fire,
a sun that burns so bright,
restores my flickering torch
with glorious blazing light.

'Love is an arrow,
barbed and swift of wing,
that lodges in my heart.
Welcome, cruel sting.'

'You should copyright your songs, Olly,' said Amelia. 'Make money.'

Wahey! Joy of joys, I had given birth to something special and wonderful. This new baby was an open heart, a wish to give everything to everyone, shout my bliss to the ceiling, hallelujah!

*

Mist smothered the cries of new lambs. It hid the solitary ash in the field and slunk over the surface, seeking nooks and crannies. Then the sun came and blew it aside, still pretending it was summer. The bare red soil basking in its warmth bore green shoots. The gorse was grown leggy. A heath fire went on for days and the fire brigade arrived to warn Oliver about Saturday night bonfires.

'All this bare soil is bad,' said Simon at assembly. 'It dries out too quickly, and every time we dig or pull out plants we destroy the mycorrhizae in the soil and release carbon into the atmosphere.' He waxed evangelical and the eyebrows rose and fell. 'We should convert to permaculture, plant ocas and mashua and camas and Szechuan pepper and saltbush.'

The room was electric. We could save labour, save the planet.

But Oliver was sullen. 'I don't know where he gets these loony ideas. No one will buy things they've never heard of.'

'You said you could sell anything to anyone for a fat profit,' said Simon.

'That's not what I said.'

Ideas flew back and forth. We voted: thirty-two for, eight against. Oliver sat po-faced.

'Right, enough. This needs more consideration. We don't base our actions on a whim. That way madness lies.' He held up an envelope and beamed. 'You've all worked hard, so in the fatness of these pursy times I'm treating you to the theatre on Friday.'

A cheer went up. Rachel told me he always bought us ice creams.

My nights were filled with crocodiles and floods. We talked about my childhood, about Gran and Lisa, about Sunday School and Guides and church on Sunday evenings, about switching from faith to boys at fourteen.

'So you were repeating a pattern when you cheated on your husband.'

I bowed my head like a bluebell.

'You're not to blame. If you betray men, it was because *you* have been betrayed by a man. You're reacting to the treachery shown to you.'

'Adam didn't betray me.'

'Someone before Adam, then.'

I pondered the string of boyfriends through teenage and

early college years. 'If anything, I did the two-timing. I called the shots.'

'Sometimes when we're hurt, we make sure it doesn't happen again. We hurt first.'

A ray of sun dazzled me.

'I thought it was better to live in the moment. What does the past matter?'

'It matters if it's affecting you now. You can't sleep and your sex life is spoilt.'

The room fell silent and I wondered if time was up.

'I've never known a woman who talked so little about her father,' he said.

*

The brandy must have been doctored the first time, because this time I remembered everything: black satin, rose-scented candles, Floris Santal, Rumi's poetry on the bedside table, the orange glow from the wall lamp, Oliver's legs peeping from the black silk dressing gown with gold pheasants. I snaked and whinnied as Simon slithered a finger down, our tongues plumbed each other's depths, hands ironed away the outside world. He clambered on top and thrust like a slaughterman with a poleaxe. Our hips gave and took with all the restlessness of our disordered lives, then came the whoosh of union and Oliver's grunts like a punched teddy bear. And Oliver's marshmallow voice telling Simon to talk to me, say how beautiful I was, telling him to turn me over. It aroused me more than doing it in my own or Simon's bed.

'You were very sexy yesterday,' said Simon the following night. 'More than with just me.'

My heart missed a beat. 'I'm afraid of hurting you. You're too good for me.'

Simon was undeterred. 'You're perfect,' he said and sank into me, and I thought of black satin and climactic grunts.

But the greater shock came the following evening.

'Eff is too bossy doing the choir.' Claire sat erect and looked towards Oliver.

'That's why I left,' said Pete.

'Me too,' said Neil.

I stared in disbelief.

'Eff's not bossy,' said Rachel. 'She has to be directive. The choir wouldn't work otherwise, if everyone did their own thing.'

'She didn't have to look at me every time she tells us to sing sharper. She thinks because she's pushing her mouth up into a smile with her fingers, that's friendly.'

'Just because she wears glasses on a string round her neck, she thinks she can push us around.'

'She hasn't been here long.'

'Yeah. Less than four months ago she was a blind. Still is, in my book.'

This last was from Pete. The initial flush of fifteen had dwindled to ten. It had made up for school. I missed school with everyone clamouring round, saying, 'Mrs Williams, Mrs Williams, tell us about the rocks', or with a stageful of children singing out their hearts, or the class play. Jonathan had come out of his shell ever since the Christmas play. 'Please, Mrs Williams, I don't want a part in the school play,' he'd said, and I pondered until I had the solution. 'Right, Jonathan. I've thought of a part for you and I will write it in for you specially. It's just three words and I don't want you to say anything yet, I want you to go away and think about it and talk to your friends, then come and tell me your answer. Right?' 'Yes, Mrs Williams.' 'Right.' The Diamond Choir made up for the loss. I had plans to take it to a nursing home, and a file with lists of music and lists of members.

Simon said, 'She's not bossy to me. You're all a parcel of

gurt big wimps.' He flushed with anger. 'She has to tell people what to do. Be like a hundred rooks up in a tree otherwise.'

'You're biased,' said Amelia, who had not joined the choir.

The debate wandered: I got special attention from Oliver and it wasn't fair. They raged on till Oliver, quick-eyed, spoke.

'I would say that a woman who is unfaithful to her husband from the off and who decrees that Mark shall have no children and who answers the phone during sex is one who likes to pull all the strings.'

A stunned silence followed.

'What, unfaithful to Mark?' Amelia said at last.

'I'll let Eff tell you.'

My toes dug into the thick red carpet. The zigzags and medallions and spiralling tendrils in the Persian carpets on the wall blurred into a mass of colours, and a ring of narrowed eyes fixed on me.

'It was my first marriage. Mark and I... He was Adam's best man.'

Through the open window came the croak of a raven.

'Says it all,' muttered Pete.

When we trooped out, Stick hung behind and put an arm round me.

'Don't do that,' said Oliver sharply. 'We must all listen to criticism. You should know that by now, Stick.'

I fled to a bathroom on the second floor.

Next day six came to choir. Oliver warned against continuing. From fifteen down to six was a consensus and I had bigger things to deal with. I nodded. Nor was he keen on the trip to Germany.

'Your grandmother's one of these people who hide what they're thinking. No doubt Mark will have told her this is a cult.'

'There's no deprivation of food, sleep or contact with family and friends,' I said.

'Precisely. Nevertheless, if you chose to go it would dash the cup from my lips.'

'I won't go.'

'Very wise. Now, about your infidelity. You do understand I was just helping you to break down your barriers? Because you do need to share more.'

I nodded again.

'I guess you like to feel in control because at some time in your life you were helpless. Perhaps at night you feel helpless.'

I hugged myself.

'Have you heard from your father?'

'No. I think the letter put him off.'

'Good girl.'

*

Misery. Oliver was away for a week in Italy flying, then two weeks in Crete and London conducting workshops and seeing his property manager. Like day-old chicks surprised by the lid of their box being lifted, we huddled together. Some felt suicidal. We hugged and hugged, cocooned by the warm wood panelling and Persian carpets. Amelia had gone with him.

'Good,' said Rachel. 'She thinks she's it, but she's no better than anyone else.'

She thought Amelia was responsible for reporting Pip.

Claire told me I had emails.

'But these are weeks old.'

Replies from friends, and one from Emma: *Thx mum, no need to worry. Having a ball (and working hard, before you say anything!) :-) x Em.*

Claire scowled. 'They were in the junk folder. Or someone didn't know who Stef was. You should tell people outside your name is Eff.'

The heat wave continued. Lambs grew woolly and birds were busy. Rachel and I got up at five to hand-milk the cows, which were docile with calves alongside and back legs roped together. On the first day Craig helped. I milked only three cows in an hour and my hands ached. Then came bottling and delivery, mucking out and cleaning up until midday.

We went to Minehead. Everywhere larches were being felled and rhododendrons cleared because sudden oak death was on the rampage. The blackthorns still wore their bridal white, and the sunny grass banks covered in primroses made me think of Jack with his open arms. Exmoor's curved summits were like nodding heads round a table and its plunging combes held dark secrets.

The town was all palms and pansies, sun shining on pink sandstone, and cider and fudge and gollies for sale. We drove to the beach to bask.

'Simon said you changed your surname to Diamond.'

'It's better than my father's name. And Oliver suggested Rachel.'

'Rachel's nicer. Rachel Diamond. What do you think about Stef Diamond? I hate the name Williams now.'

The sea whispered beyond the sand and mud. It was comforting, here at the periphery of the world. A flock of gulls scrummed over a polystyrene box of chips. In the harbour the shackles of a sailing boat tinkled. I told Rachel about the nightmares, my aloneness at night. Even in Simon's bed I felt alone. The night terrors pecked away like a griffon vulture and the only pacifier was Oliver's calm voice on the MP3 player.

She squeezed my hand. 'Something awful from your past

is intruding into the present. We all go through it. When you open your mind, all the bad old stuff comes out.'

We hugged, then sat looking out to sea, waveless and enticing.

After a while we drove to Hilda's. There would be a surprise for me if I came on Tuesday, she had said over the phone. The surprise was Jack, who shot up both hands to be picked up, and clung until the tea tray arrived. Lisa was at a conference for the day. He laid his head on my shoulder and patted my back, and all the learning about living in the present was forgotten, replaced by anguish at the missed moments. When Gran and I played the mandatory Diabelli he stood beside me, studying the black symbols dancing on the sheet music. Afterwards I sat him on my knee, taught him two-fingered chopsticks, then added the treble part. Gran and Rachel clapped.

'Brilliant,' said Rachel.

On the wall was the photo of Hilda's parents. They looked radiant, her mother sitting on a field gate, father leaning his elbow on the gate. The smell of cinnamon wafted through, and out came the cakes.

On the doorstep Jack said, 'When will I see you again?' and the words sounded strange in the mouth of a four-year-old. Surely this wasn't what Oliver meant about being like a child?

Gran hugged me so tight I wondered if I had made a mistake.

'Do you mind if I don't come to Germany, Gran?' I looked at the ground. 'Sorry.'

42

Hilda was crestfallen. Her euphoria had evaporated like tiddlers in the shallows when a shadow falls across them. But no careless words could take away love, ever. She played a sonata she had written for Fred while Jack played with his trains. The notes were in blue ink on hand-drawn staves on a single sheet of rough, yellowed paper sellotaped to a piece of cardboard. The sellotape was dry and brittle and hung loose in places. Tears ran down. After Jack had gone, she typed:

School chose me to take part in the Olympic Youth festival following the opening ceremony, a huge honour that took over my life. Berni was envious. Of course I was still seeing him, secretly. We shared a passion for fitness and sport. Our motto was a healthy mind in a healthy body. We looked after our bodies while my parents lazed around, even though they met while Papa was on a walking holiday. At thirteen Berni could sprint sixty metres in eight seconds and swim for an hour in the freezing Wannsee. I could endure only a quarter of an hour when it was so cold.

Every night I kept myself supple in my room with exercises. We rehearsed for months, at first individual school teams, then massed on various sports grounds, and one day a week for the last two months a military truck took us from school to the stadium. Mama made my white costume. We were proud and full of ourselves, we would show the world the new spirit of Germany, its strength, its unity and its peaceful, loving nature. We knew we were important. We were the worst kind of prigs.

Near the time of the Olympics, the gypsies and the No Dogs or Jews signs disappeared from streets and parks and benches and cafés. Two years earlier on a class outing in the Grunewald forest with the pungent smell of pine trees, we walked past a couple sitting on the grass with a Thermos flask and enamel mugs. It was a sunny day and two pre-school children were climbing on a log nearby. The whole class bellowed, 'Juda verrecke,' Perish Judah, except for myself and two others. Back in school the teacher said, 'Why didn't you join in?' I said, 'I didn't know them, they might not be Jewish.' My friend Herta was Jewish. One girl said she started to shout, but the boiled sweet in her mouth slipped down her throat and half-choked her. The other one didn't come back to school and we heard she had moved away. So when the signs were removed just before the Olympics, I was puzzled because by then I would gladly have shouted out with the rest.

The whole spectacular began at nightfall with the tolling of the massive Olympic bell on the gate tower, which made me swell with pride. A hundred thousand spectators watched electrified as thousands of us surged down the Marathon Steps onto the stadium. We were part of a great whole, bound together by our aims. Under the spotlights we performed dances in swirling circles. We held white half-hoops which curved over our heads, to keep perfect spacing. Then the boys in different-coloured gymnastic uniforms formed the five rotating Olympic rings while we in our white costumes formed the background. Older boys and girls did their scenes. In the final scene with torch procession, everyone in the stadium sang the Ode to Joy from Beethoven's Ninth – All Men Become Brothers – while the great spotlights panned across the field and soared upwards to the heavens to form a dome of light. It was so successful we did three encores on other nights.

43

A cold lump sat in my stomach, throbbing like a frog's throat pouch. I clasped my hands tight to stop them shaking. The marbled opaline shade of the desk lamp was lit up white against the dark of the night and the gold bar gleamed. The bronze eagle on its base was poised, wings swept back.

'So, mia uccellino. How are we doing?'

The frog burst: 'People dislike me now they know about me and Mark, even Simon is cool and he never was before, I missed you while you were away, the nightmares are worse and—'

He took both my hands in his. The orange hexagons and pineapples in the carpet had legs like lobster claws. He pressed a button on the desk.

'Do you think I'm wise?'

I nodded.

'The fool doth think he is wise, but the wise man knows himself to be a fool.'

I stared, uncomprehending. There was a knock at the door, and Craig appeared, wearing rustling combat trousers, stroking a rudimentary beard.

'For fuck's sake, Craig, shave it off. And fetch Simon, please.'

He poured me a glass of Courvoisier and squeezed my shoulder, and in no time Simon was leading me into the room of rose-scented candles and black satin and I exploded with joy, O Fortuna, one hundred and twenty voices filled my body with sound, and the smell of Floris Santal and the warm burgundy timbre of Oliver's voice from beside the bed excited me more, veni, veni, venias, we were sailing, sailing, the horns blared with raw fever, so raw that everything held its breath for a moment before the final amen. Amen. We dissolved like Swiss chocolate. We lay dovetailed.

*

The heat was unrelenting. The May flowers came out long before May and the first curly tips of bracken poked through. We formed a fireman's chain to water crops and sang as we passed the buckets along.

Simon raised the subject of the drought one balmy evening. The low sun lit up the Persian carpets on the walls in all their brilliant carmines and ultramarines and viridians.

'Why has no one mentioned it? If it's this dry in future, we need to rethink, otherwise there'll be no water, no crops, no naught. We should share ideas with like-minded communities.'

Oliver sat in a tangled web of string. 'There are none.'

'I've found a few online. In fact, we've exchanged emails.' The veins on Simon's forearms protruded and his eyebrows danced as he spoke. 'We're invited to go and visit two up country and they want to come here. I thought three or four of us could go.'

'You thought.' Oliver was a silhouette in the sun's last burst of light. 'And what made you think I'd welcome this idea?'

People shifted on their cushions.

'I've talked it over with others – Rachel, Donna... I know Donna agrees.'

Donna sat hunched into the wall like Sally the greyhound resisting the order to jump into the bath.

'Well,' said Oliver. 'What does anyone else think? Do we want another Graham?'

'Hardly,' said Toe.

Simon knitted his eyebrows. 'It's only a visit.'

'In my experience,' said Oliver, 'others are judgemental

about what we do here.'

'Ignorant, criticising,' said Pete bitterly.

Neil, who looked like an exotic bird with his bright green jumper, blond hair and beetroot cheeks, said, 'My friends and family criticised everything, told me I should cut the umbilical cord.'

'Probably jealous because they didn't have an umbilical cord,' said Oliver.

There was a low-pitched hum of agreement. I was part of the hum.

'We only have to flippin' listen,' said Simon. His fists were clenched. 'Where's the problem?'

Amelia said, 'You're the one with the problem, Simon. Who are these people anyway?'

The debate raged on. Simon shouted the loudest.

Finally Oliver said, 'Enough. I don't want blinds interfering. Now let's move on.'

Simon burst out, 'You're a megalomaniac, Oliver.'

Oliver bristled like a compact hayrick ripe for spontaneous combustion. Melanie and Amelia, who had sat like crouching, ravenous dogs, sprang up and advanced towards Simon.

'You ungrateful little shit.' Amelia's face was blotchy with rage. 'You were a gibbering wreck till Oliver took you under his wing. You didn't know a soul in London and he gave you a job and free elocution lessons. He's treated you like a son. You're the megalomaniac, Simon.'

'You think you're better than us because you know the land,' said Melanie, jabbing the air with a finger.

'I don't think so.'

Others chimed in:

'You make out you're this nice warm person, but you keep yourself apart.'

'You sneak off doing your own thing.'

'Have you forgotten how you sang Oliver's praises on that forum?'

'Too big for your boots.'

Simon sat stiff as clods of sun-baked earth and listened to the torrent open-mouthed. Oliver, who had watched keen-eyed, asked my opinion.

I looked past Simon's shoulder at the cinnamon streaks and swirls in the marble fireplace. A coldness came over me, like the mists swirling over the bogs. I let my eyes meet his. 'I think he should apologise.'

Silence. Everyone watched Simon. He clamped his lips. Oliver asked Rachel to fetch a chair. The multi-coloured patchwork skirt flared as she got up and her bare feet pattered down the stairs. She reappeared with a chair.

'Since you're so great, Simon, you can stand on the chair for the rest of this and every session until you see that you are not.'

Simon sat motionless. His Adam's apple slid down his throat. Then slowly he pushed the hair back from his furrowed brow, stood up, dragged the chair into place and stepped up. His head hung down, lips parted like the cast sheep. My bare toes stroked the carpet back and forth. Simon said nothing more all evening.

That night I slept alone with a rock in my heart, curled up like a pill woodlouse.

*

The following evening Simon sat beside me at dinner. A curt hallo was all I could muster. I upended my fork and pirouetted it in mash and gravy, forming a grainy coffee-coloured morass.

'Does this mean we're finished?' he said.

'Don't know,' I mumbled.

'I thought we had something special going.'

I let half a dozen peas lie on my fork, shrunken, dimpled, misshapen things. 'It was just sex.'

Afterwards we trailed upstairs and Simon stood meekly on his chair. Amelia proposed a scarecrow to ward off rooks.

'Nah,' said Toe. 'Just put Simon out there.'

The mirth exploded.

Simon didn't come to me that night, nor any night, nor did I go to him.

*

With May came rain in abundance. It tumbled off the hills, crashing and foaming like some thundering, avenging god. The bogs shimmered with nodding white heads of cotton grass, the woods were lush with bluebells, ramsons and bracken, and the rivers were full. The Devil is in the rivers, Simon would have said, except that he didn't say much these days.

'So much for your drought, Simon.' The rain had turned Oliver's Afro into a gorgon's head.

Simon stood on the chair with head hanging down. He said nothing in discussions and after assembly joined the queue outside the office to collect the weekly allowance when everyone had gone.

One evening Simon spoke from the chair: 'I want to quit.'

There were gasps from the floor.

'You're hardly in a fit state to leave, Simon,' said Oliver from the web in the bay. 'Looking at you now, I see no improvement over the fucked-up man you were when we first met.'

'I have family and old friends.'

'We all know about your family, Simon. What that man did is wicked. You wouldn't treat a dog like that.'

'We've mended our differences.'

'The leopard doesn't change its spots. A blind is always a blind. I feel very hurt that you want to leave. You're like a son to me. If you left now, I'm afraid what might happen. Are you trying to kill yourself? How does anybody else feel about Simon quitting?'

'I feel hurt,' said Toe. 'I've known you for more than ten years, we made this place together, we made it work. You were the rock on which this community was built. And Oliver's been like a father to you. It's a stab in the back. I would never have believed you were a quitter.'

'The traitor in our midst,' said Amelia.

'You need to come down a peg and see how small you are, Simon,' Pete said with a sneer.

'Too big for your boots,' said Neil.

'Perhaps he's thinking of setting up a rival academy,' said Melanie.

All this went on for an hour with hardly a word from Simon, till Oliver intervened:

'This is not a prison. Anyone is free to quit, however much it pains me. All you need is to wait six weeks for a full discussion to help you survive. I would be responsible if anything untoward happened to you. Do I have your word you'll give it six weeks?'

Rain hammered on the windows.

'Okay,' Simon said at last in a raspy voice.

Oliver looked round. His eyes alighted on Meredith, the would-be poet and actor who had been in love with Toe. She had moved in the night before.

'Meredith. Go and give him a big hug.'

She stood up. 'What, on the chair?'

'No, you nincompoop. Simon, get down and put the chair against the wall.' He complied. 'Now hug him.' He wouldn't let go. 'Now everyone who feels sorry for Simon, touch him.'

We rose as one and mobbed him, a laughing, jabbing scrum. He wept openly.

Meredith swapped to mailshotting and paired him whenever possible. Every evening we hate-bombed and love-bombed Simon into the small hours. But the loud remarks and guffaws had gone, the humour had gone. He was a broken man.

*

I took to sneaking into the music room to play, but the piano or viola on its own was incomplete. The notes were right but my heart wasn't, and the sound trickled into the vast space and was lost, like the long, empty nights waiting to be filled. I lay on the parquet floor and stared at the blank ceiling, the blank walls, a dot in the void. All these friends, and none filled the emptiness. What had happened to the open minds so highly praised? 'They're open-minded,' I had shouted at Mark. 'The trouble with an open mind,' he replied, 'is people put things in it.'

'It's nice to see Meredith back,' I said to Oliver in my next session. 'Is she all right?'

His eyebrows lifted. 'Meredith just needs a good fuck. Now what about you?'

I bit a nail and blushed. 'I don't belong. I'm lonely,' I moaned. Though I was never alone. 'I can't sleep. I can't—'

'Eff?' He sat erect, veins in his temples throbbing, mouth set hard, eyes ice-blue and fixed on me. 'Who has done this to you, chick? These are classic signs. Who has done this?'

'I don't—'

'Think, Eff. Think of the times your father came into your room at night. He must be the one.'

'But I was his favourite. Lisa was the one he was always angry with.'

His Adam's apple moved up his throat. 'Absolutely classic, mia cara. Your avoidance behaviour convinces me. Your father is your crocodile. You've repressed it, my dear. But think how you felt in the nightmare and cling to those feelings. Trust your feelings. Your feelings are your truth. Trust me, I know what I'm talking about.'

I frowned. The orange pineapples and hexagons in the carpet were a seething mass of lobsters and the sphinxes on the mantelpiece dug their claws into their bases. I thought of sun-doused afternoons and cricket-hunting expeditions. Just me and Daddy, never Lisa. Didn't Lisa want to come? 'This is our field,' said Daddy. I was his little field cricket because the shiny black creature stood at its burrow entrance and warbled, shrill and sweet. Our field, where crickets ticked and sang and chirped and scraped their messages of love to the sun. Our field, where we nestled in the long grass and he dotted my hair with pink centaury flowers and made buttercup bracelets because I was beautiful, he said. Our field, where the grass hid us from the world and the crickets carried me to another place, untouchable. The grass seeds stuck in my long hair like a seedcake, and those that escaped my mother's combing fell out onto the pillow at night. Now at last I saw his face *in flagrante*: a quivering storm, a hideous jigsaw of spasms going every which way, a veritable Tourette's phantasmagoria of snarls and smirks and frowns and leers. I panted like a butterfly landing on the ground, wings pulsing up and down.

Oliver stroked my hair over and over, then pressed the button on his desk and asked Pete to fetch Rachel or Stick. I sat in the waiting room. The tremulation which had started in my knees radiated out till, if the hairs on my head had had a cricket's chirping mechanism, they would have sung. I fell into Rachel's arms.

'My father…' I gasped.

*

The sun was still belching out heat from its position near the horizon.

'Remember,' Oliver said as we put on neutral masks, 'the mask has no attitude, no past, no future, only the present. Just be yourself. No speaking and no sounds.'

When he told us to imagine the breath moving down the front of the spine into the groin, it was my father's breath I felt, and I felt too his rough, calloused hands creeping inexorably down.

'Now imagine fire. The fire is in your belly. Off you go.'

The fire consumed me, ate me up. I leapt and lunged, trying to escape. Simon was repellent, towering over me with blank face, a monster hiding behind the mask. Others trod round me gingerly as if I were spouting fire, might singe them to cinders. They did circle dances in small groups and I was the lonely child watching from the corner of the playground.

'How can I be myself when I don't know who I am?' I said in the round-up. Like the aerial roots of Gran's Swiss cheese plant, fumbling for the ground which was not there.

Oliver said, 'Behind the mask is nothing.' A smile played about the corners of his mouth. 'Remember the onion. An actor's mask is liable to become his face. Perhaps you'd like to tell the group what you discovered today.'

All eyes stared. Craig's combat trousers stopped rustling. The only sound was breathing.

My voice shrivelled. 'Daddy raped me.'

Rachel squeezed my hand and everyone looked sympathetic. Rachel, Donna, Stick, Melanie, Claire and Neil said they too were sexually abused by their fathers.

At the end Oliver summed up: 'It's okay not to know who you are. It means you're open-minded. You won't find out who you are if you have preconceived ideas. I'm pleased with today's work. I've tried doing this with blinds, to disastrous effect. Caviar to the general. So give yourselves a pat on the back.'

The sounds of Amazing Grace were like a warm sea in which to float, cradled by the love of my friends. I had indeed been blind, but now could see.

Pete hugged me. 'Sorry I had a go at you about the choir.'

'Me too,' said Neil.

'You were never a blind,' said Pete. 'You're a real diamond.'

I stretched my mouth into a smile I did not feel.

*

Silver birch trunks gleamed in the moonlight. The deep wet mire was churned up by horses' hooves. The blood in my head hammered like a galloping horse, and my mother's arm encircled me as I clung to its mane. My father's shape appeared. The cold air chilled my sweat.

'Mummy, Mummy, can't you see the Erl-King with his tail? He's going to get me.'

'Be quiet, Stefanie,' said Mummy as if I were some annoying little insect. 'It's only the mist.'

My hair bounced up and down and my legs were splayed so wide my skirt rode up to my knickers. The black hair and steel-rimmed glasses came close.

'Come and play with me, darling. I'll make you buttercup chains and show you how to make sounds like grasshoppers and crickets.'

'Mummy, Mummy, can't you hear the Erl-King?'

'There's nobody there. It's only the wind rustling in the leaves.'

Mummy was betraying me. That was what grown-ups

do.

The pale blue eyes in the mist leered up close. 'Let's go hunting for the field cricket, Stefanie.'

'Mummy, Mummy, the Erl-King says if I go with him we'll find a field cricket.'

'Don't be silly, Stefanie, you don't get field crickets in forests.'

The face was inches away, I could see strong arms and legs and a big fat dick waving before us.

'I love you, my darling, you're beautiful,' he purred. 'You know I won't hurt you, but' – here his voice became a snake-like hiss – 'do as you're told, or I'll have to make you.'

I screamed and wriggled. 'He's touching me, he's hurting me.'

'I can't see anything,' said Mummy, holding me tight to stop me wriggling while the Erl-King came and came and came.

*

I was so taken up with myself, I didn't notice Simon had gone. He hadn't waited six weeks.

'Good,' said Oliver. 'Now we needn't bother with all that organic nonsense.'

Silence.

'We need the income, Olly,' said Amelia. 'We do forty veg boxes a week as well as meat and milk and the market and restaurants.'

'I have a better idea.' He grinned like a chimpanzee. 'Horses. Plenty of demand and more money.'

'But if we stop using the land for cattle,' said Toe, 'some farmer in Brazil will cut down rainforest to keep cattle and ship beef thousands of miles to Britain.'

'Toe.'

'Yes?'

'Stick to medicine. I'm not responsible for what some stupid little Brazilian peasant does.'

The group fell silent, till someone said Simon had taken the dog. Oliver was furious and lapsed into brooding and stroking his chin. Suddenly his eyes lit up.

'We'll have a swaling session to clear the old growth. I like a good burn.'

Amelia said, 'It's prohibited after the fifteenth of April, Olly.'

He snorted. 'What? Can't I do what I want on my own land? I'll have a word with someone I know.'

'It's not the Park Authority, Olly. It's Natural England.'

'Natural England. Who are they, for fuck's sake?'

A week later the cattle had gone and horses were in the fields. Three extra people would work on mailshotting, promoting courses, books, CDs and downloads.

*

Dear Stefanie,

We were utterly shocked by your letter. I know it's not your fault your mind has been filled with these ideas, but I am begging you please to look into your heart for the truth. You know I could never do such a thing, it goes against every tenet of my faith, and it breaks my heart that you could even think of it. Your mother has taken it badly, she is under close supervision by the doctor for her blood pressure, on very strong drugs, and I can't tell you how worried I am. Please think hard about what you are saying. We are devastated by your accusation, so much so that I've only now been able to take up a pen and reply.

Your mother and I are praying for you.

All our love in Christ Jesus,
Dad.

'I've never known a single perp own up straight off. You know what to do with the letter.'

I put a lighted match to the screwed-up letter in the pewter dish and gazed into Oliver's eyes as the flames danced, then recounted the Erl-King nightmare.

'I know what you're going through, chick. I was molested in the park when I was twelve. It sent me into a depression lasting four years, fucked me up, but' – he stretched out both arms sideways with upturned palms – 'what does not kill me makes me stronger. It made me devote my life to helping others. We must all build today's sandcastles from yesterday's sand. Tell him not to write again. Tell him you never want to see him again.'

'Cut him off?'

'Why would you not?'

'He's getting old.'

'What's that got to do with it?'

'I feel sorry for him, I think.'

The index fingers of his clasped hands on the desk pointed at me in a steeple and he rolled his eyes. 'Heaven preserve us. Right. See what the group think.'

The anger in the room was like a blast furnace. There was no dispute, only consensus: cut him off.

Toe said, 'I can't believe you'd contemplate talking to him.'

Rachel said, 'Don't bother replying. You were so sympathetic to my situation. Be kind to yourself for a change.'

'But I feel sorry for him.'

'I hate you, Daddy, don't leave me,' Oliver said with a sigh.

*

Rachel perched on the edge of the sofa and watched every twitch of my face like a guard dog.

'Sadie sends her love.' Gran gave the teapot another stir, replaced the tea cosy and poured. 'I've heard from your parents.' She sipped her tea and looked at me askance. 'Do you think your mother knew?'

'She's not very observant. Once she walked past me in the street.' I laughed, then grew serious. 'He blames her blood pressure on me. As if I were the perpetrator.'

Rachel grunted and stowed her chewing gum in the giant rush bag.

Gran offered cinnamon cakes freshly baked for our coming.

'She wants to see you, darling, on her own.'

'Does she blame me too?' I sneered.

'I wouldn't think so. She just doesn't want to be punished along with your father. She'll even drive down on her own. You know she always lets your father drive. That's how desperate she is.'

Rain lashed the windows. Rachel flicked her head.

'I'm going outside for a smoke, Gran,' I said.

Gran stared. The last cigarette she'd seen me with was before I had Sadie.

Round the side out of the rain, out of earshot, Rachel twirled her hair.

'Say no. She'll just try to persuade you you're wrong about the Academy.'

I lit up and inhaled furiously.

'It's not fair springing it on you. Everyone would say don't go. Tell your gran you'll let her know.'

A great tit sang its endless piercing 'Teacher, teacher, teacher, teacher' through the rain.

When we reappeared my fingers were trembling. 'I'll let

you know about Mum, Gran.'

She suggested duets, but I declined and made excuses to leave. Gran handed me an envelope containing a picture of me by Jack. I glanced at it, stuffed it back in the envelope and left.

44

Hilda looked out at field-grey clouds. The piano needed dusting. Stef and Lisa used to quarrel over polishing it and Hilda had to draw a halfway line in the dust. The ebony case never shone so brightly as it did then. Nor had Stef ever looked so displeased as she had just now at Jack's picture. Grasping at any comfort, Hilda played and sang Schubert's Litany For The Feast Of All Souls. Her voice faltered in the second verse but she played on, and in her head Papa's voice sang the words, of the false friend who deserted him, disowned him. In some way Stef had died too and she was powerless to bring her back. She could only hope Stef would hear the distant whisper of love. Against the softly rocking piano line, a slender thread of voice pleaded, come back.

She doubted Dan had done such a thing, but dared not say so. Poor Margaret, caught between husband and daughter. Her voice pleading with Hilda to mediate was frantic. Now Hilda herself was caught between daughter and granddaughter, her family disintegrating. John never wrote from Australia. His wife was the one who wrote. Too much *Weltschmerz. Die Stunden gehen, die Wunden stehen*, the hours go by, the wounds stay. If only Fred were here. If only she could believe in a god. Fred would say that one very faulty god was quite enough, thank you. Better to trust your instinct, listen to your heart. But we did listen to our hearts, Fred, we did, we did.

Afterwards she typed:

Papa was arrested. I asked Mama when he was coming home. She didn't know. After five weeks she found out he was in Sachsenhausen concentration camp. He sent letters once a month and a card at Christmas, censored, of course.

Mama never talked about it. Through the bedroom wall I heard her crying every night. Hanno missed Papa. I thought he would be re-educated and then come home. Six months after his arrest he was dead. I cried. I couldn't believe it. For all our differences, I knew in my heart that Papa loved me and I loved him. I became quiet, confused. One day Hanno and I arrived home from school to find Mama and Oma waiting with one suitcase each, packed. We could grab any last-minute things we wanted. I chose the hermit's picture, the letter from Hitler and the amber. Hanno chose his knife with the words Blut und Ehre, blood and honour, on the blade. We said nothing, not even to ask where we were going. She locked the front door and we took the tram to the station. No goodbyes. Was this how it was for Veronika? And Eva? And others?

The train journey was exhausting. When we boarded the boat higher than a house I was terrified. Hanno and I exchanged looks, but neither dared ask. Oma kept her head bent with her headscarf on and never made eye contact. Out at sea I exploded. 'I should have run away,' I spat at Mama on the boat to England. 'Tante Gudrun would have taken me in.' She didn't reply.

We lived on the outskirts of London and Mama found new piano pupils. I bitterly resented England. It was a year before I understood what I had left behind, what I had been, what I had done. My kind English teacher gradually showed me. I was horrified and couldn't bear to hear any more about it. From then on I did my utmost to be non-sporting, solitary and questioning. I refused to sing in school assembly. I resisted being roused against my wishes. We changed our surname from König to King, and Hanno became John, but I was stuck with Hilda. There were many Hildas in England, but it was too like my original name of Hilde, short for Hildegard. For years I insisted people call me Margaret. I learnt to speak English like a native. I didn't want anyone to know I was German. I wouldn't go out with Oma because she couldn't speak English.

When war broke out, people called us krauts and we had to bolt down the letterbox after someone threw in a petrol-soaked rag and a match which went out. The landlady downstairs was ostracised for housing us. Then we were to be interned. The police came for us and people lined the streets, shouting and throwing stones. A crowd of angry locals on the Isle of Man greeted the boat and tried to turn it away. In 1941 Hanno and I joined the British Army and Mama was released. I worked with the ambulance crew at the front. That was how I met Fred, born Friedrich Heinemann. In 1942 Hanno was allowed to fight in a tank regiment and Fred went to the swamps of the Far East where he contracted the bronchitis which eventually killed him in a London smog. Hanno came home with tales of comrades screaming in burning tanks. 'I am proud of you, Hänschen,' Mama said with a lump in her throat. Two years later he was killed. She never got over it. Every day when she put crumbs from the baker on the windowsill for the sparrows, as she had done in Berlin-Wilmersdorf, she said, 'Hanno loved to watch the sparrows come,' and Oma shook her head. But they never talked about Papa.

At the beginning of May 1945 I was home on leave and went with Mama to see James Cagney in *The Roaring Twenties*. We sat in the fourth row. The newsreel came on. It showed the liberation of Bergen-Belsen. People were crying, a woman fainted, and a man in the front row threw something at the screen. We couldn't stand it. We walked out, we never saw James Cagney. I couldn't look at Mama afterwards. If she asked anything I looked at my shoes and mumbled. I stayed in my room and I was glad to get back to the front. The pictures are still in my head. Bulldozers, heaps of corpses, skin and bone. Thousands strewn across the ground. An arm moving among them. The glazed eyes of the living. I cannot bear those pictures and yet I must. The big eyes. This was the country I had loved. I cannot bear it but I must. I see it now as clearly as then, the eyes staring at the camera, and I keep thinking of Papa. Papa could have been one of those nameless, hopeless creatures, with the empty eyes that said, Too late. You've rescued us, but you're too late. And I was a part of that.

45

A new crucifix hung at my mother's throat when Stick and I walked into the café.

'Do you mind if we sit outside?' I said.

'No. I could get the dog out of the car.'

'You brought Sally?'

'Your father doesn't like me travelling alone.'

I burst out laughing. 'And Sally looks so fierce.' The laughter died. *He* decided on all matters great and small.

We sat with our coffees on faded brown plastic chairs by the sea wall among the palms and yuccas, next to the four-feet-high plastic ice-cream cone. The sun shone on the distant sea. Screams came from Butlin's Chair-O-Plane.

My mother reappeared with the Barbour jacket fastened over her pleated woollen skirt, and the dog lumbered up to Stick.

'Oh. You're smoking.'

I blew out a trail of smoke.

'Sorry, I didn't introduce you. Stick – my mother.'

Stick smiled and stroked the dog. 'What a lovely dog.'

'I found her by the roadside, looking lost.'

'She's good at making you feel sorry for her.'

'Yes, I couldn't just leave her there.'

A cloud passed over the sun and we shivered.

'It's good of you to come all this way,' I said.

My mother smiled tentatively. 'I'm used to this journey.'

I bit a nail till it tore off. Stick twiddled with her pendant O and we each rolled another cigarette.

'Oh, I nearly forgot.' My mother took out a paper bag. 'I picked these this morning. You don't have strawberries where you are, do you?'

'We do. In a polytunnel and outdoors in the walled garden.'

'Oh. You don't want mine, then.'

'Yes, please. They smell lovely, thank you.' I sniffed, holding the cigarette at arm's length.

The dog nudged Stick's hand with its nose and she resumed the stroking. The dodgems bell sounded. Stick and I blew out smoke in tandem.

I went inside to order more coffee. My mother was smiling and talking to Stick like one of the waifs and strays she liked to gather in her missionary zeal.

'So.' I took a deep breath of sea air. My mother looked up. 'I know it's shocking not to notice what's going on in your own house, but I don't believe you knew. He was cunning.'

She stared. A steam train whistled and chuffed, about to depart. Stick stroked the dog more vigorously.

'We were devastated,' said my mother.

I prickled and Stick shot me an anxious glance.

'You don't believe me.'

'It's not that...'

'You'd rather believe him.'

'It's just that... How come you have this idea after all these years?'

'I repressed the memory.'

'But... when did he do it, and where?'

'I'm not sure yet, but I know something happened. I can feel it, and I trust my feelings. My feelings are my truth.' Across the channel the Welsh coast was garish yellow with rape fields. In a moment of inspiration I said, 'It was in a field where he used to take me. Just me, not Lisa. Regularly.'

My mother's lips quivered. 'Darling, please don't cut us off. I can't bear it. It's killing your father.'

'I'm not cutting you off, only him.' I spat out the last word.

Stick's bony knee nudged my thigh. 'I can't believe this. You don't believe your own daughter.'

'Okay.' My mother bit her lip. 'May I come again?'

'Of course.' But not if you take that attitude, I nearly added.

Sally got a warmer goodbye than my mother. The two forlorn figures trailed to the road.

I said, 'And God said, Let there be guilt. And there was guilt. And God saw the fucking guilt, that it was good.'

*

There it was again, the chirp of a grasshopper or cricket, a whirring like a fishing line being reeled in. Impossible. It was only May, too early. Everything was early after the spring heat wave, but still... I couldn't identify it. I scurried along the old byway. The first whortleberry plants poked through the grass and the gorse as ever was flowering. I followed the sound. The insect was a ventriloquist – this bush, that bush. I didn't know why I was following it, except that I was angry with my mother and it reminded me of *him*. That fucking bastard had taught me so well to distinguish the species, and now I knew why. Let's go hunting for the field cricket, Stefanie. A cuckoo called across the goyle, the heather was alive with twittering birds and a stonechat perched on a bush and chuck-chucked. The grasshopper was always ahead, leading me on. The cloud-shadow on the moor hurried off like a curtain being drawn back and the sun lit up the grass. But behind and alongside, charcoal-grey clouds were coming. Back there, rain smudged the moor. I stumbled onwards, compelled by the chirping, the memory of what he did.

Ahead of me was the sorcerer: a grasshopper warbler on a gorse bush. Its whole body shook as it sang. As soon as I spotted the bird it flew off. I had walked for hours and had no idea where I was. Apart from a few stunted birches that had lost their silver, it was endless moor, and now rain. Clouds raced past and visibility was only a couple of metres. Rain ran off my cagoule in rivulets, stung the eyes and blotted out the way ahead. I didn't care what Oliver said about not being on our own, I had to walk through my anger, exorcise that man.

My mother had upset me, as had Jack's picture with the wonky egg-shaped head, arms with giant hands coming from the head, triangle dress, and stick legs with shoes like three-petalled flowers. A yellow sun with rays beamed from one corner and in the other was a yellow moon. And above the big curved smile like a tiny toothbrush moustache were two pink strokes side by side: 'Don't tell,' said the angel. In a hollow was a colossal old beech with branches outstretched, trunk wrinkled like an elephant. What did Simon say? A prayer said under a beech tree rises straight to heaven. I stood underneath, utterly miserable. The cold and wet had soaked through to the skin. 'Please God get him out of my life.' Hunger gnawed. Rain dripped through the pale green foliage onto a large puddle, but inside my jacket I rolled up and lit a cigarette. As I puffed, the drips plop-plopped and they played a tune. My heart leapt. It was the tune of Love is a Flood – my song. Whatever my father had done, I had this gift from Oliver, and from all of my friends at the Academy.

Rain leaked through my collar, and my jeans and boots were awash. I shivered and set off again, singing my song. The cold hand of the Erl-King clasped my neck. Thick mist skulked past and muffled his voice. I had no idea where I was heading.

When it grew dark, a dim light shone ahead, held by a dusky little figure. I shouted and ran towards it, but every time I got near, it moved away. Surely the person must hear? But he or she kept veering off like the grasshopper warbler as if to tease. The ground was all hummocks and hollows and pools, barely visible. I tested the hummocks for weight-bearing, but the water on my eyes tricked me and my feet sank in black water. Deeper and deeper in I went with sluggish steps, I stumbled with hands outstretched and the Erl-King was getting me, the mire was sucking me in, making me a part of itself. The black slime fondled my bare legs, slithered higher and higher. Panic! No one would find me, I would sink and sink and be found a thousand years later, my body and the black cagoule with the Diamond logo perfectly preserved. My cries were lost in the mist and the Erl-King murmured, 'You are mine, mine.' Shapes loomed up and vanished. A big black St Mark's fly with dangling legs landed on my face. I was as helpless as a cast sheep.

*

Voices clamoured while I stood in the middle, shame-faced. I hardly remembered them coming, whether the shouts had been my own or others', yelling and screeching in the mist as they were yelling and screeching now.

'What if we hadn't found you?' said Toe with Captain Mainwaring glare.

I explained about the grasshopper warbler in a small, high-pitched voice. 'It made me think of my father.'

'All the more reason not to go off alone.'

'Attention-seeking,' said Melanie. 'We should have left you to it.'

The chorus jeered, brickbats flew, I stopped defending myself. It was all deserved. Oliver ended the hue and cry.

'Eff, if it weren't for your recent trauma, I'd be furious. Don't ever do that again. You are hard work.' He ran a hand through his hair. 'I think we all need a joke after that. If you see a conductor and a violist on the road, which do you run over first?' He beamed. Everyone looked baffled. 'The conductor, because work comes before pleasure.'

The chuckles filled the room like a henhouse with a fox.

*

The grey stuff had all sunk to the bottom of the clouds like a baby considering birth. Oliver said there would be no one on Lynmouth beach at that time of day and Oliver was right. A lazy sea slurped at the shore and a haze greyed out the headland. The gritty grey-brown sand trickled between our toes. Fifteen adults and five children stripped off behind great megaliths encrusted with black and orange lichen at the far end of the beach beneath towering cliffs, draping our clothes over the rocks. I changed into my costume and turned. Everyone else was naked. They stared at me, some giggled and they gathered round. With difficulty I averted my eyes from all the genitals.

'Do you have a problem with nudity?' said Oliver.

I kept my eyes fixed on his face, feeling the fire in my own. Angry clouds loitered.

'I don't mind what other people do,' I lied.

'We feel uncomfortable with you wearing a costume when no one else is,' said Oliver.

There were murmurs of agreement.

'But what if someone comes?'

'You can see them coming a quarter of a mile off.'

'But I don't know why anyone would have a problem with me wearing a costume.'

Amelia said, 'You're the one with the problem, not us. You're making us feel bad.'

'I don't mean to.'

My love of the sea dwindled.

Oliver said, 'Eff, for fuck's sake stop being a diva. You're as bad as Graham. Just take it off.'

The clouds were marching across the Bristol Channel. The children left the circle and chased each other. Slowly, head bowed, I stripped off and stood with the sag bag of flab hanging below the waist.

'So that's what it's all about. I think we'll have a little round-up about Eff's stretch marks.'

To my horror there followed a dissection of the hated silver scars.

Oliver, the last in the round-up, said, 'You're being ridiculous, Eff. Nobody cares if your scars look like a map of a floodplain. Half the people here can't see without their contacts anyway. Right. Chase you all to the sea.'

We raced en masse, shrieking, down to the water's edge. He pinched first Stick's and then Craig's backside to squeals of laughter. In the water he grabbed Melanie's breast. Nobody minded. The water was cold: only June and this was nearly the Atlantic. But for me any covering was welcome.

*

Trr, trr, trr, trr, trr. It must have been hot that day, because the short-winged conehead's chirp was pitched high, bursts of crystal alongside where we lay. Daddy had put centaury flowers in my hair, tiny pink stars with yellow stamens like panting tongues, and made a chain from open-hearted buttercups which his big rough hands hung round my neck. The cricket hesitated, just the odd trr, then stopped. The black eye on the side of its head was agog. Fellow coneheads chirped like high-pitched engines ticking over in the stillness, but quietly.

From the ditches came the crescendo of common green grasshoppers like football rattlers. The male grasshopper wooed his female for a fortnight before she yielded. Too much zeal and she would kick out.

Louder than any, the great green bush-crickets sang like a room full of shrill printers. Who else could sing for three minutes without stopping, and when they did stop, only for a second?

Faster and faster they all sang, sawing, purring, ticking, trilling. I floated among the thistle seeds above my body and watched with disinterest as Daddy pierced me. The Titian-red dress was round my waist and my pants were impaled on a grass stalk. He gasped, his lips moved but made no sound. Only the crickets were loud. I lay impassive, letting him use me.

The sun glared and the crickets notched up their chirping frequency. Daddy's gasps turned to grunts as if he were in pain, grunty-grunts. He stopped and his heaviness slumped on top. A grass spike tickled my leg. The conehead resumed its purring as if nothing could interrupt its serenade, this glorious sun would shine forever.

'You're beautiful, Eff,' he murmured.

No! This was not Daddy. Daddy called me Stefanie. This was Pete and he had razor-short sandy hair and brown spaniel eyes and tasted of envelope gum and his collarbones stuck out like the bony haunches of a cow. He rolled onto his back, flinging out arms and legs and unwittingly crushing the little noisemaker. The grass curled over us like a nest. It smelt like new hay. My tongue lay in my mouth like a frozen sparrow. I had wanted to make love in this field, enjoyed it to begin with. Then I went limp, as dead as the dried-up cowslip flowers that clung to their stalks. It felt like rape. I was dirty and disgusting, a discarded condom. I used to be good at sex. This must be my punishment. Daddy hated punishing me, it hurt him more than it hurt me, but he had to do it because he loved me. Had-to, had-to, had-to, had-to. Pete picked the grass seeds out of my hair.

'It's all right,' he said.

He was lying, it was not all right. I twirled and twirled a blade of grass round forefingers and snapped. A tiny beetle gripped the top of a swaying stalk, wobbled and spread its wings, but hung on. The crickets stepped up their pace, in requiem for their dying fellow.

*

'Why subject yourself to this torture, Eff? She feels guilty about farming you out when you were a child. Why see her again?'

I bit a nail, which tore below the quick.

'No doubt your grandmother tried to persuade you.'

'No.'

He tapped a tattoo on the desk with both hands, beginning with the little fingers. 'What shall we do about these flashbacks?'

What we did was black satin and Floris Santal and late-night blues music, and the walls hummed like the grass with a thousand strumming forewings, but Oliver's smooth fingers stroked my arm while Pete and I coupled and the fondant voice eased away my fears. Pete's skin glowed orange from the wall light as he filled me with song, and Oliver's grunts punctuated Pete's final strangulated gasp.

Next day after sheep-shearing we did the symphony of emotions. Pete was joy and I was distress. He grinned, held my hand and uttered yelps and gasps while I let out the raging in my head, whistling, crackling, banging, yowling, neurons firing like a box of fireworks with a lighted match thrown in.

That night in Pete's bed I thought of cool black satin and blues music.

'You never tell me what you're feeling, Eff.'

'I don't know what I'm feeling.' Feelings? I wasn't sure I had any – a desire for revenge, fear of my own unpredictability or just hatred that had grown unseen like a violet in undergrowth. All winnowed away. I detected nothing. I was conscious of those things sometimes, but more often I was blank. Or confused, or something. Feelings? How could I distinguish feelings amongst the tangled heap of mixed-up things, when love and hate were forever indissolubly mingled? Anyone who proclaimed love must be viewed with suspicion.

Pete stiffened. 'You can cry, you know. Or is it too big a grief?'

Too big a grief? Grief? As I considered, my eyes brimmed.

'It's as if you were waiting for my permission to cry.'

Not as if – it was exactly that. I no longer knew how to behave, what I should think and feel or what I did think and feel. I was an emotional magpie, stealing pieces of sentiment from others, except that they had to tell me which pieces glittered.

*

Claire stood in a flared black skirt with bold yellow flowers in the middle of the circle and blushed as scarlet as her painted nails.

'What if I want to keep it?'

The group sighed.

'Do you really think you're ready?' said Oliver. 'You're still a child yourself.'

'But I'm thirty-seven. This could be my last...'

'Let's hear from someone who's been a parent.'

I talked about sleepless nights and crying. 'You'd do a better job than your parents, but would it be good enough?'

Donna curled her toes and said, 'Hm. You probably need to resolve your own issues first.'

'You two didn't.'

Oliver said, 'They're a bit more ahead in the game than you are, Claire. They're not invisible. Is that why you want to be pregnant? So you'll be noticed?'

Claire's face puckered.

'Who's the father?'

Claire was tight-lipped.

Oliver groaned. 'How do you expect us to help if you don't tell us everything? We're not doing this out of some prurient interest in your sex life.'

A guessing game followed. Claire frowned at the carpet.

'It was Ian, wasn't it? I knew it.'

Ian was the father of two children living in the village. He had a partner who, Oliver once declared, was a camel burdened by the traditions of a thousand years.

Tears flowed from the shifting eyes. Oliver moved onto one half of his voluminous cushion and patted the other half. She sat on it and he put an arm round her shoulder and took her hand.

'Listen, you wouldn't want a child when you're not ready, would you? You have to think of the child, not what *you* want. You've been such a good little worker and made prodigious progress in your spiritual growth. I'd hate to jeopardise that.'

Claire wailed. Oliver clasped her tighter.

'I know, I know, you're the last person this should happen to. You've led a truthful existence. You've been a real lion. Of course it's not my style to tell you what to do, but you heard what everyone thinks.' He reached behind and pulled a tissue from a box. 'Dry your eyes now, you've got a pretty face normally, and a good figure. Heaven forfend that you should get a belly like Eff's.'

Claire blew her nose. Oliver patted her knee.

'Good girl. We'll make arrangements this afternoon. Go

back to your place now.'

She stood up and rejoined the circle, and the skirt ballooned and fell back like a flapping spinnaker.

*

'You're all slugs this morning. Let's have some energy for our visitors' sake. Follow me.' Limping with long, gangling stride and clapping hands, Oliver set off round the music room, shouting, 'How much wood would a woodchuck chuck if a woodchuck could chuck wood?'

In a circle we clapped and stamped and chanted, faster and faster, tripping up on the words and giggling, including the five new people.

'How much wood?' shouted Oliver, shoving Meredith in front of him.

She hit the floor with arms outstretched and sat nursing her arm.

'I think I've broken my wrist.'

'Meredith's being a drama queen,' Oliver said and carried on.

She left.

Oliver clapped hands above his head and strode round screaming, 'How much wood would a woodchuck chuck if a woodchuck could chuck wood?' The voices bounced off the oak panelling, rubbish words half-wrong, shrieking as if this were the most important question in their lives.

At last we sat on cushions in a semicircle, eighteen of us. Oliver sat tall with legs apart on the piano stool, hands on thighs.

'Claire.'

Claire stood and sang Somewhere Over The Rainbow. The fine swirls of the piano's walnut case were not matched by its tone: some notes had slipped below concert pitch again.

But the real surprise was Claire. From the mouth of this soft-spoken woman, this mouse, came a flood of bel canto so plaintive I had tears. The rest, apart from the newcomers, stared into space with parkinsonian masks.

'Well done, Claire.' He played top F. 'Now sing on this note, 'Oliver loves and cares for me.'' Claire sang the words. 'Never mind about making a nice sound, put some feeling into it. Scream.'

And scream she did. Harsh overtones belched forth from sweet-voiced Claire. I glanced round anxiously. Nodules could permanently damage the vocal folds, but no one else reacted. After several bouts of screaming herself hoarse, Claire sat down. I sat motionless with shock.

'The angel's in the marble, Eff,' Oliver said to me. 'Fear not, the virtue of my methods will be revealed at tomorrow's performance.' Others laughed. 'Donna.'

Donna sang Let My People Go.

Oliver surveyed her. 'Fetch the bat.'

From upstairs she fetched the baseball bat and put her cushion by the piano. 'What shall I say?'

'Let me go.'

She whacked the cushion on each word and Oliver told her to shout louder each time, then put the bat away. Upon his instruction Neil and Pete one either side took an arm and pulled while Toe grabbed her crotch from behind. Donna screamed 'Let me go' over and over and thrashed from side to side. The three men smiled. Oliver watched solemn-faced.

'Right. You three sit down.' Oliver played top F without looking at her. ''I am not a dog.''

Donna screamed on one note, 'I am not a dog.'

'Louder.'

Oliver kept his finger and eyes on the piano while Donna screeched like a howler monkey, over and over.

'Keep going.'

I stiffened and looked round to see if others were cringing, but they were unmoved, except for two of the new people, a man and a woman.

When Donna sat down these two stood up.

'I'm not putting up with this any longer,' said the man, whom Oliver had introduced as 'a property speculator and therefore capable of earning an infinite amount of money.' 'This is supposed to be a voice workshop, not some twisted psycho screaming workshop.'

They stomped to the door, put on shoes and left.

'Now we've sorted the sheep from the goats we can get on. Rachel.'

Rachel started singing Schubert's Ave Maria.

He interrupted. 'It's in bloody Latin. Sing something normal. Sing All By Myself.'

She sang it beautifully, but then followed the mandatory screaming on top F to the words 'Fuck off, you fucking fucker'.

'Don't sing it, yell. Let's have some commitment.'

I clapped hands over ears to shut out the dissonant overtones. And the language. Coming from Rachel's mouth, sunny Rachel who smiled even when the sky didn't, Rachel with the angelic voice that turned heads and softened hearts. For eight years I had sat next to her in choir, and she might moan about Janet's smelly crimplene dress or the harsh demands of the musical director, but there were none of these obscenities.

'Eff.'

I leapt up and sang O Lord, Whose Mercies Numberless. An uncomfortable silence followed.

'Are you religious, Eff?'

'No.'

He searched my face. 'Well, that's good, then.' The room breathed a sigh of relief and he played five notes up and back down. 'Sing that to 'la'.'

I complied and Oliver played the beginning note one higher. After I reached my top note, I hesitated and he repeated the next beginning note.

'It might strain my voice.' I bit at a nail, forgetting about the false nails glued on to stop the habit.

'Rachel, tell Eff I've done this workshop for years and no one has suffered damage.'

'It's true.'

Others nodded.

'But if I'm tense—'

'For fuck's sake, Eff, I've told you it won't.'

He flicked his arm in an angry gesture and his watch flew off across the room. He played the note again. I sang, rising to a hoarse squeak. We started one note higher and I uttered two hoarse squeaks at the top, and more, till we came down the scale again. My shoulders relaxed, but as soon as I got down, Oliver hit C above middle C and told me to scream as loudly as possible 'My wounded soul'. The screeched words sounded like some creature of the night facing a horrible death, and silence reigned in the moments between screams. Oliver kept one finger on the piano and now faced me with a hypnotic stare while he ascended the scale one note at a time, and I just kept on screaming myself hoarse. There were rasps and scratches, then nothing. My voice had cracked.

'Well done, Effi.' Oliver's face relaxed into a weak smile. 'I shall call you Effi from now on.'

I beamed and returned to my place in the semicircle of approving faces.

When we finished with Amazing Grace, no sound emerged from my mouth.

*

I prodded a chicken skin flap, shocked and worried my voice was wrecked forever. Claire and Rachel too were hoarse. After so much screaming from everybody, I was in shock. Too much pain in one room. I kept my head down, hoping no one would talk to me, twirled a chicken morsel in a gravy pool and watched the swirls of brown liquid, the channels where the gravy rushed in to fill up to the level. Like looking through a window at people laughing and chatting, merry people, together people, in each others' lives, not in my life, feeling a groundswell of loneliness, and when I left the table I took the window with me, saw everything through the window. Others liked me, but they were always others. They could not get in and I could not get out. My father had ruined my life in so many ways. That evening I mimed the singing round the bonfire.

But next morning a growl emerged, a strange, weak, low voice I had never heard before, from deep down in the belly. I balked at the Sunday afternoon performance. Sitting in the front row of chairs in his bottle-green brocade frock-coat, Oliver waved a hand impatiently.

'Just do it.'

I glanced at Pete and Rachel, but they stared into space. I stepped forwards, sang in the alien voice which had no power, then looked round, as embarrassed as a laryngectomee with a new prosthesis. The audience clapped and Pete smiled, as if no one had noticed the weird sound. I sat down, relieved and elated.

'I feel as if my voice has grown up,' I told Pete afterwards.

46

Berlin was hot. The Gestapo headquarters at Prinz-Albrecht-Straße 8 had been bombed away, but Hilda remembered the grandiose portal topped by statues and approached by wide stone steps. The green vans pulled up and disgorged their victims through the door, so-called criminals and enemies of the people. All that remained was part of a basement wall. At first she was lulled into nostalgia by blown-up photos of the Weimar Republic, splendid turn-of-the-century buildings, old trams, people in their Sunday best, the Romanisches Café with its high vaulted ceiling where Papa went. Her pleasure vanished on seeing the remains of cells, white-tiled from floor to ceiling. Where Papa went.

The public humiliations had started straightaway and became regular entertainment. 'I was a betrayer and bloodsucker,' said one placard round a man's neck. 'I am expelled from the people's community.' 'I defiled a Christian girl.' 'I voted no.' 'I forbade the pupils to say Heil Hitler.' In one photo a woman sat on a chair on a platform in the marketplace and was shorn bald. Thousands watched. Some grinned sheepishly, some laughed, some strained to see over the heads. On every face was mockery. Not one showed sympathy. A man in the front row smiled serenely. The SS guards were bad enough, but the smug faces were worse. I was there too, thought Hilda, mocking, feeling the ripple of Schadenfreude, marching with the processions and laughing. Afraid it might be me that was humiliated, thought un-German. First dancing bears, then people. A photo showed a man with a large placard round his neck riding on an ox, and children and adults walking alongside. Most were not looking at him. They stepped out proudly and chatted with excitement. The solidarity of it all. The children swung their arms and stepped out in time with the SA men. Hilda was part of that. It could have been Papa on the ox. After Papa was arrested, she and Hanno were ostracised. Inge made excuses to avoid her, girls in class sharpened their tongues or whispered and turned their heads to glance at her. But these were trivialities compared with the suffering and death of millions now on display. She knew some of it from the Belsen-Bergen film, but now it exploded into her face with the full horror.

The gypsies, Roma and Sinti, who disappeared from Berlin streets before the Olympics, were installed in a camp outside the city. How civilised it sounded: the government had given them their own city. And how easy to deport them from there to misery and murder. Here they were with their families, harming no one, while staff of the Office for Combating the Gypsy Problem posed on the stairs with swastika-themed railings in chillingly self-righteous formation. Gypsies, Jews, homosexuals, asocials, habitual criminals, socialists, communists, Jehovah's Witnesses and anyone who criticised the regime – there was no end to the number of enemies of the people. In one set of photos eleven men were marched to a long gallows with eleven nooses; lined up; stood on one long board while nooses were put on; the board was kicked away. One young man was too light, so a helper pulled on his ankles to tighten the rope. The crowd watched. Always the crowd. A girl of about Hilda's age gawped. In another photo a group of Latvian Jewish women and children had their backs to the trench on the edge of which they stood, waiting to be shot, and further up the body-filled trench, an officer pushed down those who had not fallen in properly. In this one event two thousand seven hundred and forty-six died. The pictures went on: Jewish people were marched in their thousands through towns to the camps and gassed, Polish people were marched into the woods and shot. Endless photos. Sick photos. She had to force herself to look and read. And then the guards from Auschwitz. They laughed, they sang along to an accordion in their idyllic mountain retreat, they sat with wine bottles. Rest and recuperation from mass murder. Every moment of pleasure in the Jungmädel was echoed by the smiles and laughter of those SS faces.

Himmler was there, the neat, mild-mannered man with smooth skin whom she and cousin Ada drooled over at the Richtfest, who said the SS's greatest achievement was to see thousands of corpses lying side by side, to cope with this and, except for cases of human weakness, to remain decent. Himmler, who said he loathed brutality.

A six-year-old epileptic girl stared out with big appealing eyes like Jack's. She was taken away, diagnosed with idiocy and murdered. She and hundreds of thousands like her. In another photo the selected patients queued up by the bus with blanked-out windows to be ticked off the list by men in white coats. Otto...

Nauseated, her resolve to stay and see everything was broken. She retreated to the cobbled streets of the Nikolaiviertel, pink and cream-painted buildings with leaf and flower scrolls, mansard roofs and shuttered ground-floor windows, lindens and old-fashioned lampposts. A fairy-tale reconstruction, nicefied like the witch's house in Hänsel and Gretel. Like Hilda's life, the cracks covered with sweets and gingerbread. She sat and drank water in the blistering heat. A woman sang the Bach-Gounod Ave Maria accompanied by a guitar in front of the Nikolaikirche. She shouldn't sing so beautifully, after such horror. Hilda took comfort in the knowledge that many resisted, many hid Jewish people, many more dissented in their hearts. But Hilda did not resist. Oh no. Hilda welcomed the new regime and invented reasons why Herta's father drowned himself in the Havel, why the girl who didn't shout at the Jewish family in the Grunewald forest left, why the hermit was not there, why Eva and Veronika left without saying goodbye, why Jewish people and gypsies and homosexuals and communists and objectors were enemies of the people. Why Papa was an enemy of the people. Those who were not with them were against them.

She sat beneath a maple to listen and confront her guilt. It started small, and then after you'd done one bad thing, it became easier to do another, or a worse one. She identified with the perpetrators. *I* marched alongside the man on the ox, she thought. *I* swung my arms and stepped out and chatted and laughed. *I* sniggered at the woman shorn bald in the marketplace. I was one of the thousands. How I laughed at such a sight because it wasn't me. *I* brushed gypsies off the streets, out of sight, out of life. They were not worthy of life. *I* burned down synagogues and shoved and whipped, *I* trod on the necks of those too old to walk, *I* shot the man with the shock of black hair and death in his face as he knelt at the edge of the pit full of jumbled zigzag bodies. *I* disinfected our country to make way for decent people. *I* condemned the naked six-year-old girl clasping her hands and looking at the camera with her head cocked on one side, *I* diagnosed idiocy and sent her off to be stubbed out, a useless eater, ballast, life unworthy of life, she would never contribute to the people's community, her death was a blessing. I did it out of compassion. *I* consigned Otto to an institution, he was not a contributor, *I* killed Otto. *I* cleaned the streets of beggars, more useless eaters, locked them up to stop them sponging. *I* beat and tortured homosexuals, tortured them to death for their vile acts. *I* persuaded myself we were doing a good thing, a right thing. And *I* took a break from mass murder for some well-earned rest, I ate and drank and laughed and made music. How I laughed, how I sang as I inhaled the fresh river air in the mountain retreat before getting back to the hard labour of choosing who to keep and who to gas.

Ora pro nobis, sang the woman in the Nikolaiviertel, pray for us sinners now and in the hour of our death. While Papa underwent who knew what torture in those sterile, easy-to-clean basement cells, Hilda danced her heart out in the Olympic Youth spectacle for all the world to see how wonderful was the new Germany.

*

Arbeit macht frei, Work sets you free, said the words in the wrought-iron gate beneath the clock tower of Sachsenhausen concentration camp. She passed through, leaving behind the smell of pines, the yellow butterfly. Most barracks were razed to the ground. The sun beat down, but the eeriness of the barren site seeped into the bones like an icy wind. In the roll-call area before her, men stood for hours in freezing temperatures, all night after Kristallnacht while ill-clad comrades collapsed all round them, dead or dying. No help allowed. A machine gun overlooked the whole area and a hole in the ground served for Christmas tree or gallows. Prisoners were made to file past hanged comrades and forbidden to look away. Surely Papa could not have looked away?

The signs on the strip next to the 300-volt fence said, Neutral zone: prisoners will be shot immediately without warning. The bodies of suicides were left for all to see. She pictured Papa launching himself against the fence and snagging on the barbed wire or crumpling to the ground where he remained as an example.

The first barracks had two wings designed for one hundred and forty-six prisoners, but ended up with four hundred. In the middle were rows of toilets and foot-washing sinks and two huge round basins with fountains, with only a few minutes to use them between wake-up and roll-call, clambering over the newly dead laid out in the washroom overnight. The lives of different prisoners were displayed: politicals, Jehovah's witnesses, Confessional Church members, homosexuals, habitual criminals, Jews, foreign slave labourers, asocials. Asocials were Jewish/Aryan engaged couples, work-shy, beggars, gypsies, vagrants, pimps, or anyone to whom some SS officer took a dislike. Photos showed them growing up, living happily with their families, then reduced to a number, a thing documented in meticulous detail. A registration card showed: height 169 cm, build slim, face narrow, eyes grey-green, nose convex, mouth curved, ears curved, teeth complete, hair dark brown, language German. Endless lists of names, lists of money and valuables taken from exterminated Jewish people for the Greater German Reich, lists of executed prisoners of war, lists of trains with origin, date and place of arrival, number of passengers and number killed, numbers of Jewish people in each territory, ad nauseam, such efficiency, detracting from the fact of murder. The letterhead on a prisoner's letter stated that prisoners may receive and send two letters or postcards a month, incoming letters must not have more than four pages of fifteen lines each and must be clear and easy to read, money may be sent only by postal order, and food packages may be received at any time and in any quantity. So reasonable and orderly, if overfastidious, showing the outside world what a good thing we were doing, showing us what a right thing we were doing. But films of survivors' drawings and descriptions of the brickworks, the most feared work detail, showed the torture, bent and weary figures, not yet dead, who did everything with hammers, shovels or bare hands, with minimal food and clothing, while guards whipped, kicked, punched or trod on the necks of any who struggled to carry cement or pull a barrow of bricks to which they were harnessed like horses. Extermination through hard labour. Behind the column returning from the brickworks came the corpse cart, heaped up. Hunger, poor hygiene and illness killed thousands within months. Normal departure, the SS called it. Hunger drove prisoners to rummage through refuse or steal, under penalty of hanging. Those not sent out to work were assigned to so-called standing units, forced to stand in thin clothes in subzero temperatures. Many died of cold. Many suffered amputations for frostbite. Six thousand Jewish men arrested after Kristallnacht had to shovel snow with bare hands, but the amputations were performed secretly by prisoner auxiliaries because Jews were not allowed in the infirmary. 'For Jews I only issue death certificates,' declared the camp doctor. Horrendous beatings were carried out in public with a baton or bull's pizzle on the back and backside while the victim was strapped over a wooden block.

Hilda stumbled to the door and sank onto a concrete bench outside, panting. Any hopes of finding traces of what Papa endured were more than fulfilled. Did she want the brutal details? But he and millions more had no voice and they deserved to be heard. The murdered could not be unmurdered, but they must be heard. One survivor said he just wanted to tell his story, but each time his family said, 'Oh, there he goes again with his concentration camp.' Next to the bench were the holes for hanging posts. For eating or smoking or loitering at work or other minor breaches or to extract confessions of intimacy between inmates, the prisoner's hands were tied behind his back, then he was hoisted up by the wrists and left hanging and screaming until the shoulders dislocated, or until he died. She moved on, sickened. Papa could have died from any of these treatments. In the middle of the site two ash trees whispered.

In the former prisoners' kitchen was a Hohner mouth organ like the one Papa gave her, and the book of songs they sang to raise their spirits, like a danse macabre among the instruments of torture and murder. 'Let our songs ring out for joy,' went the Sachsenhausen camp song, 'after the darkness comes happiness.' She imagined Papa singing to fellow prisoners and being caught and made to sing while he struggled to pull the brick-cart to which he was harnessed. On the wall a blown-up photo showed a group of officers surrounding a man kneeling and bent over with his face close to a boot. They stood with hands on hips or arms folded and the Kommandant laughed. The wooden block for the beatings was in the middle of the room, with a foothold in which the victim's feet were locked. He had to count out the blows in German, usually twenty-five. If he miscounted, he must start again from the beginning. If he passed out, it carried on. Anyone averting their eyes was dragged out and whipped as well. Sometimes they were carted off and never seen again. Was this how Papa died? 'He never betrayed anyone,' Mama told a friend after his death. 'He preferred to die.' Hilda moved from one exhibit to another – the gallows, the corpse sledge, the neck-shot facility disguised as a height-measuring rod, with a slit that lined up with a slit in the wall. Men in white coats stood by, while behind the wall a guard shot into the neck. More than ten thousand Soviet prisoners of war were killed this way in ten weeks. Orchestral music at full volume drowned out the shots. Outside the execution building they queued up, unknowing.

A photo showed a sign on the barracks. 'There is a way to freedom,' it read. 'Its milestones are: obedience, hard work, honesty, order, cleanliness, sobriety, truthfulness, self-sacrifice and love of one's country.' Guards pointed to the ovens and joked, 'There is a way to freedom, but only through this chimney.' When the crematoria were busy, the stench spread over the camp and beyond, and thick flakes of soot floated down onto clothes, hands and faces. And Hilda was part of all that.

She told herself the terror worsened in time, it was less terrible when Papa was there, and some prisoners were even released. A man in the flat above had returned from Sachsenhausen, subdued and with one arm hanging loose. She moved on to the computers and read of torture and mass murder. With their ludicrous racial theories they made rubber face masks and casts of Roma and Sinti heads and took blood samples. Dr Friedrich Mennecke came to select the sick in mind and body, the unworthy of life, who believed they were being transferred to Dachau for light work in herb plantations, not to Sonnenstein for gassing. A letter from Dr Mennecke to his wife said another hard day's work was over and he was sitting alone in his hotel and had just had cod and boiled potatoes with mustard sauce and half a bottle of 1934 Crettnacher Eucharienberg, and the work had gone quite fast, he had done thirty-four out of sixty-eight residents... A telegram from the Kommandant informed a widow that her husband died of pleurisy. How to survive: be invisible. Don't witness SS violence, don't address a guard by the wrong title, don't look away during hangings or beatings, don't be tall, don't be short, don't have gold-rimmed spectacles, don't show gold teeth, don't move near the window in the barracks at night, don't talk to Jews. Papa couldn't even talk to his friend Anton, if he was still there.

An old man on video spoke of hunger: Hunger, terrible hunger, he kept repeating and stared at the camera with big watery eyes, hunger, unbearable hunger. Another spoke of the savage beatings on the block, how the blood spurted out and the flesh was ripped apart, then the whole camp had to file past the victim. 'Blood and flesh,' he said over and over in a strangled voice. 'Blood and flesh, blood and flesh.' Years after liberation, in their minds they were still prisoners, couldn't cope with freedom. They were speaking out now, but they never wanted to speak about it again, ever. After the darkness came no happiness.

She staggered out into the sunshine. The ash trees whispered their taut tremolos into the emptiness. So quiet, no shouting or screaming or beating or shooting. The dead were shouting, but the words were lost in the ether. 'Your father has done something wrong,' Gisela had said. 'He'll learn his lesson and come back reformed.' The long, hollow tones petered out, guttered into silence.

She skipped half of the camp and cut across to the Soviet monument at the centre of the site. It bore eighteen red triangles, like those worn by the political prisoners, which included Papa. But for the homosexuals, Jews, Roma, Sinti, Jehovah's Witnesses, habitual criminals, asocials and foreign slave labourers, who all died by the thousand in this place, there was no commemoration at all. A hooded crow strutted nearby. Somewhere a lark sang in a reedy voice.

The pathology building had two autopsy tables covered in white tiles, neat and sterile like the Gestapo's basement cells, and the walls were tiled to head height. All cleaned up now, before visitors came. The bodies were moved down a ramp into the basement to be stacked up to the vaulted ceiling. It wasn't built while Papa was here, but she saw him lying on a tiled table, his back ripped, blood spurting out and splashing the wall tiles while he sang Dein Ist Mein Ganzes Herz, looking her in the eye through cracked round glasses. As the body count rose, there was only time to cut them open and stitch them up again, and on the wall was posted a list of seven possible causes of death to choose from.

After the Nazis, the Soviets found twenty tonnes of ashes in the pit of the crematoria, and more tipped into the Hohenzollern Canal. And six suitcases full of dentures. Then they continued using the camp themselves for five years and another twelve thousand died.

For seventy-five years Hilda had wondered what Papa suffered, how he died. There was more to see, a sickening more, but she left it. The dark chords of this place would haunt her for the rest of her days. Like a failed sonata it was full of wrong notes, sharp, biting notes that confounded all the euphoria of the people's community. Blood and flesh, blood and flesh.

*

The spider plant on the dining-room windowsill back home had two new babies. The carriage clock uttered four ticks a second. Cars went by. Life went on, but guilt remained like a termite city, a labyrinth of underground tunnels and rooms, dark gardens where fungi were grown, storerooms for fermented fungi, nurseries where the young were fed, where millions of termites laboured in the dark and came out at night via exit holes on the edge of the city. They kept the whole structure at a temperature of between thirty and thirty-one degrees Celsius by building a giant cooling tower from a soil and saliva mixture, with flues and galleries and pores to exchange the stale, warm air for fresh, cool air. Such was Hilda's inner world: teeming, indestructible guilt-termites crawling, overrunning, tickling, scratching, biting. After a life of remorse she wanted forgiveness from the one she had wronged. He had already given it, but it was not enough. She had told no one this story. Not Hanno, not Mama. Not even Fred. She must tell, as though words on screen or paper could pardon. She told herself she was only thirteen at the time, she was swayed by the movement, she didn't think. All true. But a slender voice said, you knew what you were doing. You didn't know the extent of the brutality, but you knew something.

One day I came home on the Wednesday afternoon, clutching my teddy bear with the swastika armband. Inge and I had made the armbands at the meeting. I was in high spirits, singing all the way up the stairs.

They were waiting for me when I walked in. Mama sat on the black and gold-striped settee in her old-fashioned dropped-waist dress, with her fair hair in an Olympia roll, and perched on the settee at her shoulder was the doll with the purple silk and lace dress. She was embroidering a cushion with a spray of pink roses and a pink crinoline lady. Beside her the standard lamp with pleated yellow shade was switched on, although the sun was streaming in. Her hand trembled. Papa sat in an armchair with his shirt collar open, sleeves rolled up, and his shiny bow tie laid over the arm of the chair. He was smoking. He didn't normally buy cigarettes, but on the coffee table was a packet of Junos and his old silver petrol lighter embossed with a picture of a leaping hind. In his other hand was a strip of paper. He asked what I had done that afternoon. I told him we learnt a new song with actions, Wulle wulle, Gänschen. We kept clapping hands and hooking arms in all the wrong places and the whole room ended up in stitches. 'We played games, did a treasure hunt, told stories, made up plays of The Brave Little Tailor and The Emperor's New Clothes.' I clutched my teddy and turned to go.

'Sit down,' he roared, 'I haven't finished.'

Mama shot him one of her looks. She pulled the handkerchief embroidered by Tante Elsbeth from the sleeve of her cardigan with the mother-of-pearl buttons. I scowled and sat down. He held up the piece of paper. I recognised it as the verse Inge and I wrote and recited as we leapt over the dying embers of the bonfire at summer solstice. His hand and voice trembled as he read:

> 'Wir halten fest und treu zusammen
> und werfen Juden in die Flammen,'

which means

> 'We stand together fast and true,
> and throw Jews in the flames.'

He glared through the round, wire-framed glasses. 'Is this what they're teaching you at your meetings?'

I said it was only a poem, at which his forearm muscles bulged, his hands clenched the air and the veins stood out on his temples. He lectured me about kindness to other people and my old friend Herta whom I shunned when Inge was around. Herta was Jewish. A few years earlier he had once said to Mama it would be a good thing if there weren't so many Jews in the professions, but I kept this to myself. Mama's head was bent over the cushion.

At the end he said, 'You can stay in for a week. You come straight home after school, and there'll be no Jungmädel on Wednesday or Saturday.'

I gasped. 'You can't keep me in. I must go. I *must* go.'

On Saturday I went to the sports afternoon and told Gisela what he said, and that he had two illegal books in a secret compartment in his bureau: Das Kapital and Heine's poems. I knew because I once searched for money to steal for an ice cream with my friends in the Tiergarten.

The following day there was a thump on the door. Mama opened it and two men in trenchcoats and fedoras pushed past her. We were having dinner of meatballs dipped in mustard with gherkins. Mama went white. No goodbye kisses were allowed. Papa shot a glance at her. He didn't look at me or Hanno. We sat with our knives and forks in mid-air. After five minutes the front door slammed. It was five weeks before she learnt that they had sent him to the new camp being built at Sachsenhausen. If Mama suspected me, she never said. I carried on going to Jungmädel, and while Papa was in that dreadful place, I sang and danced in the great Olympic spectacle.

Six months later two Gestapo men arrived at the door demanding money in return for a cardboard urn containing Papa's ashes. It was the first we heard of his death. They were supposed to invite the next of kin to see the body laid out and request consent to cremation. The Kommandant had signed the form.

After Mama's death I found a letter from a friend exhorting her to ring any time, and not to do the ultimate act of selfishness, because they had survived when so many of their friends had not and because it would be unbearable for Hildegard to have the blood of two parents on her hands. Mama never confronted me.

Hilda pulled out the large brown leather suitcase, took out a letter, sat on the bed and unfolded it. The paper was frail and tanned, with pieces torn out of the edges. Her hands trembled and it ripped at the creases. It was written in Sütterlin with e's that look like n's, h's like f's and s's like nothing else. She read:

My darling Hilde,

I want you to know that whatever happens to me here, I do not blame you and I will always love you.
                    Your Papa.

She wept and wept and wept.

47

More horses appeared.

'But we need those fields for the sheep when they lamb, Olly.'

'Let them roam. They're tough enough.'

'But it takes ages to check on them out there.'

'Well, that can be your job, then, Amelia.'

'But I've got the admin to do.'

'On second thoughts, you do the kennels. You'll be good with clients. Take Meredith with you.'

Amelia was speechless and red-faced.

'Meredith quit,' said Toe. 'She quit with Jeremy.'

'Did she? Oh yes, I forgot.' Oliver's mouth drooped. In a whine he said, 'They don't need me any more when they get boyfriends.'

'But I hate dogs and I hate their shit.' Amelia had found her voice at last. Her lips quivered.

'Calm down, dear.'

'But who'll do the admin?'

Oliver looked round. 'Claire.' He smiled. 'Claire did an admirable job while you were away.'

Disbelief was written on every face. Amelia marched out. Toe started after her.

'Leave her.'

The next day was Oliver's birthday. At assembly we hid gift-wrapped presents behind our backs, then when he walked in, smirking, we shouted 'Surprise' in unison and held them aloft. Before he reached the bay, we clamoured round.

'Children, children.' He raised a hand. 'Leave them here and go to your places.'

The opening took twenty minutes, and one Aztec eagle

face was watched for signs of pleasure by the full community, as the children were allowed in for this event. Not just signs of pleasure, but the sign of the greatest pleasure. Choose mine, choose mine, we thought, not content that he liked a present. No one else's present must be liked more.

'He didn't like mine much,' I said to Rachel, 'and I thought green was his favourite colour.'

That evening we stared at leaping yellow flames and sparks drifting upwards on the hill. My voice had returned, though raspy. Amelia stood beside Oliver, smiling. Everyone was connected and everyone belonged. Like the flames we wove in and out of each other, and all tiredness from the day's work seeped away, forgotten. The fire's warmth melted us and the sounds floated over the valley. A gold contrail crossed the sky.

*

'Sorry I'm late. Be with you in a minute.'

Oliver wore his tweed hunting jacket with the cinched waist and brass buttons. After ten minutes he reappeared and I handed over my mother's letter.

'You're not going to see her, are you?'

I bit at a false nail, thick and hard. 'S'pose not. My gran would want me to. Not that she'll say anything.'

'Well, if she doesn't say anything, where's the problem? Just tell your mother. Or don't bother.'

I laughed. 'My fucking mother keeps writing when I don't want her to, while my daughters ignore all my emails.'

'More sinned against than sinning. People with kids at university only hear from them when they want money.'

I told him about a recovered memory: I was wearing a Titian-red dress with broderie-anglaise hem and yoke, my father's favourite, holding a shiny new coin which he had given me. He often gave me coins to play with, to keep if I was good. And I had been good. My voice shrank.

He asked about my sex life. I stammered.

'Come on, I've seen it all. I want to know how it feels when Pete enters you. Is he touching the right spots? Is it Pete you're feeling or is it that bastard of a father?'

I frowned at the window-catches. Mist blotted out the view beyond. I nodded.

'We'll do more work on that, then.'

He gestured towards the letter. I screwed it up, threw it in the pewter dish and set fire to it.

*

Some people voiced discomfort about Oliver's recent focus on hunting. He had set up a room to receive guests from the hunting fraternity because they needed these people's support. Besides, nature was raw in tooth and claw. He planned to hold a Hunt Ball in a marquee with special lighting effects and a band on the far field beyond the ash tree. It was expected of the owner of a large estate. He was confident his licence application for band and alcohol till two in the morning would be approved. The last dairy cow and calf were off to market on Wednesday, so it would be all hands on deck to clean up that field. Silence fell.

He took a luxury chocolate from the box he was holding and passed it round, smiling. 'Courtesy of Morrisons. Are we lions or mice?'

Voices muttered, 'We're lions.'

'Any other issues?'

Rachel put up a hand. 'Last Friday and the one before, Angela and I drove past Effi's house and we saw this woman coming out at eight in the morning. Toe and Stick said it sounds like the one they saw with Mark, just the two of them out cycling. We're bringing it to the group rather than just you, Effi,' she added.

'She's sleeping in your bed, Effi,' said Oliver.

I sat up and clenched my fists. 'Fucking cheek,' I exploded like a poppy seed-head bursting and scattering its contents far and wide.

Oliver smiled. 'She's very sexy when she's angry, isn't she?' He suggested I write and tell Mark to buy me out or sell up.

The reply was a long time coming. The farm work was tiring and tedious: picking raspberries, blackcurrants, whitecurrants and the last of the strawberries, and peas and broad beans. Finally the letter came:

Dear Stef,

Sorry I've taken so long to get back to you. I will buy you out straightaway, on one condition: you agree to spend three days talking about your situation. A counsellor will supervise and Gran has agreed to let us use her living room, and a bedroom for you. Your parents and Lisa are excluded, and there would never be more than two people and the counsellor and yourself there at a time. Gran prefers not to take part, but she will if you want her to. Of course you could walk out any time. If, at the end, you still want to stay at the Academy, I will give you the average of three valuations.

The counsellor said to make it clear this would be a discussion, not a lecture, and no bullying. You would be listened to fully, as well as your listening to others.

Whatever you decide, I wish you happiness.

Love Mark

*

I whipped downhill like a sparrowhawk in for the kill. Stick's mountain bike was swift. Tears from the wind in my eyes flew out sidewards. At the top of the next hill I threw down the bike, collapsed onto the spongy turf and panted at the hills, glared at the sun, then leapt back on and rode till my calf muscles ached so much I yowled. The sea came into view: it glittered angrily, it bristled.

When I showed Oliver the letter he strode round the kitchen, crashed lids on saucepans, slammed cupboard doors, brought his fist down on the worktops.

'Fucking manipulative bastard.'

After ten minutes he rang the elephant bell and people arrived bewildered from all corners of the estate. The cries of outrage when I read out the letter filled the room like rooks darkening the sky before they settle.

Don't go, was the consensus.

'She'll be like a fly walking into a Venus fly-trap,' said Amelia. 'He has no right. It's her entitlement.'

'She should sue for divorce now,' said Pete. 'She'll get her half anyway without his tricks.'

But Oliver said I'd have to wait two years, and Mark could ruin me financially by delaying for years, refusing to produce documents and so on.

'Mark's not like that,' I said.

'My dear, Mark is an idiot, full of sound and fury, signifying nothing. I'd worry, if you went, you might not cope with these people, and I would hate to lose you.' He paused. 'However, it's your best option, Effi.'

Rachel twirled a lock of hair over and over into a ringlet. 'But they'll sway her against us.' She turned to me. 'They'll make mincemeat of you, they will. What's the point?'

Oliver said, 'So she can get the money which is her due.'

The group fell silent. Oliver told me to ask the counsellor's name so I could google him and go forearmed.

For two weeks we dissected what a cult was and what it

was not, all the while passing round stolen chocolates. Oliver allocated the thief each week, or we voted by a show of hands. A cult was authoritarian, but we were democratic – we debated things and voted. We ate royally. We kept ourselves to ourselves by choice because we liked each other's company. Anyway, we did the market stall and went downtown or to the village shop. We lost contact with family and friends because we wanted to. But lots of us had friends and family come for weekends. Nor were we prisoners.

'It's our choice to stay,' said Amelia. 'Why go anywhere when we have it all here?'

'You were happy to go with Oliver.'

'Only because he needed a retriever and a secretary.'

The arguments flew back and forth till Oliver said, 'Enough. Remember what this is all about.'

He directed me to push Adrian, a man in his seventies, round the room by the shoulders and shout 'You ruined my life,' 'You took away my childhood.' Next everyone pushed a partner round and the room turned into a deafening, Boschian hell. A week of hugging and singing and dancing and viola playing followed, a week of perfect togetherness, perfect order.

On my last day the sky hung like a heavy tablecloth, thick and muggy. Clouds the colour of galvanised iron skulked low in the sky. Pete and I left the quad bike and walked to check on the sheep in the woods. Suddenly Pete touched my arm. A hind ambled across the path. It stopped, long neck craning round, ears proud, dog nose pointing at us. We stared at each other. None dared move. I was the intruder here. Before we came and claimed ownership, before John Knight bought the Forest from the Crown and tamed the land, they were here. Then it wandered on. The pale rump gleamed in the darkness under the tree canopy.

At the mire restoration site the ditch block was barely visible and a pool had formed, with dragonflies and mosses and swathes of cotton grass with nodding heads. Purple bell heather and ling were in full flower. The bracken was turning, but the gorse bloomed yellow as ever. We stopped to admire the endless moor. A raven flew over.

'I love all this,' I said. 'I'm dreading tomorrow.'

He put his arms round me, huggy as the sheep already since the June shearing, and kissed me. 'You'll be fine. You know you have to go.'

In the morning Oliver presented me with a locket containing a photo of his head and fastened it round my neck. 'It'll be gruelling, but you'll soon be back here on terra firma. Just tough it out. We're all rooting for you. Remember, always listen to your heart. The heart has its reasons which the head does not know.' He studied my face. 'Of course, what you could do is pretend you agree, swallow their lies, stay there till the house sale is completed, then come back. That way you bag the money without suffering three whole days of them trying to break you down.'

He threw back his head and laughed, then hugged me tight.

48

In Gran's living room Mark and I faced each other like the prelude to a cat-fight. Then he pecked me on both cheeks. A short, stout man with grey hair stood up. The waistband of his trousers squeezed his waist into upper and lower billows. He offered his hand.

'Hallo, Stef. I'm Denis.'

'I prefer to be called Effi.' I ignored the hand. 'And I'm only here under duress because my ex-husband is refusing to cooperate over my half of the house into which he's moved his girlfriend.'

He flinched.

We sat at right angles on wingback chairs, and I cold-shouldered Mark on the sofa, who was not allowed to intervene. We could break when I wanted. Gran was somewhere in the house or garden. The bowl next to the television had been filled with fresh potpourri of rose petals, orange peel and cinnamon. I steeled myself.

Denis was tentative. What were the good things about the Diamond Academy? What did the group believe? How had I changed since moving in? I warmed to him. He didn't try to crush me and I regretted being rude. We celebrated life, I said, worked on ourselves to make a better community, help each other and protect the earth. The earth had never felt so close till I visited the Academy. I loved working on the land, dry soil trickling through my fingers or sticky wet lumps. Seeing a deer the day before, I felt at one with the world, part of a bigger scheme. It was magic.

'I understand he's rented out all the pasture for horses now,' said Denis.

'Yes. You have to work to understand it. We're not

spoonfed.'

Mark stared at his trainers.

'So looking after the land is less important?'

'No. Yes. We had a discussion. We still have the sheep and this season's crops. We'll see what the future holds. Nature is raw in tooth and claw.'

'Would it surprise you to hear Mr Diamond has sold the hunting rights on the estate to a landowning company in perpetuity?'

I frowned. 'I'm a newcomer. I don't know everything. How do you know?'

He opened a green box file and took out a document dated two weeks earlier. I gasped at the price and leant back against the cushion.

'The quest to work on ourselves is the main thing. Hunting rights don't matter.' The hind came to mind, its long neck craned round, ears proud, dog nose pointing at us, eyes staring. And the herd of deer Mark and I had nearly run into. The way their pale underparts gleamed in the dark.

'I understand you took three thousand pounds from your joint account.'

'I left the car.' I glared at Mark but his eyes were fixed on the floor. 'It was for the extra counselling and it was worth every penny.'

Denis had contacted ex-members. One paid fifteen hundred pounds, another eight thousand, and two paid four thousand each. Graham was asked to leave after two months, but refused a refund.

I grasped the locket. Graham had caused a lot of trouble and people disliked him.

Denis watched like a cat intent on its prey. 'Two people sold their homes and put it all into the Academy, with no lien should they leave, no comeback.'

'I need a break.' I would have walked out there and then, but for wanting my fair share of the house that woman had usurped.

In the kitchen Gran was putting the red and purple-chequered tea cosy over the pot.

'I won't ask anything,' she said.

'Good.'

The air was sultry and the sun struggled to get through. The sunflowers hung their heads, looking for sunshine in the ground. I carried two bowls of fresh raspberries, bleeding and covered in cream, to the wrought-iron table by the pond. A huge gold-ring dragonfly came to inspect me, its buzzing wings touching my bare arm. I rolled and lit a cigarette. It wasn't fair, telling me these things without my hearing the other side of the story. Gran appeared with the tea and the sun burst through. The great green bush-crickets on the thistles crooned, on and on like this man Denis.

Back in the lion's den, I talked about the shepherd's cottage and snow covering the door and window, that at first I was upset at being cut off, but Oliver came every day. People there made sacrifices for others. Denis asked for examples.

'I can't think of any offhand. Just being ourselves is a gift to others.'

'So is the aim self-improvement or is it more helping others?'

'Both. How can I help others if I don't work on myself? The others are what makes me who I am. We depend on what they think of us to determine who we are. That's what Sartre meant when he wrote, 'Hell is other people.'' My forefinger wagged and I settled into teacher mode, pleased with myself for remembering that one. 'We're all made up of a plurality of selves, false selves, and different ones come to the fore at different times. Each one pretends to be the true self. If we don't see that, we're blind.'

I leant back with a satisfied smile.

'But you do help each other?'

'Certainly.'

'Because ex-members told me it was common practice to humiliate people in front of the whole group.'

I stiffened. 'It's helping, not humiliating. Nobody wants to know their faults, but they need to.' Denis was infuriating. Half a day of this rubbish was more than enough. 'There's no primrose path.'

Mark examined his feet.

Denis asked about the name game, its benefits. I huffed and puffed and scowled in Mark's direction. I couldn't remember what I was accused of because it had made no sense, but that was my failing, not the group's. The benefits were elusive. Words struggled to escape like the flailing arms of a swimmer dragged down by the undertow.

'I learnt that I was attention-seeking.'

Mark exploded. 'Rubbish. You're not attention-seeking. They were attacking you for nothing, not giving you any attention you sought.'

Denis raised a hand to silence Mark, but I snapped back.

'Mark, you're an idiot. You're full of sound and fury, signifying nothing.'

Both men stared.

Mark left with Denis at lunchtime, and Gran and I sat under the clouds which now curtained off the sun. The great green bush-crickets were silent again. All morning I had twisted and turned like a swallow, never stopping. The afternoon was more of the same, without Mark there. 'Why did they do that?' Denis asked repeatedly, and I wanted to crawl under the big grand piano.

We stopped at four. My head whirled with questions of

money and farming and a baying group. But the group loved me, and it had felt so good being held, and now I was bereft.

The sea was quiet; the beach was empty. I stripped down to my costume and strode in, breathed out and carried on walking, fought to stay down like a bucking pig unstunned on the slaughter-hook with its throat slashed, then burst from the surface and thrashed and thrashed in crawl stroke. When I stopped, only a muffled hiss filled the air. There was comfort in the tired limbs and emptiness, though the head raged. I turned on my back and floated, and the warm sea cradled me like a lazy giant's hand. A piece of soft, slimy seaweed nibbled at an arm.

'By the way,' Gran said at dinner, 'your old school has had another Ofsted inspection. The head was sacked and replaced by a caretaker head.'

My face lit up. 'So I was right all along.'

'I thought you'd be pleased.'

I read through Denis's papers in the humid plant jungle of the conservatory. Four lawsuits against Oliver for extortion of singing school fees without delivery of appropriate teaching were settled out of court, on condition that plaintiffs not talk about it. But two other ex-students had drawn up affidavits. A woman was made to drink from a trough on hands and knees. Another was forced to describe a rape in intimate detail. The men had to wear their hair short and no beards. One man whose worst fear was other people seeing his anus was made to drop his pants, turn round and bend over for all to see. A promiscuous woman had to sleep with every man there. A man behaving like a baby had to wear a nappy and eat only liquidised food. Money was spirited away to tax havens or numbered accounts and charitable trusts. I gasped at the figures. And why so many changes of names of companies and directors?

Gran played Chopin and the puzzles trickled away. She fondled the keys with the lightest of touches, like an ant milking an aphid for its sweet fluid, swaying and lingering over the caramel sounds, or cascading over the keys for joy. The music washed away the day's turmoil, washed away Denis and his sharp elbows.

An email from the Academy read: *Dear Effi, our thoughts are with you. Be strong and listen to your heart. Love Oliver.* My heart melted.

Then I was alone in Gran's spare room, tossing and turning as questions rushed to the fore. The amber glow of a street lamp and my father's lowering figure invaded the space. At last I could stand it no longer. I wrapped myself in the quilt and stole into Gran's room. The triptych of mirrors on the dressing table and the brass finials on the wrought-iron bed gleamed in the moonlight that fell through a crack between the curtains. I bent over the sleeping form and stared at her face close up, willing her awake, in vain, then curled up on the floor, comforted by her nearness.

*

Gran smiled as she laid out breakfast in the garden, with tablecloth and jugs.

'We'll put up the folding bed in my room tonight.'

Breakfast was an island of peace, of forgetting the day before and the day ahead. We sat on the wrought-iron chairs with cheese rolls and coffee with cream, while birds flitted to and from the feeders or sang from the apple trees. Come ten o'clock, I was dreading the rigmarole. They thought I was brainwashed, but they were the ones doing the brainwashing, taking me out of my habitual environment and bombarding me with this stuff. It wasn't fair, not giving Oliver the right to reply.

Denis arrived without Mark. He had a disarming way of apologising, or appearing to. We discussed money.

'But it costs a fortune to run a place like the Diamond Academy,' I said.

Accounts and other documents copied by an ex-member showed that Oliver owned twelve properties in the home counties and vast portfolios of shares.

'Mr Diamond's income seems out of proportion to that of the members.'

I fumbled with my locket. Listen to your heart. The heart said, Don't listen to this man. If Oliver were here, he'd explain. 'I don't understand financial matters,' I said aloud.

'But you understand that, for example, a part-time GP earning forty thousand a year receives an allowance of only three thousand? Or that a part-time lawyer earning fifty thousand a year receives only four thousand?'

'All I know is that Oliver has been very kind and helped me hugely.'

'Do you think ex-members' testimonies are examples of kindness and helping?'

I shrugged. 'Isolated incidents. How do I know they're true? Sometimes people make things up out of spite.'

He sighed and settled into his chair. 'If they were true, would you call them kind and helpful?'

I bit at a false nail. 'It's being cruel to be kind. Half the things they complained about are irrelevant anyway. I've never seen anything like that.' Though stripping off was a harsh punishment for a scissor-leg headstand.

Gran was among the raspberry bushes, bending and picking. Her calmness soothed me from a distance and I was wary. 'She's trying to manipulate you,' Oliver had said when she wrote to ask if I'd decided about Germany. But Gran had said nothing against Oliver.

*

In the afternoon Simon arrived and I blushed, but he smiled and said hallo as if nothing had transpired between us. He looked happier, if still sunken. Shamefully, we had consigned him to oblivion since he left. I asked after his father.

'Better than naught,' he said with a grin.

He came with the infamous Graham, a man in his late forties with short red hair and rimless glasses, who shook hands warmly. His expulsion from the Academy had shaken him to the core. 'I cut off most of my family because I believed they were manipulative and abusive. But they welcomed me back with open arms.'

Simon nodded and clenched his fists and the veins on his forearms bulged. 'Me and my parents had our differences, but Oliver's take was a parcel of old trumpery.' The eyebrows knitted together. 'You were there, Eff, when he pressed me to call my father a tyrant and a wanker. And that beggaring toad turned you against your family.'

'He never said a word against Gran.'

'He advised against the Berlin trip and he convinced you your father sexually abused you.'

I bristled. 'I don't think that was down to Oliver.'

'He said about your crocodile dream, 'Absolutely classic. Your father is your crocodile.' Think about it, Eff. He criticised your parents neck and crop.'

'That's not true.' But as I spoke I pictured Oliver screwing up and setting fire to my father's letter, flames leaping from the pewter dish.

'Not just you, mind: Rachel, Donna, Melanie, Claire, Neil and others, all persuaded they were sexually abused. Stick's probably the only one who was. People like Oliver cloud the issue of real abusers being so prevalent. It's not what he did to you, Eff. It's the poor beggars that really have been abused and get disbelieved because of his kind. Makes me mad.'

Like chuggers they ranted till Denis raised a palm. 'Hang on a minute. Give Effi a chance to speak.' He rested his chin on his hands and waited before saying, 'Did Oliver suggest your father could be your crocodile?'

The absinthe drinker on the chimney breast stared vacantly and the locket hung heavy. The grandfather clock chimed the half-hour.

'Yes,' I mumbled.

Graham produced a video of a workshop he had copied. He stood in the middle and the group took turns naming one bad thing about him. Most said he was difficult, and when he challenged this as too non-specific, Oliver said, 'You have just proved the point.' 'But then I can't win,' said Graham. Oliver said, 'You're right, you can't win. That's because you're fucked up.'

Graham pressed Pause. 'I feel sick watching this.'

Denis asked what I thought. It reminded me of Simon standing on the chair. I was one of the pack of hounds, joining in with gusto.

'It looks... shocking.'

'So why did you stay after that, Graham?' said Denis.

'I was used to it and all my friends were there.'

Simon said, 'I thought they were my friends till Diamond made me stand on a chair for weeks for calling him a megalomaniac. No one defended me.'

I felt the heat in my face. I, Simon's own lover, had betrayed him, like one of Robespierre's spectators furiously knitting while heads rolled. Was it fear or what? I wept, bitterly. 'Forgive me, Simon,' I said.

'I forgive you.'

'Is that how you feel?' Denis asked me. 'All your friends are there?'

The months of suppressing feelings had made me unsure whether I had any. I poached others' sentiments, plundered others for thoughts and feelings, plagiarised them. 'I think so.'

'I never heard from none of them after I left,' said Simon. 'Nine years we lived together. No phone call, no email, no naught.'

'I'm so sorry.'

'I don't blame you. I was the same. We only contacted quitters if we thought they might come back. They were outcasts, traitors.'

After Graham's ordeal everyone hugged him.

Simon also had two short videos, secretly copied at night, the only time he wasn't watched after saying he wanted to quit. One was of Claire six years ago. She complained people didn't like her, men didn't like her, and Oliver ordered her into the middle. For half an hour people told her she was whiny, no fun, never said or did anything unless someone else suggested it, she was dull, she was difficult, she was unattractive.

'But I want a child,' she howled and the screen went blank.

Claire stood before me, aged thirty-seven, wearing a billowing black skirt with bold yellow flowers and sobbing uncontrollably while I and others, urged on by Oliver, bullied her into an abortion.

Simon had borrowed four thousand pounds from his father on the understanding he could earn it back, but Oliver claimed he had earned only three hundred. Graham too lost four thousand. A man named Richard sold his home and put two hundred and fifty thousand into buying the estate, which Oliver refused to return. 'What do you expect me to do?' Oliver said. 'Sell the manor house?' The group said

Richard was unreasonable.

'That rapacious bastard'll be after your share of your house, mind,' said Simon.

On the doorstep I said, 'I'm ashamed of how I treated you, Simon.'

He hugged me. 'I did it to others.' He handed me a piece of paper. 'Ring any time.'

Then I was alone with Gran. Thoughts of leaving the Academy slithered into my head, but there was nowhere to go after neglecting old school and college friends and neighbours. The Academy had seemed wonderful, community-spirited, close-knit. But how close-knit was it to shun departed members? I wanted to believe because it felt good to believe, to belong. Act as if you believe, and you will believe. Without the Academy my life was meaningless. I was no longer a teacher, a mother, a wife... a friend? I had no idea what I was. Oliver's voice kept telling me I was fucked up. I had been corseted, not cosseted.

Watching the news was strange – out there was a whole world of wars and earthquakes and floods and droughts. After dinner Gran and I sat outside in the oppressive heat and imbibed the almondy smell of meadowsweet. We talked about food and drink, sleeping arrangements, the sultry air, the garden, shops that had closed down, the young jobless roaming the streets, the blackberries out already because of the hot dry spring. Anything but the Diamond Academy. Indoors, I frowned at the photo of Gran's parents by the piano. I had always sensed that my mother's version, that Gran's father died in the war, was wrong.

'Sorry about Germany, Gran. Did you see your father's grave?'

She stared out at the clouds. 'My mother left his ashes behind when we moved to England. She said they often mixed them up at the crematorium.'

'I've never asked you this before, Gran. How did great-grandfather Stefan die?'

She broke down on the sofa. I hugged her tight. 'I don't know. I can only guess. He died in a concentration camp. The death certificate said pneumonia, but everyone knows that's a lie.'

Then she told me about the ash trees of Sachsenhausen, the white-tiled autopsy room, the white-tiled basement cells of Gestapo headquarters, the crowding, the squalor, the brickworks, the wooden block and the laughing Kommandant, and blood and flesh, and blood and flesh, and blood and flesh. Everything.

Finally she straightened and blew her nose. 'Since I found out Josef Mengele's favourite piece was *Träumerei*, I have not played or listened to it. But now' – she stood and drew herself to her full height – 'I am going to play it. My father would have wanted it.'

Her fingers barely touched the keys. After the rising crescendo she played the long top note so softly it was unbearable. I listened enthralled. There were no words to say what either felt. I knew only that something had happened when I asked that question.

*

'I may have made a mistake, Gran,' I said next morning. 'But I miss the group. I don't know what to think.'

'Well... I can't tell you what to think. If you have doubts, you must leave. Whatever you decide, you'll still be my beloved granddaughter. Maybe I shouldn't say it, but you used to know what you want, darling. You used to be happy on your own.'

But I had invested my whole being in the Academy.

'I'm going for a swim,' I said.

I came together in the sea. A cold spot shifted something. In the pale morning sun I beat the water this way and that, pushed and shovelled it, smacked it to see the spray arc overhead, rose and fell in abortive leaps of butterfly stroke, tumbled over and over, coming out of the water like a whale and dropping back. Then I sank into utter darkness and floated face down.

Everything was still but for the occasional languid lift of a finger. No emptiness, no fullness, no need to think. In this happy, unquestioning state I stayed till I needed to breathe and with a gulp lifted my head.

A cloud of unthinking went before me as I walked along the beach. The air was balmy, the barnacled limpet shells indented my feet and waves shushed at the shore. The sea was big.

More ex-members came with more statements, videos and tales of abuse, all similar stories, and similar to my own, if I would but admit it. Each one was told they were fucked up. I grasped at my neck, but the locket wasn't there.

Sadie appeared and we hugged tight. I trembled.

'You didn't reply to my emails,' I said.

'I wrote with my new address. Or you could have used my uni address.' She sounded like an exasperated parent. 'I rang and asked for Stef and they said there was no one of that name there. They wouldn't let Mark in, twice. They threw him out.'

'Threw him out?'

'You missed my graduation.'

I gasped and hugged her again. 'Darling, I'm sorry.'

Mark arrived and sat next to Sadie.

'I emailed, wrote a letter and went twice in person. They said you didn't want to see me. It's a bit strange after what Oliver said when I saw him last autumn. 'You seem like a good bloke to me,' he said, and he was amazed you thought the photo was genuine.'

I glowered. 'Clearly it was genuine, since you've moved her into my house.'

'Stef, I only started going out with her in March. Oliver said you were just menopausal. 'Take her out for a romantic dinner,' he said, 'wine and dine her a bit. All women love that.' Those were his words.'

'He told me *you* thought I was menopausal. All women...? You...' I slumped in the chair. 'Why are you doing this, Mark? This counselling thing.'

'Because it's wrong, what he's doing. Because I care about you still.'

He talked about the name game and other things.

Denis leant forwards. 'What do you think about that?'

I slouched hopelessly, exhausted.

'I think I made a mistake.'

Denis reached over and squeezed my arm. I wanted to fetch my stuff but he shook his head. On no account should I go back. Let someone else get it. I felt powerless to resist. Sadie and Mark hugged me. I would stay at Gran's another night and ask Gran to let my parents know. My poor father. My poor mother. All lies. Would they forgive me?

Sitting on the floor in the spare room I felt nothing. As if I had passed through a black hole and emerged on the other side in an anti-world of non-existence. Yet here I was, my sweaty hands touched my legs, the carpet was somewhere beneath me, my body was in the room. But I, Stefanie, Stef, Eff, Effi, that indefinable something that makes up a person, was not there. I was nowhere, lost. The thing in the room was something else. Mark and Sadie and Denis were in the house, but more distant than I could grasp. And Gran... Somebody else had had lunch with Gran in the kitchen. It wasn't me.

I had wasted a year of my life, lost a husband, missed my daughter's graduation, cut off my parents, cut off my sister and I felt nothing.

The MP3 player showed 'Oliver'. I couldn't bring myself to delete it. It was all I had of his voice. I listened to The Spinning Song and pictured the group dancing with hooked arms and laughing as they sang the strange words. On the side was the locket. I picked it up without opening it, afraid to gaze on the gorgon's face, dropped it in the bin, tottered towards the door and went downstairs, trembling and giddy. My hands and feet seemed not to touch the handrail and stairs. The wallpaper pattern by the stairs was fuzzy and my head pounded. At the bottom I turned into the dining room to face Emma, Sadie, Denis, Mark, Gran and Simon and clutched the edge of the table covered in sandwiches, vol-au-vents, drumsticks, ocean sticks, tomatoes cut like water lilies. Through the blur it looked a mess, as if someone had vomited over the table. Mark popped a champagne bottle and filled glasses.

'To Stef.'

'To Stef,' chorused the company.

'How did you know you were going to celebrate?'

'We didn't,' said Mark. 'We just hoped.'

Everyone laughed.

I hugged Emma. 'I'm sorry.'

'No problem, Mum.'

49

But who would rescue me from my rescuers? There was only myself – such a burden, such a millstone – and what was to stop me doing the same all over again? The Diamond Academy had robbed me of thoughts and feelings. Yesterday's friends and lovers were today's traitors. The plague I'd escaped could erupt again at any time in Mephistophelean form. Somewhere another flock lay in wait, insidious leaders with smiles and promises, and happy bands of followers. I was cast adrift like a limpet sliced off its rock. Behind the mask is nothing, Oliver had said, and now my mask had slipped. I was several different persons all called Stef, all acting a part. Who would be on stage today? Nobody. No face. Bare as the moor. Only one feeling did I recognise: shame. At being hoodwinked. How could I be so stupid? Worse, they say hypnosis can't make us do something against our will, so I must have wanted to be a puppet, to betray Simon, be mean to Claire, leave Mark, cut off my parents, accuse my father…

50

On his deathbed Shostakovich understood. It was lonely tiptoeing through the birch forest, ice crystals in spikes on every branch, each tree a plucked string, and strange, a strange place. The viola slithered down while the silver piano notes percolated through the veil. The air chilled my eyeballs and even in the frost-whiteness the light was feeble. The light was dying, out of my grasp, so in a spasm of rage I leapt, and leapt again, just to show there was life in this bleak landscape. The viola shrieked, screamed. Creatures of the forest? No, it was coming from within. I was shrieking inside, screaming, who am I? I am a betrayer of my own flesh and blood, blood and flesh, blood and flesh, blood spurting everywhere, red on white. The left hand on the piano, the iron hand, announced a solemn bass in memory of those taken away. The viola scraped a high tremolo on the bridge, a gauzy whisper. It was eerie, made no sense. A demon behind was catching up, breathing down my neck, leaning into every moment of my lovemaking. The ash trees of Sachsenhausen whispered, a white-tiled autopsy room, white-tiled basement cells where sound was muffled, blood could be washed off. Victims tried to be invisible, give the right answers, do nothing to draw attention. Then the viola strode away, not knowing where, but Oliver was leading so there must be light, must be. A sudden firm note of the piano, the viola cried out, the piano ran and ran all over the keyboard until it trickled away, as everything that had once been believed trickled away, leaving an empty shell.

But joy, singing and dancing, linking arms, and there they all were, Amelia with her coloratura laughter, Simon's guffaws, a heart-warming danse macabre. All knit together so closely they could forget name games and standing on chairs. Four hundred men crammed into a block sang and sang, no room to dance, or were made to sing while straining to pull a brick-laden cart, harnessed like horses, mirth, we want mirth, come on, sing, you filthy swine, sing or feel my whip, and feel it anyway for my pleasure. An officer relished the spectacle, ordered photos of it for his album with glee on his face. Too much laughter. Laughter is permitted only when I say. A long note trailed into infinity.

And after came the march from brickworks to camp, followed by the cart heaped up with bodies. Lives sucked out. Something had died in Gran and me. The piano was calm, the viola glided into something less anguished, more even. This was the way forward, no more straining for the light that was not there. Old wounds burst open, never healed by time, but there was always a father's letter of forgiveness, always caring family and friends. The firm tread of the viola and the lilting refrain of the piano at once saddened and gladdened us. Searing cries died away into nothingness. We were silent long after, still hearing the dark sounds.

51

The sky was milky and the meadow still silent the following day. The storm had passed over without breaking. I sneaked into the dining room to check email, but there was nothing from the Academy. I missed the fluidity, the excitement of not knowing where the group might go, what it might do.

Lisa came with Jack. She held out pink roses for me and Jack put up his arms for a cuddle, laid his head on my shoulder and patted my back. We sat with coffee and Garibaldi biscuits in the conservatory while Jack played with the trains.

'Are you looking forward to teaching again?'

'Yes,' I said, though the thought of twenty-five clamouring voices terrified me.

'It'll be easy getting a job now your old head teacher's been discredited.'

'Yes.'

'You can go wherever you choose, wherever your heart takes you.'

But my heart was in a remote place on Exmoor. Listen to your heart, said Oliver, knowing that he possessed it. The head said, do as you're told. The heart said, I am nothing.

'What happened to you?' Gran shot her a look, but Lisa would have her say. 'You were always the strong one. I looked up to you, you were my mentor. You were so... certain.'

'I thought I was.'

'When I came and helped your class with sewing and reading, they thought the world of you. You had them eating out of your hand. What happened? Why did you get caught up in it?'

I spread my arms helplessly.

'Didn't you see it was abusive? After all, you're not

stupid.'

'No. I don't know.' Doubts about Simon standing on the chair, Melanie taking off her top, the voice workshop, and yes, the name game, had seeped away because the others accepted that behaviour. Worse, they applauded it.

'That man...' Lisa fumed, hands fluttering in search of answers. 'What are his frustrations? Why does he have to surround himself with admirers?'

My hackles rose. Did Oliver look round and see twenty-five Olivers gazing back at him? Perhaps he was once good for people, found himself admired and began to take advantage. He'd wanted to be a singer and with his voice he could have been. I felt sorry for him. He cured Melanie's headache. 'He wasn't always a bully.'

Lisa spluttered droplets of tea over her lap. 'I thought you'd learnt more than enough about him to change your mind.'

'I have. But maybe he started out meaning well and the admiration went to his head.' Lisa had no right to attack.

52

Gran answered the doorbell. She lingered in the hallway before coming into the living room.

'Two of your friends are here,' she said frostily.

My face lit up, dulled, lit up again.

'Please don't invite them in,' she added and walked off towards the kitchen.

Pete and Rachel were smartly dressed all in black and marched down the drive one either side of me, shoulder to shoulder. A Yorkshire terrier sat in a window on the other side of the street and yapped. In the Land Rover I sat between them without speaking. Denis had said, mull over everything from the three days, but it was fading and in its place was a symphony of emotions, three rows of people howling, exulting, yelling, moaning, screeching, singing. My nylon swimming costume hugged my body under my clothes and on my lap was a rolled-up vermilion red towel. Rain had started. The wipers swished hypnotically.

We parked in town. Rachel and I sat motionless while Pete fetched a ticket.

'You can leave your towel in the Landie.'

'No.' I clutched it to my chest.

Majorettes high-stepped down the street in the rain. The sequined nine-year-old sex kittens in uniform twirled their batons, shook pink and silver tinselly pompons and gyrated to some cheesy love song.

The people in the café looked ordinary: two women with pushchairs, three people on their own reading newspapers, people in twos and threes, and a couple like matching china dogs. I sat at a table in the middle, facing the counter and the menu blackboard, while Pete and Rachel sat opposite.

The other three middle tables each had one person facing the counter and blackboard, like school. Rachel's giant bag was at her feet.

'I'm leaving,' I said. 'Have left,' I corrected.

'Perhaps you need a break. Oliver thinks you're fucked up by what your father did.'

I buttoned my lip. I doubted my father had done any such thing. Sorry Dad, sorry Mum, I was a rat. Don't argue about that, Denis said. Take your time. I raged against Diamond for eclipsing the appalling damage done by real abusers and increasing the likelihood of real victims being disbelieved.

'Oliver's sorry our choir flopped.' Rachel's eyes searched mine. 'He'll make sure it succeeds in future.'

'I'm not coming back.' Keep telling them you're not coming back, Denis said.

Our coffees arrived. I told them everything, the accounts, the properties, the videos, the testimonies.

'I'm not coming back,' I shouted. Keep telling them.

The staff behind the counter looked across.

'Those people have a personal vendetta against us,' said Pete. 'They've mounted concerted campaigns before.'

'It's like those articles Mark found,' said Rachel. 'Oliver explained it all to you. It was all false, remember?'

'What about Richard's two hundred and fifty thousand pounds?'

They denied it. A lie.

I stared at Pete, the earnest brown eyes, thinking of black satin and Floris Santal and wondering what that was all about. Don't get sidetracked, Denis said. I gripped the table. The clock above the blackboard said ten o'clock. The tide would not be far enough in to swim for another hour. The squelch and shrish of the coffee machine and the crash of cups on saucers and meaningless piped music crowded my ears. Pete cupped his hand over mine.

'We're all thinking of you. We miss you terribly.'

'I'm not coming back.' Denis said.

The china dogs looked across. They thought I had lost a lover. I had.

'I might go back to choir,' said Rachel. 'Will you?'

'Maybe.' The clang of spoons on glasses behind the counter reminded me of dinner at the Academy. I looked up, expecting to see the Oliver-faced T-shirts. 'They're doing the *Matthew Passion* next.'

'I will if you will.'

I frowned. 'It's my all-time favourite.' I clutched the towel on my lap. Be true to thine own self, Oliver said. Denis said, Oliver said. But what did I say? If only I had the certainty of Haydn's amen. The sea smelt strong. I leapt up. 'I'll see you there.'

I rushed out. My heart was split in two. Come back, come back. No, don't come back.

I clambered out of the sea onto a boulder, skin ripped off both knees, hair coarsened and flattened by salt water. Soft, slippery bladderwrack squelched underfoot and between toes. The rain had stopped. I jumped in, shuddered, then thrashed forwards with strong strokes, swam backstroke, swam on my side, somersaulted over and over, lunged forwards again, paddled with hands and feet. Finally I turned over and floated. Mindless, absorbed in the magnanimous, all-embracing sea. The chill water lapped at my skin. Raw and simple.

I paddled close to the shore, then rose up, leaving behind a furrow as I strode through the shallows, and sat on the sand, hugging the towel. The sea was a shifting impressionist picture, bits constantly changing places. Deceptive stillness, gentle with floating gulls but deep with child currents lashed up by parent winds while the earth-ball beneath spun giddily. The sea was this big thing that moved to and fro. Gyres raced round the edges and piled up water, pulling, pulling. I was small in a big universe. The sea whispered words of appeasement, distant swishes, inviting: come back in.

Back at Gran's, she asked me to stay another night. Later I would go home, see Sadie and Emma and hear their news. Then I would go and see my parents. Gran went into the other room to do her memoir while I went for a shower.

After the war we were still hated. A neighbour declared the German nation should be exterminated, see how they liked it, so Mama and I left Oma in London and went back to Berlin. Whole streets were unrecognisable, just shells of buildings. The Quadriga on top of the Brandenburg Gate was damaged, an arm still raised in victory, and on the east side was a picture of Stalin as high as a house. The lovely trees in the Tiergarten had been bombed or cut down for firewood and vegetables were grown instead. Everywhere were people pulling handcarts piled high with belongings, and lines of women passing buckets of rubble, blithely getting on with it and joking. All the roadways were clear, and white with dust. Soldiers sat on the walls and ogled the women or threw sweets to children. All that remained of the Kaiser-Wilhelm-Gedächtnis-Kirche was one truncated spire like a hollow tooth. The park where Papa carved his and my initials in the linden tree was gone. The Atrium Beba-Palast, my old cinema, had only the lower part of its façade. Mama tried in vain to contact Papa's fellow prisoners. We found our flat. The geraniums in the window boxes were dead, and when Mama knocked we could see new occupants sitting on the black and gold-striped settee and the doll with the purple silk and lace dress perched on the arm, and their photos in the hallway. Mama said we wanted to move back in. They laughed in our faces. 'You left,' they said. 'You didn't go through what we did. We endured the whole war. You had it easy.' Mama's face was black. 'You...' she gasped. 'You have no idea what we endured.' I tugged at her arm, afraid she'd have a stroke. 'You have no idea,' she shouted back. 'You have no idea.' I shepherded her away.

When we reached the park she collapsed on the ground and howled. That howl lives with me.

55

Gran was practising the primo part of The Arrival of the Queen of Sheba when I came down. I sat beside her.

'Let me have a quick practice first, Gran.'

My fingers stepped over the keys like the tentative advance of a cricket through long grass. The false nails clickety-clicked on the keys so I ripped them off and did a few scales.

'Right.'

We launched into it in a blaze of pomp and grandeur, darted in and out of each other's space, elbowed each other and grinned, heads nodding together on the beat. Gran's elegant wrists lifted and lowered like a cat softening its sleeping pitch. I fumbled in a solo section, but no matter. Up and down the keyboard we chased each other, leant forwards in the thoughtful bits, straightened our backs in the declamatory bits. We breathed together, swayed together. The energy made us want to play faster but our fingers were stiff, so we put all our passion into the piano and crescendoed to an almighty close.

Later I checked for emails. There were none. Don't email them, Denis said, but I wasn't going to snub them by not saying goodbye. I wrote:

Dear all,
Sorry I've left. Will miss you all, but the Academy is not what I thought it was.
Love...

How to sign off? Stef, I wrote at last, then deleted it and put Effi. Then I deleted that and put Eff. No, I had always been Stef, so I put Stef, then stared at the feeble letter. I deleted love and put best wishes. A fury and a hatred of Oliver was sneaking in, the way he kept telling me I was fucked up, a savage hatred of him for stringing me along and of myself for being strung along, but at the same time I could hear his oily voice saying Effi and it melted me. I could say love to the others, I loved them all individually. But together... An explanation was too much trouble. Don't reason with them, Denis said. Cling to everything you've seen and heard in these three days. So should I put Stef or Eff? I had enjoyed being called Eff, the familiarity and intimacy. But Stef was my real self, and Eff was something that happened with Oliver and the group. I snatched up a piece of paper, cut two eye-holes, held it to my face and looked at the screen, which had reverted to a black screen saver and showed Atlantean shoulders and a magnified body. This person was a stranger. I took the paper away from my face. Nothing, a terrifying nothing. Not Stef, not Eff, not Effi. Not Stefanie. I left the email unsigned and pressed Send.

Annoyingly, I found myself humming Amazing Grace and stopped, fearful of demonic forces lurking in the music. That tune belonged to another world of mists and grassy knolls and inky water. I wandered through to the kitchen where a freshly baked cherry cake stood on the worktop. Beside it were the red and purple-chequered tea cosy and a bright green smiley-faced toy engine. Gran was outside picking more raspberries. I took a plastic box from the cupboard and went to join her. The sun was shining again and the great green bush-crickets shrilled like manic hissing pistons. A pair of crows were mobbing a raven, circling it and butting it till it disappeared over the horizon. Gran looked up and smiled, her mouth enlarged like a clown's by raspberry juice.

'I feel I could dig a whole garden now,' she said.

Acknowledgements

To Andy Brown, Sam North and Philip Hensher, my
tutors who gave me the impetus to begin this novel.
To all of my family for their support and encouragement.
To all who gave feedback, including Gill Michell, Hazel
Albarn, Lizzie Robinson, Margaret Barnes, Ann Castell,
Sue Tong, Fenella Montgomery and Tara O'Sullivan.

Above all, to Robert Peett for believing in this book and
for working tirelessly to improve it.

Historical resources:
Evans, Richard J. *The Third Reich in Power*, London:
Penguin Books, 2006.
Giordano, Ralph. *Erinnerungen eines
        Davongekommenen*, Cologne: Kiepenheuer &
        Witsch, 2008.
Hannsmann, Margarete. *Der helle Tag bricht an*,
        Munich: Goldmann Verlag, 1982.
Metelmann, Henry. *A Hitler Youth: Growing up in
Germany in the 1930s*, Staplehurst: Spellmount, 2004.
Naujoks, Harry. *Mein Leben im KZ Sachsenhausen
1936-1942*, Berlin: Dietz Verlag, 1989.
Wolf, Christa. *Kindheitsmuster*, Munich: Luchterhand,
1993.
And many others.

About the Author

Judy Birkbeck studied German and French at Reading University, and Creative Writing at Exeter University, and works as a technical, legal and commercial translator from German, French, Russian and Spanish. She is currently working on another novel and has short stories published in literary magazines. She was born and bred in London, and lives in Yorkshire.